Can I See You Again?

"*Can I See You Again?* is a heartfelt, humorous look into the nature of true love and the winding, twisty—and, in this case, muddy—roads we often take to get there. Morgan perfectly crafts a story that will hold you in its grip until the very last page."

—Kristy Woodson Harvey, author of *Lies and Other Acts of Love*

The Someday Jar

"Allison Morgan's charming debut *The Someday Jar* is much more than just a fun read, it is a reminder to seize opportunity when it comes, to believe in yourself, to never settle, and most importantly, to actively fill your life with wonderful experiences that will become cherished memories. *The Someday Jar* is a book to read today, not someday, and Morgan is clearly a writer to watch."

—Stacey Ballis, author of *Wedding Girl*

"A reminder that the idealism of childhood dreams is something we should always hold on to, this novel sparks hope with its whimsical story. From heartwarming to heart-wrenching, the ups and downs of the main character's journey, through romance, loss and new beginnings, might just inspire readers to follow some long-lost dreams of their own."

—*RT Book Reviews*

continued . . .

"The perfect blend of humor, inspiration, motivation, and romance!"
—San Francisco Book Review

"A breezy, fun-filled dream of a read . . . Strongly recommend for fans of contemporary fiction."
—The Reading Nook Reviews

Berkley titles by Allison Morgan

THE SOMEDAY JAR
CAN I SEE YOU AGAIN?

Can I See You Again?

Allison Morgan

BERKLEY BOOKS, NEW YORK

BERKLEY

An imprint of Penguin Random House LLC
375 Hudson Street, New York, New York 10014

This book is an original publication of the Berkley Publishing Group.

Library of Congress Cataloging-in-Publication Data

Names: Morgan, Allison, author.
Title: Can I see you again? / Allison Morgan.
Description: Berkley trade paperback edition. |
New York : Berkley Books, 2016.
Identifiers: LCCN 2015045574 (print) | LCCN 2015050072 (ebook) | ISBN
9780425282458 (softcover) | ISBN 9780698405400 (ePub)
Subjects: LCSH: Man-woman relationships—Fiction. | Dating (Social
customs)—Fiction. | Mate selection—Fiction. | BISAC: FICTION /
Contemporary Women. | FICTION / Romance /
Contemporary. | GSAFD: Love stories.
Classification: LCC PS3613.O725 C36 2016 (print) | LCC PS3613.O725 (ebook) |
DDC 813/.6—dc23
LC record available at http://lccn.loc.gov/2015045574

PUBLISHING HISTORY
Berkley trade paperback edition / August 2016

PRINTED IN THE UNITED STATES OF AMERICA

10 9 8 7 6 5 4 3 2 1

Cover photographs: *Woman* © Ilina Simeonova/Trevillion. *Woman's hair* © Victoria Andreas/
Shutterstock. *Front door* © David Papazian/iStock/Thinkstock.
Cover design by Sarah Oberrender.

To Oma

one

"I can't believe this is happening," I say to my secretary, Andrew, who's seated across my desk.

"Want me to pinch you?"

"Stay away from me." I laugh, lifting my hands to stop him as he jumps from his chair. "Dr. Oz said squeezing the skin can cause blood clots. Or something like that. And, anyway, it's hard to celebrate if I'm dead."

"Nonsense." He quickly nips my elbow, then steps away to answer the phone.

I'm not dreaming, but my God, it's surreal that in less than two months' time my very own book, *Can I See You Again?*, will hit the shelves. *The shelves.* After two years of manuscript revisions and enough rejection letters to wallpaper an Ikea, my book—which is my hardest-fought and proudest accomplishment—will be published. If I weren't wearing my new black pencil skirt, I'd run outside my office and spin cartwheels along the shore. Well, that and no one wants to see the fabric split clear up to my waistband. Again.

Comprising tips and suggestions to find the one-and-only,

my self-help debut chronicles a handful of my most memorable matchmaking love stories (my favorite being the couple who married at seventy-seven years old and went bungee jumping on their honeymoon) along with funny anecdotes about first meetings that didn't go well—one guy arrived in a U-Haul, tossed his date a pair of gloves, and told her to grab the far end of his sectional. Another guy brought his date to a funeral.

Not only will a successful book broaden my business and its footprint, but the bags under my eyes from late nights fixed at the computer—honestly, seeing one's reflection in a laptop monitor at two a.m. should be a crime against women's rights—tears of uncertainty pooled on my keyboard, and callused fingertips from typing, deleting, and typing again will culminate in something tangible. Something *I* created. Something my grandmother Jo will be proud of.

Behind my computer, I reach for the framed and faded snapshot of her and me sitting side by side on her porch steps outside the home my G-pa built nearly forty years ago. I'd asked her one afternoon, as we tilted our heads together and smiled for Mom's camera, "Think I could write a book?"

"Oh, Bree, I do. And I'd be first in line to buy it."

I can still smell the hint of black cherry on Jo's breath when she kissed my cheek good-bye.

It's hard to fathom that fifteen years of Saturdays have passed. Harder yet to believe it's just the two of us now. She's the only family I have left. And though Jo hides it well, her once-infectious smile has flattened into a thin line of disappointment, and it doesn't take a body language expert to recognize the layer of sorrow clouding her eyes.

So along with sidebars and strategies, curse-filled rants, doubt, and resurgence, I've infused my heart and soul into *Can I See You Again?*—not to mention a sizable chunk of my savings account for a publicist—and there's nothing I want more than to celebrate the release of my book with Jo, high-light a joyful connection from our past. Ease the sting of all that I ripped away.

Andrew returns and leans against my desk. He's dressed in black jeans and a fitted gray vest wrapped over a white button-down shirt topped with a paisley bow tie. His dark brown hair is shaved close above his ears and grown longer on top, gelled into perfectly white-tipped spikes (he bent over his bathroom sink and dipped the points in bleach).

Andrew has been my closest friend since our junior year at UCSD; we shared the community bathroom in an off-campus apartment complex along with a wicked fight three weeks into fall semester—who knew that turning my hair dryer on and off as I readied for my seven a.m. class rather than leaving it on until my hair was completely dry had him teetering on the edge of sanity? I told him he had the slumped shoulders of a wall-flower. He told me to shave my forearms.

The following day he bought me a sleek, *quieter* hair dryer, lent me his favorite sweatshirt, and showed me how to apply lip gloss. We've been tight ever since.

Same can't be said of his parents. Once they learned of his feminine ways and sexual preferences, they enrolled Andrew in football camp, martial arts classes, shooting range lessons, anything and everything manly with hopes of toughening him up. It didn't work.

"Jo's on the phone," he says. "She sounds kinda flustered, didn't even want to talk about what happened on *The Bachelor* last night." Andrew picks at the label of my granola bar. "We *always* talk about what happened on *The Bachelor*."

"That's strange. Let me see what's going on." I press line one, grateful he loves my eighty-year-old grandmother as much as I do. Though, how can he not? She's spunky and adorable with her floss-like silver hair coiled and secured with a butterfly clip. She makes the best snickerdoodle cookies in all of San Diego County, and though neither admitted it, while she was recovering from her hip surgery four years ago, I'm pretty sure the two shared a bag of Fritos, a can of bean dip, and a tightly rolled joint. "Hi, Jo. Everything okay?"

"Oh, my heavens, Bree, I don't know what to do."

Andrew's right.

All the same, I smile at the trepidation in Jo's voice. Bless her heart, she's grown a bit forgetful and fearful in her golden years, and though I visit every day, it's not uncommon for her to call panicked because she misplaced the TV remote or can't find her other slipper. But no matter, I'll call or stop by a hundred times a day if need be. Anything to keep her close and content. Anything to soothe the strain of the last fifteen years. "What's wrong?"

"The postman just delivered a letter."

"Yes, okay." *That's kind of what they do.* "What does the letter say?"

"It's full of tiny, fancy words. I can't make sense of it. But *final notice* is written in red ink, right across the top. It says I owe a lot of money. Can you come over?"

"Yes, of course. But, don't worry, it's likely a scam of some sort. Remember the silly water filtration system that telemarketer practically strong-armed you into buying a couple years ago? I'll come by after work. Need me to bring anything? More sandwich meat? Still have enough green apples?"

"I'm fine. Just hurry."

"I will. And in the meantime, try to relax. Make yourself a cup of that lavender-sage-flavored tea you like. I put more in the pantry. I'll see you after a bit."

"She okay?" Andrew asks.

"Yeah, just got a threatening letter." I jot myself a note to pick up a piece of her favorite double-chip-chocolate cake. Chocolate cake makes everything better. "How do people sleep at night, preying on old people?"

"Armpits of society." Before heading toward his desk, Andrew points at my computer screen and says, "You know, most people screw around shopping on Amazon or watching YouTube videos of hairless cats. You're the only person I know who sneaks glimpses of the *New York Times* bestseller list during business hours."

"The best of the best land here." I tap the black-and-white Web page filling my screen. "This stuff is interesting."

"Apparently you've never seen a hairless cat eat a raspberry."

"Get back to work," I chuckle. But rather than closing the Web page, I click on this week's current number-one bestseller, *Fallen*, triggering memories of Jo and me, anteing with raisins, Ritz crackers, pretzel sticks, or her favorite—liqueur-filled chocolates—scrolling through the *Times* Web page, wagering on the upcoming week's bestseller rankings. We'd bet which novel jumped to the top spot, which fell below twenty, the number of times *Love*, *Forever*, or *Dead* appeared in titles, how cute we thought the male authors might be.

It never mattered who won. We combined our snack piles and munched on the winnings, laughing at nothing special, enjoying the afternoon with just us two.

My office door swings open and my client, Nixon Voss, steps inside.

"Hey, Bree." He settles into the chair across my desk in smooth dark jeans, nearly swallowing the leather slingback with his long California tanned frame. Nixon tugs at the cuffs of his pale pink button-down shirt, a color not many men can pull off. "How are you?"

With a crumpled smile, I grab my cell phone and aim it toward Nixon, showing him the lengthy text from another of his disappointed dates. "Are you out to set a record?"

"It's nice to see you, too. Heard it may rain later, but it's a beautiful morning so far, don't you think?"

I pause, then say with a voice matching the teasing tone in his, "So sorry. Can I get you a cup of coffee? Multigrain bagel? A conscience?"

"Do you chastise all your clients like this?" He silences his ringing phone with a thumb pressed against his pocket.

"Just the ones who break hearts in the double-digit range. How many does this make now? Eleven? There's no bonus for the most dates, you know. No punch card where you get the twelfth free."

"Now you tell me. All this time I've been holding out for a Bree Caxton and Associates bumper sticker."

I swallow my laugh and flip open his date's file; she's a blue-eyed ballet instructor whose toned thighs make me regret the wedge of Oreo-crusted cheesecake I ate for breakfast this morning. "Where'd you take her? And don't say for coffee."

"Then I won't say it."

"You know, it'd be easier finding a lasting match for a death row inmate."

"Better get cracking on my espionage plan, then."

"You realize you're trying to impress these women?"

"And they should be trying to impress me. But why suffer through dinner if we can't muster a decent conversation during a cup of coffee?"

"Because women like dinner. Dinner shouts to the world that you chose her, above all others, even if just for the evening. And trust me, a valued woman is more likely to open up. In *all* ways. Dinner is the slow seduction."

"Slow seduction?"

"Stop laughing. I'm serious." I flick a stray paper clip in his direction.

He reaches for it, but the wire fumbles through his grasp. "All right. Dinner. Slow seduction. I'll try to remember that. Excuse me one sec?"

I nod the go-ahead and he pulls his persistent phone from his pocket. It occurs to me that in the handful of times we've met, Nixon's phone is always cemented inside his palm, securing a deal, ratifying a contract, persuading a client to jump onboard. When does he find time to play Game of War? Or nap?

No doubt, Nixon's a sharp, diligent businessman with an iron-will dedication to his company. So it seems fitting, as he taps at his keys, that his phone's alert is a series of three rigid bumps like the hammering of a nail.

I flip my phone end over end while thinking about how revealing ringtones are. When waiting for a dentist's appointment or manicure, I try to peg other people's chosen signals based on their magazine selection, shoe style, tattoo, or haircut. It's a silly little game I play. Totally judgmental and founded on nothing besides conjecture. But, what the hell, I get a kick out of it. And, given that my livelihood depends on my ability to read energy and body language, I'm happy to report that the last nine out of ten times, I've nailed it. Not to mention, I predicted three out of the last four *Amazing Race* winners. Hard to say if my intuition stems from my psychology degree, books I've devoured on human behavior, or my being born on Halloween.

Whatever the reason, I'm grateful for the instinct and over the last six years, I've not only met hundreds of fascinating people but also capitalized off their unique characteristics.

"Sorry," Nixon says, pointing at his phone, "small fire at the office."

He types his reply and I consider my own ringtone, realizing

I don't differ much from the predictable. My dark blond hair is draped around my shoulders in loose curls and my makeup is minimal. I'm happiest with my butt in the sand or curled up on the couch with a crossword puzzle and bag of peanut-butter-stuffed pretzels by my side. I love to walk, I hate to bike, and I'm a pointed toe away from conquering an eight-angle yoga pose.

So it's no surprise that my ringtone is a Fratellis song, by an organic indie rock band I fell in love with after my boyfriend, Sean, took me to their concert last spring. We drank too many Blue Moons, danced until a blister formed on my pinkie toe, and then, wired and giddy, fooled around like teenagers in the back of his Audi A4. Which, by the light of day, isn't as fun as it sounds. I limped around for the better part of a week with a cup-holder-shaped bruise on my left hip.

Allowing Nixon another minute, I sort through my mail, tossing away pamphlets advertising last-minute Ensenada cruise deals, free cash, and low auto insurance rates. I then order three rolls of Christmas-themed wrapping paper from my landscaper's granddaughter who's fund-raising for a field trip to the San Diego Zoo. They're $24.95—*per roll*—but who can say no to a pigtailed second-grader with a gap between her front teeth?

Nixon still types.

Okay, that's long enough.

"Medical emergency?"

He says nothing.

"Beached whale?"

"Hmm?"

"Should I take cover because we've launched into World War Three?"

Nixon lifts his focus to offer a what-the-hell-are-you-talking-about scowl.

"We're discussing your life, remember?" I point at his phone. "What's more important than love?"

"Look." Nixon clicks off his screen. "I appreciate your help. I really do. But you know this whole arranged-dating thing isn't me. I'm here because my mom forgets I have a business to run and insists . . . *actually, commands* . . . that I have a date on my arm for my cousin's wedding. If I don't, she'll have to explain to friends and neighbors, the caterer, the florist, and anyone else within earshot that the Voss family name is in jeopardy because I haven't married and spawned a grand-child, which in her eyes is equivalent to the earth slipping off its axis. So, according to my mom, if I don't have a girlfriend at the party, I'll be responsible for the end of humanity."

"Be nice." I fiddle with a file, trying not to laugh at Mrs. Voss's expense even though Nixon's not off base. I recall her phone call several weeks ago—she noticed my billing statement on his counter and jotted down my number—explaining with an unwavering tone and heavy Spanish accent that each passing day is one less she'll be alive to spend with her grandchildren. And the *Amado Jesús* can strike her dead before she'll allow *niños* without marriage. She's giving Nixon until his cousin's wedding before *Mamá* steps in and finds a daughter-in-law herself.

Yes, her approach is abrasive, but I admire her conviction, her certainty. All she wants is to share her love with her family. Who can fault a woman for pinpointing exactly what she desires from life? And, though Nixon may disagree, he's a lot like his mom, confident and steadfast. But the two differ in the sense that work *is* his baby. Poor Mrs. Voss, how is she supposed to spoon-feed mashed sweet potatoes to a Fortune 500 company?

"Let's be honest." I tuck my hair behind my ears and drop my elbows on my thick glass desk. "You're not here because your mom said so. You're here because you're a thirty-five-year-old man with no one to share your life. Your house is cold and sterile. There's probably expired milk in your fridge. And more than likely, gray hairs are sprouting up in inappropriate places. Your comfort zone is shrinking and, at the end of the day, you're alone."

"Shit, Bree. Don't sugarcoat it. Give it to me straight."

"I know it sounds harsh."

"It sounds like you're stalking me."

"Only when your shutters are open."

He laughs.

"All kidding aside, love isn't easy. Don't get discouraged because we've had a few misfires. And don't let my casual attitude fool you. I take my business seriously. And I'm good at what I do." I thumb toward the wall behind me, which is blanketed with framed pictures of some of the happy couples I've introduced over the last six years. "I've attended countless weddings. Seven of my clients have named their firstborn after me, and the newly married owner of Dutch's Safe Haven Zoo dubbed his last rescue in my honor."

"Well, you know you've made it when that happens. What was it? Majestic lioness?"

"It really doesn't matter."

"California condor?"

"You're missing the point."

"Rarely seen snow leopard?"

"A squirrel, all right?"

"Squirrel?"

"Yes, I know. Nothing that unpredictable can be trusted. Moving on"—I scoot toward the edge of my seat—"I've facilitated relationships between aging lounge singers and triathletes. I've married pilots to prison guards, CEOs to sanitation workers, vegans to paleo dieters. Bree Caxton and Associates is one of San Diego's most prolific matchmaking companies. I've devoted my life to finding love and I have a ninety-eight percent success rate." I lean closer toward him. "Do you realize, Nixon Voss, you're my two percent?"

"Are you really afraid of squirrels?"

"I wish you'd take this seriously."

"Is it the soft, bushy tails or the doelike eyes that terrify you?"

"Very funny." I reach for his date's head shot. "Here is a perky blonde with a Colgate-worthy smile. She's adorable. *You* chose her. So tell me, what killed it?"

"I don't know. She seemed too obvious, a little young."

"Young? That's what I've said for months. And for months, you've overridden my choices and selected girls—eleven to be exact—that aren't your right match. And for some crazy reason, I've allowed it." Mrs. Voss's voice plays through my mind. *Mi familia.* "Your mom is right. No more."

"No more what?"

"This." I wave his date's picture in the air. "You *think* you want a twenty-something model/actress with big boobs and a tight ass, but you're wrong."

"How are big boobs and a tight ass ever wrong?"

"Think of it this way. You're a venture capitalist who negotiates with financiers across the world, right?"

"Right."

"You speak three languages and have a master's degree in business."

"I do."

"How can you expect to find a connection with some barely legal play toy? It isn't probable. You don't share the same energy. Girls that age don't care about exchange rates or investment returns. They don't care about variances in sea levels or the shipping economy. They care about bikini waxes, polishing their nails with the color of the season, and mango-flavored vodka. That's who they are. That's who they *should be*." I point at Nixon. "But that's not you."

"It's not?"

"It's not. You need a thirty-something, strong, independent, *less obvious* woman who is filled with a driving passion. Someone who challenges you."

Nixon leans against the chair's backrest and studies me for a few seconds from head to toe. My neck muscles tighten from his scrutiny.

A mischievous corner smile curves his lips. The same smile that I'm certain paved Nixon's way into countless women's panties. Not that it matters to me, but the smile does have its charm.

"So . . ." he says, "I need someone like you?"

"What? No, not like me." I reach for a pencil, though I've nothing to jot down. "Well, yes, technically, I suppose . . . exactly like me." *Bree, what have you done? You've given Nixon the wrong impression with your sassy "you're my two percent" garbage. Some expert you are, leading the poor guy on.* I pull the lapels of my blazer closer together, then with the eraser tap the framed picture of Sean and me paddleboarding in Cabo. "Sorry, Nixon, not me. I'm here for you *professionally.*"

"Whoa, I'm totally kidding. Did you think . . . me and you?" He laughs loud enough to grab a glance from Andrew seated across the room.

It isn't that funny.

"You're too old anyway," he says.

I shoot him a look, without admitting that his comment stings, more so since I filled out a health insurance questionnaire two weeks ago. Thanks to my thirty-first birthday last year, I had to check a lower box. A *lower* box.

At what age will my eggs shrivel up?

"I'm just giving you a hard time," Nixon says. "You've made yourself clear." He nods as if about to say something more but stops. For the briefest moment, his jawbone clamps tight and he stares at his feet.

I've struck a nerve.

Two seconds ago I considered kicking Nixon in the shins—

hard—but now, a wave of loneliness washes over me. Not for me. For *him*. Nixon's a good man. Yes, a tad smug, making a mockery of my livelihood, but all the same, he deserves a loving relationship, someone to hold hands with when shopping for air filters on Saturday afternoons or to snuggle close to watching *Arrested Development* reruns on lazy Sunday mornings. The type of effortless connection I have with Sean.

Out of the corner of my eye, I catch a glimpse of the dozen white roses he sent me last week, the day before we met with a financial advisor. As I think about my boyfriend of four years, a sense of calm replaces my unease. I think about how his beach-colored hair reflects the season, dark like wet sand in the winter and light as dry sand in the summer, a result of surfing and impromptu weekend volleyball games. His skin bronzes the color of a mocha latte, and we mark the calendar noting how long his swim trunks tan line lasts. January ninth is the record. My sun-screened Irish-skinned body never makes it past October first.

We hardly argue—aside from him getting upset when I fall asleep during a Tom Cruise movie (try as I might, his acting is like a horse tranquilizer to me), or the few times I didn't laugh at one of Sean's lame lawyer jokes. Honestly, the one about the public defender, the prostitute, and the lamppost isn't that funny. But at the end of the day, there's a treasured comfort level that we share, a priceless familiarity. *History.*

In my purse rests the Post-it note Sean stuck on my office door this morning before I arrived at work.

Antonio's. 8:00 p.m.

Leave it to Sean, scrawling a note about our evening. That's so him. Such an adorable little quirk he has, writing everything down on stickies. I swear there isn't a day that goes by where

I don't find something scribbled and stuck somewhere: on his apartment's medicine cabinet, the dash of his Audi, the upper right corner of his latest deposition. I suppress my smile as I remember the one time I found Sean naked in my bed with a smiley face drawn on a Post-it and stuck on the tip of his—

"Bree?" Nixon redirects my attention. "Wasn't it you who chewed me out for not being present?"

"Sorry. Yes, let's continue with your situation. You're paying me to find you love, so it's time to let me call the shots and—"

"You win." Nixon raises his hands in surrender. "My cousin's wedding is a few weeks away, and my mom will see right through me if I show up with a piece of arm candy. Get my mom off my back so I can focus on work. You pick the woman this time."

"Finally!" I raise my fists in victory.

"Settle down, crazy lady." He laughs. "Just find me my lovely."

I sit upright, pulled like a puppet on a string, caught by the tenderness of his words. *My lovely.* "Why, Nixon Voss. Underneath this smooth-talking, systematic, number-crunching, all-business-all-the-time exterior is a mushy center."

"There's nothing mushy about me."

"A soft underbelly."

"I don't think so."

"Beneath your thick crust, you're as gooey as a marshmallow."

He smacks his knees, then stands. "And that, folks, is my cue to go." But before turning away, Nixon braces his fingers on my desk's edge. For the first time, I notice tiny specs of brown sprinkled in his blue eyes and catch a whiff of his Giorgio Armani cologne. I recognize the woodsy scent because I bought Sean a bottle last Christmas.

He exchanged it.

"So, how long until the release?"

"My book? Six weeks. October eleventh, to be exact."

"Claiming your spot?" He nods toward the bestseller Web page.

"Oh, no." I feel my cheeks blush. "I . . . no . . . I don't expect to make *the list*. Heck, I'm thrilled just to get my book published. The *Times* is something my grandmother and I follow. We keep tabs on the big guys."

"Well, good." He points at the screen. "Because that list isn't the only threshold of success. Be proud of your accomplishment. I am."

He is? "Um . . . thanks, Nixon, that's very sweet." I reach for my pencil again.

"So, you'll find me the right woman?"

"You know what they say, twelfth time's the charm."

"Sounds good. See you later."

"God, that man is highly attractive," Andrew says, joining me at my desk. "One of those silent but deadly types."

"What are you talking about?"

"You know, the kinda guy that's aloof and guarded just enough to be sexy, but not conceited." He watches Nixon leave. "You don't see it?"

I follow his gaze, stifling a laugh. *Yeah, I see it.*

The paper clip is stuck to Nixon's butt.

That's what he gets for calling me old.

two

I work through lunch interviewing prospective new clients. The one that looked to "bump uglies with a banging chick" was shown the door. I pay my electric and credit card bills online, order a sugar-pearl KitchenAid mixer off Bed Bath & Beyond's wedding registry for one of my soon-to-be-married couples, then type a quick e-mail reminding a client with a date tonight not to drink too much Pinot Grigio and mount the bronze horse outside P. F. Chang's. Like last time.

"Andrew?" I glance in his direction. "Bring the profiles, will you?"

A moment later, he sinks into the chair, then opens his laptop on my desk's edge.

When I hired Andrew six years ago to help answer phones, I never expected him to stay on this long. Figured I was a stepping-stone to bigger and better things and once my business established itself, he'd pursue his teaching interests or venture into something kid-related, a mentor or guidance role of some sort.

"Teaching little nuggets, that's where my heart belongs," he's said more than once.

But one month rolled into two, one year into another, and now I can't imagine this office without him. Plus, clients love Andrew—one hairstylist we married to a plumber drops off hair gel and fancy shampoos all the time, while an insurance adjuster we paired with a veterinarian takes him out for ice cream every year on his birthday. Andrew's an integral part of my company, and I'm damn glad to have him.

"What are we looking for?" he asks.

"Who do we have for Nixon?"

"Besides me?" Andrew teases, clearly aware of the Bree Caxton and Associates strict no-dating-the-clients policy.

"What happened to the FedEx guy?"

"Didn't I tell you? When he picked me up the other night, I looked down at his feet and said, 'Now that's a nice-looking pair of Crocs.'"

"You did?" I say with an arched eyebrow.

"Of course not. Has anyone *ever* said, 'Now that's a nice-looking pair of Crocs'?"

"Oh, sweetie," I say between laughs, "I'm sorry."

"It's okay. I read my horoscope today and it said true love is on the horizon." Ever since the lucky numbers on Andrew's daily forecast won him a thousand dollars from the California lottery a couple of years ago, he lives and breathes by their predictions.

"That's promising."

"More promising if it listed his GPS coordinates."

"Well, how about for now we search for Nixon's potential true love, twenty-eight to thirty-five years old, career type, educated."

Andrew opens the client database and clicks through a few head shots before a particular woman comes to mind. "Find Sara, the art curator."

"Nice choice," he says. "Thirty, college educated, likes to travel. And look, she lives close, in Pacific Beach."

"What's her coffee preference?"

Andrew scrolls to the answer. "One sugar."

"Excellent." Had he said something fussy like a half-caf soy latte with medium foam and a whisper—not a sprinkle, nor a smidgen—of cinnamon, I might have reconsidered Sara as a viable candidate.

Coffee preferences are a lot like ringtones.

"She looks like Sandra Bullock," Andrew says. "Remind me why she's still single."

"Married her college sweetheart who developed second thoughts on their second anniversary. She drove her anger and free time into her career at the gallery and has been single ever since. Look at her, she's perfect for Nixon." I return to my chair. "Let her know he'll be calling. Better yet, see if she's available to stop by my office today. I'd like to meet with her in person, make sure we've cleared the air from last month's fiasco."

"Cut yourself some slack. The guy's background check came back clean."

"True, but spending a Saturday night decked out in heels and a classic black shift dress, dodging taunts by drunks, druggies, and derelicts while being fingerprinted and questioned by the cops because your date picked you up in a hot-wired car is less than an ideal evening."

"Sounds more exciting than holding hands with a Croc-wearing delivery man." Andrew closes the laptop. "Want me to call Nixon, too?"

"Yes, tell him about Sara. And remind him, no coffee."

"Got it." He scribbles a note, then looks at me. "What's so funny?"

"Nothing. Just remembered something I said to Nixon." *Dinner is the slow seduction.* "Oh, and mention that bar and grill with the fire pits on Prospect."

"Because they have high tables, right? And people are more attentive when seated at a high table."

"My little boy is growing up."

"Told you I'm more than a pretty face. Now remember, we've got three dates scheduled for tonight. I'll follow up with them tomorrow morning. And this month's meet-and-greet is at the Marston House, right?"

"Yep."

"Am I including Nixon on this list?"

Sara's charming smile comes to mind. "Nah, he'll be off the market soon."

An hour later, I'm buried in another client's file when Andrew places a manila envelope on my desk. "This just came for you."

"Thanks." I tear open the package and dump out a thick stack of papers filled with "tiny, fancy words," as Jo's sweet, albeit frantic voice had said.

"What are those?"

"Forms for Sean and me to sign. We met with a financial advisor last week and decided to pool our savings accounts to obtain stronger financial holdings, solid margins, and more advantageous yields."

"Sorry, I fell asleep while you were talking. What did you say?"

"Ha. Ha." I skim through the paperwork, noting the spots for our signatures. Okay, a blue chip mutual fund might not be the sexiest thing in the world, but it's what I love about Sean, his sturdy footing. Just like with the flowers. In all our years together, he's sent no other color but white. Some people crave surprises in a relationship, the mystery of the unknown. Not me. I cherish Sean's consistency. His dependability. His control.

I return the documents into the envelope and type Sean a

quick text, hoping to catch him before court. He's arguing a lucrative case against a real estate developer facing tax evasion charges. He's worked on the case for months and every night this past week. Poor guy, he's so stressed and busy I've hardly seen him since we met with the advisor.

Got the docs. Joint account . . . we're such grown-ups. :)

I'm about to call Jo and check on her when my office door flings open and Randi, my publicist, blows into the room with the force of a jet turbine. She marches toward me in ankle-strapped stilettos and a cheetah print dress stretched taut across her ample chest and hips. A black leather purse, which appears the same diameter as the front tire of her Lexus IS C, is slung over her shoulder and a cell phone is pressed against her ear. She settles into my guest chair, rolls her eyes, and says to the caller, "When I schedule a goddamn lunch appointment, you show up on time. You are *not* the Queen of Sheba. And I wouldn't wait twenty minutes for her fat ass any more than I'll wait for yours. Uh-huh. Okay, fine. Love you, too, Mom."

Mom? I bet Randi's ringtone is an air horn.

I peek at my day calendar but find nothing written about an appointment with Randi. "Sorry, I don't recall a meeting today."

"Oh, honey, we don't have one. But have I got news. Have. I. Got. News. First, I crunched some numbers on your projected sales."

"Did you?" My fingertips drain to white as I brace my hands on the edge of my desk for support. *Stay calm, Bree. This is the moment you've waited for. You've written a good book. A helpful book. Randi wouldn't come in person if the expectations were bad. Right?* I try to hide the rising pitch in my voice but end up squeaking like a pubescent boy. "And, so the numbers . . . ?"

"Yes, the early response is promising."

"Really?" I relax my pose and my heart starts beating again. "That's great news."

"If you're happy with mediocrity."

"Well, no, I—"

"Promising numbers aren't enough. We want mind-blowing numbers. And that means we have a shitload of work to do."

"In that case, I'll pull on my boots."

She doesn't laugh.

C'mon . . . that's funny.

"Now, remember, when you hired me, you hired the best. In the nineteen years I've been in this business, only a handful of my clients haven't reached the list."

"What list? Wait . . . you mean . . . the *bestseller list*?"

"No, my grocery list. Of course, the bestseller list. Isn't this why you hired me?"

"I hired you for recognition, sure, but I never . . . I never thought I'd have a shot."

"Every book has a shot." She taps her glossy red acrylic nail on my desk. "You're familiar with the escalator clause in your contract, aren't you? A twenty-five-thousand-dollar bonus if you reach the bestseller ranking."

"Yes, but honestly, I glossed over that section, never thinking I . . . I . . . really?" *Stop trembling, Bree.*

"Honey, I made a bestseller out of a French Provincial cabinetry poem book. So, if you follow my advice, I mean follow everything that I suggest to the letter, then, Bree Caxton, *Can I See You Again?* may very well land on the top twenty."

"Oh my God." *This is wild.* I picture Jo clutching my book against her chest with one arm and hugging me tight with the other. Andrew and me dancing like idiots, waving my book in the air. A line of eager readers waiting for my autograph. *Slow down, Bree. You're getting ahead of yourself. Way ahead of yourself.* Then all the variables and could-go-wrongs zip back and forth through my mind like a *Fast and Furious* movie car chase. Worry spreads through my veins like a virus. "You're not pulling me along, right? Please don't say I'll make the list if it isn't true."

"I *never* joke about money. The book's quite good, you know."

"You read it? I didn't think you'd—"

"My assistant said it didn't suck. Remember now, I stand to gain from your success. So, no, I'm not stroking you."

"Tell me what to do."

"That's my girl." She winks. "This brings me to part two. Guess who landed you a five-week installment profile in the *National Tribune*?"

"Seriously?" Oh, for Pete's sake, I can't hide it. Now I'm *really* trembling. "No, way? That's a national newspaper."

"The newspaper's equivalent to *People* magazine with damn near the same reach. You'll be featured in the *Close-Up* section of Sunday's edition as well as, and maybe most importantly in today's digital media age, the online version, which has an enormous following and receives something ridiculous like thirty-five million hits a month." She crosses her legs and straightens her hem. "You can thank me now."

"Thank you, thank you." *This is incredible.* I resist the urge to climb on top of my desk and pound my chest. "How'd you do this? That newspaper saves those weekend profiles for celebrities, famous chefs, people like that. I'm a newbie, a nobody. How'd you secure this?"

"Gave the editor a blow job."

Oh, dear Lord.

She laughs. "I'm kidding."

I fear she's not, but I shake the thought—*and image*—from my head and focus on the opportunity at hand. "Wow, Randi. This is fantastic."

"Listen up. Lucy Hanover of KMRQ, you know, the radio host?"

"Of course. She's the Oprah of morning talk shows."

"KMRQ is an affiliate of the *Tribune* and Lucy reads the paper religiously. The *Close-Up* section is her favorite. She can make or break a new author by mere mention of their name on her show. She falls in love with you during this segment and you're golden."

I stand and pace behind my chair, rubbing my forearm with my opposite hand. "Randi, this is unbelievable, but I must admit, five weeks? What's the story? What do I talk about?" *Aside from the fact that I can recite the Budweiser beer slogan, I'm not that exciting. Oh, wait . . . I do know a couple of card tricks.*

"You and your life. They want to know the ins and outs of Bree Caxton and Associates. What makes this business tick. What makes you tick. How you find love so well for the desolate."

"I wouldn't call them *desolate.*"

"I don't give a rat's ass what you call them." She pulls out a contract from her bag and flips to the signature page.

I quickly skim through the document and sign.

"You need to be on point for the next five weeks," she says. "Be at my beck and call."

"I can do that."

"This article, along with a blog that my office will initiate and manage, Lucy's influence, and a few appearances that I'll arrange will get you noticed by those who matter."

This is amazing. I've worked so hard. *So hard. Wait until I tell Jo.*

"Okay, gotta go." Randi gathers the contract. "I've made myself clear, right? For the next five weeks, I'm your center of influence."

"Absolutely."

"All right, then. Go out tonight and celebrate because for the next five weeks, you'll be a busy girl."

"Will do. I already have plans, actually. I'm meeting my boyfriend for dinner."

"Make sure your workspace is in order."

"Sorry?"

She forms a triangle with her thumb and index fingers, dancing it over her lap. "Your workspace. Your playground. Your—"

"Um, yes, got it, thanks." I flinch at such intimate references. What am I saying? I flinch at all of Randi's references.

"I'll be in touch with more details in the morning. Clear your schedule; the first interview is the day after tomorrow. And don't wear that outfit. You look like a Banana Republic mannequin."

And like the silence of a departed jet plane, the whirlwind of Randi is gone.

Andrew drums his hands on my desk. "I knew it. I knew it. I knew it. Your forecast said something to this effect just the other day. Or maybe it was Jo's . . . I can't remember. Anyway, you're gonna be famous."

"I don't know about famous, but can you believe this? The bestseller list. Never in a million years did I think that possible. And twenty-five thousand dollars? God, what I could do with the money. Buy a new copier for the office. Ramp up my advertising campaign. Pay off my credit cards." Successful business aside, the lease on my ocean-view commercial space is a killer. "If I *am* dreaming, please don't wake me."

"You're not dreaming. This *is* happening. You've earned this. My boss and best friend, a bestselling author—"

"*Potential* bestselling author."

"Shush." He swats the air with his hand. "I'm super happy for you."

"Thanks. I am, too. Phew! What a day." I slide open the top drawer of my cabinet and search for a client's file.

"That's it?"

"What do you mean?"

"Aren't you going to run a hot lap around the office, scream and flail your arms? Buy yourself that new Vuitton clutch? Anything?"

"Let's not get too excited. You heard Randi, there's a lot to do." I pause, then close the drawer. "Okay, just for a second."

We laugh, hopping up and down around my office like a couple of bunny rabbits.

"You landing that interview, among all the other candidates, is karma. Good things happen to good people." Andrew slides a stray hair away from my face, then taps my chest. "And you, Bree Caxton, are good people."

"Remember, I'm not alone in this. Congrats to you as well. You've been right by my side the past few years."

"So, you're buying me the Vuitton clutch?"

"Nice try."

"Well, then, how about I get off early this afternoon?"

The clock reads four p.m. "Big plans?"

"Two-for-one special today at Sun-Gun Salon. Thinking of inviting my dad, too, just to hear the terror in his voice. 'Spray tan? Men don't get spray tans,'" Andrew says, mocking his father's throaty timbre. "'Come spend the day at one of my job sites, swing a hammer or dig a trench. Hard work, that gets you tan.'"

"It's not a bad idea, you know." I fiddle with the cuff of my blazer. *How'd Randi know I got this at Banana Republic, anyway?* "Your dad's got a big crew of guys. Cute, strong guys, I'd imagine."

"Well, all the more reason for an even tan."

"All right, go ahead, get out of here."

"Thanks. Oh, I almost forgot. Sara called when you were talking with Randi. She's working at her new gallery and can't get away. She asked if you could stop by after work. She's only two blocks away."

"Shoot, that doesn't leave me much time before dinner," I mutter to myself. Along with the chocolate cake, I want to pick up a copy of *Fallen* for Jo before stopping by. I check the clock again, deciding that I'll feel a heck of a lot better if Sara and I talk face-to-face, making sure she doesn't hold any ill will toward me or my company. "Call her back and tell her I'll be there within half an hour."

"Will do." He returns a minute later with Sara's address. "Here you go. She's expecting you. The gallery's on the corner of Grand and Claremont, next to Einstein's Bagels."

"Got it, thanks."

"Okay, I'm leaving." He slides his leather satchel onto his shoulder. "Have a fun night. Take care of you."

"Take care of you." I repeat our favorite line from *Pretty Woman*, the movie we watched instead of me studying for spring finals, senior year.

Twenty minutes later I stroll along the boutique-lined sidewalk toward Sara's gallery. Sean hasn't responded to my text and court should be over by now, so I make a quick call.

"Sean Thomas." He answers on the first ring. I hear the courthouse door swing open and the sound of city traffic fill his background, much like my own.

"Hi, babe, done with court?"

"Just finished."

"How'd it go?"

"We won."

"Congratulations." This is a big case for Sean, a cash cow in billable hours, and with this verdict, he's established himself as a landmark on the map of the litigation world. So why does he sound so distracted? Almost irritated.

"I'm heading to the office. I've got a few things to tie up."

"Sure, of course. But real quick, did you get my text about the documents?"

"I did."

"Great, so I'll bring the forms to dinner. We can toast to our new adventure with a glass of Champagne." I laugh into dead air. "Sean?"

"I gotta run."

"Okay, see you at Antonio's."

We click off before I tell him about the interview. No worries, we can chat about our day over entrées.

I reach the floor-to-ceiling double glass doors of Sara's gallery and stride into the sparse space with its trendy exposed piping, deep plum–painted ceiling, and snow-white walls. Only a few sculptures decorate the floor and a half dozen paintings, blanketed under opaque tarps, lean against wood pallets. The smell of lacquer thinner lingers in the air.

"Bree, thanks for coming by." Sara's footsteps echo against the floor as she walks toward me in a Chanel cream pant suit, bright red ballet flats, and long dark hair pulled back into a sleek ponytail. Laden with class—twenty bucks says she has a Norah Jones ringtone—she's perfect for Nixon. Why didn't I think of her sooner?

"Sara, it's nice to see you."

"You as well. Though you wouldn't know by the mess, we're only a couple days away from opening. Can I get you something to drink? I have a bottle of Cristal that I'm dying to uncork."

"Sounds delicious, but no, thank you." Cognizant that not all my clients want the world to know they've employed a matchmaker, I survey the room and once confident no one is within earshot, I say, "Sara, I want to apologize once more for the atrocious date you had."

"Certainly one of my more interesting evenings, I'll give you that." Her eyes veer to the left and I fear she's still upset. Then she shrugs and says with a hint of her southern background in her voice, "But I learned there are no outstanding warrants for my arrest and they didn't make me change into one of those god-awful orange jumpsuits, so that's the takeaway, I suppose."

We share a laugh and relief spreads a smile across my face. "A silver lining for sure. All the same, I'm here to make it up to you. I wanted to tell you in person that a very attractive, self-made, and felony-free man, with kind eyes and a snarky sense of wit, will be calling you soon. He's one of those silent-but-deadly guys." I plagiarize Andrew.

"Ooh . . . quiet but sexy. I love that type."

"Yes, apparently it's a popular characteristic. Anyway, his name is Nixon Voss."

Her cheeks cast a rosy glow, matching her shoes. "He sounds wonderful."

"I think you'll find him to be a great match, and I'm eager to see what you think of him." I clap my hands together and say, "So, we're good? No hard feelings?"

"My goodness, no. All is forgiven."

"Great. I'll be in touch." I glance around the room. "This is a lovely space. You'll do well here."

"Thank you. You'll have to come by when we're finished."

"I'd love to. Let me know what you think of Nixon."

The heavy glass door closes behind me and I wave good-bye to Sara before stepping away.

She waves back with an eagerness inspired by the promise of possibility.

With a smile as wide as the Pacific Ocean, I think about how grateful I am for the people in my life. Sean and his family, my friends, my clients, Andrew and Jo. Even crazy Randi. And, with a little more hard work, something the success of my business proves I've never shied away from, I might find myself with a bestseller on my hands.

Maybe Andrew's right. Maybe good things do happen to good people.

three

Two hours later, the warm fall breeze tickles my calves as I climb into the backseat of a hired Uber town car. I'm bathed, wrapped in cream lace La Perla lingerie and a burgundy sheath dress, and have readied my *workspace*. Jo's book and a boxed slice of cake rests beside me.

So does a cellophane-wrapped dog bone stuffed with some sort of colorless, but unfortunately not odorless, poultry paste for Martin, Jo's gray-and-white, seven-year-old shih tzu. I picked up the treat at the pet store across the street from Sara's gallery.

My driver, a young woman whose long side braid rests on top of a fuchsia hibiscus tattoo fanning over her right shoulder, winds her way through the streets of my grandmother's neighborhood.

I've often considered a tattoo. Went as far as scheduling an appointment years ago on my nineteenth birthday but backed out at the last minute after my friend said I'd get herpes from the needle. Thank God I believed her, because my cowgirl phase was short-lived and a horseshoe with a dangling star inked around my right calf would've been a horrendous mistake. In all the years that followed, I haven't thought of anything worthy to embed into my skin. Until now. I giggle to myself, imagining *bestselling author* inscribed in bold cursive letters across my chest.

I reach for the copy of *Fallen* and thumb through the first few pages, recalling the many Saturdays Jo and I spent together during my early teenage years, lingering in bookstores or lounging on her sofa, snacking on fruit candies and soaking up every #1. We shared a yellow highlighter and marked our favorite lines in each book, writing comments in the margins, giggling at the saucy parts.

"Here you are," the driver says.

We've pulled curbside to Jo's house, a single-level home with a grass lawn, smooth-glass windows, an aged terra-cotta tiled roof, and ivory siding repainted a dozen times over walls that wrap around and safeguard my memories of laughter and love. I stare at the home I've spent countless hours inside, with its same seashell wreath hanging on the front door, same squeaky porch swing Jo and I nearly laughed ourselves off when Dad shocked himself tightening screws on the doorbell, same fake rock where the hide-a-key is buried, same pale-yellow room I lived in after my parents died.

Jo said she'll stay in this home until the day she dies. Begged me not to stick her in a center for "old geezers" once the time comes. "I'd rather sip on a bottle of brandy and fall asleep in my recliner, pretending your G-pa is holding my hand," she'd said. "Promise me, that's the only way I'll leave this house."

I promised, then asked her to talk about something less depressing.

Martin barks at my knock. His nails scape along the wood floor as he stampedes down the long hallway toward the door. I can't help but take a step back.

Over the years, I've brought Jo's four-legged companion all sorts of treats. Bought him squeaky toys, filled his water bowl, cleaned up his turds, and yet each time he sees me, he snarls at me with the ferocity of a wolverine.

"Bree?" Jo says, opening the door as wide as the chain lock allows. "Is that you?"

Martin pokes his furry head through the gap, jingling the bells on his lime green collar as he yips at my feet.

Martin doesn't like me.

I don't like him.

We both like Jo.

"Oh, thank goodness you're here. Come in. Come in." Jo unfastens the chain, scoops Martin into her arms, and opens the door. She stands in a lilac bathrobe cinched tight around her narrow waist.

I'm taken aback by the fact that she hasn't dressed for the day, nor clipped her hair in a bun. I can tell something is wrong by the way she shuffles her slippered feet into the kitchen with its original white cabinets and gold appliances and the faint smell of grilled cheese and corn on the cob.

I set my things on the counter and, as always, confirm that her daily pill box is empty, then glance at the *Life Alert* monitor box resting beside her telephone, verifying that the power light blinks green. The remote is slung around Jo's neck and I'm comforted knowing she has this medical warning system. One push of a button and a nurse calls Jo. If there's no response, the call center dispatches a paramedic and then contacts me. Jo's required to check in with medical staff when she wakes each morning and again before she goes to bed.

"Read this." She hands me the paper, then pets Martin's head with the nervousness of a prostitute in church.

"It's okay, Jo, whatever it is, we'll—" But my comforting words vanish as I recognize the embossed Internal Revenue

Service eagle insignia in the upper left-hand corner and read the words written in bold across the top: NOTICE AND DEMAND FOR PAYMENT. FINAL NOTICE OF INTENT TO LEVY AND NOTICE OF RIGHT TO A HEARING. Jo's property address is listed and a balance due of $47,746.29.

Oh, Christ.

"What does it mean?" she asks.

"I'm not sure." The rest of the letter is full of legal verbiage—and Jo's right, it might as well be written in Mandarin. What does "Deferred Acceptance" mean, anyway? It's hard to tell if the claim is well founded. Maybe Sean can give me some insight. No reason to get overexcited. I stuff the letter into my purse. "I'll check into it. I'm sure it's nothing. Don't worry, okay?"

She nods, unconvinced.

"In the meantime, I've got something that will cheer you up." I open the lid on the chocolate cake as if unveiling a newly discovered Picasso. "Doesn't this look yummy? Oh, and this is for Martin." I hand her the bone, then reach to pat his head, but his lip quivers, revealing the glint of his pointy canine.

Another time, then.

She unwraps it, then sets Martin on the floor with his new prize. He picks up the bone and prances toward the living room.

I pour her a glass of milk and grab a fork before moving toward the sink and tackling the dirty dishes. "The weather's nice, don't you think? They mentioned rain later, but I don't see any storm clouds," I say, with hopes of lifting Jo's mood.

It didn't work.

Through the window's reflection I see the concerned look still plaguing Jo's face.

And she hasn't touched her cake.

Okay, now *I'm* worried. Jo never turns down a slice of sugary bliss.

The letter and its verbiage come to mind, dates and warnings and warnings and illegible signatures. But the more I think about the notice, the more I think it can't be legitimate. The IRS doesn't send a letter out of the blue and say you owe them a bundle of money, pay up now or else. *Right?* No, of course not. They have guidelines and rules, timelines and statutes to follow. This letter is a fraud, albeit a realistic attempt, but fraudulent nonetheless. I scratch at a chunk of egg caked on a plate with disgust. Whoever sent this deceitful letter is a horrid human being and I'm going to turn them in. They can't get away with this. God, how many unsuspecting older people actually mail in a check? Well, we'll get their money back. All of it. Sean will save the day. Justice will be served.

Twenty minutes later, after I've turned on *Wheel of Fortune* and put a load of towels in the wash, Jo walks me to the door. She just now studies my dress. "You're dressed up fancy. Where you off to?"

"Having dinner with my boyfriend. You remember Sean?"

"Who?"

She's met Sean before, many times. In fact, the two watched the final ten minutes of the presidential debate a few weeks ago while I called her homeowner's association about a cluster of bees nesting by her front hose bib.

She doesn't seem to remember.

A sense of urgency overcomes me as I grasp her frail hands and small wrists, the skin thinning over her cheekbones. She's smaller than I remember, shrinking with each passing day, and I'm reminded again by the physical proof that so many strained years have passed. I pull her close and hug her.

Martin gets wind of my affection.

He doesn't like it.

He charges toward me and clamps his jaw around my ankle.

"Aagh!" I scream, and flick my foot, but the little snot-wipe bears down with a fierce grip.

"Martin, no!" Jo claps. "Off." She then scurries toward the living room and returns waving his bone. "Martin, come here, boy. Want your treat?"

He releases me and trots toward his master, sitting erect, proud, tail wagging.

Suck-up.

I examine my foot, grateful to discover he didn't puncture my tender skin. I'm fine. The same can't be said for my sling-backs, whose straps are now poked with tiny teeth marks.

"You okay?"

"Yeah, I think so."

"I don't know what it is about you. He's so good with everyone else. Maybe it's the heels."

Or maybe he should be stuffed down the garbage disposal.

She grabs Martin and follows me onto the porch. "You'll take care of the letter for me?"

"Yes, of course."

"Let me know the minute you know anything, okay?"

"Okay. But please try not to worry. We'll get it straightened out and have a laugh. I'll call you tomorrow." I climb into the hired ride.

My scar itches. It does this at random times: typing an e-mail, pouring detergent into the wash, watering the plants.

I trace my fingers along the four-inch shameful reminder snaking the inside of my right forearm and hidden underneath the sleeve of my dress. I keep it covered. *Always.* If no one sees it, no one asks questions. If the scar is out of view, I don't have to watch the mixture of shock and thank-God-it-isn't-my-family flicker in the eyes of strangers who claim it's none of their business but are dying to know what happened. If the mark is concealed, I don't have to rehash the moment I broke my family apart.

I glance out the window and wave good-bye to Jo.

The car pulls away but I'm unable to leave behind the pained expression weighing Jo's face.

It's far too familiar.

four

It's a typical clear evening in La Jolla. I roll down the window and inhale the smell of the ocean and the sounds of bell-ringing beach-cruiser bicycle riders. Happy-hour crowds spill into the sidewalks of open-air restaurants as we drive along Mission Boulevard, which curves and bends with the shoreline toward Antonio's, a boardwalk bistro in Pacific Beach.

Maybe it's the fact that I'm on my way to Sean or the excitement I feel about our joint adventure, but I allow the fresh air to blow away my anxiety regarding Jo, and I settle into a good mood. All around me are groups of friends laughing and couples holding hands. The streets are alive and colorful. The moisture in the air soothes my skin. I feel sorry for people still at work, boxed inside four walls with stuffy air and stuffy people. Or worse yet, those not in love. Outside, on the streets, savoring the evening, enjoying each other, is the place to be. I love this town.

Stopping at a red light, I watch a wave of pedestrians crossing toward the beach, no doubt heading to catch the notorious green flash, a vibrant spot on the horizon visible for a second or two before the sun dips good night into the ocean.

Halfway across the walk, a tan blond-haired girl with cut-off denim shorts and a turquoise bikini top flips her long hair and laughs at the shirtless surfer-looking guy beside her. He grabs her by the hand and they jog barefoot toward the curb, with a six-pack of Rolling Rock beer and a blanket folded over his other arm.

My mind drifts to the countless evenings Sean and I have spent at the beach, his hand on the small of my back, guiding me across this very street with our own blanket and cooler in tow. We've lounged away seasons of sunsets sipping wine and wiggling our toes in the sand while he read depositions and I reviewed client files or edited my manuscript.

But among those many evenings, there's one in particular, a night three and a half years ago, six months into our dating, that stands tall above the others.

"Watch this," Sean had said, pointing at the horizon. "Don't blink or you'll miss it."

"We've seen the flash before."

"Just watch." He slid his arm around me.

I can still feel the strength of his hand on my shoulder. The tumbling in my stomach as he stroked his thumb up and down my summer-kissed skin. The tiniest friction from his stubble when he leaned over to kiss my shoulder and whispered for the first time, "I love you, Bree."

I forgot what I was supposed to be looking at. The flash might have been the brightest, most expressive of the entire year. I didn't see it. I stared into Sean's eyes and repeated the words. *I love you.* Any other day, I would've been concerned with who watched, judged, but at that moment, I didn't care. The world around me stilled and I kissed him. My focus *was* him. My green flash was this man.

We shared a bottle of wine, then made love in a secluded spot by the pier. More than his tender words or strong hands blanketing my skin, or maybe *because* of them, an awareness saturated my body like a wave soaking deep into the sand. The first time in years that I allowed myself to *feel*. My parents' death sucked joy, anger, curiosity out of me. I had nothing left. Sean wrapped his arms around me and somehow my pain and guilt seemed less consuming if we shouldered it together. On that night, a balmy Thursday evening in July, I felt a flicker of possibility. The chance at a life not threaded with regret and shame.

My vibrating phone jars my thoughts. I read a text from Nixon.

> *Hope Sara likes coffee.*
> *Meet for coffee and I'll strangle you. Go for dinner . . .*
>   *cheapskate.*
> *Okay . . . but if the date sucks, you're footing the bill.*

Unable to stop the smile shaping my lips, I type, *Then don't let it suck.*

If all goes well in the coming days, he'll share a romantic dinner with an art curator. A woman of poise and intellect. Beauty and brains. A complement to him. Sara may very well be the woman who breaks down Nixon's all-business-no-time-for-love approach to life. She may be the one to peel away his layers and soften his resolve.

And who knows? Maybe their love story will become a feature in the newspaper article. Or better yet, a chapter in . . . dare I say it . . . my self-help sequel. Maybe soon I'll be ordering a second sugar-pearl KitchenAid mixer.

As I catch a glance at the manila folder peeking out from my purse, the possibility of *my* evening hits me. Sean and I are signing papers, coupling our money, binding our *future*? We have had *the talk*. A number of times. Even stopped at the engagement ring section of jewelry stores, dog-eared pages of wedding dresses in bridal magazines, and scrolled through the *Ten Most Romantic Honeymoon Destinations* on Yahoo's travel website. Hell, we've dated longer than some marriages last, and the only reason we don't live together is that we agreed that with his civil litigation firm gaining traction and the attention my book and my company have demanded the last few years, it hasn't been the best time. But now my debut is all but stacked on the shelves and his law firm is a solid contender.

I inhale a deep breath, trying to settle the anticipation swirling through my head.

Did meeting with the advisor and discussion of a joint account trigger something within Sean? Is he ready for a shared last name? Monogrammed checkbook covers? A forever plus-one on RSVPs?

"Ma'am?" The driver motions that we've arrived.

"Oh, yes, thank you." I step out of the car and nearly prance along the sandy and sunny boardwalk toward Antonio's with a bubbly excitement for the evening ahead. There's nothing better than being in love.

Once I'm inside the dimly lit restaurant with floor-to-ceiling windows overlooking the ocean, complemented by the smell of grilling steak, garlic, and fresh fish, the familiar hostess says, "Mr. Thomas is already seated."

"Thank you." Before joining him, I pop into the restroom and comb my fingers through my hair, pinching my cheeks so they flush pink. I smooth my dress, pleased with my toned belly and sculpted thighs. Hot yoga has paid off.

Ready and eager to find Sean, I walk past the classy bar with its dark wood trim and glass shelves lined with polished liquor bottles and head toward the dining room decorated with rich linen tablecloths and waiters decked in bow ties. Antonio's is where Sean and I came for our first date. It's where we've come for each birthday and anniversary thereafter. It's the place we bring his parents when they're in town. It's the place we cele-brated Sean's first won trial and my book contract, sitting at the same curved leather booth by the window, sharing unhur-ried conversation and a bottle of Chateau Montelena Cabernet Sauvignon. Sometimes two.

Antonio's is our place.

Comfortable.

Warm.

Familiar.

So why is Sean gulping whiskey like a dehydrated Death Valley hiker sucks down water?

five

Experts say we lose our hearing bilaterally at a rate of two or more decibels per year. The average person is partially impaired by age fifty-four. Perhaps mine is deteriorating faster. Perhaps I have the eardrums of an old woman who spent her working years as an airport traffic director, never wearing the brightly colored ear protectors. I tug at my earlobe. That's it. It's the only possible explanation. I'm growing deaf. I mean, Sean didn't actually *say* what I think I heard, right?

I force a little laugh. "What did you say?"

He sits across from me sporting a white button-down shirt, slightly wrinkled at the bend of the arm. His tie rests a touch to the left and his suit jacket is slung over the booth. Sean pushes his empty glass aside—one of three, I now notice—and taps his finger on the stack of documents I placed on the table. "I'm sorry. I don't know how else to say it. But this isn't working."

"What isn't working?" I pray to God he's referring to his TAG Heuer carbon composite watch, a thirty-five-hundred-dollar present he bought himself a few years ago after he won his first trial, or maybe a misspelling in the paperwork's word-ing, but in my heart, I know that's not true.

"Us, Bree. Everything. This." He sweeps his hands across the table as if to imply that our complimentary sourdough bread basket is also part of the problem.

"I . . . I don't understand." My words are thick and confused, like the night I caught Dad sliding a dollar under my pillow, my baby tooth clutched in his other palm. "Where is this coming from? It makes no sense. We're good. We're happy. Aren't we?"

Though the truth is revealed in his creased brow and clamped jaw, the gentle shake of Sean's head squashes any remaining doubt.

I close my eyes tight and try to breathe.

This can't be real. This can't be happening.

But no matter how many times I blink my eyes clear, I still see the certitude on Sean's face.

This is happening.

"I'm not ready to sign papers. I'm not ready to link our . . ."

"Our what? Our futures."

"Yes."

"But *you* wanted to pool our money. This was your idea. You sent me flowers the morning of our appointment. You said to meet here tonight."

"Yes, I know. But ever since we met with the advisor . . ." He pauses and runs his fingers through his hair. I'm momentarily elated, noticing his widow's peak has widened. The crown of his head will be bald by fifty. Something I overlooked in love. That, along with his small hands. "I didn't expect the appoint-ment and the relevant discourse and the commingling of funds and these papers to . . . I don't know . . . change things for me. I feel stifled."

"Stifled?"

"Yeah, claustrophobic."

"So you're breaking up with me?"

"I'll admit the timing is less than ideal, but I decided if we came here tonight, to our first date spot, it'd be cyclical somehow and the best way to prove that this isn't about you. It's me. It's all my doing. Hell, you're perfect for me."

"You're breaking up with me, because I'm perfect for you?" For a lawyer, he's got seriously flawed thinking.

"Bree, I'm so sorry." He clasps my hand. "If you'll let me explain—"

"What else is there to explain? You love everything about me but don't want me in your future, and please will I get the hell out of your life." I flick his hand away and stare into the eyes that until this moment were seductive and gravitating, definitive and sound. Eyes that I'd assumed would always be mine. "You've explained enough." I slide out of the booth, waving the documents in the air. "And you want to know the most pathetic thing of this evening? I thought you might propose."

"Bree, wait."

I march out the door, dragging my dignity like a dead tree branch behind me.

The predictions held true. The clear sky has turned cloudy and started to rain. As I hurry along the boardwalk, my tears blend with the weather and within seconds, La Jolla's beautiful night has turned into a thick, sticky, soaked mess. Like me.

I've wished many times in my life that I weren't afraid to drive. Wished the accident didn't haunt me, stunt me. Because Sean calls after me and I'm forced to stand in the doorway of the women's public restroom, frantically texting for an Uber car to whisk me home, as rain bounces off the concrete, splashing my shoes and calves.

I spot the Uber car and quickly scramble into the backseat,

shivering and apologizing for the pool of water saturating his leather seat.

He turns on the heat. "You okay, ma'am?"

No. "Take me home, please."

Half an hour ago I thought I'd done it. Climbed the summit of love. Trekked past the loose and jagged rocks of dating and uncertainty. Crested to the solid ground of comfort and trust. And now, I find myself slid down to the mountain base. My ass cut and bruised. The snowcapped peak of my future has disappeared behind the billowing clouds.

I grit my teeth, forcing myself not to cry in this man's presence, but a few minutes into the drive my shoulders collapse and my tears flow faster than the raindrops splatting the car windows. My head spins with questions. *Four years together and now I'm suffocating you? Why, Sean, why?*

Standing in my entryway ten minutes later, I strip off my wet clothes, head into the living room, and crank on the gas fireplace.

As the fire flashes to life, warming my cheeks, knees, and toes, I wrap myself in a blanket and head toward the fridge, finding another one of Sean's notes stuck above the fridge's ice dispenser.

Horseradish.

I trace my fingers over his letters. As I stop on *d*, something clicks inside me. *Of all the dumb-ass habits.* I snatch the note from the fridge and rip it into shreds, admitting to myself that I've always hated his little reminders. Why can't he remember a damn thing without writing it down?

I pop the cork off a bottle of Champagne I keep chilled for our special evenings and take a long, comforting swig.

Halfway—okay, three fourths—into the bottle, I lie spread-eagle on the floor, deciding my life without Sean will be good. Damn good. No more reaching for my toothbrush only to discover it's wet. No more annoying Fox News piercing the promise and hope of the crisp morning air. No more scattered bits of shaved black hairs in my bathroom sink.

It's then I notice another Post-it stuck to the baseboard underneath my end table. Damn things are like cockroaches. But my breath catches in my chest as I read Sean's words.

L'Straut Jewelers . . . ask Bree.

L'Straut Jewelers is the most sought-after jewelry store in San Diego. It's where he bought his watch. It's where we playfully tried on several engagement rings, marking our favorites. It's where they recorded my ring size.

A proposal?

I'm not sure if this discovery makes me feel better or worse. Both, I suppose. Though I'm not clear when he wrote the note, somehow I'm grateful knowing that the four years we spent together, regardless of what happened tonight, were genuine. He loves me. Or at least did.

I scramble up the stairs and climb into bed. Three cinnamon-scented candles flicker on my dresser, but I still smell Sean. The scent of his spring-fresh shampoo lingers on my sheets.

I can hear him, too. I can hear him curse when he scrapes his shin, inching my dresser away from the wall after my diamond teardrop necklace slipped behind it. I can hear him whistle the theme song to *The Office* as he fastens his belt or ties the laces of his polished shoes. I can hear him snore, vibrating the mattress the tiniest bit when he breathes in and out.

I pull the covers over my head and bury my ears into my pillow, hoping the doctors are right, hoping my hearing will fail and I won't listen to myself crying to sleep.

six

There's not enough concealer on the planet to mask the bags and dark circles under my eyes the following morning. I look like I drank too much Champagne, then spent the night tossing and turning and washing my sheets at four a.m. . . . Oh, that's right, I did.

With eye drops, aspirin, and a coffee the size of a milk jug, I walk toward work only to find myself trapped at an intersection behind a young couple making out. *It's eight forty-five a.m., for Christ's sake!* I step aside only to bump into another guy murmuring into his phone, "I miss you, baby. Can't wait for tonight."

Ugh.

I cross the street, and though I marveled at the beauty of La Jolla's streets on my way to Antonio's last night, this time I see crooked cracks and seeped stains in the sidewalk. Flies circle trash cans overstuffed with Starbucks cups and McDonald's wrappers. Muddled newspapers, plastic bags, and crumpled leaves are smushed into storm drains. The stench from car exhaust and rotten grease traps heavies the air. I hear nothing but honking horns, screeching brakes, and a homeless woman yelling obscenities at a man in a black jogging suit.

La Jolla streets have lost their charm.

So has love.

Trudging into my office, I shut out the outside world and shift my focus to what I'm good at. Diligence. Center. Control.

An e-mail from the financial advisor lights up my screen.

> *We're ready to activate the Thomas/Caxton account.*
> *Documents signed?*

Great. Now I have to explain to a relative stranger that my life fell apart.

But rather than feel any more sorry for myself, I reply, *Change of plans. I will be the only one investing. You have my account info. Wire the funds as we discussed and move ahead accordingly.* I scan and attach the signed paperwork, then click send with a sense of achievement.

"Dang, girl. Must've been some night," Andrew says, smoothing lotion onto his slightly orange spray-tanned hands and settling in the chair opposite my desk. "Let me hear all the romantic things Sean did for you last night. Tell me the naughty parts. Twice. Three times if they're really naughty."

"Let's get to work. We've got a lot to do today."

Andrew's smile vanishes. "You okay?"

Am I okay? The words grate my nerves like knuckles drawn across sandpaper. How many times did Mom's banking colleagues or Dad's poker buddies ask me that at the funeral? The words evoke a familiar emptiness that makes me a little sick to my stomach. And just like I did then, I reply to Andrew with a bit more snap than necessary, "Where's the coffee cup Sean bought me from Anthropologie?"

"The one with your initial?"

"The very one."

He returns from the break room and hands me the mug.

I clasp my fingers around the cool handle of the oversized cup, examining the ceramic's smooth glazed ivory-colored finish. With my thumb, I trace the swooping letter *B* inked in black.

The night Sean bought this for me, we'd grabbed a quick dinner at Bella's before walking hand-in-hand through the Mercado, an outdoor mall canopied with globe lights strung from shop to shop above the cobblestone walkway. Through the window of Anthropologie, I spotted the new red-and-cream Aari duvet on display. "Ooh, let's pop in for a sec."

Sean followed me inside and stood close while I contemplated. "I love the pattern, but worry the red is *too* red. I don't want it to clash with the sunset picture over my bed."

He reached for the price tag and choked on his words. "Five hundred and ninety-eight dollars?"

"It's embroidered."

"It's a blanket." He shoved his hands in his pockets, stepped behind me in a wrinkled-in-all-the-right-places American Apparel T-shirt, and whispered in my ear. His breath tickled my neck as he said, "Will you sleep naked underneath that five-hundred-and-ninety-eight-dollar blanket?"

Now, months later, I sit at my desk and tap the mug's base against the palm of my other hand. It's a quality cup. Well constructed. Sturdy.

Geronimo! I pitch it into the trash can. The mug echoes like a firework as it smacks the bottom. The ceramic splinters into delightful black-and-white shards.

My version of retail therapy.

Andrew gasps. "What are you doing? You love that mug."

"Hand me the vase."

He glances at Sean's bouquet, resting defenseless on the sideboard. "What? Why?"

"Just give it to me."

He hurries between me and the vase, shielding the glass with his spread-eagle arms. "Sit down and tell me what happened. Don't take it out on the Waterford."

"Okay." I exhale a long breath. "That's sound advice. Thank you."

"Yes, good. That's better. Let's take a second and relax." He settles into his chair. "Now, very calmly, tell me—"

I sneak past him and snatch the vase, smashing it into the bottom of the trash can with a satisfying *thud*. Water splashes onto the floor, showering Andrew's feet.

"Bree, what the hell's gotten into you?"

I scour the room, tapping my foot like a jackhammer. What else did Sean give me that I can destroy? Ah, yes, the picture frame. I line up with the trash can, poising for two points, but notice Andrew blotting water droplets off his suede loafers. The same loafers he bought last Friday after saving for three months. With the frame in my lap, I slump into my chair. "Sean broke up with me."

"Cocksucker."

I almost laugh at such a foul word coming from the mouth of a man who fixed a piglet eraser on his favorite pencil.

"Says he doesn't want a joint account and thought last night, at Antonio's, was the perfect place to end our relationship, some circle-of-life nonsense." I stare at the Cabo picture and Sean's yellow swim trunks that we'd bought at the hotel gift shop after discovering he'd packed none.

"Bree, I'm so sorry."

I grab the frame and slip the photo free from the glass. "Who says 'I want to share my financial future with you,' then dumps you a week later in a corner booth? In *our* corner booth." I tear the picture into pieces, then sprinkle them into the trash can.

Andrew crouches beside me and wraps his arms around me. "I'm sorry, hon."

My tears trickle again.

Andrew cries, too, and I love him a little bit more for it.

"How did I miss this?" I say. "How did my life fall apart in a matter of seconds?" I shake my head. "Obviously, I'm not quite the expert in love like I thought."

"Stop." Andrew points his finger an inch away from my nose. His face is fierce like an alley dog defending a bone. "You're amazing at your job. No one does it better. Don't for a second think your personal life has any impact on your professional life. Don't give Sean the credit." He pulls a petal from my hair. "As a matter of fact, Sara left a message this morning about Nixon. They talked last night and had an instant connection. You did that, and you've done all of this." He gestures above me at my wall of happy couples.

"I knew he'd like her," I say between sniffles.

"And, by the sound of her voice, she likes him, too. They have a date this weekend."

"Yeah? That's good."

"It *is* good." He wipes mascara away from under my eyes. "Don't ever question your abilities, understand? Sean's the bad guy. Not you. You know what would make you feel better?"

"Nachos."

"If you stand tall, don't let Sean be the victor."

I'm empowered by his confidence and the conviction in his eyes until I get a glimpse of his water-spattered loafers. "Oh, Andrew, I'm sorry. Are your shoes ruined?"

"Nah, I like polka dots anyway." He picks up a few petals

and picture shreds decorating the carpet. "I'm gonna get a broom and sweep this up."

Andrew's advice brings me comfort, and several minutes pass without any thoughts of Sean until I hear the Fratellis song playing on my cell phone.

I let it ring—the third call since last night.

Sure it's childish to avoid him. And a bit immature to ignore his pleading outside my front door before work this morning. He could've let himself in with his key and I appreciate the fact that he didn't because I'm not ready to hear Sean's voice or look at the lips that less than twenty-four hours ago were mouthing the words, "I feel claustrophobic."

It occurs to me as the song plays over and over that the ringtone no longer soothes me. The lead singer's Scottish voice no longer sounds smooth and easy, seductive and familiar. Now, his voice screeches in my ears like a dentist's drill coring out a cavity.

I click on the settings tab and search through the choices for a new sound. I want something unique, something true to Sean's character. Unfortunately they don't have a selection labeled *ass-wipe*—what would it sound like anyway?—but they do have one called *donkey*. Close enough.

Sean leaves a voice mail and a *hee-haw . . . hee-haw* sound resonates from my phone.

Excited over my small victory—*Go, Bree!*—I absentmindedly press the play button.

"I know you're mad. You have every right to be. But please, can we get together and talk? That's all I'm asking. I love you so much and I always will. Baby, please, just talk to me."

I press play again.

Baby, please, just talk to me.

"Oh, Bree." Andrew returns. "It'll be okay. I promise it'll be . . . oh, no."

"What?"

"Randi's here."

"What? Where?" Through the office window I see my publicist walking toward my front door.

"Go pull yourself together. I'll delay her."

I swallow the last four years of my life wedged deep inside my throat and hurry into the bathroom with hopes that my face doesn't look red and blotchy.

No such luck.

Not only do I feel like crap, but as a bonus, I look like crap, too. *Lucky me.*

But as I splash water on my face and stare at my reflection, I see behind my spotted skin and puffy eyelids; I see *me.*

Andrew's right. I'm a successful businesswoman on the verge of launching a nationwide interview and a debut book. How many people can say that? And what about all the other positives in my life? Hell, I've traveled through twenty-five states, stuck my head out of the Statue of Liberty's crown, and just last month ran my sixth half marathon in under two hours. An armful of accomplishments, to say the least.

Suffocating you, eh, Sean? Well, fine. Go ahead and spread your wings. Fly away, high in the sky. Hope you choke on all the fresh air.

"Good morning," Randi calls from across the room. "I received the particulars from the paper. Let's sit, I'll explain."

Andrew winks at me and offers a nod of encouragement before handing Randi a cup of coffee.

"Ah, you're heaven sent. And with a tight ass I could bounce quarters off of." Randi sips her coffee, leaving behind a red lipstick imprint. "Well, let's get to it. My contact at the *National Tribune* told me each installment will focus on a different aspect of Bree Caxton and Associates. For example, one might touch on your background, another on the company's mission, and another will highlight your matchups, that sort of thing. Sounds fun, don't you think?"

"Sounds great." And it does. *This is good. Concentrate on work.*

"Once they get some feedback, they might make changes or venture down another path, but for now, that's the initial plan. I have the specifics for the first week."

"Fire away."

She slides on her jeweled reader glasses—something she likely denied needing for as long as possible—and refers to an e-mail on her iPad. "Tomorrow's interview will start with you. They want to highlight the woman behind the business before shifting to your work and your success."

"Okay." Easy enough.

"They'll ask why you do what you do, that sort of thing. They'll interview you here, let me find the time." She scrolls through the rest of the e-mail, then pulls off her glasses. "Good Lord, they'll arrive at eight a.m. What a god-awful time of the morning to be presentable. Don't worry, I'll bring Bloody Marys." She returns her glasses to the bridge of her nose. "They'll ask about the book, and we want them to. But we don't want to give too much away about the content or offer too many of your tips. We want to tease the readers. Lift the skirt and show a little leg, but not the kitty in the middle. Make sense?"

Oddly enough it does.

"They'll want a photo. So do something with your bangs."

Andrew nods in agreement.

What's wrong with my bangs?

She removes her glasses again and looks at me. "Come to think of it, your eyes are red. Your face is splotchy and swollen, too. Have you gained weight? Are you preggo?"

"No."

"Stoned?"

"God, no."

"All right, then. I guess that covers it for now." She takes a long sip of coffee, then stands, noticing the broken vase and flowers in the trash can. "What happened?"

"That . . . um . . . ?" I'm searching my mind for a way out, something plausible and convincing, but I draw a blank under her demanding glare. The only thing that comes to mind is Sean. And the fact that he's no longer *my* Sean. But I can't tell her that. I can't walk around proclaiming to be a master at love and relationships, then say, "Want to hear a funny story? Last night my boyfriend dumped me."

Actually, it's not that funny.

Andrew comes to my rescue. "Damn vase had a crack in it. Water leaked all over Bree's desk. Even dribbled on my shoes."

"That's right. Ruined a picture, too. I didn't want it spilling all over everything else, so I dropped the vase into the trash can." Would've shattered it with a baseball bat had I the chance.

Randi gathers her purse. "For a moment I feared you'd say you had a fight with whoever sent you those flowers. Or worse, broke up."

Andrew's laugh borderlines on a cackle. "That's hilarious."

"Aspiring bestsellers say all sorts of things to make it to the top. Remember that bogus memoir from the druggie years back? Went on Oprah and everything only to find out he made everything up. All of it." She glances at my naked ring finger. Her lips draw tight and she narrows her eyes on me, forming a thin line across her brow. "Just to be clear, you do have someone in your life, right?"

"Yes. Yes, she does," Andrew says, avoiding my openmouthed stare.

"Why did I even ask? You're too beautiful not to. I'll see you tomorrow, eight a.m. sharp." Randi hurries toward the door, turns, and says, "I look forward to meeting your man."

"My what?"

"Your man. The paper wants him here as well."

I tug at my ear. "Um, why?"

"It adds the element of credibility, proof that a successful matchmaker who preaches and orders people around is in love herself."

Is this a nightmare? I bite down hard on the inside of my cheek, but I don't wake from a bad dream. Nothing changes except for now I have a sore spot in my mouth. "Um . . . Randi, wait."

"Yes?"

"You see, uh . . . tiny problem . . . and you're gonna get a kick out of this." I start to laugh.

"Spill it. I've got work to do."

"Yes, that's just it. My boyfriend, the man who exists and is madly in love with me . . . like, over-the-top crazy about me, well . . . he's . . . he's working. Can't get away, I'm afraid. Such short notice and all."

My neck itches the moment the words leave my mouth. A side effect of when I lie. It's why I never play poker and always dodge Jo's asking me if I think Martin is "the cutest thing in the whole wide world."

Randi folds her arms across her chest.

She doesn't believe me.

"Very important man," Andrew adds. "A doctor."

"Doctor?" Randi says. "That's interesting. Tell me more."

"He's a . . . a . . . urologist," Andrew says.

Urologist?

He nudges my shoulder and whispers, "Say something."

"Um . . . that's right. He has a surgery scheduled tomorrow morning. A penis transplant." *Did I just say that?* I scratch at my tender skin.

Randi shrugs and says, "Well, I'm sorry, he'll have to figure something out. It's a condition of the contract. Didn't you read page six?"

"Yes, but I don't recall specific mention of a boyfriend requirement."

"It mentions you providing access to all aspects of your life, professional and personal. Now, I made myself clear. Did I not?"

"He'll be there," Andrew says.

"He sure as shit better be. Or the deal is off. Toodles." The door closes behind her.

"He'll be there?" I practically shout at Andrew. "Who will be there? Who?"

"At least I didn't say he had a scheduled penis transplant. Do they even do such a thing?" Andrew covers his crotch with his hands.

"What have I gotten myself into? Why didn't I just tell the truth?"

"Oh, c'mon. It's a tiny white lie."

Easy for him to say. A tiny white lie got me caught smoking cigarettes after school instead of attending my Girl Scouts meeting in fifth grade. A tiny white lie got me fired from Burger-a-rama my sophomore year. A tiny white lie got my parents killed.

"This is going to come back and bite me in the butt. In case you forgot, I have no boyfriend. Oh, God. I'm having a heart attack." I press his palm against my heart. "Feel that? I'm having my first chest pain."

"You can't back out now."

"Christ, Andrew, how am I going to get through this? How am I supposed to find a boyfriend in twenty-four hours?"

seven

My panic attack subsided. My chest pains stopped, too. So I'm not getting out of this jam with a heart attack. *Can't a girl catch a break?*

"What about him?" Andrew points to a tall man in a navy blue suit, with a frosting of gray hair above his temple, sipping a Bud Light at the bar. "He's cute."

Andrew persuaded me to close the office early and numb the pain of my shitty day with a pitcher of happy hour margaritas. "For the last time, I am not going to hit on a guy and ask him to stop by my office tomorrow morning and then say, 'Wanna pretend we're crazy in love and you're the country's leading expert in penis transplants?'"

"I know it sounds nuts." He chuckles at his pun. "But you don't have much choice."

"What if he's a serial killer?"

"Do you honestly think a mass murderer pops into T.G.I. Friday's for half-price chicken wings?" He sips his drink. "You could ask Sean."

"I'd rather you squirt acid in my eyes, thank you very much."

"C'mon, he screwed up. Let him make it up to you."

"That's enough tequila for you." I slide his margarita over toward me.

He slides it back. "It's not a bad idea."

"It's a horrible idea. Sean knows he hurt me emotionally; there's no way in hell I'll admit he's hurting me professionally, too." I fiddle with my napkin. "It wouldn't work, anyway."

"Who, Sean?"

"No, him." I point my straw toward the man at the bar. "He moves his hands too much when he talks, and he drinks Bud Light. Hard to respect a guy who drinks watered-down beer." *Sean drinks Guinness.* I force thoughts of him from my head. I am not going to let him sour my evening. I release a long sigh. "This whole situation completely, unequivocally sucks booty."

"Good thing your fake boyfriend is a urologist."

"Technically, he'd need to be a proctologist. And that's not funny."

"Yes, it is." Andrew winks. "Pick another guy here, then."

My phone rings. The caller ID reads Lawrence Chambers.

"I gotta take this." I step away. On top of my breakup and the fiasco I webbed myself into, Jo's IRS letter that I'd convinced myself was a scam still niggles at the back of my brain. Thanks to my ex-boyfriend's ill-timed mental breakdown— not that there's ever a *well-timed* mental breakdown—I can no longer ask him. So this morning I e-mailed his colleague that I remembered him mentioning.

"Lawrence Chambers is a bulldog," Sean had said.

Not sure if bulldog is a good or bad thing, but the way Sean carved into his steak, tearing it into pieces, suggested Lawrence might be worth a call.

"Hello, Mr. Chambers, thanks for phoning back."

"My secretary said something about a tax lien?" His voice

is slow and thick like a cup of cold diner coffee. Something tells me he sits relaxed in a leather wingback chair, stroking a too-short tie, and inhaling puffs of an expensive cigar with a vintage set of law books lining the wall behind him.

"Yes, I'm inquiring on my grandmother's behalf. It's possible I'm overreacting, but the letter says to contact the IRS to prevent loss of property. My grandmother thinks it's the real thing and frankly I can't tell myself. I just want to make sure."

"Is it a 1058 form?"

I pull the letter from my purse and refer to the number on the upper right of the page. "Yes. Is that significant?"

"E-mail the document and I'll make a few calls to confirm the validity."

"Okay, I appreciate this."

"To be clear, you're officially retaining my legal services?"

"Yes, I guess so."

"I'll need a check for twenty-five hundred dollars. That'll get me started."

Jesus. How much to get you finished? Earlier today I received confirmation from the advisor that the bulk of my savings account was transferred into the investment fund. Deducting another $2,500 squeezes things a bit tight. But with no other choice, I agree.

"My secretary will forward the contract," he says. "I'll be in touch."

"Okay, thank you. Um . . . Mr. Chambers . . . should we be worried?"

I'm too late.

He clicked off.

"Don't frown like that," Andrew says as I climb onto the bar stool. "Botox is expensive."

"Look at this."

Andrew scans the letter before handing it back to me. "You

know my literacy rate is barely higher than a scrappy eleven-year-old. What does it mean?"

"I'm not totally sure. It's the letter that upset Jo yesterday, and I have a feeling it wasn't her first notice. That call was from a lawyer I hired."

"This amount, nearly fifty thousand dollars, she owes that?"

"That's what I'm afraid of."

"What'd the lawyer say?"

"He's getting back to me." I skim the letter again. "But I don't think it's gonna be with good news."

"Does she have the money?"

"Not unless she knocked over a couple 7-Elevens that I don't know about. She and G-pa took out a reverse mortgage on their house years ago. There's no equity in the property. As far as savings, she's lived off her social security and my G-pa's pension for years. I take care of the extras. So no, she doesn't have the money."

"Okay, well, you said yourself there's a lot of swindlers out there, feasting on old people. Let's wait to hear from this lawyer guy before freaking out. How about we focus on your more immediate threat?"

Hee-haw . . . Hee-haw . . . hee-haw.

"Speak of the devil," he says.

I silence my phone without looking at the screen.

"You can't ignore him forever."

"Says who?"

"Says you, if you weren't acting so stubborn."

"Is it wrong that I want him to suffer? That I want him to stew in misery and lose sleep and wear the same shirt for a week and get all pale and sallow and sunken cheeks and have his friends tell him he looks awful and smells awful before begging me to take him back?"

"No. There's nothing wrong with that at all." He clinks his glass with mine. "Okay, so as far as the paper goes, what about asking a favor from an old boyfriend? What about that guy from college? Tim or Todd or something?"

"Troy."

"Yeah, what about him?"

"Married."

"Happily?"

My scowl reveals my answer.

"I could ask one of my guy friends."

"To do what? Fall in love with me in a few hours?"

"Most people do." He nudges my shoulder with his hand. "C'mon, now, we've got to think of something."

He's right. I called Randi a couple of hours ago and explained . . . okay, begged . . . that my boyfriend couldn't make the interview and can't we exclude that provision from the contract? I sounded professional and resolute.

She had none of it.

The TV signals that it's six p.m. I swallow the last of my margarita. "I better go."

"You're still going?"

"To my Q&A? Of course I am. Why wouldn't I?"

"I don't know, maybe because your life is a total wreck at the moment."

"Thank you for reminding me. I'd forgotten for five whole seconds." I slide my purse onto my shoulder. "Being with the group will clear my head. Besides, you know I haven't missed but one or two meetings all year. They need me."

"You need them."

It's true. I started the weekly Q&A sessions months ago as an added service for my clients, an impromptu way to pose relationship topics and bounce ideas around. We meet at the library and even though the same handful of people show up, a small group of my older clients, I don't have the heart to cancel, because one, I'm a sucker for happy old people and number two . . . well, I guess there's only one reason. They smuggle in a Thermos full of wine and we share a few insights about relationships, but the conversation always turns to laughter and memories from their younger years. I'm like an adopted daughter to them. At least, that's how I feel.

I kiss him on the cheek and say, "I'm off. Take care of you."

"Take care of you."

Twenty minutes later, I walk through the sliding doors and into the library. The hushed corner chats and soft-stepping librarians do nothing to drown out voices ricocheting through my head. *Please, baby . . . talk to me. Final Notice. Five-week spread. Bring your man.*

But as I turn the corner and wave at my handful of attendees sitting around a square table in a glass-walled conference room, sneaking sips of Chardonnay from their matching travel tumblers that Gwen, the *youngest* older lady, bought on clearance at BevMo, my mood lifts.

"So, you *are* stalking me."

I spin around and see Nixon stepping toward me in a black T-shirt, weathered jeans, and leather-soled flip-flops. I've never seen him in casual clothes and I'm pleased to notice he's got strong forearms and solid feet. He looks good. Sipping-a-Corona-in-a-hammock good.

For half a second, I let my eyes wander down his shirt, which stretches tight against his biceps and drapes over his stomach. I imagine him grasping the back neck collar and pulling the shirt off overhead in one smooth move, revealing a tan chiseled chest. I wonder what his skin smells like after a day at the beach.

"Bree?"

"Um . . . hey, there, Nixon." *His skin after a day at the*

beach? Where the hell did that come from? Last time I say yes to a Grand Marnier float in my margarita for only two dollars more. I shake clear my thoughts and smile, deciding the laid-back look will be a nice side of Nixon for Sara to see.

It's then that a sandy-haired six-, maybe seven-year-old boy darts from the comic book section, dragging a Quicksilver backpack. He grasps Nixon's leg. The two share the same shape nose.

His son? He never mentioned a boy. A child is a game-changer. As his love facilitator, I need to know about these things, about all aspects of his life.

"Who are you?" the little boy asks.

"I'm Bree." I smile at him. "Who are you?"

He says nothing, leaning closer against Nixon's thigh.

"Your son?"

"No." Nixon tousles the boy's hair. "My nephew."

"Ah."

"This little dude takes reading lessons once a week and then we stuff our face with pizza."

"Uncle Nixon lets me have soda."

"We don't need no stinkin' teeth. Am I right?" Nixon jokes. The two high-five.

"I've never seen you two here before."

"His instructor switched the time. We were coming Thursdays."

The boy, totally bored with our conversation, begins to search through his backpack.

A *swoosh* sound from an incoming e-mail triggers Nixon to reach for his phone. He scrolls through a message, ignoring me and the library's TURN OFF YOUR CELL PHONE sign.

"What happens if your phone isn't within reach? Panic attack? Shortness of breath? Spotted vision?"

"My work is important."

"Speaking of important, ready for your date with Sara?"

"Actually, I have a budget meeting—"

"Don't you dare."

"Okay, okay." He tosses his hands in surrender. "I'll take her to dinner."

"You better. And, from what I'm told, she already likes you, so don't screw it up."

"Thanks for the vote of confidence."

"Walk a bit after dinner. Give her plenty of space, don't crowd. Compliment her shoes." I glance at the boy before whispering. "And don't spend the evening picturing what she looks like naked."

"Now I'm definitely not going."

"I'm serious. Remember, you're taking a new approach to dating. You're no longer picking dates based on their bra size. No more girls with HOTTIE bedazzled across their Lycra-clad butts. And don't bring your phone."

"Uncle Nix." The boy tugs on Nixon's sleeve. "I forgot my library card. We have to go home and get it."

"Your lesson starts in five minutes, buddy. We won't make it back in time."

"But I have to have my card to get into Kid Town. After my lesson, I get fifteen minutes in Kid Town. Mom said I could play the Xbox today."

"We'll knock, they'll let you in."

"No, it's a rule. We have to go home. C'mon." He tugs at Nixon's shirt again.

"Wait a second." I unzip my wallet and offer the boy my library card. "You can borrow mine. I don't need it today."

"No, that's okay," Nixon says. "I can get him a new one."

"Not unless you brought a decade's worth of electric bills and a hair follicle from your great-grandfather. They're kinda strict around here."

"But you won't be able to play the Xbox," Nixon's nephew says to me.

"Do they have Ms. Pac-Man?"

He shakes his head.

"Then no worries. I like to chomp the ghosts."

The inkling of a held-back smile twists the edges of the boy's lips as he takes the card from my hand.

"Well, we better get you to practice. Thanks, Bree."

"No problem. Have fun."

"Isn't he a handsome man?" Gwen says as I enter the conference room.

I peek through the glass at Nixon.

He playfully punches his nephew in the arm as the two walk away.

Just like I thought, a mushy center.

eight

"For the love of God, why are we having this conversation again?" Randi says, at ten minutes to eight o'clock the following morning.

Is that smoke billowing from her ears?

"Don't you hear me?"

Yes, because you're yelling at me.

"The paper has a very specific vision. And, as we discussed already, the contract is binding. If your boyfriend doesn't show, then this interview is off and so is your chance at a bestseller." She stirs her Bloody Mary with a celery stalk.

I wrestled in bed all night long, tossing and turning (that makes two nights in a row), uncertain what to do. But once the sun crested and light spilled into my bedroom, I decided not to lie. I won't lie. I will tell the truth. Yes, I want my book to do well, but not at the expense of deception.

"This isn't hard to understand," she snaps.

"I'm sorry to be difficult, but there's no way—"

"Bree, can I talk to you for a moment?" Andrew interrupts.

"In a minute," I tell him. "I know the contract says—"

"It'll just take a second." Andrew steps closer.

Andrew and I have an agreement that the other one is to step in if a client or salesperson overstays their welcome and we need rescuing. But surely Andrew can appreciate the difference here?

"Please, Bree," he says, a bit more agitated.

What is his problem? "Sorry, Randi, I apologize for the—"

"I need to speak with you now!" Andrew nearly shrieks, waving his hands in the air as if trying to scare away a bat dive-bombing his head.

Good Lord. "Excuse me, Randi." I join Andrew in the break room. "Are you kidding me right now? What is so important? And don't you dare say you called me over just to tell me Netflix released another season of *Supernatural*."

"You can't tell the truth."

"Yes, I can. Don't worry, I'll still be at Randi's beck and call and I'll convince the paper to continue with the interviews. I just don't need a boyfriend beside me to validate my expertise." I start to step away, but Andrew grabs my arm.

What the heck?

"*Can I See You Again?* has got to become a bestseller. Think of Jo."

"What's with you?" I peel his fingers off my arm. "Is this about her letter? I appreciate your concern, but we don't even know if the letter is legit."

"We do now. Your attorney just e-mailed. The letter is the real deal."

"It is? Damn. I feared this would happen. Okay, well—"

"And he can't stop the auction."

"Auction? What auction? He said, 'auction'?"

"He did. If you don't come up with the money, Jo loses her house."

"Oh my God." I press my hands against my forehead and

pace back and forth in front of the sink. "Her house? They can't take her house. Can they take her house? Are you sure he said 'auction'?"

"I'm afraid so. I checked the business account. You can spare maybe ten grand."

And, thanks to my investment deposit and the lawyer's retainer, same goes for my savings account.

Wish I hadn't blown my $10,000 book advance on ten days in Wailea with Sean, especially since the sex on the beach was hardly worth the sand in inappropriate places. Stupid, stupid, selfish Bree.

But, Jesus, my G-pa built that house. Their handprints are cemented in the sidewalk. My mom's growth chart is penciled on the wall behind the laundry room door. "I promised Jo, Andrew. I promised that she'd never have to leave that house. I've taken so much from her . . . and now her house . . . what am I going to do?"

"I have fifteen hundred in a CD," Andrew says in a voice so tender it nearly splits my heart in pieces. "She's my grand-mother, too, you know."

And he means it. He really does. Given the arm's-length distance at which his parents keep him, Jo's the only family he really has.

I reach out and stroke his hand. "Thanks, love, but I can't take your money."

"They're here." Randi steps into the break room. She swallows the last of her drink and tosses the empty cup into the trash. "Do not make me look like a goddamn fool. Your guy has exactly thirty seconds to walk through that door." She storms out.

Auction. Auction. Auction.

"There's a way to come up with the rest of the money, you know," he says.

"How? Sell my body on the street corner?"

"The escalator clause."

He's right. If I pool together my available funds and Andrew's sweet contribution, the bonus will put us at the mark. It'd be enough.

"That means my book has to make the list."

"It does."

"And I have to find a boyfriend."

"That, too."

"And I have to lie."

"It's the only way you can save Jo's house."

"Bree, let's go," Randi orders.

"What are you going to do?" Andrew asks.

I have no idea.

⁓

"Hello, welcome," Randi says, greeting a woman hidden behind a pair of tortoise-shell sunglasses. Her hair is platinum and straight and angled sharp below bronzed cheekbones. She's a sauntering blend of sophistication and edginess, dressed in black leggings, a taupe cashmere tunic, and sleek nude stilettos.

"It's good to see you, Randi." A chunky ivory bracelet slips toward her elbow as the woman slides her glasses on top of her head.

"No way. It's Candace Porter," I whisper to Andrew, who stepped close. "I recognize her from past articles in the *Close-Up* section. She won the Excellence in Feature Writing award the last three years. God, Andrew, Candace Porter is one of the most well-known journalists in Southern California. She was the first to interview that transgender football player, remember?"

Not to mention, she's married to a Los Angeles Kings hockey player and the pair is often spotted at trendy bars, hotels, and restaurants. Not only does she write for the paper, but photos of her frequent the *Who's Who* section.

She's the kind of person that you love to hate until you get to know her and find out she donates her time at soup kitchens and Red Cross fund-raisers. Then you just hate yourself for not doing the same.

The impact of the situation hits me. This is a bigger deal than I thought. Only a chosen few are spotlighted in *Close-Up* and even fewer are interviewed by Candace Porter. And she's here for me. *Holy crap!* Her platform and its reach . . . *Andrew's right, I can't screw this up.* I wish I'd taken Randi up on the offer of a Bloody Mary.

Following Candace inside is a rail-thin, surfs-before-work-looking young man decked out in a Metallica T-shirt and Volcom pants with tattered hems. He carries a duffel bag over his right shoulder.

"Who's that?" Andrew asks.

"Don't know."

"Wonder if he needs my help," Andrew jokes. "Or my phone number."

Candace scrutinizes my office, then points to my saddle chairs in the lobby and says to the guy, "Scotty, angle those forty-five degrees for better symmetry. Bring in the plant and rust-colored rug from my trunk. We'll start here."

"I'm on it." He disappears outside.

Most people may not appreciate Candace's presumption of sauntering into my office and rearranging my furniture like she owns the place. Not me. I'm impressed by her foresight. Look at her, positioning chairs. A classic move to create a comfortable setting. *Well done, Candace.*

"Okay," she says, "where's the woman of the hour?"

"Right here." Randi sweeps her hand in my direction. "This is Bree Caxton. Owner and operator of Bree Caxton and Associates."

"So you're the puppet master, pulling the heartstrings until they're tangled with love." Before I have the chance to answer, she raises her index finger, then jots onto a notepad she pulled from her pocket. "Until they're tangled with love. Love that line."

"Nice to meet you," I say, pumping our handshake. "And, now that I see it's you, I'm a bit nervous."

"Don't be. This won't hurt a bit."

How I wish this were true. I know it's a matter of time before Randi or Candace asks where the other half of my equation is.

"Can I get you anything? Coffee? Tea?" A red pen to strike out page six of the contract?

"No, thank you. Give me a couple minutes and then we'll get started."

Scotty returns with a tall vase of artificial peonies and a rolled-up rug.

"Right here, on the table." Candace points, then repositions a few of the branches as Scotty unrolls the carpet. She slides my watercolor waterfall picture a few inches to the left and fluffs up the chair's cushions. "Okay, I think we are all set. Ready, Bree?" She motions me toward the seat on the right.

"Yes. Ready." I pop in an Altoid and force a smile. *He's terribly sorry, but my boyfriend couldn't make it today. Those are exquisite earrings. Turquoise? First question, please.*

Scotty unpacks his camera with its massive lens, then kneels beside me. Stubble from a missed morning shave dots his chin, and his breath is heavy with stale coffee. "May I?"

"Um, sure?"

Scotty picks at my bangs.

"I told her to do something with those," Randi says, shooting daggers at me while pointing at her watch. "Where is he?" she mouths.

Before I have the chance to drown myself in the toilet, Scotty poses his camera inches from my face and snaps a few test shots.

I'm totally nervous now. I don't know what to do with my trembling hands. I tuck them underneath my thighs, but consider the weak impression I'm giving off and fold my hands, resting them on my lap, trying not to squeeze them tight. *Really sorry, he can't make it. But let's get going, shall we? Time is money.*

But as Candace places a voice recorder on the table between us and flips over a few pages of her notebook, my nerves settle. Maybe Candace won't ask about my boyfriend. Maybe my relationship status isn't that big a deal. The contract doesn't specifically say, *Must have a boyfriend.* Perhaps Randi's playing hardball with me. Acting safe. After all, she's looking out for sales and the more bases covered, the better.

The more I consider her perspective, the more I convince myself that I've gotten all worked up for nothing. This article is about me. Not Sean. Maybe the subject of my love life won't even come up.

I take a deep breath, exhaling my apprehension. Candace is right, this interview won't hurt a bit. After all, we'll discuss familiar territory, and I love talking about love. Facilitating relationships is what I do best. I almost laugh out loud at my foolish anxiety of moments ago. I mean, honestly, I can't imagine one single question thrown by Candace that'll rattle me.

She clicks off her recorder. "Where's your boyfriend?"

Except that one.

nine

Jo's birthday is November second, two days after mine. On the day between my twelfth and her sixty-first birthday, a Saturday, nineteen years ago, we went to Chili's for lunch, then visited Barnes & Noble at the Southcoast Plaza Mall. We wandered the afternoon through the romance, humor, and young adult sections, skimming the back covers, critiquing the author photos, reading the first few pages of each book.

Jo sneaked off to the restroom and as I turned the corner into the women's fiction aisle, I spotted our favorite author—well, mine because Jo liked her—signing copies of her latest novel. Jo hadn't seen her. The circular table beside me fanned piles of her book, a World War II love story about a nurse and high-ranking officer who crosses enemy lines to be with her. I picked up a copy. $24.95. Mom had given me twenty dollars for the day and I'd already spent eleven bucks on a necklace from American Eagle.

But I couldn't pass up this opportunity. An autographed book would be such a great birthday gift.

But how?

Waltz up to the author, an older woman with stark chin-length hair and houndstooth blazer, and ask for a free book? Signed, no less. *Yeah, right.* But at the same time, I grew heavy with disappointment, fearing I'd have to walk away without a copy of something Jo would cherish.

A woman in a beige sport jacket stood first in the long line. After thanking the author, she stepped toward the cookbook section a couple of aisles over. She set her book on the shelf's edge and dug through her purse for her ringing phone.

I knew it was wrong.

I knew Jo would step from the bathroom at any moment.

I knew I hadn't much time.

With the slyness of a coyote, I snatched the book, tucked it underneath my sweatshirt, and sprinted outside to a nearby bench. Fueled by the rush of defiance, I didn't stop to think that Jo would question how I got the signed novel.

I crouched low, peeking every few seconds for my grandmother, certain that after she searched the store, she'd come look for me out here. I'd tell her I felt hot and needed a breath of fresh air, then surprise her with the book. Looking back, it didn't make sense, but I wasn't worried at the time.

But a minute later, Jo wasn't the person standing by the bench.

A large man with buttons threatening to burst from his overstretched white shirt, a loosely tied tie, and a crooked name tag that read *Manager* loomed over me. His menacing shadow nearly reached the escalator.

"Miss, I believe you have something that doesn't belong to you."

The book's owner stood a few paces away with her fist wrapped tight around her purse strap.

"I . . . I don't know what you mean." My voice quivered.

"The book."

"What book?" Jo asked, approaching us.

"She with you?" the manager asked.

"Yes. What's going on?"

"She stole my book," the lady said. "It's under her sweat-shirt."

Jo studied my face, no doubt seeing the desperation and regret churning wild through my eyes. She spun around and asked the lady, "Did you see her take it?"

"Well, no, not exactly, but I saw her standing there and I took my eyes off the book for one second and next thing I knew it disappeared. And your girl ran out of the store."

"Hand it over. Now!" The manager tugged at my sweat-shirt, dragging me off the bench.

I kept my hand pressed tight against my stomach.

"Don't touch her." Jo smacked his arm and moved between us, lifting me up. "We're done here."

"I don't think we are," he said.

"Fine. Call the police," Jo snarled at the man. "I'd love to explain how you harassed a young girl based on speculation. I'll be damned if you lay another finger on my granddaughter."

He stepped back.

"Ma'am, I'm sorry you lost your book," Jo said. "Let's go, Bree."

Now that I think about it, maybe that moment first taught me the power of body language. For Jo's five-foot-three-inch frame stood tall, rooted like an oak tree, against the towering manager. She spoke with a backbone and a certainty I didn't have. Jo taught me to be strong.

No doubt I deserved to get punished. Jo should've ratted me out and let me suffer the consequences, scare me straight so I'd never steal again. Funny thing is, at that moment, I wasn't frightened. Not even when the manager yanked me off the bench and the book slipped, nearly plopping on the ground, or when he threatened to call the police. Jo stood by my side. She defended me. She loved me. I needed nothing else.

The two of us walked away a united front. And, as we did, I marveled in her confidence.

She knew I stole the book. But without saying a word, she drove me to the library and I deposited the novel in the drop box. We never spoke of it again.

Now, with Jo in mind, a surge of motivation pushes through me.

I will convince Candace, with the same adamancy as Jo, that this interview is about me. No one else. I'm an expert in this field and I don't need a man to validate my worth. I am Bree Caxton, a proven puppet master pulling the strings of love.

And I hope Sean gets chlamydia.

Problem is, my self-assuredness lasts for about twenty seconds, long enough for me to notice Candace scowl at Randi and say, "I don't have time for this."

"I, too, was under the impression we were ready to go." By the look on Randi's face, she'd like to dig her celery stalk out of the trash and bitch-slap me with it.

"It's clearly stated, Bree," Candace scolds. "This interview is about you and your life. Including your love life."

"I understand." A bead of sweat slides down my spine like a raindrop following a pane of glass. *C'mon, little brain . . . think.* "He's, um . . . running a bit late. The surgery ran long . . . um, the blood and the scrotum . . ."

Scotty's face draws pale. "Jesus."

Andrew buries his head in his hands.

"Listen, I have a full schedule with no room for excuses. I carved an opening in my schedule to accommodate this story. We're going to press in two days and if you can't meet the terms of our arrangement, then we have no arrangement." She stands to leave.

"No, don't go. I . . . um . . ." I could stand quickly, tell them I'm sick, came down with a bit of the flu. Maybe sneeze for good measure. But that only delays my predicament. *Buck up, Bree. Where's the backbone of a moment ago? Just tell the truth.* "Okay, truth is, I don't—"

"Oh, pardon me," a man's smooth familiar voice says, "I didn't mean to interrupt."

Nixon stands behind Candace in the doorway, dressed in a suit the color of ash and a crisp shirt matching the whiteness of his eyes. I smell the amber scent in his aftershave. My library card rests in his palm.

Candace doesn't acknowledge him. She plants her hands on her hips and says, "I'll ask you one more time, Bree Caxton. Where is your boyfriend?"

Looking back and forth between her and Randi, Andrew, and Scotty. I think of Lawrence Chambers's e-mail.

Auction.

Lose her house.

Without realizing what I'm doing, I feel for my scar. The toughened and raised pink flesh tingles as I follow the mark, seeing the hint of my mom's narrow hands and slender fingers in my own. I'd never noticed the similarities until the night I sat rigid in the backseat of Dad's Jeep Cherokee with arms folded across my chest in an adolescent act of defiance. Illuminated by the dashboard lights, Mom's thumb massaged Dad's vein, bulging above his temple, soothing his anger as he drove us toward home.

I think about the screams and shattered glass, the hissing fluids, the smell of fuel, the sirens, the twisted steel. I think about Jo falling to her knees in the hospital waiting room when the doctor told us that Dad and Mom, Jo's only daughter, died. I think about the deafening silence between us two as we packed away their plates, linens, and clothes, removed the pictures from the walls and closed their front door. I think about the mistake I made and how our lives have never been— *and never will be*—the same. I think about how it'd feel to no longer be burdened by shame.

Auction.

Lose her house.

Right here. Right now is my chance to prevent it.

A tiny white lie.

"All right, Scotty, let's go." Candace turns to gather her things. "We'll run that piece on wild horses in New Mexico."

"No, please, don't go."

She stops. "What is it, Bree?"

I know it's wrong.

I know I haven't much time.

I know I've taken Jo's daughter and son-in-law from her, and I can't—*I won't*—let the house disappear, too.

I march past Candace and curl my hands around Nixon's arm. "Here he is. This is my boyfriend."

ten

"He's your boyfriend?" Candace asks.

"He is," I confirm.

"I am?" Nixon's bicep flexes. He starts to pull away.

I squeeze tighter. "Listen to him joke. He's so funny. One of the many reasons I love him so, so much." My neck itches. Tiny spikes of heat prickle my skin, right underneath my chin, and I clench my teeth, fighting like hell not to scratch it.

"My, my, aren't you the cat's ass?" Randi says, moistening her lips.

Out of the corner of my eye, I catch Nixon's facial expression. His eyes are narrowed and suspicious, like he made a wrong turn into a seedy neighborhood. I don't dare look at Andrew, whose gasp almost blew my cover.

"Well, I'm glad you finally made it," Candace says. "We were beginning to wonder if she had a boyfriend at all."

"Oh, that's funny." I laugh louder than I should. "Candace, can we have a minute? Nixon needs to um . . . wash his hands or something. Surgery and all."

"Real quick," Candace says. "We're behind schedule as it is."

I escort Nixon into the break room.

"What the hell is going on?"

"I know it's ridiculous and I'm very sorry, but please, do me this one favor."

"Pose as your boyfriend? Are you kidding me?"

Heat creeps along my throat, spreading to the other side. "I'm not kidding."

"Why is your neck so red?"

I claw my skin like a raccoon tearing at a bag of trash. "I break out in hives when I lie. My friends think it's cute."

"Puppies are cute. Mottled skin is not cute."

"Well, I can't help that I'm so transparent."

"Listen, I've got a lot of work to get done today." He checks his watch. "And a conference call in an hour."

"This won't take long. I promise." Another lie. I have no idea how long this will take. The stinging spreads behind my neck, underneath my hairline.

"Why would I do this?"

I explain my book, the interview, the contract requirement.

"So . . . again, why would I do this? You have a boyfriend. Sean, right?"

"As a matter of fact, I don't." I stare at my shoes. "He broke up with me a couple nights ago. Apparently, I *stifled* him. And you know the really sad part of it? I thought we were forever."

He flicks the library card against his other palm. "Nothing is forever."

I'm held by his look, which is tough but tender, like a lion with a thorn stuck in his paw. *What's made Nixon so cynical?*

The matter at hand redirects my thoughts. "Sean screwed up my personal life, but there's no way in hell he's going to wreck my professional life, too. I've sunk my teeth into this book. Now comes along this interview, which will expose my efforts and potentially catapult me to a bestseller ranking. And I know you said the bestseller ranking isn't the only threshold of success, but right now, for me, it is. I need that ranking. I need the money that comes along with it."

"Why, what's the money going to do?"

"My grandmother owes back taxes and her house is at risk. I *can't* let that house go. *I can't.* The house means everything to her and she means everything to me. And more than protecting the roof over her head, it's my chance to maybe . . . just maybe . . . erase a little bit of my guilt." My voice dwindles to a whisper. I shake my head and wipe the tears forming in my eyes. "Sorry, I didn't mean to ramble. I know this isn't your concern. It's just, I'm in a terrible spot and I need a boyfriend now. If I blow this, I blow everything."

Nixon's phone chimes with yet another message. He scans the text and types a reply before saying to me, "My nephew scored the highest ever on his test yesterday."

"Yeah?"

He slips the phone into his pocket. "And you prevented a meltdown."

"Kid Town is serious business."

He hands me my library card, casting a long glance at Candace, then back at me. "My grandmother, Noni, loves to cook. She makes these fried apple slices dusted with powdered sugar. Ever had them?"

I shake my head.

"They're awful. Greasy on the outside, squishy on the inside, taste like cardboard, no flavor whatsoever. But every year on New Year's Day, rain or shine, she makes them for me, has for as long as I can remember. She's a tiny thing, only about four feet tall, needs a step stool to reach the upper cabinets. She scoots that damn stool from one side of the kitchen to the other, spending the whole day frying and dusting apples. Sugar gets all over the floor." He tugs his ear and says with a half grin, "I love my Noni. I don't like fried apples, but I love my Noni."

Almost got him. "Please," I beg.

"It's that important to you?"

"More than you can imagine."

"One interview?"

"One and done. They won't even ask you more than a question or two. You're here to confirm my credibility. You're just a prop."

"Boy, you know how to pump up a guy."

"Obviously you're more than a prop, but you know what I mean. The other interviews will focus on my work and stuff. Today is just an intro to me and my life. Will you do it?"

"Under one condition."

I press my fist to my lips, trying not to smile. "Name it."

"You come to my cousin's wedding."

"Me?" I'm taken back. I thought he'd say a month of free dates, a car wash coupon, or an actual Bree Caxton and Associates bumper sticker. Pose as his girlfriend? I didn't see that coming. "Why me? Why not Sara?"

"Because I might like Sara. And, aside from the fact that my mom will corner Sara and cram the benefits of prenatal care and breast-feeding down her throat, the wedding is on a Friday, as if people don't have jobs to consider. Something about it being the same day they met. I don't know." He frowns. "Anyway, it's lousy timing because I have two deals scheduled to close that day. It'd be a hell of a lot easier not having to worry about a budding relationship."

"So you want me to come, but you're going to blow me off once we're there? Sneak off and work?"

"More or less."

"Boy, you know how to pump up a girl."

"It's the terms of my agreement."

"But if they think I'm your girlfriend—"

"You're only there to prove my credibility. You'll just be a prop."

"Ha-ha."

"Help me get my mom off my back for the time being. If Sara and I work out, then I can say you and I broke up and bring her into the mix down the line."

"I don't want to trick your family."

"Why not? You're proposing to trick the country."

"Touché."

"Bree, let's get started." Randi waves me over.

"And no pictures of me in the paper," he says.

"You said *one* condition."

"The last thing I need is my face plastered in this article."

"I can't guarantee that."

"Then I'm out."

"Fine, fine . . . I don't know how I'll do it, but no pictures. Do we have a deal?"

We shake and I can't resist sliding my arms around his neck for a quick hug. "Thank you, thank you, thank you!"

"Settle down. And put some cream on your neck."

"You ready?" I ask.

"What type of doctor am I, anyway?"

"Urologist."

"Of course I am. I can't believe I'm doing this."

Me either.

I can almost see the nervous sparks bouncing off my body as we join Candace and the others. This may very well be the most asinine thing I've ever done, even dumber than the time Andrew and I drank half a bottle of Fireball and he dared me to lick a lightbulb to see if it was hot.

It was.

"Ah, finally," Candace says. "Do we have another chair for . . . I'm sorry, I didn't catch your name?"

Nixon hesitates. He won't want his real name in the papers any more than his face.

"Nick," I interject. "His name is Nick."

"Nice to meet you. Have a seat." Candace plants herself across from us in my desk chair.

While Candace sifts through a few notes, I lean toward Nixon and whisper, "Don't sit like that."

He faces straight with one leg crossed over the other in a figure-four position. "What are you taking about?"

"It looks like you're mad."

"I *am* mad."

"No, you're not. This'll be fun."

"Fun is snowboarding in Taos with a twelve-inch layer of virgin powder. This here, is not fun."

"Uncross your legs and turn toward me. Especially your feet. Feet are a dead giveaway."

"My feet?"

"We need to give Candace the best impression. Trust me, I know this stuff."

"And what about you? You're sitting straighter than a ventriloquist's dummy."

My knees, calves, and ankles are pressed together. My hands are folded in my lap. And, yes, my back is straight. "This is called good posture, thank you very much. A nonthreatening pose. C'mon." I smack his knee.

"I'm comfortable. I'm not changing my position."

"Fine. But right now your feet are telling Scotty you're into *him*."

Nixon uncrosses his legs and turns toward me.

I giggle.

"Ah, look at you two, laughing. What a handsome couple." She turns on her recorder again. "Okay, everyone ready?"

"Absolutely," I say.

"What we'd like to do today is highlight both your professional and personal life. Get to know Bree, both in and out of the office. Sound good?"

"Sounds great."

"So, Bree, why matchmaking?"

"That's easy, love."

"Love?"

"Yeah, I'm a sucker for it."

"Everyone loves love."

"I suppose. But not everyone gets to facilitate it. Not everyone gets to watch the journey of two people and witness a connection of spirits. I mean, the smiles, the banter, the first touch, the bright eyes, all of it. I witness the beginnings of a potential family. What's better than that? What's more powerful than love?"

"How'd you get started in matchmaking? Childhood dream? Family business? Is there some sort of school that trains for this type of profession?"

"None of the above. I went to college with a journalism degree in mind, but my sophomore year I took a psychology class that focused on kinesics, you know, nonverbal communication, and it hooked me. I switched my major and started utilizing what I'd learned, setting up friends and classmates for fun. Word spread and before I knew it, people offered to pay me to find them a date. One thing led to another and here I am."

"Fascinating." Candace jots a few notes. "So, tell me, what are some of these nonverbal communications that you take notice of?"

"Well, for starters there are six universal facial expressions." I count them off on my fingers. "Happiness, sadness, fear, disgust, surprise, and anger. And at any given time, we indicate, whether consciously or not, one of these expressions."

"Really? This is quite interesting. What else?"

"Eighty percent of communication is nonverbal, so you can imagine there are a ton of clues. For example, a woman might flick her hair or lift her chin when walking by an attractive man."

"Or suck in her stomach." Candace pats her own with a short laugh.

"Exactly. Whereas a man might puff up his chest and walk with an erect back. We all do it, in one form or another. Nonverbal communication speaks louder than words."

"Okay, so how do we know if someone rolls their eyes because they're annoyed or simply trying to get a stubborn eyelash out?"

"Good question. It's a given that a long gaze from a woman indicates she's interested, but we shouldn't make a sweeping conclusion based on one signal. Clusters of—"

Randi fake-coughs and catches my attention. "Bree, don't show the kitty."

Right. "Let me assure you, Candace, there's much more to matchmaking and enabling a lasting connection than body language. I employ several factors when matching two people. I discuss this and other influences in greater detail in my book, *Can I See You Again?*"

Randi offers a thumbs-up.

Score one for a shameless plug.

"Say I were a client of yours. What services am I provided? I mean, with all the online dating sites available, why you?"

"There are a lot of choices online, that's for sure. But often these come with risks. Whether it's physical, financial, or psychological, safety is an element of concern. Along with background checks, I offer another layer of service. I meet personally with each one of my clients. We talk at length about favorite restaurants, books, movies, how the price of cable has shot through the roof, which teams will or won't make the playoffs. But I'm not relying one hundred percent on their answers for my assessment. I'm reading *them*. I'm determining what counter-type personality will best suit them. These are innate truths that a computer program can't recognize, let alone decipher. With this insight, I can pair up two people with extreme confidence."

"So you're saying you have some sort of inherent ability?"

"Something like that."

"Okay, then what? The pair meets for a date?"

"That's the goal. But not everyone is comfortable with a blind date of sorts, so, as an alternative, I host a reception once a month geared to like-minded clients at a venue compatible with their common interests. For example, a couple of months ago I pooled my more adventurous, outgoing clients and kayaked the seven caves of La Jolla, then met for a barbecue on the beach. And, later this week actually, my more conservative, educated clients are meeting at the historic Marston House Gardens. Now, I'm not saying online dating is bad, I'm saying I'm better."

Candace doesn't laugh or crack a smile, and I take a second to once again consider the seriousness of the situation. I've got Nixon, a man whom I hardly know, pretending to be madly in love with me. Then there's Candace and her Stretch Armstrong–like professional reach who can make or break my future. The balance of Jo's house hinges on the success of *Can I See You Again?* It's a wonder that I'm not cowering in the corner like a beaten dog, frightened by the influence Candace has on my future.

But just like that day outside the bookstore with Jo, I'm not nervous.

Is it because we're discussing a topic I'm knowledgeable about? Is it because I'm adamant about making this book a success and ambition is outweighing my nerves? Am I trying to prove a point to myself that I can and will survive without Sean? Or am I comforted by . . . Nixon?

My eyes drift toward him as he nonchalantly peeks at his watch.

I'm grateful he's helping me. And even more thankful that Candace hasn't asked him any questions. I've kept my word. Nixon is a prop.

"So, Nick, let's focus on you for a moment."

And, so much for that.

"Me?" He points to himself. "No, I don't have much to contribute. Let's keep the attention on Bree."

"Let's not. What do you think of Bree's profession? Do you ever get jealous knowing she's surrounded by single men?"

"Not in the least." Nixon's voice is purposeful and convincing. "Bree's good at what she does. She treats her clients with professionalism and respect. She takes her job seriously." He leans back and says with a softer tone, "Plus, look at her, she's a beautiful woman. Only a fool would jeopardize that."

I smile at him, appreciating the compliment. Even if it's for show.

"Last question. Bree, how are we to know? For those of us who can't read body language or pick up on subtle nuances that you've got this built-in eye for, leave us with one indicator that a new relationship is . . . sustainable, for lack of a better word."

"Oh, that's easy. The first kiss."

"How so?"

"The first kiss reveals everything about a relationship; it's body language at its finest. It's the moment energy is mirrored and synchronized. Or at least, that's the goal. See, if the first kiss is *mirrored*, then unconscious feelings of affirmation and trust are immediately established. We think, hey, this person likes me, and *is* like me."

"So, what about you two?" Candace asks.

"Sorry?"

"Tell me about your first kiss."

For the first time during this interview, I grow nervous. My thoughts clam up and I'm unable to think of a clever way to respond. "Um . . . can you repeat the question?"

"Your first kiss. Clearly it was a good one."

"Um . . . right, let's see . . . it . . . um, it—"

As if rehearsed a thousand times or an ordinary, everyday gesture, Nixon grasps my hand and turns it over. Cradling my palm within his own, he slowly draws the tips of each of his long fingers across the pale, tender skin of my exposed wrist, triggering sparks up my arm. Then, without releasing his embrace, Nixon leans toward me and says, "Bree tasted like Christmas morning."

"She . . . uh . . . wow," Candace says.

I know he isn't serious, but Candace is right . . . *uh . . . wow.*

A few seconds pass before I realize he's released me and I've covered my wrist with my other hand as if to . . . what? Solidify the moment in Candace's eyes? Guarantee my scar isn't seen? *Preserve* Nixon's touch?

Um . . . anyway.

"Can't think of a better way to finish for today." Candace stands.

Yes, finish. Good idea.

"Great stuff, you two. I think the readers are going to respond quite well to this article." She slips away to answer her cell phone.

"I've gotta run," Randi says. "This is great material for your blog. I have a damn good feeling about this. You might be the easiest client yet." She inches toward Nixon. "If things don't work out with Bree, call me." She tucks her business card in his shirt pocket.

"Can I go now?" Nixon asks, turning his phone's ringer back on.

"Yes, thanks a million."

"My cousin's wedding. Don't forget." He hands me Randi's card.

"When is it?"

"A couple weeks. I'll text you the exact date."

"Okay. Be sweet with Sara tonight. No coffee. Dinner only. And, remember, don't check that dang thing all night." I gesture toward his phone. "In fact, leave it at home."

"Nick, Bree, one more thing before you go," Candace calls from across the room with a phone pressed against her ear, "I want a picture of you two."

I spin Nixon around and push him away. "Hurry, get out of here. Go, go, go."

He scurries out the door.

Andrew claps his hands as he rushes over. "Awesome job."

"I didn't sound like a braggart?"

"Not at all. And that stuff with Nixon . . . er . . . Nick . . . totally convincing. If I didn't know better, I'd think you two *are* dating."

"Where'd Nick rush off to?" Candace asks.

"Emergency surgery."

"Can he come back later? I'd really like a picture for the paper."

"No, sorry. Full schedule today. And tomorrow. And the next day." *Do not scratch your neck, Bree. Do not.*

"Well, shoot. All right, then, Scotty, let's go."

They head toward the door, but Candace spins around and says, "You know, Bree, living in the public eye it's hard to meet new people, let alone date. So, I sought outside help and met my husband through a service similar to yours. We've had eleven great years together and two beautiful children. That's why this article intrigues me. I have a special place in my heart for people like yourself, helping others find joy in their lives."

"Thank you, Candace. That means a lot."

"And, if you don't mind me saying, I see a lot of my husband's best qualities in Nick. He's a charming man. I don't know where you found him, but I wouldn't let him go."

eleven

"Thank you for seeing me so quickly, Mr. Chambers." I sit across from him in his spacious and well-lit office, flanked with a framed vintage map of Paris on one wall and shelves of casebooks—like I suspected—organized in numerical order on the other. Our view of one another is obstructed by client files and law books littered with Post-it notes (must be a lawyer thing) stacked high on his desk. Plus, my chair sits an inch or so lower than his, enough to position him in the domineering position (probably another lawyer thing).

When I visited Jo this morning, I didn't tell her about this meeting. Or Lawrence's e-mail. She asked about the letter status and I said I hadn't heard a definitive answer, which is true. Sure, Mr. Chambers's e-mail threatened an auction, but I'm still holding on to the possibility this is an error. A misdirected computer entry. Maybe the bill was satisfied years ago and this is a simple accounting oversight.

"My pleasure. You received my e-mail?"

"I did, but is it possible this whole thing is a misunderstanding? I mean, certainly there's a chance she doesn't owe the money. My grandmother pays her taxes."

Lawrence's chair creaks as he leans forward and props his elbows on his desk. A tuft of curly black chest hair peeks above his shirt collar. "I can assure you, Ms. Caxton, she owes the money. Let me explain how this works. Basically the 1058 letter states two things. First is notification that if payment isn't received, the IRS intends to sell the affected property to pay off the neglected tax lien. And second, you have a legal right to a hearing before said auction. This is your opportunity to plead your case and in some instances, make payment arrangements. Unless you can prove differently, the IRS will move forward with proceedings. They consider tax dodgers—"

"My grandmother is no criminal."

He stiffens at my tone. "You need to hear me out, Ms. Caxton."

You need a breath mint, Mr. Chambers.

Shush, Bree. Focus.

"Sorry." I clasp my hands on my lap. "I just don't understand how they can do this, just up and take her house. Why didn't they contact her sooner? Why wasn't there a warning of some kind?"

"This is not *new* news. Typically tax liens remain on the books for a near decade before the IRS takes action."

"Did you say a decade?"

"Yes, the IRS is actually quite lenient. They don't pursue tax liens of this magnitude until they near the ten-year mark. They created the initial tax lien against your grandmother nine years ago. The IRS has sent, and your grandmother received, registered letters the entire time."

"Nine years?"

"Nine years."

Jesus. I'd never seen one letter. Jo must've thrown them all away. "Well, my grandmother is old and alone. She thought the letters were junk mail or something. Oh, God. Clearly, they won't hold that against her. They can't take her house. Tell me they won't."

"I can't promise you that."

"I . . . I . . ." I'm choked with panic. *Hold it together, Bree.* "Okay, then what do we do next? You said something about a hearing."

"You have the right to appeal."

"Yes, great." I nod and sit straighter. "Let's start the paperwork."

"Already have. I'll need you to provide a few additional documents. I'll e-mail you the requirements."

"Okay, thank you. Think it'll work?"

"The appeal? Depends on how you look at it. You're essentially challenging the IRS's right to levy, which I've never seen overturned, so, basically all you're doing is buying time to find proof for dismissal or come up with the money." He refers to his computer. "And the liability with penalties and fees is nearly fifty thousand dollars."

"We don't have that kind of money."

His nod implies what I fear.

"So it's true? My grandmother's house could be sold to some stranger with a checkbook?"

"Yes, that is a very likely outcome. But let's not jump ahead of ourselves. Let's get through the hearing first, then go from there, shall we?"

His attempt to sound hopeful falls flat. I know from listening to Sean over the years that the IRS doesn't often make mistakes. And is even less forgiving.

"So if the appeal is denied, how much time do I have?"

"It's contingent on timing of the ruling, but traditionally, you'll have about thirty days."

Same time as my book release.

I picture Jo standing on the sidewalk, wrapped in her lilac robe, watching some money-minded investor bulldoze into her home, strip off the apple wallpaper, rip out the carpet, and toss her appliances and her memories into a foul-smelling Dumpster parked on the lawn.

My fingers ache from my grip on the armrests.

Andrew's right; the escalator clause is the only chance I've got.

Can I See You Again? has got to make the list.

twelve

A couple of days later, I fumble in the dark of early morning and answer my phone. It's Andrew.

"Did you read the article yet?"

I bolt straight up in bed. "It's Sunday, isn't it?"

"Yes, you fool. What day did you think it was?"

"I can't believe I forgot. I fell asleep without setting my alarm." I don't mention along with my worries about Jo—trying to decide the best way to break the news to her—that Sean left me another voice mail last night, a long detailed ramble about how much he loves me and how bad he feels, reiterating it's him, not me. *Blah-blah-blah.* Nor do I tell Andrew that I listened to Sean's message thirteen times.

"Hurry up and get downstairs."

With the phone pressed against my ear, I open the front door and see the tri-folded and rubber-band-bound copy of the *National Tribune* at the foot of my porch steps. Never have I been more excited to see the paper in my life.

People say print is making a comeback, and the glare of the computer screen is losing its appeal. For me, the charm never left. I love ink-stained fingers, the smell and the feel of the paper in my hands. Same goes for a book, especially those aged with yellowed pages and cracking spines, found in the cramped, sagging shelves of used bookstores that often reek of body odor and hot sauce, wondering where and with whom these stories have been shared.

I rush toward the steps in my pj's and reach for the paper. My sprinkler valve kicks on, spraying my feet and ankles with cold water. "Aagh! Damn thing." I nearly drop the phone. Worse yet, the newspaper.

"Haven't you got that fixed yet? I gave you the number of my plumber."

"I called him, but he charges $167.50. An hour. That's insane." Okay, yes, I charge as much, but Bree Caxton and Associates is totally worth it. I mean, you can't put a price on love. Just ask my happy couples.

I head inside and fling off the rubber band, dumping a landfill's worth of hearing aid and mortgage lender advertisements on the floor until I find the *Close-Up* circular. "Look at it, Andrew," I say as if he's beside me on the couch and not on the phone miles away. "It's gorgeous."

Close-Up is inked in bright red and the cover boasts a full-body picture of Julia Roberts outside her New Mexico ranch. The title of her latest movie is scripted along the bottom edge. On the right side of the page, underneath the wording about avocados and their weight loss benefits, there's the caption that beats my heart so fast, I swear it's going to burst through my skin. *Fall in love with Bree Caxton, page 4.*

With jittery hands, I flip to the page and find a picture of me—*me!*—sitting at my desk, laughing at something said in the distance. The article text wraps around my photo.

"Look, there's the cover of my book." In the lower corner, *Can I See You Again?* is splashed in bold black against a hazy background of a man knocking on a woman's red front door with a bouquet of roses clutched behind his back. It's fresh and playful. "Randi must've e-mailed it to her."

With Andrew still on the phone, I read the article, growing more and more excited—if that's even possible—with each paragraph.

Bree Caxton is one of Southern California's most prolific matchmakers. Over the last six years, her diligence and inherent ability to decipher body language and energy has facilitated hundreds of meaningful relationships for lonely men, bashful women, divorcees, widows, and widowers. With a near-perfect success rate, she's touted as the go-to gal for love.

"It's so strange to read my name in the paper. I'm such a big shot."

Both professionally and personally, Bree's proven herself not to shy away from hard work, a trait evident within her soon-to-be-released book, Can I See You Again? *Her self-help debut chronicles a handful of Bree's most triumphant connections along with tips and suggestions for those of us still looking for a happily-ever-after.*

I laugh and giddiness whirls through my mind as I continue to read. "This is a great piece, don't you think? Candace touched on the important aspects of my company with a light-hearted spin."

Part of me wishes Sean were here, sharing this moment with me. True, he prefers the *Los Angeles Times* to the *Tribune*, but all the same, he's witnessed firsthand how hard I've worked to get here. Maybe a quick call?

"The phone is going to ring off the hook now." Andrew captures my focus, and I shake off thoughts of reaching out to Sean. God forbid I stifle him any more. "Are you still reading?"

I've known Andrew long enough to recognize the caution in his voice. Maybe Andrew's acting protective because Candace questioned the company's limited scope, wondering if Bree Caxton and Associates is as successful as claimed, why we haven't branched into other cities.

It's the last paragraph.

It doesn't take the eagle eye of a reporter to see that Bree's found love herself, a walking example of what her clients so desperately seek. Her boyfriend, Nick, spews sex appeal and is the kind of man neighborhood women pray will take his shirt off when mowing the lawn. But more than his stellar looks, the charming man wanted to take a backseat to her moment in my spotlight, let his woman enjoy the bit of fame. Sitting beside her, the compassionate and deliciously handsome Nick hardly took his eyes off Bree as she answered my questions. The electricity between the two could light up the Las Vegas strip. Should I have left the two alone?

Follow along with me for the next four weeks as I delve deeper into the life of Bree Caxton. We'll learn a few of her proven techniques for finding love, what keeps her so in tune with hearts and minds, and, perhaps most importantly, find out what Nick's like in the sack?

"Oh, God, Andrew."
"I told you, you were convincing."
"Nixon's not going to like this."

"I bet he's amazing."

"Sorry?"

"In bed. I bet he's slow and selfless, methodical and assertive. I bet he's—"

"Okay, you've painted a clear picture."

"What do you think?"

"I haven't."

"Oh, c'mon. You haven't once thought what it'd feel like to have his powerful arms and legs wrapped around your naked skin?"

"Of course not." Okay, twice.

"Whatever. Well, congrats on the article."

"Thanks. Talk to you tomorrow."

"Take care of you," we say in unison, and hang up.

I start to text Nixon: *Boy, that Candace, she's quite a hoot, eh?* But I delete it. *In the sack? Ha. Ha.* I erase that, too. Maybe he won't see the spread.

And maybe he lives under a rock.

⤔

It's several hours later and I'm abuzz with energy. Either from my third cup of coffee or because I forced myself to cast aside the worries heaving my mind and focus on the positive. After all, it's not every day I'm featured in a national newspaper. Nixon held up his end of the bargain quite convincingly. From here on out, I'll mitigate any more discussion about the two of us and focus on my company and my book sales. *Bestseller list, here I come.*

I clean the ceiling fans, water my half-dead plants— anything living around here leads a rough life—while waiting on my last batch of pumpkin cream cheese muffins to cool.

My cell phone rings. It's Sara.

I think about her last date and how poorly it went. *Please,*

Lord, don't let her be calling with bad news. "Hey, Sara, it's good to hear from you. How are you? How'd the date go with Nixon last night?"

"Sorry to bother you on a Sunday, but my God, Bree. That man is a dream come true. Where did you find him?"

"Picked him from a perfect-man tree."

She laughs. "You must've. I can't believe he's single."

Funny you mention that.

"What did you two do?"

"Well, he took me to this trendy grill on Prospect. Ever hear of it?"

Good boy. "Yes, it's nice."

"I had this amazing farro salad with roasted beets and lemon-dill yogurt. You'll have to try it."

"Okay, I will." Minus the beets, lemon-dill yogurt, and farro.

"The food tasted amazing but didn't compare to our conversation. He's so attentive, didn't even answer his phone although I heard it vibrate several times."

Good boy.

"Plus, he's funny and adventurous. Did you know in his early twenties, he spent two summers on a sailboat in Hawaii?"

"No, I—"

"As a deckhand, on a tour boat thing, sailing around the islands. He loves to travel. He's hoping to visit Greece by the year's end. Oh my gosh, what if he took me with him?"

One step at a time, Sara.

"And, he smells good, too, like a man."

"Yes, well, I'm so glad—"

"We walked down to the beach after dinner and talked and watched the moon. The perfect romantic evening. And he's such a gentleman." She sighs. "Though, I have to tell you, when we were sitting in the sand, I wished he weren't *such* a gentleman."

Good boy. "So, do you—"

"He must work out or something because his shirt fit in all the right places. And, I'm not afraid to say, I pretended to trip just so he'd catch me." She laughs again. "And have you seen his eyes? They're so blue, just like the sky in a painting I purchased the other day. I sure hope he asks me out again. Has he called you? Has he said anything?"

My God, I chuckle to myself. Does the woman breathe through her ears? How can she continue talking without stopping for a breath?

"Bree?"

"No, I haven't talked to him. But it's Sunday, I'm—"

"God, I hope he calls me again."

"Now, Sara, I'm glad it went so well, but let's not put too much weight on a first date. We don't want to get too worked up."

"You're right. I'll settle down. If I can. Oh, my gosh, I haven't felt this giddy since my teenage years. My goodness, Bree. I want to shout to the world, tell everyone I know. You're the best matchmaker ever."

thirteen

I can't put it off any longer. I need to tell Jo the truth about her house. So, after a confidence-boosting pep talk to myself—not with megaphones and high kicks, but several spirited chants of *You can do it, Bree!*—I slide into my skinny jeans and well-worn UCSD alumni T-shirt that I bought for half price the day after graduation and make my way toward Jo's. I promised I'd tell her once I had a definitive answer, and *auction* is pretty dang conclusive.

On the way to Jo's house, my Uber driver stops at a red light.

Andrew's seated at a window booth of Ryoko's, a classy Japanese restaurant decorated with concrete counters, teak chairs, and a young business crowd during the lunch hour on weekdays. Dressed in dark pants and a mint green collared shirt that Andrew hung on our break room door after picking it up from the dry cleaner on Friday, he slides his water glass out of the way, making room for a plate of colorful fish the waitress sets before him.

What the heck? I've tried to get Andrew to eat here for years. But he's refused, claiming he hates sushi, afraid of it, actually.

"Raw fish?" he's said in the past. "Like eyeballs, squid guts, and parasites swimming around my stomach? Sounds delicious."

The pillar blocks my view of who he's with, but by Andrew's straight back and nervous smile, it's someone he's trying to impress.

The light turns green and as we drive away, I crank my neck, trying to see who is sitting across from him.

Strange.

A minute later, my phone rings with a number I don't recognize. A 442 area code. I hope it isn't Sean disguising his phone number, but, at the same time, I'm tired of hiding from him. I decide to play ball.

"Look, Sean—"

"*Hola*, Ms. Caxton?" A woman's Spanish-laced voice interrupts me.

"Yes?"

"This is Regina Voss, Nixon's mother."

"Oh, yes, hello. I'm sorry, I thought you were someone else."

"*No hay problema.*"

"How are you?" I straighten my posture, even though she can't see me.

"Fine, thank you. I apologize for calling on the Lord's day, but this wedding seems to swallow my weekdays. I'm just now getting a chance to make a few calls."

"No, worries. What can I do for you?"

"Well, I'm in charge of the reception seating chart and placement cards. It's insensitive to have a reception without placement cards, leaving people to just mill around, don't you think?"

"It's nice to know where to sit."

"*Sí.* You understand the importance, then. The printer needs the names tomorrow. I selected a lovely embossed ivory card stock, and my son hasn't returned my calls. He promised to bring a date and I figured you'd know her name. Have you found him a girlfriend?"

On paper, yes. And she's awesome.

"If not, I've got three women lined up to call."

"I really shouldn't speak for Nixon, Mrs. Voss. How about I make sure he calls you right away?"

"*¡Maldito sea mi hijo!*" she snaps, before releasing a long sigh. "I'll go ahead and invite one of these women. He leaves me no choice."

"No, that won't be necessary. He's planning to bring someone to the wedding."

"Are you sure?"

"Positive."

"*¡Maravilloso!* Tell me; what does she look like? Is she quite lovely?"

Almond-shaped eyes, buttermilk skin. And if I do say so myself, I kill it in a backless dress.

"Actually, Mrs. Voss . . . it's me. Nixon is bringing me."

"*¿En serio?*" She gasps. "Well, isn't that interesting? I didn't know you two had a connection."

"Yes, well, as they say, one thing led to another."

"*Sí. Sí.*"

Nothing but dead air suspends between us.

Oh, no. Have I overstepped? Is she mad?

"B-R-E-E, is that correct?"

"Yes."

"Lovely, I'll tell the printer."

Thank God.

"I'm glad to see my boy is in such good hands. I look forward to seeing you at the wedding. You seem like a charming young woman."

"Thank you. See you in a couple weeks." I hang up with a smile on my face until I remember I'm a fraud. A complete joke.

My God, my skin can't take much more of this. I dig deep into my purse and yank out my tube of Cortizone cream. Extra strength.

Ten minutes later, I'm dropped off at Jo's. We're gathered around her kitchen table. She munches on a pumpkin spice muffin, alternating bites with Martin, who sits on her lap.

The good news is he hasn't nipped at my heels. But to be safe, I've tucked my legs underneath themselves—I'm not giving that four-legged piranha any opportunity to chomp.

"So." I slide the *Close-Up* circular toward her. "Did you have a look?"

"Yes, it's good. But who is Nick? I thought your boyfriend's name was something else, Stan or Shane or something."

For once, I'm grateful for her foggy memory. Rather than confuse her or say Sean's name out loud, I pop up and refill her water glass.

Jo angles the plate toward Martin, and he licks it clean.

"He's probably done. Let me take that dish to the sink."

"No, no, he's not done. He likes it."

"Likes to lick his own butt, too."

"Be nice, now."

My courage to tell her about the auction is wavering. Come to think of it, she hasn't asked me about it the past couple of days. Is it possible she forgot? *No, Bree. Get it over with.* "So, listen, Jo—"

Martin jumps off Jo's lap, runs down the hall, and barks at the door.

"He needs to go doo-doo. His leash is on the counter."

"You want me to take him?"

"You brought the muffins."

"I didn't feed him the muffins."

He barks again.

"Hurry, before he tinkles on the floor."

But I don't like Martin. And Martin doesn't like me.

"Grab a couple doggie bags, too, for his messes."

And I certainly don't like Martin's messes.

Martin dodges and snaps at me as I try to fasten the leash onto his collar.

"Stay still, Martin."

"See, that's the problem," Jo says. "Your tone is all wrong. You can't yell at him; talk sweet."

"It's hard to be sweet when he's trying to bite the flesh off my hands."

"He's doing no such thing."

Jo's joints crack as she kneels beside us. "Let me see that."

Martin sits, facing her, tail wagging.

Suck-up.

With a click the leash is attached. "See, it's that easy."

I take the lead from her hand and open the door, but Martin won't budge. I tug a little—refraining from yanking him hard and swinging him above my head like a lasso—but he's fixed in place.

"Go on now," she says to Martin. "Be a good boy."

He moves no more than a fraction of an inch, so Jo scoots him across the threshold with her foot. "Take care of him now."

"This isn't such a good idea. How about—"

"When you come back, you can tell me what Nick is like in the sack."

"Jo!"

She winks and shuts the door.

"You heard the lady, let's go."

To my surprise, the little fur ball trots alongside me with his nose lifted in the air as if he's king of the sidewalk. He strolls toward a nearby rosemary bush, stopping for a moment to sniff. He then pulls on the leash, springing toward a cluster of red-flowered lantana.

"Okay, okay. I'm coming," I say, finding myself laughing.

Martin buries his head inside the plant, pulls it out, shakes his ears, and sneezes off a red petal.

"Bless you."

He heels by my side.

Well, look at this. Maybe this won't be so hard. Maybe Jo's right. Maybe *my* bad attitude resonated with him and we both needed a fresh start, to clear the air, literally. Maybe with this walk, we'll gain a new respect for each other. I mean, look at us, two peas in a pod. Now that I think about it, he's kinda cute, quite lovable.

Martin squats and poops on the sidewalk.

And quite disgusting.

I bend to pick up the stinky pile just as he kicks his spindly little legs, scattering the Tootsie rolls across the sidewalk and into the rocks.

"Jesus, dog. What are you doing?" I gather his messes while trying not to gag—this is why I don't have a dog—and tie the bag closed. "You are gross."

At the sound of my voice, Martin lunges toward me, barking and snapping at my ankles.

"Ouch!" I try to flick him away. "I just picked up your poop; you should be nice to me. Stop biting me, you jerk."

He circles me like a shark, gnashing his teeth, wrapping the leash tight around my legs.

"That's it, you little turd." I untangle myself. "I'm trading you in for a goldfish." It's only when I'm free that I notice Martin's dangling collar.

He slipped loose.

Oh God, no.

I search all around me.

He's gone.

In a panic, I whistle for him. "Martin? Come here, boy." I

search the walkway and under the hedges lining the curb. I sprint toward the grassy area up ahead, screaming his name. "Martin! Martin!"

He's not here.

This is bad. Very bad.

A woman hurries toward me and I'm already thanking her in my mind, grateful for another set of eyes.

"Glad I caught you," she says.

"Yes, thank you. If you'll search around the playground and I'll—"

She hands me a flyer for a community barbecue next Sunday. "What gluten-free item shall I put you down for?"

"No, I'm not . . . I'm looking for my dog." I shake the leash in the air.

"We have a leash law."

My phone rings. *Hee-haw.* I'm tempted to answer. Sean once found my earring back in the hall closet carpet. But, just like with the newspaper, I don't want his help.

"I gotta go," I say to the lady. "Martin, where are you?"

Ten minutes have passed and Jo's sidekick is nowhere to be found.

I'm dizzy with desperation when a teenage boy calls from the opposite side of the grass bowl. "You looking for him?" He points at Martin, sniffing behind a trash can.

"Yes!" *Oh, thank God. Such a relief.* I hurry toward them. "Thank you." I bend down and reach for Martin.

"Come here, you little numb-nuts."

He spins away, flashes his teeth, and growls.

"He doesn't like you," the kid says, before riding away on his skateboard.

Martin darts—faster than I thought his stumpy little legs could move—out from under my grasp. He ducks between two mailboxes lining the curb. Martin chases into the street.

A UPS truck approaches.

Oh, shit.

"Martin, no!"

I dash after him—faster than I thought *my* stumpy legs could move—and scream, "Martin! Martin, come!"

The truck gets closer.

I can see it now, walking back to Jo's without Martin, only his collar and leash in my hand.

Jo will kill me.

Worse yet, this will kill *her*.

I arrive at the curb's edge, fearing the worst.

But someone is watching out for me—or him—because I don't see the furry fella pancaked on the asphalt.

The brown truck continues down the street.

Thank God.

But only a fraction of a second passes before I realize Martin's still gone. It's almost dark. *What am I going to do?*

Fifteen minutes later, the sun has fully disappeared and I'm dripping with sweat after scouring the entire complex, the pools, the fitness area, and the playground twice more. But I've found no dog.

I consider hanging myself with his leash, for it's all I can do to take one step in front of the other as I make my way back to Jo's. I'm such an idiot. How do I lose a seven-pound shih tzu? I won't be able to look Jo in the eye.

Twice now, I've broken her heart. What's my encore? Sweep out her legs and break her hip?

Jo opens her door and notices the leash. Before she says anything, I start to explain. "I'm sorry. I don't know how it happened. One second he stood beside me and the next he slipped out of his collar and took off. But I'm going to keep looking. I bet someone in the complex found him. I'll post signs. I'll knock on every door. I promise I'll find him. I— Wait a second . . . what is that noise?" I peek around Jo toward a muffled gnawing sound coming from the hallway behind her.

Martin is splayed out on floor, chewing on his bone.

Little shit.

"What if something happened to him, Bree? What if he . . ." She shakes her head as if to erase the thought. "He's my baby."

"I know. I feel awful."

"I'm tired." Her tone is clipped. "I need to rest."

"Sure, of course." I start to leave but stop, remembering that I haven't told Jo about the auction.

She walks toward the living room, not inviting me in, but not shutting me out. And anyway, I need to tell her the truth. Yes, I'd rather stick my arm in an alligator's mouth, but I promised to keep her updated. And since Martin is okay, now is as crappy a time as any.

Jo settles into her well-worn recliner, switches on the table lamp, and reaches for a book.

Martin abandons his bone and curls himself beside Jo's feet.

She smiles at her companion, then focuses on the pages.

I'm gripped by the moment.

It's a normal, natural practice between the two. Nothing unique or extraordinary. The nightly ritual of an old woman and her faithful dog. But that's what strikes me. The simplicity. Jo's sat in this chair hundreds, maybe thousands, of times. The cushions shape to her frame. The carpet is impressed from Martin's habitual spot. She's comfortable in this home, guarded by the four walls. She belongs here. It's familiar. Safe.

The auction threatens to take her sanctuary away.

"Bree, why are you just standing there?"

Bestseller is inscribed across the book held in her hands.

I'm reminded of the possibilities for *Can I See You Again?*

"What on earth is wrong?" The wrinkles around her eyes seem deeper than a couple of hours ago, her skin pallid.

She *is* tired.

"Nothing's wrong." I drape the nearby blanket over my grandmother's legs, deciding not to mention the current status of the house, because maybe . . . I won't need to. Why remind her of the situation, disrupt her peaceful evening, have her fret and lose sleep when my numbers are up and this bestseller ranking is no longer such a pie-in-the-sky aspiration? Why worry her, just yet? "Get some rest." I kiss my grandmother's cheek and walk out the door.

No, I don't tell Jo the truth.

But I don't break her heart again, either.

fourteen

Randi greets me as I unlock my office door the following morning clutching a purse twice as big as the other day. "How's my favorite client?"

"I bet you say that to all the girls."

"Honey, haven't you heard? You're a sensation, more popular than the morning-after pill at a sorority house. The calls and e-mails to Candace's department yesterday and this morning damn near jammed up the phone lines. And the buzz keeps growing."

"Are you serious?" We walk inside.

"Your editor already e-mailed me. She saw the article, too. They're upping the first run of *Can I See You Again?* by ten thousand copies. I also sent a copy of the manuscript to Lucy Hanover at KMRQ last week. She likes what she's read so far. I have a call in to her asking if she'll have you on her show. You're on your way to a bestseller debut, no question."

"You're kidding."

"Awesome," Andrew says, walking toward us.

"Did you say something? I can't hear you over the angels

singing." I point at my head. Thank goodness I hired Randi and things are on the upswing. With the dang IRS debacle consuming my thoughts, I could use a little upswing.

Andrew hurries to answer the phone and Randi follows me toward my desk. "So here's the deal: Given the popularity of the first interview, the paper's raising the stakes. They've developed an expanded vision for the remaining installments."

"What does that mean?"

"Not entirely sure. All I know is that you are a sensation. Candace is on her way in to discuss."

"Now?"

"Yes, they're very excited."

At the very same moment, Scotty holds the door open as Candace parades into the room with a Peet's coffee cup and a beaming smile. "Hello, everyone. Can you believe what a beautiful day it is? Why are we all working?"

"Mimosas by the beach, anyone?" Randi says, half joking.

"That is tempting, but thanks to you"—Candace points at me—"nothing short of a journalist's dream, we have loads of work to do."

"Randi said the article was well received?"

"We haven't entertained this amount of feedback since our cover of George Clooney's wife."

"Wow, really?"

"You should see the mass of e-mails."

I peek at Andrew; he clicks from one ringing line to the next.

"We've received a sizable amount of calls and inquiries regarding your professional life." Candace pulls out a folder from her bag. "So I've decided to split this exposé into two parts, your personal life and your professional life."

"Okay."

"Naturally, we'll want to know more about you and your sexy man."

Ah, crap. "Um, no, no, there's nothing more to say. We're quite boring, actually. Grocery lists and laundry, that sort of thing."

"Readers are enamored by you. Well, you and Nick."

"Me *and* Nick?"

"Yes. Readers latched on the two of you like you're Brangelina or something. Now there's an idea. Ever thought of combining your names? Nickee? Brick? Anyway, we want to learn more about the love you two share." She waves her hand in the air. "But that part's easy."

Not as easy as you think.

"Now, the tricky part concerns your professional life. We're going to exploit your talents. Prove to the readers just how capable you are."

"What do you have in mind?"

"A test case."

"Sorry?"

"The paper and our readers are going to follow along, week after week, as you find love for a brand-new single, off-the-street candidate."

"Ooh, now that sounds interesting," Randi says.

Candace scoots toward the edge of her chair and points at my front door. "The next person to walk through that door will become your new client. You'll interview or do whatever it is you do to find a match for that person. We'll observe and report for the readers. Together, as a nation, we'll watch them fall in love, week by week, under your guide. See if you really are as good as you say."

"You want me to find a match for some random person that walks into my office?"

"You got it. The paper will cover all the expenses, of course."

"What if the next guy is a heroin addict?"

"Do you get many heroin addicts?"

"Well, no."

"Then there's no problem. Not only will we read in each edition about you and Nick celebrating your love, thus learning through observation the workings of a solid relationship, but we'll shadow a lucky individual as he or she *falls* in love over the course of this segment. It's a win-win. You up for the challenge?"

"Of course she is," Randi pipes in.

"It does sound kinda fun," I admit. *Except for the part about Nick and me celebrating our love. Not sure how to handle that.*

"Great. Now we want to keep this as controlled as possible. Obviously, we aren't going on the dates, and we ask that you don't either, or manipulate the process in anyway."

"She'd never compromise her professional ethics," Randi assures Candace. "Right?"

"Right," I confirm. *Unless you count Nixon.*

"I don't doubt that for a second. All the same, after the initial setup, I'll meet with the client after each date or meeting or whatever it is you arrange and interview him or her. This way, you'll learn of the success or failure of the new relationship when the article is released, just like everyone else. Make sense?"

"Sure does."

Candace folds her hands on her lap. "I don't mind saying, this idea is genius. I'm quite excited. All we need now is our guinea pig."

"I wonder who the lucky girl or guy will be," Randi says.

"Thing is, we're appointment only," I say. "We don't get many walk-ins."

To prove me wrong, the door swings open.

We all turn to see a man step inside.

A man with a swimmer's build, slightly windblown hair, rigid jaw, and a pressed jacket. A man with a raspberry-colored birthmark behind his left ear and a chicken pox scar to the right of his belly button.

A man with my broken heart held in his palm.

My hands curl into fists.

Sean.

fifteen

This can't be real. This must be a bad dream. To hell with Dr. Oz and broken capillaries. Pinch me. *For Christ's sake, someone pinch me!*

"Hi, I'm Candace Porter with the *National Tribune*. And, you are?" she asks.

"Sean Thomas."

"Are you a client here?"

"No. I'm here to speak with Bree."

"Sorry, but you'll have to make an appointment," I say, moving around Sean and pushing open my office door, stepping on his toe as a painful—albeit childish—reminder of what he threw away. I gesture outside. "And no, we don't validate. Good-bye."

"Bree? What are you doing? This man is lovely." Candace grabs Sean by the arm and pulls him farther into my office. "You've come to the right place. Shut the door, Bree." She waves me inside. "This darling lady, Bree Caxton, is one of San Diego's best matchmakers."

"Yeah, I'm told she's pretty great."

"Oh, she is." Candace peeks at me and says with a little laugh, "Listen to me, I'm supposed to be an objective reporter, but I can't help but sing your praises." She gestures for Sean to have a seat, then sits beside him. "You can talk to Bree all you want, but first I have a proposition for you."

"Really?"

"I'm writing a piece for the *National Tribune* about Bree Caxton and her exceptional talents as a matchmaker."

"Really? That's great."

No. No way. He can't do that. Obviously Sean hasn't seen yesterday's article, likely didn't know to look as we talked only about his claustrophobia at dinner, nothing about me or the *Close-Up* interview. But now it's too late. He's not allowed to sound interested and proud. He's not allowed to cheer me on.

"Yes, and we've decided to put Bree in the hot seat and test her methods. For the next month, we'd like to chart the progress of a new client finding love. We'd like you to be that client. The paper will cover all of your expenses. How can you pass this up?"

Uh . . . he can, quite easily.

"All you have to do is say yes to love."

"Yes to love, huh?" Sean says. "Would Bree be involved?"

Don't you dare, Sean Michael Thomas. Don't. You. Dare.

"Heavens, yes," Candace says, "along with a couple of interviews with me in the coming weeks, and, of course, dating beautiful women. That won't be so hard, will it?"

"Doesn't sound like it."

What are you doing? You broke up with me like twenty minutes ago, you big jerk.

"Wait a second," Candace says.

"Yes, great idea," I say, raising my palms like a crossing guard stopping traffic. If I had a whistle, I'd blow it hard into Sean's ears. "Let's take a second and discuss the many, many reasons why this won't work."

"You have that shindig coming up soon, right?"

"My social?"

"Yes, that could be Sean's debut." Candace clutches his forearm. "Bree will interview or prep you, or however she readies a client, and then, showtime."

"All of this will help Bree's company?" Sean asks.

"I should say so. Shall we get started?"

"No!" My sharp tone catches Candace off-guard.

"No?"

"Um . . . no . . . you see, there's not near enough time to coordinate realistic and compatible matches. And love shouldn't be rushed. So this won't work." *Ever.* "Thanks for coming by." I move past him and open the door once again.

"Bree, don't be ridiculous." Candace scoots me away from the door. "Sean, do you have a few minutes now?"

"I do."

"Candace, I—"

"Remember, Bree." There's a stinging quality to her words. "When you signed the contract, you agreed to be accessible *anytime* during the course of this installment. Come now, no time like the present. Find this handsome young man love. This is fun. Won't this be fun?"

This will not be fun.

"I'm excited to watch you work your magic." Candace jars my thoughts. "It brings back memories of my husband and my first dates. Now, you go about your normal routine, I'm just here to observe."

Andrew's answering the phone, Randi's stepped aside

replying to an e-mail, and dammit, I can't escape through the air conditioner duct. With no other choice, I slide into my desk chair, forcing myself not to recall details of the night Sean and I made love here. Nor do I acknowledge his gaze at the missing nick of baseboard when the chair's wheel bonked into the wall.

Has he no shame? No conscience? How can he do this to me? Well . . . fine . . . whatever. You want a date? I'll find you a date. Someone who'll get you drunk and shave off an eyebrow. Or two. Better yet, how about an unshaven Russian women's wrestling champion who'll wrap you in a headlock with her tree-trunk arms. Bet you'll feel stifled then, eh?

Andrew catches my eye and, through his own, I read—*Auction. If you don't come up with the money, Jo loses her house.*

"Bree, are you ready?"

Christ, I'm backed into a corner. Ugh. Okay, calm yourself, Bree. Take a breath. Switch gears. Concentrate.

"Uh, yes." I reach for my new-client questionnaire and sit tall. *You can do this. For Jo, for the book, for the house.* "So, Sean, is it?"

"Yes."

"Isn't that a woman's name?" I say this, knowing it'll touch a nerve. He shared the name with a freckled girl in third grade. The other kids colored hearts and rainbows on his lunch box. And lots of times over the years, mail has come addressed to *Miss* Sean Thomas. Once he received a three-dollars-off coupon for Kotex.

"It's a man's name."

"Oh." I pretend to scrawl something important, but doodle *jerk.* "Okay, then, first things first. What type of man are you looking for? Soft and passive? Or rugged and well-built? Maybe a brick layer with meaty hands?"

"A woman, thank you."

"My mistake. I pegged you swinging for the other team."

"In his dreams," Andrew mutters so only I can hear, before busying himself with a file he's walked over with and pretending to organize.

"No, I'm not into guys. I'm into girls who are kind and merciful. A woman who listens and appreciates all perspectives."

"You like doormats, then?"

"Hardly. I like someone with grit. Someone who will discuss things and doesn't walk away when times get tough. A woman who gives a man a chance to explain."

"What else is there to say? And what if she doesn't care about his reasons, anyway? What if he made himself crystal clear?"

"Hmm," Candace murmurs, scrawling away at her notepad.

"Then I'd say she's being closed-minded and failing to see his side of the story. I'd say she hasn't taken into account that he's hurt, too. And he misses her. And he doesn't want to be kicked out of her life."

I scribble *jackass*. "Then maybe he shouldn't have kicked her out."

Sean's tongue pokes into his cheek and he folds his arms across his chest. His classic sign of irritation.

Ha! I got him riled.

"Clearly, I'm out of my realm," Candace says, "because I do not see how this helps find Sean love."

"Look, Bree—" Sean starts.

"You know, I've got all I need here for today."

"You do?" Candace scrolls her pencil down her notepad. "I didn't get much out of that. If you don't mind, Sean, I have one question. And I guess this proves the difference between Bree's abilities and mine, but she didn't ask you anything about appearances. I'm curious, what type of woman do you find attractive?" Her pencil is now poised.

"That's easy." He stares at me. "A woman with gumdrop green eyes, silky hair that smells like jasmine, a sense of humor mixed with sweet and spice, and a smile that makes me forget what day it is."

That's not fair.

Candace writes quickly on her notepad and says with a laugh, "Almost sounds as if you're describing Bree."

"Actually, Candace, mind if I chat with her for a moment, in private?"

"Go right ahead. It'll give me a second to make sense of my scribble."

Sean follows me into the break room. I position myself close enough to speak softly but not close enough to feel his breath drift over my skin.

It's funny, Sean and I have never stalled for good conversation, something I've always been proud of. I looked forward to long plane rides or traffic jams because I knew we'd banter back and forth, laugh, challenging each other on capital punishment (he's against), allowing dogs in grocery stores (I'm against), or which person should get voted off Survivor (the annoying ones).

But as I stare at the man I thought certain to be *the one*, for the first time, I don't know what to say.

"You haven't returned my calls. Or my texts."

"You're surprised?"

He swallows hard. "Look, Bree. I don't know where to begin. It kills me to know you're so upset. I've been beating myself up ever since."

"Aww . . . you poor thing."

"I just want to talk with you."

"Why?"

"I . . . maybe I . . . made the wrong decision." He scratches the side of his nose.

The bastard is lying.

"You should go."

I start to move past him, but he grabs my wrist and says, "Look, I'm confused, okay? I . . . I didn't mean to hurt you." His fingers slide toward my hand, and this time I don't flick it away.

This time for a few seconds, I let his thumb caress my skin and allow myself to remember how good his touch feels. "Let me help you with this newspaper thing. I don't want it to be like this."

"You think *I* want this?" I grind my teeth together and stare at the floor, willing myself not to cry. "Four years together, Sean. Four years. And you broke up with me, just like that, and at our favorite spot."

He hangs his head low and nods before saying, "You're right. I fucked up. I made an impossibly bad call. I thought the timing had some sort of symmetry . . . I don't know. But can we please put this behind us and move forward? Just give me some time. Can we at least be friends?"

"Friends? Like go to Antonio's again? Sit in our usual booth? Order our usual wine? Clink glasses and laugh, pretend that night never existed?"

"We can get through this." He squeezes my hand.

He's not wearing his watch. Which I find odd, as it's his most prized possession, polishing the face each morning and again in the evening before tucking it safely in its case with gentleness as if it's an injured baby bird. He's worn the watch every single day except when he had the clasp repaired last year.

I hate that I know so much about him.

"You can't do this interview, Sean."

"You won't return my calls. I just want to talk to you."

Tears form in my eyes and I shake my head. "Please, Sean."

"Okay, I'll back out. But meet me for dinner?"

The logical part of my brain says *Absolutely not*, but the sappy side is caving, reminding me how difficult it is to find love and how much harder it is to let go. "No dinner. Coffee."

"When?"

"After work."

"Sean, Bree?" Candace calls. "Ready to finish up?"

Sean loosens his grasp and we rejoin the ladies. "Actually, Candace, I appreciate the opportunity, but there's been a change of plans. I'm not going to be the guinea pig."

"What? Why on earth not?"

"Something more important came up."

"Oh, shoot. Is there any way I can convince you otherwise?"

Nixon steps inside my office.

"No, thanks," Sean says. "Let that guy have the spotlight."

Candace laughs. "I don't think Bree would appreciate that too much."

"Why not?"

"Because that's Bree's boyfriend."

Oh, crap. This is about to get *very* ugly.

"Your boyfriend?" Sean's tone turns razor sharp and I almost check for blood dripping off my skin.

See.

"Yes, and they're adorable. Thanks for considering the proposition. Back to the drawing board, eh, Bree?" She heads toward Nixon and says, "Now, why am I not surprised to see you visiting your little lovebird?"

"A fucking boyfriend. Really, Bree? How long has this been going on?"

I take offense to his criticism. After all, he started this mess. "It's really none of your business."

"No?"

"No."

"You sit here and make me feel like a dick when all along you've been cheating on me."

"If you'll let me explain—"

"What else is there to explain?" Sean sneers, repeating the very same words I said at Antonio's. "Candace?" Sean spins around. "Forget what I said. I'll do the interview. And all the dating that comes with it. Seems as if I'm very single."

"Wonderful!" She returns her attention to Nixon.

I grab Sean by his wrist. "What the hell do you think you're doing?"

He brushes my hand away and I'm struck by the reversal of roles. The other night and just moments ago, he clutched my arm, begging for reconsideration. "Letting you find me love."

"This is thrilling." Candace joins us, leaving Nixon in the sitting area. "What fun it'll be to watch Bree's brilliance unfold. Need anything else from Sean for the moment?"

The last four years of my life, please. Oh, and another vase to bust over his head. "No. Not one thing."

"Sean, I need you to sign a few release documents real quick, but I've left my briefcase in my car. I'm parked right outside. Walk with me?"

"Sure, of course."

"Bree, I'll be right back," Candace says. "You don't go anywhere either, Nick. I have more questions for you two." With keys in hand, she steps outside.

"Won't this be fun, Bree?" Sean marches toward the door, shoulder-checking Nixon.

"Hey, watch it, man," Nixon says.

Sean doesn't respond, just pushes open the front door, slamming it against the stucco.

"Sean?" Nixon asks.

"In the flesh." I clasp my hands together to keep them from trembling. "The paper just made him my client. I have to match him with a girlfriend. A *girlfriend*. If I don't, then I look like an incompetent loser and I can say good-bye to my business and a bestseller and Jo's house. But if I do find Sean a match, and he falls in love . . . then . . . I don't know . . . I don't want to talk about it." I rub my aching temples from an instant headache. "What are you doing here, anyway?"

He waves the rolled-up article in the air. "I'm wondering why people at my office are gathered around the conference room discussing what I'm like in the sack."

"Don't you mean what Nick the urologist is like in the sack?"

"What's the difference?" He tosses the circular onto my desk.

"Oh, c'mon, it's not like your picture is in there. Plus, it's not even your real name. No one will ever suspect it's you."

"Why does Candace have more questions? I signed up for one interview, remember? 'One and done' is what you said."

"Yeah, well, apparently you're a big hit."

"I don't want to be a big hit."

"People love you." I poke him on the arm, trying to spin the situation and my mood.

He couldn't care less.

"I couldn't care less."

"You can't cut and run."

"I can, too. I don't have time for this nonsense. I hired you to find me a girlfriend, not thrust me into the nation's eye for a public dissection of my sex life. I'm sorry, but this is your deal."

I fold my arms across my chest and pout like a spoiled toddler. "Then I'm out. I'm not coming to the wedding."

"You said you would."

"Yes, but the more I think about it, the more I realize I entered into a lopsided arrangement."

"What are you talking about?"

"Nick, Bree?" Candace returns from outside and calls us over.

"Um . . . just a minute." I smile at her, then say to Nixon, "A wedding is a big deal. It's hellos and hugs, it's family and friends. It's five hundred bucks for a new dress and new shoes that I'll spend hours searching for and will likely never wear again. It's a manicure and pedicure. It's overnight and—"

"Whatever. I'll go alone."

"Do as you wish, but your mom called and I told her you were bringing me. The seating chart is finalized and placement cards have been ordered. Nice stuff, embossed ivory card stock."

"Why would you do that?"

"Because you *were* bringing me. But if you back out, then so do I, because, think about it, I'll need to get my hair done and—"

"If I agree to this interview crap, will you stop talking?"

"Well, not during the interviews."

"Guys, I really need to get rolling." Candace grabs Nixon by the arm. "Come along now, you two can make googly eyes at each other later."

"Yes, come along, baby."

We sit across from Candace, as she has arranged the chairs in the same pattern as the other day.

"Such luck that I caught you both here." She settles into her chair. "I want to get a jump start on the next article. Readers are dying to know more about you two. Buckle up, we're about to delve deeper into your relationship."

"Deeper?" Nixon asks, glaring at me.

"Scores of women asked about your private life, how you two keep the attraction going, and where Dr. Nick works. Tell me, do you work for a hospital or your own practice? Scotty can't find a urologist named Nick that matches your description."

"This is insane," Nixon whispers, and starts to stand.

I press my hand on his forearm, forcing him still. He nearly lifts me off my chair. Damn, he's strong. I glare at him.

He glares back.

"You know, Candace, his work doesn't need the publicity. Let's focus on the other questions, shall we?"

"Yes, I suppose we can. Let's see, now." She skims through her notes. "As I said, hundreds of women sent in their phone numbers; some included photos of themselves. One girl posed half dressed in some sort of bumblebee costume and another not dressed in anything at all, just her phone number penned across her belly. My, my," she says before looking at me, "if I were you, Bree, with all these interested women, I'd hold on to him tight."

"Don't worry, I will." And, I am. *Literally.*

He pries at my fingers.

I cover his hand with my other, digging my nails into his skin.

He doesn't flinch.

What is he, some sort of robot?

"Look at you two. Can't keep your hands off one another." She flips open her notebook and clicks on her recorder. "So the paper's decided to engage the audience and ask you *their* questions." She refers to her notes again. "Where do I start?"

Nixon frees my hand, his skin blotchy from my clasp. "Listen, there's been a misunderstanding."

"What kind of misunderstanding?" She bounces her gaze between Nixon and me.

"You see, Bree and I—"

"Can't decide where to go on vacation this year. I'm thinking Hawaii, but in his twenties, Nick spent a couple summers there as a deckhand, on a tour boat thing. He's leaning toward Greece. But, you know, we'll figure it out." I laugh a little longer and louder than necessary, ignoring the instant flash of heat brewing along my neck.

Nixon's frown grows deeper, but he remains seated.

Thank God.

"Either place is lovely." She sorts through more printed e-mails. "Lena from right here in La Jolla wants to know: Do you two live together?"

"Nope," I start before Nixon has a chance. "We believe in marriage first."

"Traditional values, that's refreshing. You don't hear that too often these days."

"Why buy the cow when you can get the milk for free?" I say.

"Especially if she has mad cow disease," Nixon adds.

"Sorry?" Candace says.

"He's teasing. Such a kidder." I smack him hard on the arm. "Be serious now, sweetie."

"Makayla from La Mesa wants to know if you have a single brother. If not, do you have a single sister?" Candace's cheeks redden. "Why, now that's an interesting proposal, isn't it?"

"No brothers or sisters," I interject, recalling his questionnaire. "But we are visiting his family in a few weeks. Nick's cousin is getting married at his parents' house. All the family will be there. Loads of fun." I pat Nixon's knee.

"And where is that?" Candace asks.

I have no idea.

Nixon tilts his head with a smirk on his face. "Go ahead, *sweetie*, tell Candace where my parents live."

Candace sits poised, ready for my answer.

A hive blossoms at the nape of my neck. "Um . . . it's a lovely place . . . in . . ." Then I remember Mrs. Voss's area code when she called the other day. 442. "Carlsbad area, north of here."

He flinches, likely surprised by my knowledge.

Now Nixon must really think I'm stalking him *and* his family.

"Nice area." Candace selects another question. "Here's a good one. Erica from San Diego says, 'Nick and Bree sound so cute and totally in love. What do the two do for fun?'"

"Oh, that's easy," I say. "We like wine tastings, movies, fiddling around one another's houses taking care of Cinderella chores. In fact, I have a sprinkler valve—"

Nixon clasps my hand. "You know, I should contribute to this conversation, too. After all, it is about *us*."

"No, you relax, honey. I don't mind answering the questions."

Please stay quiet, please.

"Actually, Bree, I'd like to hear from Nick. Tell me, what do the two of you do for fun?"

"In or out of the bedroom?" He laughs. "Or should I say the parking lot of Whole Foods? Am I right, *sweetie*?" Nixon runs his fingers through my hair. "What this girl can do with an olive."

Please tell me he did not just say that.

"Oh, my." Candace writes a few notes.

I whisper to Nixon, "What are you doing?"

"Just playing along."

"Laying it on a bit thick, don't you think?"

"You roped me into this song and dance. Now we play it my way."

Good Lord, I've created a monster.

"All right, so aside from . . . um . . . Whole Foods"—Candace clears her throat—"what else do you two like to do? Like, say, for example, what are your plans for this weekend?"

"Well, my little Breester is quite the adventure buff. So, I'm thinking rappelling."

Dangle from a tiny rope? I'd rather slather myself in strawberry jelly and crawl into a grizzly bear's den. "Um, too bad, baby cakes, I called, and they're booked, so—"

"Jet-Skiing," he says.

In the ocean? Hasn't he ever watched Shark Week? I catch the light in his eye. He's enjoying this. *Okay, funny guy, no reason you should have all the fun.*

"Unfortunately, that's out, too. You see, Nick has this skin condition on his butt that gets flaky in salt water, so—"

"So . . ." He wraps his arm around my shoulder and pulls me close.

I do not like the look in his eye. I do not.

"We signed up for a Tough Mudder."

"Tough Mudder? What's that?" Candace asks.

Yeah, what's that?

"It's a twelve-mile military-style obstacle course, designed to play on common fears like heights, space, and water, that sort of stuff. It tests mental strength and physical stamina."

"Sounds quite challenging," Candace adds.

Sounds like torture.

"It is, but, my Bree, she's resilient. Besides, it's for a good cause, raises money for the Wounded Warrior Project. It's this Saturday morning in the mountains east of San Diego."

"All for charity, that's wonderful." Candace gathers her papers and stands.

We join her.

"Well, as I said last time, I'm no expert, but it seems as though you two have it all figured out, an excellent example of your professional skills overlapping into your personal life."

"She's my peach." He smacks me in the ass.

I will kill him.

"Do you have all you need, Candace?" Randi asks.

I'd forgotten she was still here.

"I believe so. Andrew, you got the information on the new client, Sean, right?"

Damn. It wasn't a bad dream.

"I do," he says.

"Now, the cocktail party is in a couple of days? And you'll have potential matches for him there?"

"Uh . . . yes, I will." I barely squeak out the words. *How am I supposed to do this? How am I supposed to find love for the man who still holds my heart? And my vinyl collection.*

"Wonderful. As I've mentioned, we're expediting the pace here and moving right along. Next week's article will feature the two of you." She motions toward Nixon and me. "Alongside will be Sean, and if Bree is as good as she says, then his new gal, too."

Gee . . . great.

"So, with that said, I'll have Sean here the day after the party, at nine a.m., for a quick interview. After that, I'll meet with him privately. Thanks again, everyone. We'll talk soon."

"I'm off, too," Randi says. "Only a little over a month before the release and I've got a lot to do."

"Olives?" I snarl at Nixon. "My grandmother is going to read this article."

"You know, it wouldn't hurt to thank me. I'm not doing this interview for *me*."

"Yes, fine, you're right. I'm grateful for your help and quick thinking. I mean the Tough Mudder stuff is classic."

"Think I'm kidding? Hope you have a decent pair of tennis shoes. I'll pick you up Saturday, six a.m."

sixteen

A few minutes later, Andrew follows me to my desk.

I collapse into my chair. "This day started off well, then fizzled into disaster."

"Yes, but on the flip side, the phone has been ringing all morning. I signed a dozen new clients all because they saw the article, and I had to print off more applications for a dozen others." Andrew glances at his watch. "It's not even eleven a.m."

"At least something's going right today."

"Yeah, about that. This may not be the best time to tell you, but Mr. Chambers called. Don't you think he sounds like an arena announcer? *Let's get ready to rumble . . .*"

"What did he say, Andrew?"

"The hearing is set for next Wednesday."

The confirmation weighs on my chest like a brick. "Okay, right. Guess it's official, then. Well, that's good, I suppose. At least then we'll know exactly what we're up against."

"Have you told Jo what's going on?"

"Not yet. She hasn't asked and"—I shrug—"what's one more tiny white lie?"

"You're not lying to her."

"I'm withholding the truth. Same difference."

"She's tough, you know? Remember when she crawled underneath her sink and repaired her garbage disposal?"

"I know she's tough, but I've never seen her like this. She crumbles at the thought of losing her house."

"Then let's not let that happen. By the way, there's an e-mail from Chambers, listing a few things he wants beforehand."

"Okay." I dig in my purse for Advil.

"There's more."

"Of course there is."

"The Gardens canceled our reception for Thursday night."

I perk up. "No, that's perfect. I can cancel Sean and—"

"I already paid the nonrefundable deposit with the caterer."

"Damn. Why'd they cancel?"

"Roof leak."

"On top of everything else and now this." I swallow the pills without water, something my dad used to do.

"Any other venue ideas?" Andrew tucks his bright yellow shirttail into his white jeans.

"No."

"What about that new restaurant on Sixth?"

"Too bright. I want somewhere classy and fresh, yet untapped."

"How about the park with the carousel?"

"No, the ticket-taker guy creeps me out. I swear he angles the mirrors to peek up girls' skirts."

"I've seen that look before," Andrew says. "What's your grand idea?"

"How about Sara's gallery? It's a great space. Not too small. Not too large." *Plus, Sean hates stuffy art galleries.*

"Definitely classy and hip."

"I'm sure she has the gallery finished by now. I bet she'd

love the exposure. Do I have any appointments scheduled soon?"

He checks his iPad. "Nope, not until after lunch."

"Great. I'm going to ask Sara in person. Wanna come?"

"Absolutely."

After a quick stop for a coffee, Andrew and I head toward Sara's gallery, pausing at the crosswalk for a red light.

"We haven't talked about it much, but how are you doing?" he asks, and I know he means Sean.

"I don't know. I'm mad. I'm sad. I'm embarrassed. I'm confused."

"Yeah, I bet."

There have been a few times that I've forgotten that Sean ended our relationship. Just this morning alone, as I readied for work, several fleeting thoughts about us grilling steaks this weekend and finishing up the yellow peppers from last Saturday's farmer's market fluttered through my mind. And without thinking, I almost texted him about catching the new Robert Downey, Jr., movie on Sunday.

But then there are moments when the truth consumes me, when reality smacks me in the face and the images of his pained expression, his parted lips as he mouthed the words "It's not working" and his eyes narrowed with pity, carve a deeper pit into my heart.

"It helps having the article and even my little fake relationship with Nixon . . . er . . . Nick to take my mind off Sean. But I must admit, I fall asleep and wake up thinking of the past four years and everything I did wrong."

"You didn't do anything wrong."

"Maybe not, but I must not have done enough right, either."

"I'm sorry he acted like such a jerk. Want me to kick him in the nuts next time I see him?"

"Yes."

"I think Sean truly feels bad for what he did."

"He should." We weave between two parked cars and cross the street.

"Yeah, he should. But, I don't know . . ." He shrugs and sidesteps a newspaper stand. "I'm just saying if he's that important to you, then don't close the door. You know better than most, a good relationship is hard to find. Give him some space and don't let your pride get in the way."

"Thanks, Andrew. I appreciate it."

"Speaking of swallowing pride, I called my parents yesterday."

"Not the spray tan thing again?"

"No." He laughs. "I asked them to lunch. For real. All this talk about Jo and family has got me thinking, maybe I'm as much to blame as them for our family's dysfunction."

"Yeah, how so?"

"Over the years, I've thrown our differences in their face, kinda gayed things up, so to speak, just to piss them off."

I know what he's referring to. So frustrated with his parents' criticism for his sexual orientation, Andrew dropped out of college late in his junior year. He cashed in his savings bonds and blew the money on nightclubs and weekends in Vegas at expensive hotels with random guys.

"All it got me was thirty-six credits shy of a degree, broke, a scar on my ankle that I have no idea where it came from, and a dad who can't stand the sight of me."

"That's not true. He just doesn't understand your choices, that's all."

"But that's the thing. That aspect of my life is not all that I am. And their disappointment in my 'lifestyle' isn't all they are, either."

"Dang, Andrew, that's the most profound thing you've ever said. Maybe anyone's ever said."

"Yeah, well, remind me of that if they slam the door in my face. I'll let you know how it goes."

"Hey, by the way, who were you having lunch with yesterday? At Ryoko's? The place you hate."

"Huh?" He bites his lip, buying time.

"What's going on?"

"It's nothing."

"Oh, c'mon." I tickle his stomach. "What's the matter? Parasites swimming around in there?"

He swats my hands away. "Let's get back to you and your troubles."

He reveals no more about his sushi lunch and I decide to let it go. Besides, Andrew can't keep a secret. I'll find out soon enough.

"What kind of matchmaker can't keep a boyfriend?" he says with a playful, inoffensive tone.

"Ha. I'm quite impressive, don't you think?" I fan my hands in the air and call out as if reading a marquee. *"Come find love with Bree Caxton and Associates, never mind that she can't find love herself."*

"If you want to work with a loser, give her a call." Andrew laughs, then wraps his arm around me.

"You know, sometimes I wish you weren't gay."

"Sometimes I wish you weren't a woman."

We hold hands all the way until we reach Sara's gallery.

The tarps have been removed, the artwork hung, the birch floors polished. A series of frameless watercolors line the smooth walls. Dominating the center of the room is a sculpture formed with industrial-style heavy black iron pipe shaped into a flying bird . . . or a hang glider . . . or maybe the movers dropped the figure on the concrete and who's to know?

All the same, the gallery is modernly sparse and fresh, yet sophisticated and trendy enough that no one will dare admit they don't understand the art. It's an ideal venue for my upscale crowd.

"Perfect, isn't it?" I say.

Andrew gazes up at a sweeping chandelier made of shiny chrome arms and covered with ivory-colored feathers. "This place is beautiful. It has an engaging sense and a great environment for mingling. We can set the bar up in that far corner."

"Yes, and arrange a few chairs in the other corner for seating."

"Bree? What a nice surprise." A bright shade of coral lipstick colors Sara's lips. She's twenty feet away and I can see the glow on her face.

"The power of a new love," I whisper to Andrew, before Sara reaches us.

"The power of *Nixon*," Andrew says. "Fifty bucks says she bought new underwear."

"Hello, Sara. You remember Andrew?"

"Of course. A pleasure to see you."

"You, too," he says. "I love those sandals."

We all peek at her camel-colored double-strapped shoes. "Thanks."

"Sara, the gallery is incredible," I say. "I'm impressed you pulled it together so quickly."

"Thank you." She bends down to pick a piece of fuzz off the ground, sticking it inside her pocket. "It's been a lot of work, more than I anticipated, but thrilling at the same time. All I've got to do now is get people in the door. So, what brings you here? Did you come to take me up on that offer of Cristal?"

"Yes!" Andrew says.

I still his clapping hands. "Not today, thank you. Actually, I might have an idea to help get people in the door. At least for one night. We're here today with a proposition."

She tilts her head. "Really? What is it?"

"Well, as you know, each month I host a get-together for my like-minded clients to meet and mingle."

"Yes, I attended the brunch at Hotel del Coronado."

"That's right. Well, I planned to host this month's party at the Gardens, but they canceled. I know it's last minute, but I'm wondering if you'd consider holding the mixer here."

"In my gallery?"

"Yes. Thursday night. It'd be great exposure for the new place."

She nibbles on her fingernail. "That it would be. But this Thursday?"

"I know, not a lot of time to prepare, but I'll handle all the arrangements: food, bar, wait staff, clean up, everything with the exception of security. I'm sure you have your own firm."

"I do."

Andrew jumps in. "We're keeping the guest list small and intimate, twenty-five to thirty people, maximum. A couple of hours, tops. What do you say?"

"I do have a few pieces from a new expressionist that I've been excited to display. This mixer will be a perfect occasion. I say yes. Let's do it." She places her hand on my forearm. "First you find me Nixon, who may very well be the *one*. I had another nice conversation with him earlier today, by the way."

Yeah, so did I.

"And, now you offer me a fantastic business opportunity. Bree Caxton, you're my new favorite person."

ᔓ

A few hours later, after my appointments have been wrapped up, client calls returned, bills paid, my mouse pad wiped clean, pencils pointed east in my desk drawer, tea bags organized in the cupboard, and anything else I can do around the office to prolong the inevitable, Andrew props his laptop on his knees. He clicks open the database. "We need to do this."

"How'd I get myself into this mess? Not long ago I bounced around happy and clueless. And now, my future rests on Sean falling in love. With *someone else*."

"Put on your professional hat and get this over with. What are the parameters?"

"Missing front tooth. Incontinent. Riddled with cold sores."

"C'mon, now, Bree. You said yourself, the success of *Can I See You Again?* hangs in the balance. It isn't going to work if you don't take this seriously."

"Fine, fine." I exhale a long breath. *For Jo, for the book, for the house.* "Okay, search for a nonsmoker, cultured, snarky, nice ass." I arch my back and pat my own butt. "But I guess you already knew that."

"Now there's the Bree I know and love."

seventeen

Before stepping inside the Q&A conference room the following evening, I run my fingers through my hair and scan the library one last time. For no reason in particular.

All right, yes.

Fine.

So what if I did walk the long way around, passing by Kid Town? I just wanted to say hi. I'm nothing if not polite. No big deal, really. Besides, I didn't even see Nixon.

"Hey, everyone," I say to the gang, setting my purse on the nearby chair.

But they don't reply.

Gwen and her friend are hunched over Ernie the oldest member's shoulder. And the two men seated on either side of him crowd close. They're focused on something in Ernie's hands.

"Don't tell me you stole another copy of your grandson's *Playboy*, Ernie. We'll get kicked out again."

"No, silly," Gwen says, pointing at what I now recognize as my *Close-Up* article. "We're reading about you!"

I feel myself blushing. "Oh, c'mon, put that away. Unless, of course . . . you don't want to."

"Why didn't you tell us?" Gwen grabs each of my hands and shakes them in the air. "A gal at my water aerobics class kept going on and on about this fabulous new series in the paper, and when she mentioned your name, I nearly sank to the bottom of the pool. I said, 'Bree Caxton? I love Bree Caxton.' The other ladies in my class all knew about the article, too."

"My granddaughter told me," says Gwen's friend. "And she lives clear out in Florida. She's following it online."

"Everyone's talking about you," Gwen says. "You're famous."

"I don't know about that."

"Excuse me." The door pushes open behind me and in walks a twenty-something woman in a powder-blue tunic, black leggings, and brown Ugg flats. Three more twenty-something women stand behind her, waiting to come in. "Are we too late?"

"Too late for what?"

"For the Fall in Love with Bree Caxton question-and-answer session. We saw the article and read about tonight's meeting on the blog."

They're here for me? Awesome. "Um . . . no, not at all. Please." I motion them inside. "We're just getting started. Have a seat, anywhere you like."

"Told you." Gwen winks, then pats a chair. "Girls, there's an open spot here."

Two of the old guys spring from their seats.

Easy, tigers, don't pop out a hip.

"Sit here, if you like," one says.

"Or here." Ernie slides out his chair.

"Are you Bree Caxton?"

I spin around and face two other women in their midforties.

Before I answer, one says, "It *is* you. You're much prettier in person."

"Thank you. Please come in."

My goodness. An audience. What a lovely and unexpected surprise. But, crap. Now I have to come up with a discussion topic. *Dating taboos? Meeting the family? Boundaries?*

Nixon's nephew knocks on the glass, drawing my attention. He presses his nose against the clear partition and waves faster than a rabbit thumps his foot.

I wave back.

Nixon hurries toward the boy, tugging at his shirt collar and apologizing to me with a crumpled smile.

"No problem," I mouth.

Whether it's Nixon's tenderness with his nephew or his easygoing attitude outside the office, there's a stirring within me as Nixon's eyes meet mine. Something that feels sharp and vibrant, cutting through the glass between us. Something I haven't felt in a very long time. Is it confidence? Comfort? Wonder?

He waves good-bye and our connection is broken.

But the feeling remains for several moments until an idea pops into my head as I turn toward the group. "Welcome, everyone. Thank you for coming. My name is Bree Caxton and for tonight's Q&A, we're talking about hope."

eighteen

As luck would have it, no giant sinkhole swallowed Sara's gallery floor. No staff mutiny. No crazed gunman running amok through the streets forcing an evacuation of the entire city block.

My mixer is scheduled as planned.

Sean will be there, polished and positive with his square jaw and deep, thundering voice.

I'm a bundle of nerves, so when my phone squeaks with a text from Andrew, I nearly drop the phone.

Soooo sorry, I'll be there in 5.

That's the second time this week he's been late. Not only was he evasive about his lunch the other day, but just this morning I discovered he e-mailed the wrong person—*twice*. And I caught him on his phone in the break room. He hung up the moment I walked in, claiming it was a telemarketer. *What is going on with him?*

Hurry, I type, then tuck my phone into the back pocket of my sleek gray trousers.

Sara greets me at the door of her gallery.

"Bree, welcome."

"This place looks amazing."

"Thank you. We barely pulled it together for tonight, but I'm happy with the finished product." She slides a single diamond pendant back and forth along her gold chain. "I'm nervous. Nixon's on his way here. Do I look okay?"

I find Candace across the room, studying an abstract painting with Randi. "Here? Like gallery-here?"

"You seem surprised. Oh, no. Have I screwed up? It's too soon, right? I shouldn't have called him?"

Dammit, Bree. How could you have spaced this? I muster a smile. "No, no. It's fine. Will you excuse me? I have a couple last-minute details to tend to."

"Yes, of course."

I sneak off to a private corner and dial Nixon straightaway.

"Breester, how are you?"

"You can't come to Sara's gallery tonight."

"Were you sick the day they taught etiquette in school?"

I bite my lip, curbing my smile. "Hello, Nixon. How are you today?"

"I'm good, Bree. Thanks for asking. You?"

"Wonderful." I pause. There's a moment of silence.

"Fine. Why can't I come to Sara's gallery tonight?"

"Because I'm hosting the mixer here."

"Yeah, I know. Sara mentioned it."

"Candace is here."

"Just so I'm clear, you chastised me for not dating and now that I am dating, you don't want me to."

"Exactly."

He sighs. "I'll look like a jerk, but all right, I'll reschedule Sara."

"Thanks. I owe you one."

"You owe me a lot more than one."

I hang up as Andrew strides close.

"Sorry I'm late." He dabs beads of sweat off his forehead with his palm before studying my face. "My, my, who was that on the phone, making you blush like that?"

"Telemarketer."

"Touché." But the little devil grabs my phone and his eyes widen. "Nixon."

"Shush." I swat his hand away and slide my phone back into my pocket.

"I knew it."

"You know nothing. Save your wizardry for someone else. We all set?"

"Yes. Looks like a few more people showed up than anticipated, but I know we're good with drinks and appetizers. The bartender has plenty of seltzer and the blackest napkins I've ever seen."

"Good."

He pauses before saying, "And Sean's girls are here.

Sean's girls. Puke. "Where are they?"

Andrew points across the room at Chelsea, a mortgage broker with false eyelashes and small ears. Standing beside her is Betty, a dental hygienist with a boob job. They're chatting with each other next to a painting of an old barn.

"Just remember why you're doing this."

For Jo, for the book, for the house. "Might as well get it over with."

"Chelsea, Betty, it's nice to see you both."

They say hello in unison.

Betty starts, "Is Sean here? I'm really excited to meet him. Andrew described him as so dreamy."

He is. Or rather . . . was.

"Don't forget about me. I'm anxious to meet him, too," Chelsea says, stepping a few inches in front of Betty.

Two gorgeous women with sculpted bodies both vying for Sean. Awesome. For Jo, for the book, for the house.

"Yes, I'm sure he's looking forward to meeting you both. He'll be here soon."

"Is that him?"

Like the gods parted the gates, Sean strides into the gallery with the sun haloing behind him, dressed in khaki trousers and a short-sleeve black rayon button-up shirt.

It's a new shirt.

He looks good.

"Yes, excuse me a moment." I step toward Sean.

He smells good, too.

Which I find incredibly irritating. "I can't believe you're going ahead with this."

"Why? I'm here and ready to say yes to love."

"My book and my business are not a joke. I desperately need this book to sell well. Jo—" I decide not to tell him. He's opted out of my life. He doesn't deserve to know. "You're making light of my future."

"Speaking of *your* future." He inches close and says with the warmth of the polar ice cap, "Is your boyfriend here? Thought maybe he and I could compare notes."

"So this is how it's going to be?"

"Hey, I'm not the one who has a boyfriend."

"I'm not the one who dumped me."

"A formality, I'd say. Because from what I'm told, you and Nick go way back. Tell me, did it ever get confusing dating us both, keeping the two of us straight?"

"Fine. There they are." I point toward Chelsea and Betty, waiting in line for a drink at the bar. "Have at it. Go on and—"

"Pardon me, Bree?"

"What?" I say in haste only to find sweet Sara. I drop my head for a brief second. "I'm sorry. What can I do for you?"

"My security team is asking for a list of attendees."

"Yes, of course. I'll have Andrew get it for you."

"Thanks." She doesn't look happy.

"Is something wrong?"

"Nixon just called. He's not coming."

"He's not?" *Jesus, Bree, listen to yourself. First you tamper with a budding relationship and now you pretend like you don't know. Congratulations, you're a total jerk.*

"Last-minute meeting. God, I hope he isn't blowing me off."

"Nah, he's just a busy guy."

"You think? I know we've only gone on one date and it's none of my business, but is he seeing someone else?"

Besides me?

She notices Sean. "Oh, I'm sorry. I completely interrupted your conversation."

"No, problem. Is this your gallery, Sara?" he asks, reading her name tag and flashing his trial opening argument smile. The same smile he practiced in the mirror for six weeks.

"Yes, it is."

"Nice place. I'm Sean."

"Sara . . . as you know."

The tone of Sean's voice has grown warmer. "Bree, you didn't answer me. Is your boyfriend coming tonight?"

"Oh, that's right," Sara says. "Nick, isn't it? I read about him in the article. You two seem so cute together."

"Aren't they?" Sean says. "Damn near the cutest thing I've ever seen."

I take it back. Sean's the total jerk.

"No, I'm sorry. He has a surgery scheduled." I cringe at how easily lies have been rolling off my tongue. I reach for my neck and scrape my already sore skin.

"Oops." Betty laughs, catching our attention. She bends over, exposing the edge of her lace stocking through the slit in her dress. She picks up the lime wheel fallen from her glass.

"I think she needs me." Sean laughs. "Great meeting you, Sara."

"You, too." She turns to me. "He seems nice."

I used to think so.

"I'm gonna buzz around the room, answer any questions about the art. Let me know if you need anything."

"Will do, thanks. And Sara, I'm sorry about Nixon." And I am. I really am.

I glance again at Sean. He shakes Chelsea's hand, then offers Betty a napkin. Look at him. I know exactly what he's doing, exercising what he calls his "mental floss," running mnemonic techniques through his mind to remember their names.

Whenever he meets someone, he assigns a label to their face. Prideful of his "gift," he'd tell me what stamps he came up with. I hate to admit it, but I'd laugh, even at the monikers on the verge of being cruel. *Rick the dick. Prissy Missy. Elizabeth lizard breath.*

He casts his eyes over Betty's ample chest.

Her name is not Betty Big Boobs.

An hour later, after the impromptu art presentation Sara offered, the party's in full swing.

Andrew mingles with the crowd, tending to minor details like "My heels are rubbing on my pinkie toe, do you have a Band-Aid?" and "A waiter asked for my phone number, should I give to him?"

I hang back, as I customarily do, studying the group's dynamic, the conversations, and, of course, the body language.

Those who found someone interesting have shrunk their personal space to no more than a couple of inches, and the typical clues are evident. The women lick their lips, trace their fingers along their palms or forearms, angle their chin toward the man, pat his arm.

The men laugh with a deeper tenor or stand with widened legs as if they just corralled the cattle and dismounted a horse. They spew strength and masculinity while at the same time are insecure, hoping desperately to read the women's clues correctly.

Not everyone finds a match. Love is trial and error, that's why a mutual relationship that ebbs and flows organically feels so good.

And when it's gone, hurts so bad.

Candace joins me. "It didn't take long for our boy to settle into a quiet conversation with a young woman."

I've tried like hell to avoid glancing at Sean, seated on a leather bench beside Betty, chatting for twenty-seven and a half minutes.

"What do you see? Any chemistry between the two?"

I don't want to look. I want to bury my face in my hands like I did at my friend's end-of-summer slumber party when we watched *The Shining*.

"Your thoughts?"

Be a grown-up, Bree. For Jo, for the book, for the house.

"Right. Well, if you'll notice, her legs are tightly crossed and aimed toward Sean."

"Why is that significant?"

"Because the farther away the body part is from the brain, the less aware we are of it. We control our facial expressions, shoulders, and hand gestures but often forget our feet. So it's what the lower body is doing that tells us what a person is *truly* feeling."

"Interesting."

"And see, she's facing him, showing off her legs. It's a position that increases her sexual allure, emphasizing her feminine shape and tone."

Jesus, this is unbearable. A root canal is less painful.

"What else?"

Wasn't that enough? I breathe deeply. "All right, see how she's sliding her thumb and finger up and down the stem of her wineglass?"

"Yes?"

"She might as well unzip his pants and pull out the real thing."

"Pardon?" Candace asks.

I said that out loud, didn't I? "Um . . . what I meant to say is, that gesture is a phallic transference, stimulating basic urges in males."

"Oh, my."

Betty tosses her head back and laughs.

She likes him.

Candace's phone rings. "Excuse me for a minute."

Andrew steps near. "Guess what?"

"Betty is a transvestite?"

"No, no." He laughs. "Our bank executive sparked a connection with the Escondido Realtor."

"Great." My tone is flat.

"Don't let him get to you."

"I thought I knew him. All this time together and I really thought I knew him. But now, watching him, I'd never picked him as the kind of guy who could discard our past so easily and move on to another woman. What do you suppose he sees in her?"

"Maybe it's her kick-ass body."

"You're not helping."

"I know, but hell, look at her. A couple more glasses of wine and *I'll* go home with her." Andrew nudges my shoulder in an it'll-be-okay way.

Sean leans toward Betty as she whispers something in his ear. He laughs, then slides his hand on the small of her back.

He likes her, too.

Bree, what have you done?

nineteen

Sean and Candace sit beside each other across from my desk the next morning. Thankfully, they arrived at the same time, so I didn't have to fill the awkward air space between Sean and me with silly chitchat. I've done an excellent job avoiding his eyes.

"So, Mr. Sean," Candace says, "looks like you found someone who captured your attention? A dental hygienist, right?"

"Yes, I had a fun conversation with her."

"Gorgeous girl. Do you plan to see her again?"

"Well, she offered me a free cleaning." Sean folds his arms over his head and leans against the chair's backrest. "Said she'd show me her instruments, if you know what I mean."

Oh, give me a break. Nobody says stuff like that. He's just trying to get at me.

"She seems like a great girl," he says, "but I'm not going to ask her out."

"You're not?" I say, feeling calmer hearing this.

"Last night I found someone even more captivating." He moves forward, meeting my eyes.

No, Sean. Please don't bring me into this.

"Really? One of Bree's contacts?"

"She had a hand in it, yes. Bree knows what I like."

Don't say any more. Not one more word about me. You'll ruin everything.

"So, tell us, what's her name?"

No, don't say it. Please. Don't—

"Sara," he says.

"Candace, I can explain, I . . . Sara?" I stare at Sean.

"Yes," he says, "the gallery owner."

Yes, I *know* who Sara is, thank you very much. But Sara? *Nixon's Sara?*

Candace jots a note. "Oh, she's lovely. Tell me what you like about her."

"She's intelligent and confident, knows how to carry herself in a room. We both love the Bay Area, and she's got a spunky sense of humor."

Other than a few minutes early in the evening, when did he talk with her? "Sara? Are you sure?"

"Bree, you sound surprised," Candace says.

"I . . . I . . . just thought he showed more interest in Betty during the evening." I didn't know he took his eyes off her boobs long enough to engage with anyone else. Actually, that's not true. Sean's not the type to ogle women. I wouldn't have dated him if he were.

"Don't get me wrong," he says, "Betty is likely one hell of a good time, but, I don't know, Sara's got something. Something interesting."

What about Nixon? My heart breaks a little for him.

"Do you want to see her again?" Candace asks.

"Absolutely."

My heart breaks a little for me.

"Sara it is," Candace says. "Bree, what happens now?"

Knowing there's potential in this match, I force myself to answer with an unemotional, nonquivering voice. "I'll call Sara and see if she's interested. She's seeing someone else, so I can't guarantee she'll be receptive." Truth is, I have no idea how she'll react. But I toss the barb out because it makes me feel better. "If she says it's okay, I'll pass on her number to um . . . Sean."

And then I'll throw up.

"Excellent. I can't imagine anyone not interested in you, Sean. Now, Bree, any advice for our man of the hour?"

Wear your green polo that makes you look like a leprechaun. Bore her with one of your drawn-out narratives about 1031 tax implications. And try not to be so damn handsome.

I squash my thoughts and say, "Well, Sean, a few first-date ground rules. No bathing suits. No—"

"Why's that?" Candace asks.

"No woman wants to be seen in a swimming suit on the first date." Or the hundredth, for that matter. "They shouldn't show off the merchandise too early."

"Makes sense."

"Stay away from religion, politics, abortion, or death penalty discussions. And lastly . . . no sex." I can hardly get the words out, for the image of him naked, tangled between the sheets, skin-to-skin with another woman shoots a rush of heat to my forehead.

"Well, it sounds like love is in the air. On all counts." Candace winks at me.

"Yes, how is Nick?" Sean asks.

"Great. Really great. So great. Never had anyone better," I sneer.

"Take care, all; it's going to be a busy week." Candace gathers her things. "From here on out, I'll meet with Sean privately, keeping tabs on the dates with Sara."

"I'll walk you out, Candace," he says. "Can't wait for my date." And with a wink he's gone.

Andrew tosses me a piece of Ghirardelli salted caramel candy. We save a stash of the treat for moments like this. Or whenever.

I tear open the wrapped square. "Why is he doing this to me?"

"Because he's hurt."

"So am I."

"Because he's scum."

I drop my head into my hands.

"I know things seem bad."

"Because they *are* bad."

"Maybe, but you no longer are doing this for just yourself. Grab the bull by the horns and find a lover for your ex-boyfriend."

I look at him. "That's such a stupid expression. Why would I ever grab a bull by the horns?"

"Call Sara and get it over with. Your popularity has created a hell storm of work. We've got a lot to do."

"This isn't easy for me, you know."

"Think it's easy to watch my best friend suffer? I'm furious with Sean for what he did, but wallowing in it just gives him the upper hand."

"You're right."

"Another piece of chocolate?"

"Make it two. Okay, three, but no more than four."

Mr. Chambers's e-mail pops into my inbox, interrupting my pity party. I click it open and skim through the list of requested documents, six total. He includes a recorded acknowledgment from the IRS regarding the hearing date and reminds me the case is set for nine a.m. sharp, the nineteenth.

Sometimes it sucks to be a grown-up.

For Jo, for the book, for the house.

I release a long exhale and dial Sara.

She answers after several rings. "Hello?"

"Hi, Sara. It's Bree."

"Bree. How are you?"

I'm fine except for the fact that you're dating my fake boyfriend and about to date my real boyfriend . . . er . . . ex-boyfriend. "Great. How are you?"

"Exhausted from last night. So exhilarated from the evening, I barely slept, recounting the evening over and over in my mind. One of your clients, Sean, bought two pieces for his office."

"Did he?"

"Not to mention, he's fascinating and funny. Cute, too. Did you know he won a skateboarding competition in eighth grade?"

Did you know he's allergic to strawberries, has a hardened speck of cartilage in his right ear from a closed piercing that I used to fiddle with on long drives, and he gets turned on when I do the splits? "Actually, Sara, Sean's the reason I'm calling."

"It is?"

"You'll likely think this is crazy, and you don't have to say yes, but Sean's wondering if you'd go out with him." *Gag.* "I explained that you've just met Nixon and won't be interested, but—"

"Why wouldn't I be interested?"

Because four days ago you were ready to freeze your eggs until Nixon's ready. "Last time we spoke you seemed excited about Nixon, and—"

"I *am* excited about him. Have you seen Nixon's swagger and my God, that sexy little crevice between his brows when he frowns?"

Yes, actually I have.

"But we've gone on one date and talked only a handful of times. Gosh, would I be a terrible person if I went on a date with Sean?"

Yes.

"Dating two men at once, does that make me a floozy?"

Yes.

"Nixon and I aren't exclusive or anything. Not like you and Nick. I'm loving the article thing, by the way; can't wait for the next one."

"That reminds me. You may be featured in the paper if you date Sean."

"Ooh . . . that's even more tempting. My fifteen minutes of fame." She giggles. "I have to admit, it's kinda fun. I've never had two men interested in me at once."

"You hardly know Sean. He might be a serial killer."

"I hardly know Nixon, either. And I don't think you'd sail me down that river twice."

Ouch. How could I have forgotten her stint in the police station? "No, of course not, I'm just looking out for my clients. I need to make sure everyone is up front and honest."

"I understand. I'll have a chat with Nixon, but you said yourself to calm down and take it slow. So that's what I'll do. I'll take it slow . . . with two men." She laughs.

"Well, I think you should know that Sean hates to play board games. He has no patience."

And he steals the covers.

"You are thorough. I guess that's why you're so good at what you do. You're truly an expert in love. Thanks, Bree. I really mean that. Just a few weeks ago I came down with a fit of the 'poor-me's', pretty down for not having someone in my life, worrying that I might never find a man to share my days and nights. And then, out of the blue, you send two charming princes my way and promote my new gallery. Honestly, I couldn't have asked for a better turn of events." She laughs. "What a dilemma I'm in now, huh? Having to spend time with two gorgeous men. Listen to me, rattling on like a little girl. I'm just anxious to find the love that you have with Nick." She gasps. "Hey, I just had a great idea. Maybe someday we can double-date. I'd love to meet your boyfriend."

twenty

"Isn't it illegal to be up this early?"

Nixon and I are stopped behind a long line of brake lights, waiting our turn to enter the dirt parking lot of an expansive rock quarry.

"Are you always cranky in the mornings?"

"Just the ones where I get up before five a.m. and am forced to crawl around on a muddy playground."

"I think you'll find Tough Mudder is more challenging than recess."

"Yes, well, don't forget, you're sitting beside the hopscotch champion, second *and* third grade."

He laughs and waves on two oncoming cars, allowing them to cut in.

Sean never does that. He ignores signals and pleas from other drivers, saying, "It's not my fault they picked the slow lane."

Nixon pulls into a parking spot, cuts the engine, and pops open the glove box. He scrolls through his phone's messages before hiding it underneath his car manual. "Want to put anything in here?"

"You're not bringing your phone?"

"Nope."

"Sure you'll survive?" I tuck mine beside his.

"I'm not the one we should be worried about."

What does that mean?

"C'mon, let's go."

Shielding the sun with my hand, I step from the car, trying to gain a sense of the craggy dirt course. Several water trucks spray the steep roads carved into the surrounding mountains. Among the mud-bogged terrain lie several sets of barbed-wire-topped trenches to crawl under, five-foot-wide pits to leap over, hay bales stacked ten high to climb over, and floating barrels to swim under. Orange flags flank the windy sharp trail until they are tiny specks and I can't tell if I really see them or not. "How far did you say this course is?"

"Twelve miles."

Daunting, but doable. I've run half marathons before. There are a few more hills than I'm used to, but it's okay. I'm pumped for the challenge. Plus, all this exercise will justify the cheeseburger, beer, and French fries dipped in ranch dressing that I'm totally eating after the race.

But my confidence dips as we join the swarm of contenders with their scored stomachs, bulging biceps, and larger-than-my-head chiseled thighs.

"Geez. Haven't any of these people ever heard of Easy Cheese and a La-Z-Boy recliner?"

Nixon laughs, handing me my registration packet and paper bib with four safety pins.

We pass underneath the entrance, marked with a fifteen-foot black blow-up arch that screams in bold letters I Overcome All Fears.

That's somewhat ominous.

We stash Nixon's keys and our packets in the provided

lockers. I'm fastening the last safety pin to my long-sleeved top when a young woman dressed in an orange Mudder sweatshirt and ball cap asks me my number. I refer to my bib. "26042."

Before I can say, 'Hey, what the hell are you doing?' she whips out a king-size Sharpie and scribbles on my forehead.

"Hey, what the hell are you doing?"

"It's your number in case your bib falls off," she says.

13149 is inked on Nixon's arm.

"Next."

"You look ridiculous," he says.

I snarl at him.

Nixon and I enter the horseshoe-shaped waiting area encircled with tents, including a first-aid station, a beer garden with "Eye of the Tiger" blaring from the speakers, and a dozen or so T-shirt and souvenir vendors. At the open end is the starting line, designated by another fifteen-foot blow-up arch.

Once again, I OVERCOME ALL FEARS is splashed across the top.

Boy, they really send that message home. But how hard can the course be?

I follow Nixon toward a tent labeled MUDDER AID. He grabs a roll of duct tape.

"So I take it we loop around the mountains, tackle a few obstacles, and end over there?" I point toward the finish line, marked with a third blow-up arch. Must've been a sale.

"Yep." He props my shoe onto his knee.

"Hey, look monkey bars." I nod toward a framed structure, one hundred yards out. "And you said this wouldn't be like grade school."

"Those monkey bars are slimed with grease and spaced about a foot and a half apart. They're built at an incline the first two thirds and if you fall, you splash into a muddy pond below." Nixon tears off a strip of duct tape with his teeth.

Well, that doesn't sound like the recess I remember.

"Whatever you do, when you get to the Arctic Enema, don't overthink it. Jump right in. Plow right out. You'll get disoriented if you linger too long in the water."

"What's the Arctic Enema?"

"Let's call it an ice bath."

"Big deal. Athletes use ice baths all the time."

"Yeah, but athletes' baths aren't canopied with barbed wire and filled with a dump truck's worth of ice." Nixon wraps the duct tape around my shoe.

"What are you doing?"

"The mud is thick, some of it waist high. It'll suck your shoe clean off."

"I know what you're doing." I prop my other shoe on his knee.

"You should, because I just told you."

"You're trying to scare me. You're still mad at me for this whole interview thing and you're hoping to rattle me. What are you going to say next, huh? That we run through fire or get electrocuted?"

He lifts his eyebrows and bites off another strip of tape.

"You're not serious?"

"See those wood beams over there, with the dangling yellow wires, what, maybe a few hundred or more?"

"The spaghetti-looking things?"

"Yep. Those wires are live. And they sure as hell don't tickle." He sets my foot on the ground. "They'll rattle you more than I ever could."

"Electrocution. You never mentioned that."

"Didn't I?"

"No. You said heights and water and cramped spaces. I would remember if you mentioned electrocution!" Suddenly *I overcome all fears* makes perfect sense.

"They give you a beer at the end."

"How can I drink a beer if I'm dead?"

"Are you scared?" he asks.

"Yes. Any sane person would be scared."

"Relax, it'll be fine."

It will *not* be fine. Andrew once left a shocking pen on my desk as a joke. I clicked it and got such a jolt, I bit my tongue. Not funny. *Oh, God.*

Andrew's right about karma. Good things happen to good people. And shitty things happen to shitty people. One tiny white lie about Nixon being my boyfriend and now I'm going to be electrocuted.

Sweat forms at the nape of my neck. "I can't do this. You win. You don't have to pose as my boyfriend anymore."

"You're out?"

"I am."

"What are you going to tell Randi and Candace?"

"I'll figure something out."

"No time like the present. They're right behind you."

I spin around and see Candace dressed in trousers and a loose-fitting button-down cream blouse.

Randi prances behind her in skintight jeans, a long black tunic, and knee-high boots.

"Oh, I'm so glad I found you," Candace says. "This place is a zoo. There must be ten thousand people here."

"And Mary mother of Joseph, ninety percent of the men are hard-bodied and half naked. Thank the sweet Lord above." Randi slides off her sunglasses, scoping out a guy dressed in nothing but Superman underwear. His bib is pinned across his ass.

"Ladies." Nixon dips his head.

"Hi, sugar." Randi traces the numbers on Nixon's bicep with the arm of her sunglasses.

He steps closer to me.

"Golly, I'm nervous," Candace says, "I don't know why, I'm not even running. But can you feel the energy here? Now, what am I saying? You two do this sort of thing all the time, surely *you* aren't nervous."

Terrified. Did you hear? I will get shocked.

A chilly breeze drifts through the air, sending goose bumps along my skin. I wrap my arms around myself, shivering with both nerves and regret from wearing just a thin shirt, sports bra, and black capris, and for agreeing to this whole thing in the first place. Why am I doing this again? *For Jo, for the book, for the house.*

"Excuse me, are you Bree Caxton?" A young woman in a black T-shirt and pink short-shorts asks. Her hair is pulled into a high ponytail and her race number is inked on her cheek.

"Yes, that's me."

"God, I can't believe I'm talking to you. I loved that article in the *National Tribune* and I'm following your blog." She claps her fingertips. "I can't wait to buy your book."

"Thank you. I appreciate that."

"It's totally cool you're here. This makes me like you even more. Good luck on the course."

"How nice," I say, with a smile.

"People love love," Candace says. "You said so yourself. And people love you. I wonder where Scotty is?" She checks her watch.

"Time to go," Nixon says.

"Already? Can't we wait another hour or two or forever?"

"Good luck. We'll find you at the finish line," Randi says.

I'll be the one on the stretcher.

"C'mon." Nixon grabs my hand, churning a tickle in my stomach with his strong grip.

We join the wave of spandex and tennis shoes funneling

into the starting corral. We're behind six or seven men, all wearing bumblebee-yellow T-shirts with *Mud, Sweat, and Beers* printed on the back. Another group's shirts say, *Does this shirt make my butt look fast?*

A tall man with a similar orange Mudder sweatshirt as the Sharpie girl hops onto a center platform and draws our attention. He clicks on his microphone and says, "Are we ready to get started?"

The group responds with cheers and claps.

The announcer says, "All right, y'all. This course is muddy. This course is tough. This course will hurt you."

Hurt me?

"Can I get a *hoorah*?" he shouts.

"Hoorah!" The crowd cheers.

"This course is not about competition."

"Hoorah."

"This course is not about your finish time."

"Hoorah."

The crowd bounces in unison. Slight at first, but then it grows into a sea of bobbing heads.

My scar tingles. Mom and Dad would've loved this. I picture Mom stretching her hamstrings, prepping to run, and Dad snapping photos of her and the course.

Candace is right, there's a dynamism floating among the contenders. You can feel the vigor, the excitement.

I find myself joining the dance.

"This course is twelve miles of utter hell designed by British special forces."

I stop bouncing. *Utter hell? Special forces?*

"Hoorah."

"Tough Mudder is not a race but a challenge. And we run this race in honor of our military."

"Hoorah."

"We dig deep for the sacrifices they've made for you and me and our country."

"Hoorah."

"When you're facedown in the mud, certain you can't scale another wall or run another mile, I want you to think about what our military men and women are fighting for. They find the will, so you find the will. They find the grit, so you find the grit. They find the strength, so you find the strength."

"Hoorah."

Okay, now I'm excited.

"All right, y'all, take a look at the person on your left, on your right, and pat them on the back."

Nixon pats my back. "Ready, Breester?"

You know, I am. My body is twitching with energy. I'm pumped. This will be fun. An adventure, to say the least. Plus, this might be good for book sales. Lots of people become famous after they're dead.

I can do this. *For Jo, for the book, for the house.* I will do this. *For Jo, for the book, for the house.* With a smack across Nixon's back, I say, "Don't cry when I beat you across the finish line."

"You think so, huh?"

"Ten-nine-eight-seven . . ." The announcer counts down.

The flare gun fires and we're off, running up the first hill.

Though I'm certain Nixon's pace is faster than mine, he strides close. Side by side we run up and down miles of hills, belly-crawl through rocky, muddy trenches, scale . . . *and tremble* . . . over crazy-tall A-framed ladders, trudge . . . *and tremble* . . . through the freezing-ass-cold ice bath, inch hand-over-hand along wiggly suspended ropes, and plod through ponds and ponds of waist-high mud.

"You good?" Nixon asks.

"I'm good."

Two hours later, after we've trekked, climbed, and swum,

I'm tired and grateful for each passing mile and completed hurdle, knowing the end is near. All along the course, I'm inspired by the difficulty and the camaraderie, people pushing themselves, cheering one another on. But my nerves snarl into a knot when the electrified spaghetti noodles dangle in front of me.

"I can't do this."

"Sure you can," Nixon says, pointing through the cables to the end. "It's the last obstacle."

The finish line arch reads I OVERCAME ALL FEARS.

Another runner bellows like Tarzan and charges into the wires. Ten feet in, he drops to the ground, clutches his thigh, and groans.

"I'm gonna throw up."

"No, you're not," says Nixon. "That guy's a wuss. Besides, not all wires are live."

"They aren't? How can you tell?"

"You can't, but look, they're spaced twelve inches apart. Snake your way through." Nixon waves me into certain death.

"If I die, I'm going to be super pissed at you."

"Go on." He laughs.

I wrap my ponytail into a tight bun, stuff the hem of my top into my capris—which is not my best look—suck in my stomach, tuck my tailbone, and squeeze my shoulder blades.

Last obstacle. Beer at the end. For Jo, for the book, for the house.

I slink between a couple of wires. No shock. Relief surges through my body. I slip through a couple more. Nothing.

I glance back at Nixon. "Hey, you're right. This isn't so bad."

"Told you."

A breeze kicks up.

The wires sway.

My elbow is zapped.

"Aagh!" I jerk away from one cable only to throw myself into another. A sharp pain zings deep inside my thigh. "Ouch!" Another strikes my belly. *Help! Help!* I'm being attacked!

The smart thing is to remain calm, take a moment and settle, then tiptoe my way toward my celebratory beer and laugh, *Ha-ha, that was close*. But as a cable sparks my ass, I panic and bounce from one hot wire to another, flailing through the obstacle like a fish trapped in a net.

I'm going to die. Die!

Nixon dashes toward me. He grabs my hand and presses it against his back. "Stay behind me."

I clutch his shoulder with my other hand.

Nixon shields me with his body. We plow through the wires, passing other runners dropped to the mud in agony. But, like a friggin' bad-ass, Nixon doesn't stop, even though, every few feet, his body flinches and his neck muscles bulge.

I'm no longer getting tagged, but there's a spark firing up my arm from Nixon clasping my hand. My gaze is on the finish line, but my focus is on his fingers, laced within mine . . . wondering why it feels so *right*.

We reach the other side and cross through the final arch.

Victory.

We're handed orange headbands with Tough Mudder embroidered in black.

Nixon snatches mine and slides it onto my forehead. "You did it." He grabs two beers and we cheer.

"I did it." Not gonna lie, I feel damn good about myself. Sure, my Nike seventy-dollar Dri-Fit shirt is snagged from the barbed wire, chunks of ice from the Arctic Enema are still frozen between my boobs, my knee caps and elbows are bloody and bruised, I nearly died from electrocution, and I'll be sore as shit tomorrow, but right now, I feel great.

"Over here," Candace calls us over. "My goodness, you two are quite a sight."

Dried mud cakes my biceps and thighs. My calves and shoulders are scraped and scratched as if someone dragged me through the bushland. Ah . . . who cares. I sip my beer. I'm a freakin' Tough Mudder.

"Congratulations," Randi says.

"Shoot." Candace shakes her head while reading a message on her phone.

"Something wrong?" Randi asks.

"Scotty just texted me. There's a broken-down semitruck slowing traffic on I-5. He's not going to make it and he's got the camera."

I'd forgotten all about the picture.

"Use your phone and e-mail me a photo, otherwise we'll never make deadline." Candace reads Scotty's message aloud. "Well, I've no other choice." She points at us. "Stay right where you are, with the Tough Mudder sign in the background." She snaps the picture before I have the chance to block Nixon's face with my beer.

"No pictures, remember?" Nixon warns in my ear.

"Um . . . Candace? Mind if I take a peek at the photo? You know us girls, always want to make sure we look okay."

"You look fine, a little dirty, but fine."

"Let me see." I nearly rip the phone from her hand. "Oh, darn. I accidentally deleted it."

"How the heck did you do that?" She frowns as I return the phone.

"Trembling fingers. I'm still jacked up from the race. Take another?"

"Guess we'll have to."

"I said no pictures, not *two* pictures," Nixon says.

"I know." Before she clicks the shot, I hurl a glob of mud on Nixon's cheek.

"What the hell?" he says, trying to wipe himself clean. It doesn't work. He smears the sludge, masking the side of his face.

I scoop another handful and fling it, covering his eyebrow and forehead, caking his skin. A chunk of mud falls from his nose and plops into his beer.

"That's it." Nixon tosses his cup onto the ground. Beer splashes my shins. He scoops two fistfuls of mud and whips them toward me. I duck, but some of the goop catches in my hair.

"What are you two doing?" Candace says.

"Bree?" Randi scolds.

"Oh, yeah. Come here." Nixon grabs my wrist and holds it behind my back, pulling me into his chest, smothering my face with mud.

I wiggle and squirm, trying to break free from his grasp, but he clutches me tight against his body.

A hard body.

I scrape sludge from his shirt and arms, careful not to reveal his race number, and smear the sticky goo along his chin and jaw.

After a minute, both of us covered in muck, he says, "Truce?"

I'm out of breath from laughing and fighting. "Truce."

Nixon lets me go.

Mud coats his face. Chunks have hardened in his hair and blanketed his lips.

I blink dirt out of my eye.

Candace gasps. "Good Lord. You two are hardly recognizable."

That's the point.

"But I need a picture for tomorrow's installment. Guess this'll have to do. C'mon, now. Get closer."

Without hesitation, Nixon drapes his arm across my back

and draws me near. I slide my arm around his waist. My head nestles comfortably against the little indentation between his shoulder and chest.

Whenever Sean and I posed for pictures like this my hair often caught underneath his armpit or his arm would lie heavy on my shoulders, kinking my neck at an uncomfortable angle. But with Nixon, it's different. It's coherent. Just like when he grasped my hand in the shock obstacle, our bodies fuse together like two pieces of a seamlessly cut puzzle. He squeezes me closer and I'm struck by the ease of our bodies sided together. We . . . *fit.*

Breaking the charm, Nixon flicks a piece of mud toward me after Candace snaps the picture and whispers, "Nicely done, Bree."

"Yeah, you, too." I stare at him. Maybe longer than I should. *Endorphins. Nothing but endorphins.*

After Candace and Randi have left and we've rinsed off at the makeshift showers, changed into the clean clothes Nixon suggested we bring, donated our shoes to the race, and grabbed a burger, he pulls curbside to my house.

"Looks like you have a broken sprinkler valve."

I glance at the water spraying my porch steps. "Yeah, I do." *I've got to get that fixed.* "So, anyway, don't tell anyone, but I think I had a good time today."

"Did you?" He hands me my phone and grabs his own. I'm certain his inbox is flooded with e-mails, urgent voice mails from anxious people, desperate for his answers, a few moments of his time. But he doesn't click it on, he doesn't check his messages. He places the phone in the cup holder between us. He listens to me.

"Yeah, well, I mean, the creators of the course should seek medical attention because they're sick and twisted. And the whole *I overcome all fears* thing is a joke because I discovered about ten fears I never knew I had. But all in all, a fun day. So, thanks."

"You're welcome. Now get out of here. You stink."

I climb up the porch steps, hopping over the water spray with a smile. I like getting up at five a.m., starting the morning with exercise, challenging my body and mind.

And the best part: I didn't think about Sean all day.

twenty-one

"Don't you just love this time of year?" I say to Andrew, standing in line the following morning at a neighborhood café known for their spinach frittata. "Women wear scarves, even though it's seventy-two degrees in Southern California. Pumpkins and fall leaves decorate people's porches. And look at the acorns colored on the menu board. Aren't they cute?"

"You're in a good mood." He plays with a strand of hair hanging above his eyes, curling from the moisture in the air. "Come to think of it, I haven't seen you smile like this since you found those Vera Wang heels for eight bucks at the thrift store. Fun yesterday?"

"You know what? It was. The Tough Mudder was actually . . . not awful. I got electrocuted."

"Seriously?"

"Yep. I belly-crawled through muddy, gravelly trenches, scrambled over fifteen-foot-high walls, and got this." I point to a zigzag scrape on my bruised knee.

"Is that mud in your hair?"

"Oh, God. Is it? My arms are so sore. I can't lift them. Get it out, will you?"

We order our coffees and two spiced gingerbread muffins, then sit at a window-side table.

"How'd it go with your parents?"

"Not bad, actually. It was semi-awkward when I got there, like a first date, but after a few minutes they lightened up and I suppose I did, too. We even laughed a few times."

"That's great. Are you going to see them again?"

"Mom asked me over for lasagna next week."

"Gosh, Andrew." I squeeze his hand. "That's really good."

"Yeah, well, her lasagna is terrible. But, you know what isn't terrible?" Andrew slides the article toward me.

"Is it? I didn't have the strength to yank free the rubber band."

He laughs and flips open the paper. *"The love-duo—"*

"Wait. It says that?" I find the quote in the article. "Love-duo, huh? That's funny. I mean, it's—"

Andrew stares at me like I have underwear on my head.

"Shush," I say, "keep reading."

"The love-duo set out yesterday to donate their time, sweat, tennis shoes, and smiles to raise money for the Wounded Warrior Project. Can they get any more adorable?" Andrew rolls his eyes. *"And trust me, readers, even though Nick's face is obscured—a rousing game of mudslinging between the two, which I imagine is their idea of foreplay—I'd say Bree's a lucky gal to be snuggled beside this man."* He sets down the article. "So, are you? Are you a lucky gal?"

"Oh, stop. It's just for show. I told you, Nixon needs me to attend a wedding, so he's helping me out with this interview stuff. It's a business arrangement."

"Uh-huh."

"Shush," I say again, smacking him on the arm.

"Hang on a second." Andrew answers a text, holding his phone under the table.

"Who are you talking to? And don't pretend it's another telemarketer." I lean over the table, trying to sneak a peek. "Why are you hiding it? Let me see."

"Go away, it's nothing."

"You keep saying that."

"Because it is."

Is it? We tell each other everything, so all this secrecy has gotten me worried. I settle into my seat but can't focus on my article. The rest of the *National Tribune* lies on the edge of our table, folded open to the unemployment ads. I can't make out the job descriptions, but several posts are circled. *Circled.*

Oh, God, is Andrew looking for another job?

Has he grown tired of matchmaking? Is he seeking a job closer to his interests? A teaching position? Something with summers off and benefits? Now that I think about it, it must be the reason he's been tightlipped, the reason he suffered through a lunch at Ryoko's. It wasn't a date with a friend. It was an interview. "Andrew—"

"I didn't know Sean went on a date already. With Sara?" He sets his phone down and points at a picture in the article.

"What?"

Andrew continues reading. "*Seems our guinea pig, Sean, might be heading down the same path as Nick and Bree. He met and enjoyed his date with Sara, an art gallery owner, last Friday night, calling her 'a breath of fresh air.' We chatted with Sara and here's what she said about Sean. 'He took me on a drive up PCH to a charming beachside bistro in Del Mar with the most amazing mahi-mahi. We talked the entire time. I never knew tax codes could be so interesting. And he's so funny. He told me this one joke about getting rid of his vacuum—'*"

"Because all it does is collect dust. Hardy-har-har."

Andrew reads more. "'Then right before the sunset, we strolled along the beach, kicked off our shoes, and built a sand castle. My goodness, I had so much fun.' Though their relationship is new, one can't help but wonder: With Bree's successful track record, could Sara be the one for Sean? Between the two happy couples, it might be a race to the altar." Andrew sets the paper down again, studying my face. "You don't seem totally freaked out by Sean's date."

"Because I've given it some thought and like you said, he's trying to get me jealous. Plus, it's only one date and hardly an original one at that. We've been to that bistro a hundred times. The mahi-mahi isn't that good. We've built a zillion sand castles. And that joke? He tells it every chance he gets." I reach for the article and check out their picture. Sara's peach sundress complements her skin tone, and Sean's dressed in his jeans and a loose ivory button-down shirt. The wind kicks up tufts of his hair. "Besides, their body language speaks for itself."

Andrew peeks over.

"Sure they're close to each other, but see here, Sean's shoulder is leaning away and his smile is about as forced as I've ever seen."

"Yeah? What about you and Nixon?"

I glance at our photo. Slime coats our bodies and clothes. Mountains, obstacles, and a sea of orange-headband-clad racers decorate the background.

Though I try to hide it, a smile inches its way across my lips.

It's then I notice my feet.

Angled toward Nixon's.

His toward mine.

I toss the paper aside. "Body language isn't an *exact* science."

"Uh-huh." He pops a chunk of muffin in his mouth. "Well, *all for show* or not, I'm surprised to hear you're going camping. You hate camping."

"What are you talking about?"

"It says right here." He follows his finger along a sentence at the end of the article. "'*Next week we'll read about Nick and Bree's romantic camping trip.*' So, let's talk about what you're wearing. You'll need something rugged but adorable. I'm thinking—"

"Let me see that." I snatch the article from his hands. Damn, he's right. Camping. "Where did Candace come up with this idea? I've never camped a day in my life. Nor do I intend to. There are noises, and spiders, and creepy things scurrying around. There are squirrels." A shiver runs along my spine. "I will never—oh, shit. Hide." I raise my napkin like a barricade and shield my face.

"What are you doing?"

"Get down."

He crouches low. "Why am I hiding?"

"Look behind you. No, wait. Not yet."

"This is crazy."

"Okay, now."

Andrew peeks over his shoulder.

"See him?"

"Who?"

"Sean. At a table on the other side of the cafe."

Sean's sitting at a table for two in dark jeans and a Padres black polo—his go-to Sunday shirt—which I know has a tiny hole in the left armpit. He slides the pepper shaker back and forth between his hands. His copper-rimmed Ray-Ban aviators reflect the sun, and his teeth shine white.

Seated across from him is a woman with thin arms and brown hair. A tailored jacket is folded on the chair behind her. *Sara.*

"What's he doing?" I ask.

"Eating breakfast." Andrew sits up and yanks the napkin away from me. "Stop acting like a lunatic."

"He's on another date with Sara."

"I thought you weren't fazed."

"I didn't know they were going on morning dates. You only go on a morning date if you're totally secure with one another. When you don't care if the sun highlights chin hairs and stuff. Plus, he's wearing his Padres shirt, Andrew."

"What does that mean?"

"He's comfortable. Are they holding hands?"

Sean looks in our direction.

I force Andrew to his knees.

"Quit it, Bree. Why don't you just go over and say hello? Be friendly."

"Walk over there and be friendly?"

"Yeah."

"What's it like to live in la-la land? Should I bring my unicorn?"

"Listen, you little smart-ass, show him that he's not getting to you."

"He is getting to me. Why do you think I'm hiding behind this menu?"

Their waiter presents a bottle of Cristal. He offers Sean a taste for his approval, pours two full glasses, then slips away.

Sara sips her bubbly as Sean rolls the sleeves of his shirt to his forearms.

"Look at him. Acting all macho. 'Hey, check out my strong arms. Want to watch me chop down a tree?'" I say in a deep voice.

Sara laughs, lowering her head and looking sideways toward Sean, exposing her neck.

Casual. Sensual. Inviting.

Andrew wrenches his hand from my tight grip.

"Oh, God, Andrew. What if this isn't a *morning* date? What if this is last night's date still going? What if they . . .

they . . . slept together?" I squint, examining the back of Sara's head. "Is that a flat spot in her hair? You know, from a pillow? Sean's pillow."

"C'mon, sweetie. Let's get out of here."

I swallow hard, allowing the truth to settle within me. Sean ended our relationship. But he's not wallowing in remorse, hollowed and ashen like I hoped. He's laughing and flirting. He's moved on.

Why am I watching this?

"You're right. This is stupid. Let's get out of here."

So much for my good mood.

twenty-two

Later that afternoon, I sit cross-legged in my closet, staring at my reflection in the full-length mirror.

It's over.

After witnessing Sean and Sara's coziness this morning, I realize I've fooled myself these last couple of weeks thinking he'd come running back, pining for me, begging for forgiveness.

Couple that with certain aspects of my life that I hate at the moment—pretending Nixon's my boyfriend, keeping the truth from Jo, spewing lies every time I open my mouth (won't someone shut me up?), and Andrew searching for another job—and I start to feel very, very alone.

I don't like when waters get rough or lives get upturned. I don't like letting go of the familiar. I mean, look at me. Even my appearance shouts that I cling to my comfort level. The same hairstyle since high school. Same purse since college. Same habits (except for smoking cloves, that was short-lived), same hue of pink toenail polish every pedicure. I don't like starting over and saying good-bye to the past. I feel safe under a veil of dependability and consistency, vulnerable to the elements without my parents', and now Sean's, protective umbrella.

Whoever said change is good is a fool. Change isn't good. Change means someone or something died.

Trust me, I know.

I glance at my scar, then decide to take a walk before heading to Jo's. Fresh air will do me good.

On a side street near the boardwalk, I spot a long-sleeved blush-colored lace dress fitted on a mannequin in the storefront across the street. Tiny pearls strung along the hemline reflect in the sunlight. The model dangles a pair of nude strapped heels from her plastic hands. *Aren't you a lovely little thing?* It'd be perfect for Nixon's cousin's wedding. Besides, retail therapy always makes a girl feel better.

Twenty minutes later, I lay the pretty frock across the Uber car's backseat and set the shoes by my feet. I'm lost in thoughts of a new shade of nail polish, jewelry, and highlights when Candace calls.

"Hi, Candace. How are you?"

"Busy, busy. I've never seen such a flurry of activity. You two are so popular."

"Really?" *Hooray! Sell, little books, sell.*

"Yes, and people are demanding a picture of Nick. So that's why I'm calling. When are you leaving for the camping trip?"

"Actually, I planned to ask you about that. What makes you think we're camping?"

"Nick told me."

"He did?"

"Oh, now, I hope I haven't spoiled a surprise. Well, too late, I suppose, all of America knows."

"When did he tell you this?"

"At the Tough Mudder. I asked him what your plans were for this coming weekend and he said, 'I'm taking Bree camping,' said you loved the outdoors."

I hate the outdoors.

"And, by the way, well done with Sean and Sara. I didn't want to tell you until the next article released, but they've seen quite a lot of one another. Sara seems to really enjoy him."

Yeah, I've noticed.

"You really do have an eye for this matchmaking stuff."

"Hmm . . . thanks." I murmur, staring out the window at the passing cars, hung up on her comment. *They've seen quite a lot of one another.*

"This success will be tremendous for your book sales. Have you decided what your second bestseller will be about?"

"Second bestseller?" *My God, that's fun to say.* "Um . . . no, I haven't."

"Let me cover the release, will you?" Before I answer, she says, "Firm up your plans and let me know when Scotty can stop by for a shot. The paper, and the readers, will have my head if I don't have Nick's sweet face in this week's article."

"Yes, absolutely." I don't mention that there's no way in hell Nixon will allow his face in the paper. I scratch the tender skin inside my wrist. *What's another lie at this point?*

"Talk to you soon, Bree."

"Yes, sounds good."

We hang up and I call Nixon. "Camping?"

"Yeah, is that a problem?"

"I don't want West Nile virus, thank you very much. I'm a city girl. Camping means bugs and open spaces. And squirrels."

"Squirrels are the least of your concerns. It's the rattlesnakes, coyotes, and bobcats you should be worried about."

"Very funny. Wait . . . you're joking, right? Couldn't you

have told Candace we're going to the movies or you're gathering tools and parts to fix my sprinkler head this weekend?"

"It's still broken?"

"Yeah. Why? Can you fix it?"

"Yes, but we're going camping."

"What if I have plans?"

"You don't. You're at the paper's beck and call for the next few weeks, remember?"

"When you say camping, you really mean a five-star resort with lavender woven in the thousand-count bedsheets, mint leaves in my chilled water, and an infinity-edge pool, right?"

"Exactly. Just totally opposite."

"First Mudder, now this. You like to see me squirm?"

"I might." I fiddle with a loose thread on my dress, tempted to tell him about the lacy frock, but decide against it. After all, it's just a dress. And he's just a prop.

"I'm not wearing a silly camouflage bucket hat with dangling fishing lures."

"We're camping, not fishing."

"And you better not drag me into the woods to shoot a frickin' elk or something."

"As I said, camping, not hunting. Bring a good pair of tennis shoes."

"Again with the shoes? I don't have a good pair anymore. Mine were ruined in a mud run some guy made me do."

"That guy sounds awesome. Get a new pair."

"Do I need duct tape this time?"

"Only if you talk too much."

"Rude."

He laughs. "Do you have a warm jacket?"

"Are you kidding? I have an awesome Burberry quilted lambskin leather bomber—"

"Whatever. Pack light. A sweatshirt and toothbrush. I'll take care of the rest. Can you get out of work Friday afternoon by four? I want to avoid the traffic."

I think for a second. "Well, I do own the company. Where are we going anyway?"

"You'll see."

I hang up and catch my reflection in the driver's rearview mirror, noticing that I no longer look saddened by my worries, I'm smiling. And excited. Excited as if going on a date.

twenty-three

I climb out from the car to find Jo opening her front door. Martin, tethered to a leash, growls at my feet.

"Bree, I didn't expect you."

Nor I you. *What happened to bridge club?* The hearing is the day after tomorrow and I need to get the documents Lawrence requested. I hoped to do it without her knowledge. "Hi, Jo."

"What are you doing here?"

"Oh, you know . . ."

Jo waves. "Oh, Claire's here. I'm on my way to my bridge club. Can you come later?" She shuts the door behind her and locks it tight.

"Yes, of course."

"Come along, Martin." She climbs into the car. Martin hops on her lap and Claire drives away.

I wait until the car disappears down the road before grabbing the hide-a-key.

Jo keeps this sort of legal stuff in her guest bedroom closet. It'll only take a minute.

Though it seems unusual and intrusive to wander through Jo's house without her here, or without a bag of groceries, the vacuum, or a load of laundry in my hand, I step through her kitchen and out into the living room with a different perspective. Like I'm visiting for the first time, seeing everything new.

I move toward her Windsor table, letting my fingers trail over the ridges and curves of Mom and Dad's picture frame, Jo's jewelry box, the empty spot sprinkled with dust, G-pa's ceramic frog.

My eyes sweep around the room, and I'm taken back to lazy movie nights with my parents, referees blowing whistles on the TV during Thanksgiving football games, the tear of wrapping paper on Christmas Eve, the sweet smell of an oven-roasted glazed ham lingering in the air.

I lie on the couch as I'd done so many Sundays before my parents died and wiggle a comfy spot in the cushion for my neck, wishing Jo sat in her recliner with a bowl of popcorn between us, wondering when we'd done that last.

Glancing at the ceiling, I find the hint of a kidney-shaped water stain Dad painted over.

He'd dribbled paint on his cheek and in his hair that day.

Mom teased, asking if he was painting the ceiling or himself.

After a minute, I head into the dining room and almost press my ear to the wall, yearning to hear the voices, the laughter, and the stories these old walls have absorbed over the years.

I move into the hallway, jiggling the linen closet door handle that sticks whenever the air conditioner kicks on, then round the corner into my former bedroom. The same heavy furniture remains: an oak rolltop desk and chair, floral curtains, and a bright yellow-and-blue-checked quilt draped over a queen bed. My room after my parents died.

I glance at my watch, realizing I've wasted too much time lost in memories and move toward the closet, quickly searching through several banker boxes for the one I recall labeled *TAX*.

After ten minutes of sorting prior years' returns and receipts, I find the documents I need.

I'm about to close the door when I notice another box marked *Libby & Sam*.

My parents.

My heart beats hard underneath my skin as I blow off the dust and open the lid. Several manila envelopes rest inside.

I unclip the first envelope and dump out a paper trail of Mom's life. There are several newspaper clippings from her school days, including an article about her third-grade class's field trip to the aquarium, multiple years' worth of report cards and the principal's honor roll list, a write-up about the Lions Club award she won for her academic success, and cutouts from her cross-country meets and track meets. There are homecoming and prom pictures, a snapshot of her holding a box outside her UCSD dormitory on move-in day, and a couple of handbills from her college graduation.

A second manila envelope contains handfuls of pictures of my parents, cheering at a Chargers game, raising margaritas underneath a *Margaritaville* sign, red-eyed and wearing *Happy New Year* paper hats with Dad blowing a kazoo. There are photos of Mom at a luncheon with friends, Dad mowing the lawn, the two of them playing Scrabble in Jo's backyard, several wedding pictures, Mom's business card, and a folded newspaper article of a city council meeting where they discussed zoning changes to the parking outside my office building; Dad's face is barely visible in the audience.

The last picture, a five-by-seven with a torn right corner, is of my dad. He leans over a hospital bed as Mom cradles a swaddled, and newly born, me.

Pressure builds in my throat as I undo the third envelope and sift through newspaper snippets of the accident. The police report. The funeral announcement. The hospital, bank, and insurance paperwork. A sympathy card from the funeral home and my parents' combined obituary.

Jo and I never said much to each other about the accident. We never sat beside one another clutching Kleenex and holding hands while we read the investigation's findings. Never attended the drunk driver's trial. Never claimed the hand sanitizer, package of gum, loose coins, and other personal items salvaged from my parents' mangled car.

In all the days and years that followed the accident, never once did Jo yell at me. She never shook me by the shoulders, slapped my face, or cursed my name.

But I'd hear her cries. Late at night, in the darkest hours before dawn, through the bedroom walls.

In the mornings, she'd pour me a glass of juice, wish me a good day, and hide her pain behind the thin disguise of a smile. Days turned into months, and we slipped into a routine of breakfast, lunch, dinner, laundry, school, and grocery shopping. Both of us knowing that drunk driver killed four people that day, not just two.

Her compassion made me feel worse, knowing she hid her disappointment and resentment toward me. So I'd climb out of bed and stand outside her door, night after night, and listen to her weep, covering my mouth with my hand, hiding my own sobs.

I deserved it. I deserved the shame.

I was to blame.

I was the reason her daughter and son-in-law were dead.

And I still am.

Several minutes pass before I tear myself away from the

box, knowing Jo might be home soon. After covering any trace of my presence, I slip outside and hide the key.

Waiting on my ride, I gaze at the house.

I've taken so much from Jo.

Please, God. Please, let me give back.

twenty-four

It occurs to me as I step inside the concrete-floored and high-ceilinged courthouse Wednesday morning that I never watched Sean in action. I never sat in the front bench dressed in a knee-length skirt and scalloped-collared shirt buttoned to the top, nodding in agreement with a well-argued point, absorbed in the proceedings, marveled by his acuity.

"Trials are boring," he'd said. "Lots of case readings citing precedent and relevance, lawyers droning on and on. Sometimes I have a hard time staying awake myself," Sean joked.

I spot Mr. Chambers studying a file outside a courtroom door with his briefcase and shiny-loafered foot propped on the edge of a bench. "Mr. Chambers, hello."

"Ms. Caxton." He drops his foot to the ground. "You have the originals?"

"Yes." I hand him a couple of tax forms that weren't legible in my e-mail. It's then I notice the tremble in my hands.

"Don't be nervous. It's a procedural matter, simple law. And

I know this judge, he doesn't draw out his cases. The whole thing will likely be over in a few minutes."

"Okay, I just wish I knew—"

"Bree?"

Sean lets go of the handle from a neighboring courtroom door and steps toward me in a black suit, white shirt, and pale blue tie, his scornfulness seemingly left behind at Sara's gallery as his leather briefcase swings in line with his stride.

"Hello, Lawrence." The two men exchange nods before Sean pulls me aside and says, "What are you doing here?"

There's no reason in hiding the truth. Sean can easily figure out what's going on by glancing at the courtroom's docket. "Trying to clear up something for Jo."

"What's the issue?"

"Jo received a 1058 form."

Lines form across his forehead as he raises his eyebrows in judgment. "Lawrence is representing you?"

"Yes. You said he was a bulldog, so I—"

"Bullfrog. I called him a bullfrog because he's an inefficient bastard and doesn't have a clue how to represent a case."

Oh.

He glances at his watch, back on his wrist. "Okay, I'll help. Wish you'd called me sooner."

I must admit, breakup or not, I'm relieved to know he's on my side. Relieved he still cares. Maybe the breakfast with Sara was nothing more than . . . breakfast.

He turns around and walks toward Lawrence. Sean's had a recent haircut. A defined tan line exposes itself above his shirt collar and I'm reminded that these past couple of weeks Sean's reveled in the sun, enjoyed the beach, spent time outdoors. Hardly wallowing in misery like he said, hardly sorry for breaking my heart, hardly confused.

I think I've seen enough.

"Sean," I call after him. "Wait."

"I haven't much time. I've got another proceeding starting—"

"I don't need your help. I've got representation."

"Bree, c'mon, this is a serious matter. Let me help you."

"No, thanks. Ready, Mr. Chambers?"

My attorney pulls open the door and I'm about to stride in the courtroom confident with a suck-it-Sean stride when Jo calls my name from behind.

She ambles toward me. "What's going on? Why didn't you tell me?"

"Jo? I . . . I'm surprised to see you here."

Her voice cracks as she says, "Some clerk lady called this morning looking for you. She told me about the hearing. I had no idea. What's going on?"

"We better get inside," Lawrence says.

"C'mon, let's find a seat and I'll explain."

Mr. Chambers sits at an oversized wood desk and we settle in the bench behind him.

"I'm sorry. I should've told you," I say to Jo. "I'd hoped to get the results of this hearing before mentioning anything. The letter you received isn't a scam. It's legitimate and binding. It's from the Internal Revenue Service and they claim you owe them nearly fifty thousand dollars."

"For what?"

"Years of unpaid taxes."

"Oh, my." She lifts her vein-laced hand to her mouth. "Your G-pa handled these types of matters. I don't have that kind of money."

"I know. That's why we're here, to figure out what we can do about it. So, let's remain calm"—I point to our attorney—"and let Mr. Chambers do his job. No need to worry about something that may blow over."

⤳

It didn't blow over.

The judge validated the IRS claim and overruled our request to negotiate the outstanding amount or settle the remaining balance with installment payments. "Given the property owner's nonresponse for a significant length of time with regard to a serious matter," he said, "the court rules in favor of initializing levying proceedings. Balance due in full by October twentieth."

Jo flinched at the smack of the judge's gavel.

"What does this mean?" she asks, as we step from the courtroom.

"It means the judge was in a bad mood."

"What about the house, Mr. Chambers?"

"You have until October twentieth to come up with the money or the IRS will auction off the property."

"But that's only a month away," Jo says.

And a week after my book release.

"I'll post the required paperwork and e-mail my bill by the end of the week."

That's it? He's leaving. No more fight? It's my grandmother's house, for Christ's sake. Sean's right. Chambers is a lazy bastard.

"This is awful." Tears glisten in Jo's eyes. "It's your grandfather's house."

"I know. I feared this might happen, but listen, it'll be okay." I explain the escalator clause, the money remaining in my savings account, and Andrew's contribution. I explain that with a few more weeks and more preorders, we'll meet the goal. I wrap my arms around my grandmother.

She wraps hers around me. "Please don't let them take it away."

The warmth of Jo's skin and her heartbeat in sync with my own reminds me of my cherished past, the years passed, and the time with her daughter that I've stolen.

I will lie.

I will continue with this charade.

I will do whatever it takes to make *Can I See You Again?* a bestseller.

I will save Jo's house.

∽

A couple of hours later, after I've made Jo a sandwich and added a splash of brandy to her tea, she retires for a nap and I head into the office.

"How'd it go?" Andrew walks over in black Converse high tops, jeans, a Metallica T-shirt, and a loose cardigan, holding a rolled-up newspaper in his hand.

I'm going to miss him. It's only a matter of time before he tells me the truth, tells me he accepted a job offer, somewhere with better perks and a retirement fund. Tears line my lids as I realize why he's kept it all a secret. With Sean and Jo, Nixon and the paper, I've got enough to worry about. Still, it's a shame. Andrew's so good at this, so good at connecting with people, calming their apprehensions about hiring a matchmaker, making them feel comfortable. My clients will be sad to hear he's left. With any luck, his new job won't move him out of this zip code and we can still meet for dollar tacos on Tuesdays, wine on Wednesdays, and . . . shoot . . . I'm really going to miss him.

"You okay?" He dabs a tear at the corner of my eye.

"They're taking her house. I have until October twentieth."

"A week after the release."

"Yeah." I slump into my chair. "Jo showed up, too. I hoped to keep her out of it. She was pretty frazzled."

"Sweet thing."

"Can't say I'm completely surprised the judge ruled as he did, just disappointed, wishing some fairy would've waved her magic wand and zapped the 1058 letter away. Or at the very least, figure out some sort of payment arrangement. But the judge was adamant. All or nothing. According to my lawyer, the judge was in a bad mood."

"Maybe this will cheer you up." Andrew sets a copy of the *Square*, a local tabloid, on my desk. The caption in the cover's corner reads: *Bree Caxton PREGNANT!* Worse yet, the picture is of me climbing into an Uber, and sweet Jesus, given the angle . . . I do look sort of pregnant.

"Are they serious? And why would this cheer me up?"

"It means your reach is beyond the *National Tribune*. Your name is catching on. People are paying attention to you."

"Let's hope that turns into book sales."

The office phone rings and I answer it before Andrew, hopeful it's Randi returning my call from this morning. I'm anxious to chat with her, desperate for some good news about my book preorders. Especially after contacting my bank and discovering that since I own my own business, the verification process for an equity loan takes longer than most and I won't receive the money in time. The escalator clause is my one and only shot.

"Hi, Randi, how are you?"

"Busy. Ready for an update?"

"Yes."

"Preorders are holding steady. I'd like to see more activity, but I'm confident that with a couple more interviews and if we get Lucy Hanover on board, and that's a big *if*, your numbers will increase exponentially. Keep on doing what you're doing."

"Okay. Yes, I'll plug away. Anything you need. Anything at all. Just name it."

"Sounds good."

"Say, Randi, I'm wondering, if my book debuts on the list, how soon will I receive the check?"

"Already spent the money, have you?"

"Something like that."

"A few days."

That's all the time I have.

twenty-five

As promised, Nixon walks through my office door at three forty-five p.m. Friday afternoon dressed in a Locally Grown T-shirt with a vintage ten-speed bike printed on the front. I know the shirt is as soft as a puppy's ear because I've groped them repeatedly at my farmer's market. A large square box is tucked under his arm.

Though I loathe the outdoors with its noises and creepy-crawlies, I look forward to this break from my worries. I'll never tell Nixon this, of course, but a little time away might be good for me. Plus, Andrew promised to keep an eye on Jo, and I overheard the two chatting about ordering Chinese food and watching scary movies tonight.

"Ready?" he says.

"Just about." I kneel on my suitcase.

Nixon sets the box on my desk and waves me off my luggage.

"Oh, thank you. Just a good tug on the zipper is all it needs."

He flops open the lid.

"What are you doing?"

He pulls out my computer and sets it on my desk. "This is the last thing you need. I told you to pack light."

"How am I supposed to pack light when I don't know where we're going?" I close the lid.

"I told you what to bring." He opens the lid again—which is totally counterproductive considering his adamancy about leaving early—and digs through my pajamas, my long socks, my short socks, my curling iron, the copy of *Fallen*, three T-shirts, my totally rockin' leather jacket, two pairs of jeans (because you never know which style will look best), and a new pair of Puma tennis shoes.

"Stop rifling through my stuff, you pervert." I smack at his hands, but with an outstretched arm, he keeps me at bay.

He pulls out my jacket, sweatshirt, and toothbrush. "At least you've got jeans on."

"Uh . . . excuse me . . . these aren't just any jeans." I pat my thighs. "These are Frame Denim in Queensway-color and they're adorable." And hopefully, offering a flattering fit that slims my thighs while lifting my rear like the Nordstrom's clerk promised. Hell, for $245 they should hoist my ass to the moon.

"Whatever. Let's go."

"What about all my stuff?"

"This is all your stuff. Except this." Nixon points to the box. "Open it."

My irritation subsides. I mean, who can stay mad when gifts are involved? "Let me guess, it's a pony?"

"Yep."

"I take it the store sold out of wrapping paper?" I joke (sort of) and tear off a strip of clear packing tape.

He holds the box in place as I pull out a very shiny, very white, and very round full-face motorcycle helmet.

What the heck am I supposed to do with this? "Thanks,

but I don't need . . ." A black-and-silver KTM motorcycle parked curbside catches my eye. A similar helmet hangs from the hand grip. "We aren't . . . you don't think I'm . . . um . . . no! Absolutely not."

He ignores me and carries my clothes outside.

"Maybe you didn't hear me. I am not getting on this thing."

"I heard you."

"I don't want to die."

"That makes two of us." He hands me my jacket, then crams my sweatshirt and toothbrush into a saddlebag fixed to the side of the bike.

"Tell you what, I'll walk."

"Fine. Head north. I'll see you in a hundred and twenty miles."

"How about we camp in my backyard? A mosquito landed on my barbecue the other day, so it'll be just like the woods."

"Get on." He slides into his dark weathered leather jacket, then swings his leg over the bike, balancing it with quadriceps flexing against his jeans.

It's not polite to stare, Bree. "Look, I'll call Uber and meet you wherever it is we're going. There's no—"

"Yo, Nick, Bree," Scotty calls, climbing out of his car and slinging a camera strap over his neck. "Wait up. My editor's totally jacked that we haven't shown Nick's face yet." Scotty pops off his lens cap and aims the camera in our direction. "I'm here for a shot."

Crappity-crap.

Without any other choice, I grab Nixon's helmet and shove it into his hands. "Quick, put it on."

Foam presses hard against my ears as I do the same.

We flip closed the tinted plastic windshields.

"C'mon guys, I can't see your faces."

Nixon starts the engine and revs the throttle.

"Sorry, can't hear you, Scotty." I pat the helmet before climbing onto the bike.

"You guys suck ass," he says, snapping several pictures.

We take off and Scotty shrinks to no more than a speck in Nixon's side mirror.

"Woo-hoo! We got away, we . . . oh, dammit," I chastise myself. "You're an idiot, Bree. You just hopped onto a motorcycle—"

"Sure did," Nixon replies in my ear.

"You can hear me?"

"Wireless microphones in our helmets."

"Oh, well, good. Pull over."

"Nope." We continue through my neighborhood.

I bonk my helmet into his. "Pull over."

"Hey! Take it easy. I'm not stopping." He throttles a bit faster.

"This is kidnapping." I'd totally flag down a cop or bystander if I weren't terrified to let go of my seat. "You underestimate me, Nixon Voss. I can complain for the next one hundred and twenty miles. I—oh, God." I cough. "I swallowed a bug."

"Good, now maybe you'll shut your mouth for a bit."

I bonk his helmet again.

"Ouch!" He laughs. "I dare you to find anything wrong with the place we're going."

"Where *are* we going?"

"You'll see."

We reach the entrance of the highway's on-ramp.

"Don't make road meat out of me."

"Trust me, will you? Now, hang on to me. Tight."

I slide my arms around his butter-soft jacket, clasping my hands at his waist. My thighs are sandwiched around his.

Okay, so this might not totally suck.

But I grow nervous again, afraid to sneeze or breathe too

heavy and risk throwing us off balance as we speed faster and the asphalt's white hash marks that I'm inches away from blur into one. "Can you slow down a little? Shouldn't you turn your hazards on? And watch out for that semitruck."

"You mean the one that's three quarters of a mile away? You're fine. Trust me. I won't let anything happen to you."

"Promise?"

"Didn't I already?"

"Nixon?'

"Fine. Yes. Final answer. I promise."

It occurs to me as I press my chest against Nixon's back, totally dependent on the man, how different his body feels from Sean's.

Yes, they share similar physiques, long and lean, but somehow Nixon's frame is more self-assured, intense. And though I never minded Sean releasing stress with biweekly hot stone massages, there's a sexy fascination to a man who unwinds outdoors, chasing the sun, throttling a powerful machine between his legs.

Okay, that sounded weird.

The more miles we travel, the more I grow to appreciate Nixon's precision and quick reaction. He weaves through cars and switches lanes with skill, revving around the Prius driver who cut us off, avoiding the pothole the size of Kansas in the middle of our lane, slowing down when the traffic thickens.

I'm enjoying the beauty and freedom of the open road, energized by the danger and allure of my exposure. And there's something to be said for listening to the sounds of the streets, the wind, or Nixon's comments on landmarks we pass, rather than Eminem rapping nasty things about his baby mama or politicians bickering on the radio.

I relax my iron grip—just a tiny bit—around Nixon's waist and settle into the leather seat.

The city is long behind us when Nixon exits the freeway and turns right onto a long, windy, mountainside road. A sign reads: IDYLLWILD 37 MILES.

"I've always wanted to come here."

Nixon says nothing for the rest of the climb. Our bodies move in sync, hugging the curls of the road. With each passing mile, the trees grow thicker and jut higher into the sky. I slip my hands inside Nixon's pockets, for the air's grown crisp.

We continue up the mountain and drive through a one-street town shouldering Strawberry Creek until Nixon turns right, slowing onto a single-lane dirt road toward Idyllwild Campground. He parks outside the registration office.

"Stay with the bike."

He heads inside and I watch three little ponytailed girls balance on a fallen log and a couple of fishermen casting from the shore of a small pond.

Nixon returns a minute later and we ride up the steep hill, passing campsites, some occupied with tents or trailers and some empty, but all with a weathered picnic table and a blackened fire ring. The smell of campfire lingers in the air.

He swings into a vacant spot at the edge of a bluff, overlooking a group of Boy Scouts busy assembling a half dozen tents.

I slide off the bike, pull off my helmet, and fluff my flattened hair. "Our cabin's been stolen."

"Brought our own. Give me a hand, will you?"

We work together unloading the saddlebags and within a few minutes our tent is up.

"Just so I'm clear, we have one tent, two sleeping bags, a package of hot dogs, buns, strawberries, and a six-pack of Rolling Rock."

"Yep." He cracks open a beer and hands it to me. "What more do we need?"

"The strawberries are a nice touch, but no down comforter?

No vanilla-pomegranate-infused bath and fuzzy slippers? At least tell me you packed a Keurig."

He sips his beer.

"No coffee? You *are* trying to kill me."

Several smoothed tree stumps serving as chairs surround the fire pit.

I sit beside him as he breaks a clump of twigs over his knee and tosses them onto the firewood piled in the ring.

"Haven't you ever fallen asleep under the stars? No TV, car alarms, or sirens. No flashing city lights. Just the mountain air and sounds of nature."

No. "For your information, Jo and I watched a PBS documentary on the journey of butterflies." I don't mention that I fell asleep six and a half minutes into the show because good Lord, those yellow flapping wings journeyed me right into a headache. "I love nature. I just love it more from the comfort of my bed."

"Well, it's supposed to be a full moon tonight. Should be a sight." With a swift move, Nixon strikes a match. The kindling smokes and crackles until catching the bigger pieces of wood. Within seconds, flames erupt, warming my shins and knees.

"I take it you've done this before."

"My parents used to bring me here. Now, I bring my nephew a few times a year."

"Where's your name?" I step toward the picnic table, graffitied with carvings. "Apparently *Molly loves Jack, Chris loves Liann, Jimmy was here, and Kaitlyn's a whore.*"

"Does it list Kaitlyn's phone number?"

"Charming."

"Hungry?" he asks.

"Starved."

Nixon stokes the fire, which has burned into flaring hot

embers. He sharpens the end of a stick with a pocketknife, jams on a hot dog, and hands it to me.

"Thanks." I suspend the meat over the fire. "So, why camping? I mean, if you're trying to get back at me for this whole newspaper thing, why not tie me to a chair and force me to watch *The Housewives of Beverly Hills*? Why pick something so far away? Wait . . . you're not planning to murder me out here, are you? Strangle me with fishing line?"

"Haven't decided." He checks his hot dog for doneness, then returns it to the fire and says with a shrug, "I don't know. Candace asked what we do for fun. I started thinking about things I like to do. Things I haven't done in a while."

"Kinda wish you hadn't visited the Four Seasons spa in a while."

"Nah, you like it here. I can tell."

"*You* can tell? I'm the master at body language. But, go ahead, Mr. Big-Time Corporate Man, explain how you can tell."

"All right." He spins toward me. "Your legs are straight and your feet have fallen to the side. Your hands rest in your lap and your held is tilted toward me."

"So, I'm relaxed. It was a long ride."

"Maybe. But you're the one who gathered those flowers." He points at a bouquet of blue and purple lantana I'd stuffed into a knot in the picnic table. "You're happy here."

His eyes reflect the setting sun. He looks peaceful. He's happy here, too.

"Well, *you* haven't checked your phone since we arrived."

"I'm not all business, you know?"

Yeah, I'm starting to see that.

I take a moment and study our surroundings, the fire, the solitude, the tent. I'm just now struck by the fact that this excursion seems more like a romantic getaway for two than payback for roping him into the interview.

But that's insane, clearly not his intention. My radar must be a click off, still hurt from Sean. For half a second I recall him and Sara laughing, totally comfortable at their breakfast. I shake the image clear. No reason to give Sean another thought. Besides, Nixon's dating Sara, too. Surely she can't resist his charms. I ask, "How are things with Sara?"

"She's nice," he says, as if describing a quilt.

"Just nice? You date eleven gorgeous women and you tell me they're all too shallow or too obvious. Then I set you up with Sara, who's sophisticated, smart, and sexy. The total package. And all you can say is she's *nice*. I can't figure you out, Nixon. What do you look for in a woman?"

"For starters, I like a woman who doesn't expect a Keurig coffeemaker while camping."

"Very funny."

"No, I'm serious. Believe it or not, I'm a simple guy and I like a simple girl."

"Simple? Like simple-minded?" I slide my hot dog onto a bun.

"No, definitely not. I mean simple in demands. I like a woman with little makeup, an easy-to-come-by smile, and shoes that won't make her complain about walking too far. I want someone who can give me a run for my money. A woman who wears confidence and nothing else."

"She'll be chilly."

"Okay, confidence and a tight pair of jeans." Thin laugh lines frame his smile. He lowers his hot dog closer to the embers and says, "At the end of the day, I want a relationship like my parents'."

My mom's nightly ritual of leaning toward Dad and kissing him before sitting for dinner comes to mind. I glance at my scar, covered by my shirt. *Me, too.*

We sit quietly for a couple of minutes, listening to the

popping of the twigs and hot dog grease hissing in the flames. This evening is comfortable. The space between us smaller.

"Nixon, if you don't mind my asking, why not tell your mom no? Why agree to this charade? Seems a lot of unnecessary trouble for you."

A long stretch of silence passes before he says, "We're a lot alike. You and me. Both seeking redemption of sorts, trying to prove our worth."

"You're a very successful man. What do you have to prove that you haven't already?"

He reaches into his pocket and pulls out a scratched silver coin. He flips it back and forth between his thumb and middle finger like a poker player fiddling with his chip, contemplating whether to bet or fold.

"My uncle Marcos, my mom's brother, worked at a Taco Bell since he was fifteen. Every day after school, he cleaned the floors, scrubbed the ovens and fryers, emptied the trash, washed the pots and pans, doing whatever they asked of him until long after midnight. Then he got up the next morning, went to school, and did it all over again.

"They promoted him to manager the day after his high school graduation, the youngest at the time. A couple years later, he bought the Taco Bell. One restaurant turned into two, two into four, and eventually he owned nine locations around Southern California and a couple in Nevada."

"Wow, that's impressive."

Nixon stares into the fire. "Even though he could afford not to, he still scrubbed the grease off the fryers, climbed on the roof and fixed the condensation lines, labored on his hands and knees, working until the day he died of a heart attack twelve years ago. He had no children and left me a trust fund." Nixon rests the coin in his palm. "And you know what I did? I gambled it. All of it. I blew his life's work, his sweat, his sore back, his swollen knees, his tired bones on blackjack tables in Vegas and Reno. Didn't take me long, a few years is all. My uncle worked his whole life, his whole goddamned life, and this coin"—he aims it toward the flame's light—"is all I have to show for it."

"So you've worked hard to prove—"

"That I'm not a total fuck-up, yeah. I've worked hard to rebuild Marco's legacy, leaving no time to focus on a relationship, but I don't want to disappoint my mom any more than I already have."

I know the feeling.

"If she wants a girl on my arm, I'll give her a girl on my arm." Nixon slips the coin into his pocket, then finishes his beer in one long swallow.

"You surprise me, Nixon. For the past few months, you've portrayed this suit-and-tie, too-busy-for-love kinda guy and yet, once or twice, this softer side of you pokes through. This mushy center. It catches me off guard."

"You've caught me off guard, too." The fire flickers in his eyes as he holds my gaze.

Should he look at me like that?

Should I want him to?

"Whoa, careful," he says.

"What?" *Was my stare that obvious?*

"An ember bounced on your sleeve. Your sleeve is burning." He flicks off the glowing coal and pats out the smoke.

"Thanks. That could've been bad." Without thinking, I slide my sweatshirt sleeve up my forearm. "Thank goodness, I—"

"What happened there?" Nixon points at my scar.

"Oh, God." I hurry to pull down my sleeve.

Nixon places his hand on my wrist. "Don't."

I haven't discussed my parents' accident in years, and with no more than a few people. Shown my scar to even fewer. But something in the warmth of Nixon's touch tells me it'll be okay.

He lets go of my arm.

Before I realize it, I start to tell him my story. "Sophomore year in high school this guy I liked asked me to meet him at a party in Oceanside. My parents said no. Defiant and totally pissed off, I pretended to have a headache and went to bed around nine p.m. An hour later I sneaked out the guest bedroom window and met my friends. We went to the party and that guy kissed me. My first kiss, actually. I remember thinking, *This is the best night of my life*."

"First kisses can do that."

"Yeah, everything was great until Mom checked on me before going to bed and discovered I wasn't home. Such a stupid kid." I pick up a broken twig. "They picked me up and the entire way home I sat in the back of the car pouting like a spoiled brat. Thinking only about myself, embarrassed my parents dragged me out of the party, thinking that guy would never talk to me again."

I toss the stick into the flames, wringing my hands, grateful that he's quiet. Just listens, doesn't judge.

"We approached this intersection and I remember thinking, *Good, the light is green. We'll get home faster.* I didn't want to be in the car a moment longer because I despised the way Mom rubbed Dad's temple and how he drove with two hands gripping the wheel. It was them against me, and I couldn't stand being trapped in the backseat with them another minute. Told myself I'd sneak out a hundred times more, just to get away. Those were the last things that ran through my mind, how much I hated them and having to answer to their rules, how much I wanted to get away from my parents." I wrap my arms around myself. "We didn't make it through the intersection. Some guy ran his red light and smashed into Mom's side of the car."

I close my eyes, remembering the screams, sirens, and smells. The nosy people, standing curbside watching the firefighters straighten the mangled metal crushed around my mom and dad while I picked at a knot in a tree umbrellaed over the sidewalk, nothing but a cut on my arm. I remember a neighbor lady wrapped in a blue robe who put her hand to her mouth when they placed Mom on the stretcher and covered her with a white sheet.

Nixon says nothing.

My tears blur my vision of the flames. "The police report said *driving while intoxicated*, but it doesn't matter what they wrote as the reason. *I'm* the reason my parents were driving across town at twelve forty-two a.m. *I'm* the reason a drunk driver plowed into my dad's Jeep Cherokee. *I'm* the reason steel crushed the life out of my mom's body. *I'm* the reason my dad died on the operating table two hours later. *I'm* the reason Jo lost her family."

"Bree—"

"No, it's okay. You don't have to try to make me feel better." I wipe the tears from my cheeks. "I'm ashamed and I miss my parents. Simple as that."

"People aren't judged by their worst moments. Draw attention to what shaped your life, don't hide from it."

"I'm not worried about being judged."

"Then why do you keep the scar hidden?"

"Because it's a painful reminder. Because I don't want to explain what happened. Because I don't want people feeling sorry for me. Because I don't want to be judg—"

"The accident wasn't your fault. You weren't behind the wheel." He stares at me with eyes as hard as flint. "Your parents and their memory should be honored, not hidden."

Maybe it's his definitive gaze or the unvarnished timber in his voice, but for the first time in my life, I almost believe it's true.

A few more minutes of silence pass, and I stare at the flames whirling in the shared space between us, unsure of what to say. Swallowing the rest of my beer, I want to make a turn in this conversation. No one likes talking about dead parents. Especially me. "Sorry, you didn't come here to listen to me rattle on about my sad story. So, enough of that. Now, where do I . . . you know . . . tinkle?"

"Tinkle? Are you four years old?"

"Ha ha."

"There's a bathroom up the road." He hands me the lantern. "Want me to walk you?"

"No, thanks. I'm fine." Gravel crunches under my feet and crickets chirp in my ear as I head toward the restroom. Though I'm still not a fan of the outdoors, especially at night, I am savoring the break from city life. The brisk air. The slow, quiet evening. And, I must admit, I'm relieved to have shared the weight of my past.

I reach the bathrooms only to find a sign that reads SORRY—RESTROOM BROKEN. USE ONE AT HOST'S OFFICE. Seriously? The office is more than a mile away.

Nixon's drunk a couple of beers; I don't want to ask him for a ride. And I sure as hell don't want to walk.

I survey what's around me. Nothing but campfire glow and billowing smoke clouds the shadows. We are *camping*. This is what campers do, right? Become one with nature. Give back to the earth.

I weave through the thick trees, sneaking a peek at the Boy Scouts' campsite below. Except for a citronella candle burning on the picnic table, it's dark. They're likely catching frogs or rebuilding a beaver's dam or something nature-y.

I set my lantern on top of a large boulder and out of sight from the road, I duck behind the rock and slide my jeans around my ankles.

This morning I never thought I'd cruise up a mountain on a motorcycle, roast a hot dog, and pee in the Idyllwild forest.

Come to think of it . . . this whole experience is liberating. Kinda free. Kinda I-am-woman-here-me-roar stuff.

And then I hear it.

The wiggle of a branch.

The *scratch-scratch* on the boulder.

My eyes adjust to the darkness and I see it.

Two beady eyes fix on me. Sharp claws glint in the lantern's light.

A squirrel.

Stay still, Bree. Relax. No sudden movements.

He scuttles closer. The scamp chitters at my feet.

Oh, God. Oh, God.

A rational reaction would be to shimmy him off my foot, calmly walk toward Nixon—after I pulled up my pants—and say, "Funny story, a squirrel scurried across my foot. Ha-ha-ha."

But the shifty bastard circles me. His tail brushes along my ass.

"Aaaagh!" I try to scramble to a stand, but my jeans tangle around my feet and I plummet backward down the bank.

End over end, my body tumbles down the hill. I bump into and over sharp rocks, tree stumps, and pine needles. *Ouch. Ouch. Ouch.* I roll over damp mud and muck, grasping at branches, twigs, anything to slow my course. Finally, I land face-first in the dirt at the base of the Boy Scouts' camp.

I look up as flashlights shine in my eyes.

One of the boys laughs. "Check out her butt."

∽

"Congratulations on the tension of the zip-ties." I lift my bound hands in the air, sitting in Bill the host's office. My overpriced jeans are ruined, stained with gunk, littered with holes.

"Care to explain why you went streaking through a camp-site full of Boy Scouts?" he asks.

"I wasn't streaking. I used the outdoor facilities because yours are broken . . . thank you very much . . . when a squirrel attacked me."

"I highly doubt that, ma'am. A squirrel only attacks if his food supply is threatened."

"Let me assure you, I did not try to eat his nuts." *Okay, that sounded very wrong.*

"Excuse me," Nixon says, walking into the office. "Mind cutting her some slack? She's a camping newbie. Never peed in the woods."

"No kidding?" Bill reacts as if Nixon said I'd been born with twelve toes.

"Forgive me for being civilized."

The host's wife walks in with Hello, I'm Helen written on her name tag. She exchanges glances between Nixon and me before covering her mouth with her hand. "Oh my gosh. Are you Bree Caxton?"

"Yes." I wave as much as the zip-ties allow.

"And this is Nick?"

He nods. "Nice to meet you, ma'am."

"All this time I've wondered what you looked like. You're just as handsome as I imagined." She nudges my shoulder. "Bet you two *do* have a great time in the sack."

"Helen?" Bill scolds.

"Oh, please, we were young once." She slides her hands on her hips. "You know, you both have inspired me. After I read about the Tough Mudder, I took myself on a long walk and jumped over two logs." She gasps. "Look at you, tied up like a criminal. Let's clip you loose, shall we?"

"Yes, that'd be great."

After a couple of autographs and an apology to the Boy Scout troop leader, I'm free to go.

"We're so glad you chose our little campground as one of your rendezvous spots," Helen says. "Holler if you need anything."

"Thank you." I slide onto the back of Nixon's motorcycle, knowing Nixon paid cash and registered under my name so no chance of blowing his cover.

"Didn't you see the boys' campsite below?"

"It was dark. I figured they weren't there. And what's wrong with those boys, anyway? Sitting around without any lights on. Shouldn't they be on their iPhones watching inappropriate Snapchat videos like normal kids these days?"

"They were studying the moon."

"Oh, yeah? They should thank me, then."

"What for?"

"I showed them a moon to remember."

twenty-six

"Bree, wake up." Nixon nudges my shoulder in the morning. I force my eyes open and rub them to life. "What's wrong?"

"Nothing, get up."

"Why? It's still dark. And cold." I bury myself deeper into the sleeping bag.

"Put this on." He tosses me his sweatshirt. "Hurry."

With a half grumble, I pull it over my head and inhale the remnant smell of the campfire. And the remnant smell of *him*.

He hands me my shoes. "C'mon."

I slide into my sneakers and pull my hair into a ponytail, grateful for the altitude, my run through the woods, and the couple of beers that helped me fall asleep quickly last night. We didn't have an awkward moment at bedtime. "Where are we going?"

"You'll see." Lit by the lantern, Nixon guides me up the road toward the mountain base.

We follow a windy makeshift dirt trail, hopping over cacti and snaking between bushes and rocks and then scrambling up a boulder fixed at the mountaintop. He sits on my right, close to me, for the rock is not much wider than the two of us.

I don't inch away as Nixon's thigh presses against mine.

He pulls a thermos and a blanket from his backpack and covers our legs.

The sun has yet to crest, but it casts an orange glow over the sleeping campground, the valley, and Strawberry Creek. Only a few birds are chirping.

Streaks of red, pink, and purple illuminate the dark sky. The sun is slowly rising and the brilliant rays warm the air as the sun, which now looks like a big yellow egg yolk, spills onto the horizon. I'm not a religious person, but there's something spiritual about watching the birth of a new day, full of innocence, promise, and hope.

"Wow, it's beautiful. I'm glad you brought me here."

We say nothing, and seconds, maybe minutes, pass before he breaks the silence. "This land is full of secrets."

"What kind of secrets?"

"See that peak?" He points past me at the tallest mountain across the valley, and then, lowering his arm, slides his hand beside my mine. He curls his pinkie around my own.

His show of affection surprises me. So does the feeling rushing through me.

Nixon.

"It's called Tahquitz Peak, named after a highly regarded Indian who fell in love with the daughter of an enemy tribe. The pair lived on opposite sides of the mountain and sneaked away to meet on that peak. Every morning, for months, they watched the sunrise together."

Our fingers are now entwined, one lost within the other.

"Now that's a love story," I whisper.

"Once her father heard about the two lovers, he forbade the union, said she could never see Tahquitz again." He slips his hand away.

"That's terrible." *Come back.* "What happened?"

"Somehow Tahquitz got word to her. The two agreed to meet the following sunrise and run away together."

"And they lived happily ever after?"

"She never came."

"What? Why not?"

He shrugs. "No one knows for sure. Some say her father moved her to another tribe far away. Some say she died of a longing heart. Every morning for the rest of his life, Tahquitz climbed the peak and waited for her, but he never saw her again. He died on top of that mountain."

"God, to be loved like that." My eyes are moist now.

"Legend says, if you watch the peak at sunrise you'll find his spirit—"

"Searching for her."

"No, scampering away from a squirrel with his pants wrapped around his ankles."

"You big jerk." I punch his arm.

"Take it easy." He laughs. "It's a true story."

"Whatever."

I snatch the thermos from his grasp. "Hey! Where'd you get this coffee anyway?"

"Bill has a Keurig."

∽

Later, as we travel home, Nixon doesn't remind me to hold on tight. He doesn't ask that I press my chest against his back or melt my shoulders into his.

I just do.

But as Tahquitz Peak fades in the distance, I begin to wonder if the mountain air confused my senses. Is the feeling resonating within me from Nixon's touch or simply my subconscious trying to mend my broken heart? But if it's the thin air, then why did I feel this way at Tough Mudder? Why do I feel this way around him, all the time? Is there something more? Do I have feelings for Nixon? Does he for me?

Far too soon, Nixon cuts the engine and we climb off the bike outside my house.

Standing curbside, I remove my helmet and comb my fingers through my hair. My lips are chapped. My throat is dry. My heart is pounding. *I don't want him to go.* Right or wrong, I want to know how he feels. Not sure if I should, even less sure that I shouldn't, I stare into his eyes. "Nixon, I need to ask—"

"Bree, let me say something first. You need to know, these past couple weeks have all been for show, but I—"

"Bree?"

I spin around toward a familiar voice.

Sean stands on my porch. "Can we talk?"

twenty-seven

Nixon hands me my bag, distancing himself from me as if I'm laced with anthrax. "I'll see you around."

Before I can say anything, he climbs onto his bike and rides away.

Sean joins me on the sidewalk. "Hey."

"What are you doing here?"

"Can I come inside?"

"I'm really tired."

"I've something important to say."

So did Nixon.

I glance down the street. Nixon stops at the intersection, balancing his bike with his foot planted on the ground.

You need to know, these past couple weeks have all been for show.

He turns right. His brake light disappears.

Sean grabs my bag. "Please, just for a bit."

I'm emotionally exhausted, too weak to put up a fight. "Yeah, okay, I suppose." I unlock the door. "Let me just change real quick."

"Take your time. I'll wait."

I'm bothered, but curious about Sean's unannounced visit. What could he possibly want? Is he here to tell me that while I meant nothing, Sara means something?

My head is fogged with thoughts. Sean and Sara's dates. The book. Jo's house. How much my life's changed in a matter of weeks. *Nixon.*

Ten minutes later, I head downstairs.

Sean sits on the couch. His hands are squeezed into fists and he silently mouths a few words. I've seen this preparation many times, especially on the nights before his trial's opening or closing arguments.

I remain at the base of the stairs, watching the man who's consumed so many of my days and evenings over the last four years. I know Sean so well. I know he snores on his right side but not his left. I know he requests a number six blade at the barber, the scar on his right elbow came from a skateboarding crash on his twelfth birthday, and Lilly McGovern was his first kiss, fifth grade, after school, underneath the slide. He cringes when his aunt Kathy adds ice to her red wine or A-1 sauce to her steak, but he loves to dip his Doritos in sour cream.

There's something to be said for knowing the idiosyncrasies about a person that others don't. A secret window into his life. *History.*

"Hey, there." He stands the moment he notices me.

"Hi."

"Thanks for seeing me." He twists his hands together. "You'd think a trial attorney wouldn't be so nervous to plead his case. Do you want to sit?"

"No, I'm fine. What did you come to say?"

"Okay, I'll get right to it. This time without you has been very enlightening. I've been on several dates with a woman who's lovely, sweet, funny. She's—"

"You're joking, right? You're here to tell me how great Sara is?"

"No, sorry, that's not what I meant. Let me start over." He wipes his brow.

He *is* nervous.

"What I'm trying to say is, Sara's everything a man could ask for."

"That isn't any better."

"But she isn't you."

"Yes, Sean, you're right. We're two separate people." I can't hide my sharp tone. "Your overpriced education is really paying off."

"See, that's what I mean. She isn't snarky and stubborn and constantly nipping at my heels. She isn't insanely determined and dedicated to her clients. She isn't obsessed with love."

"Are you complimenting me or insulting me?"

He takes a step closer. "She doesn't make me laugh. She doesn't make me excited to get up in the morning and see what the day holds. She doesn't make me a better person. All she does, all any other woman does, is remind me that I once had something so great, so imperfectly perfect. She reminds me that I don't want to spend another day, another minute, another millisecond without you." Sean bends down on one knee. He holds out a stunning two-carat square-cut diamond ring.

Oh, my, God.

"I know this won't be easy. I know I have a lot of work to do to earn your love and forgiveness, but please, let me spend the rest of my life proving how much I love you. Be my wife. Marry me."

My mouth falls open. Holding this opportunity in my hand, this chance at a family and a future, I'm a mess. My thoughts are confused and suffocating, as if I've fallen into a frozen pond, frantically trying to get out from underneath a layer of ice, desperate for air.

"Sean, I don't know what to say."

"Say yes." His smile is anxious, eager, endearing. "Say yes to love."

The angles of Nixon's face come to mind. The smell of his skin as I leaned against him on the bike. The wonder and strength of his stare warming my skin like the morning sun cresting over Idyllwild.

But then his voice punctures my calm. *You need to know, these past couple weeks have all been for show.*

What is wrong with me? Why am I wasting a single thought on a man who's playing a part? Sure, Nixon and I have spent a lot of time together, but he's only holding up his side of the bargain. Our relationship is a business arrangement. Our love is a sham. Not even real. It's nothing. Why can't I get this through my thick head?

On the other hand, Sean and I have years together. Like Antonio's, we're comfortable and familiar. And, except for his momentary insanity, we haven't had many bumps in the road. Maybe what Sean said is true. Maybe he did need to explore someone else to make our relationship healthier, to appreciate all that we have, to feel safe. Maybe I did, too? Maybe my fascination with Nixon is no more than my ego trying to ease the wounds of my battered heart.

In a sense, Sean dumping me made our bond stronger.

My scar reminds me yet again of the pain from having something so precious taken from me. It's hard to let relationships go. Even years after the accident, I still grow angry when friends complain about wearisome Sunday night family spaghetti dinners or obligations to repeat their mom's silly traditions like watching *Elf* while decorating the Christmas tree. I would be thinking, *Be grateful you have a family. Be thankful for the consistency, something and someone to count on.*

No doubt, my parents would've loved Sean. Dad would've

appreciated Sean's work ethic, a lawyer himself, patting him on the back and complimenting his impressive caseload, talking judgments and statutes, then cracking open a couple of beers and watching the game highlights or brushing another coat of paint on the house trim.

Mom would've enjoyed Sean's casual attitude and light-hearted sense of humor. I picture the two of them walking to Peet's for morning coffee, then strolling the long way home alongside the shoreline, hunting for beach glass, sand dollars, and coral. Sean tucking Mom's "keepers" in his pockets.

They'd be happy for me. For Sean's proposal. For the promise of my future. I have a mental image of their approving nod.

"You're smiling. That's a good sign." He winks. "Bree, baby, please say yes."

My eyes linger on the ring for several moments.

I think of his note. *L'Straut Jewelers . . . ask Bree.*

Equally powerful as hearing Sean utter the words *marry me,* if not more so, are the actions and thoughts that led up to his decision. It's that revelation that charms me the most. The moment he decided, *she's the one.* Honestly, is there anything more raw and meaningful than that awareness? I'm the person Sean wants to share his life with. Forever.

Ever since my parents passed, I've craved, *needed,* someone to count on, someone to share my past and future with. If I say no, then aren't I walking away from exactly what I long for?

"Sean, I want to be completely honest with one another. Clean the slate." I pull him up to a standing position. "Why did you break up with me?"

He slides the ring midway onto his pinkie and grabs my hands. "I got scared. I don't think I've told you much about my parents' divorce, but they fought constantly over money. How much this or that cost, why Dad bought a motorcycle when Mom wanted to redo the kitchen. Money ruined them, tore them apart." He strokes my hands with his thumbs. "So, when we met with the financial advisor and discussed portfolio projections and interest rates, I thought of them. Their fights and tension gummed up my head. I feared the same might happen to us. I freaked out." He wraps my hands behind his back. "I'm not perfect. I've made mistakes, but I love you. I love you more than anything."

As I stare back at the man I've known intimately for four years, I'm taken back to the moment by the beach and the green flash. The first time he said he loved me. He's right. We've come so far together. With a cleansing breath, I decide right there and then that mistakes are just that, mistakes. What type of person does it make me, not to forgive and forget a quick moment—albeit painful—over the years of wonderful moments?

"We have history. Good history."

It's as if he read my mind.

"I want to bounce our grandbabies on my knees and take them to Disneyland. I want to have Sunday dinners and weekend soccer games. Let's start a family. Marry me, please."

I press my body closer toward Sean, silencing the petty worry in my mind. Besides, if I want any chance at a solid future, I have to trust him. "Yes, I will marry you."

"You have no idea how happy this makes me."

He slips the ring onto my finger and kisses me long and slow.

I'm reminded of his taste, his comfort, his rhythm.

"Do you have any Champagne?"

"Drank it the night we broke up."

"Well, no matter. There are better ways to celebrate, anyway. How about you and I go upstairs and I show you how much I missed you?" His lips are on my neck. "It's been a long time since I've had you."

"Um . . . actually." I inch away. "It's just . . . I had a really long weekend. I'm beat and our reunion should be special and . . ."

"Say no more. You're right. We're starting over. I want things perfect. No reason to rush. We have our whole lives." He slides the bangs out of my eyes. "I'm leaving tomorrow for my conference in Denver. Terrible timing, I know. But how about this? When I get back, I'll book us an oceanfront suite at La Valencia. We'll share a very sexy, very romantic dinner for two. We'll make new memories. Sound good?"

"Sounds good." And it does. It really does.

He laughs and reaches for the door. "Wait until we tell Candace. Won't she be shocked?"

"No!" I practically shout. "You can't say anything."

"Why not?"

"It will ruin everything."

"Our engagement ruins everything?"

"Yes."

"Ah, the paper."

"Our little hiccup happened the night before my first interview and the paper demanded I have a boyfriend by my side, so I panicked and asked Nixon."

"You mean this whole time you and Nixon were pretending?"

"Yes."

"You never slept together?"

Does my imagination count? Stop it, Bree. Stop it right now. "No."

"Damn, that's good news." Sean lifts me by the waist and spins me around.

"Okay, right, great. But put me down. Candace doesn't know. She can't know. Nor can anyone else. I have to continue dating Nixon and you have to keep pretending you're dating Sara."

"How long?"

"A couple more weeks, until the last interview posts."

"It kills me not to share the news with the world, but I'll

play along. For a couple weeks. Mrs. Sean Thomas. God, I love the sound of that. All right, I'll let you rest. I'll see you the moment I get back from Denver. I love you, Bree." He kisses me and steps out my front door.

"I love you, too."

My sprinkler kicks on, soaking his shoes and pants.

"Shit!" He prances toward his car.

But I shouldn't laugh.

I shouldn't cry, either.

twenty-eight

"What the hell are these?" Jo asks, the following morning, dressed in a lavender-colored velour suit and sitting at her kitchen table.

"Roasted kale chips."

"Where are my Swiss Rolls?"

"You don't need that processed stuff."

"I'm an old woman. I've earned the right to eat whatever I want."

"Kale is good for you."

"I think she's trying to kill us," she says to Martin, who's nestled on her lap, and feeds him a chip.

He spits it out.

"See."

I laugh and remove the pineapple and pepperoni pizza from the oven, sliding a slice onto her plate. "Eat this. It's full of grease and artery-clogging cheese."

"Now, this is what I'm talking about."

I chew on a slice while unloading the remaining groceries.

"Did you know? You and Nick are winning the 'Who Is

Cuter?' poll by eleven points." She sits at the table, pointing at the *Close-Up* feature opened in front of her. She's grabbed a yellow highlighter, poised to mark her favorite sentences. Just like we used to do with the bestsellers.

I've decided not to read the articles ahead of time. I'd rather listen to the write-up through her words. See the story through her eyes.

"And that score difference sure says something, considering we've never seen Nick's face. I mean, look here, you're both wearing helmets, for Pete's sake."

"He's camera shy." I head toward the fridge for milk, passing Martin.

He growls.

I growl back.

"When do I get to meet your boyfriend?"

Which one? "Um . . . soon." Obviously, I'm eager to tell Jo about Sean's proposal even though she'll be puzzled. I'll need to explain why Nixon posed as Nick and as my boyfriend. And that technically Sean's my boyfriend and he dated Sara who's also dating Nick . . . er, Nixon, but now he's my fiancé, Sean that is, and . . . geez. Maybe I should draw a diagram because I'm a little confused myself.

I'm glad I left my engagement ring at home. Just seems easier.

"This Sean is a handsome fellow, too. Don't you think?"

"I do."

"It says he and Sara spent an afternoon . . ."

At the San Diego Zoo. Sean told me about it. He thought it'd be a good, more platonic environment than, say, a sunset harbor cruise or a romantic movie in the park. Next week he plans to meet Sara at the Del Mar beach cleanup. Which I think is genius. What girl wants to make out or get cozy while picking up stinky beer cans and soiled diapers?

Yes, tricking Sara is a crappy thing to do. But Sean promised to keep himself at arm's length emotionally—and physically—these next couple of weeks so when he says they're not connecting and breaks things off, it won't come as a complete surprise. And I find comfort knowing that the practiced lawyer that Sean is will lace his words with sugar and accountability, shielding her feelings so that Sara walks away feeling victorious and better off without the likes of *him*.

Plus, she's dating Nixon, too. Isn't one charming guy enough?

Speaking of Nixon, he and I haven't seen or spoken to one another since he dropped me at my curb. Yes, it's been less than twenty-four hours, but still. I haven't thought about him. Once or twice is all.

God, I'm so grateful Nixon cut me off and I didn't end up blabbing like a hormonal teenager that afternoon. Imagine how embarrassing it would've been had I said—*out loud*—what I felt. Correction. What I *thought* I felt.

I fold Jo's empty grocery bags and stack them in her pantry. Maybe I suffered from altitude sickness? That's a thing, right? I know Idyllwild is no Mt. Everest, but still, spending day and night outside in the thin air, hiking to an even higher elevation in the morning, eating two nitrate-filled hot dogs. It's no wonder I became delusional.

Well, that's that. What does it matter now, anyway? Sean's shiny ring, tucked safely in my nightstand at home, illuminates in my mind. *I'm getting married.* One thing is for sure. My emotions are jumbled no more.

"Look here, they're feeding a giraffe." Jo grabs my attention.

I sneak a peek over her shoulder. Sara's hair is gathered into a low ponytail and her half-smiling, half-cringing face is turned away from the giraffe's foot-long tongue as he nibbles a carrot off her extended hand.

Sean stands beside her, and though he's laughing, his arms

are crossed against his chest. His body is closed. Means his mind is closed, too. *Good boy.*

"What poll are you talking about, anyway? I don't remember Candace saying anything like that."

"It's on your blog."

"You're following my blog?"

"Of course, I am. It's not every day my granddaughter becomes a bestselling author." She winks.

"Eleven points, you say?" I pour us each a glass of milk.

"Yep." She returns to the article, following along with her index finger as she reads. *"We can only wonder how the lovebirds spent their weekend in the mountains."*

He brushed his hand against mine.

"Did they watch for shooting stars under the crisp night air?"

I wrapped his sweatshirt close around my skin.

"Snuggle close in a tent made for two?"

The sunrise. Just us.

"Hello?" Jo waves the paper in my face. "Anyone home?"

"Huh? Oh, yeah, sorry." *What is your problem, Bree?* I shake my mind clear. *And who does Nixon think he is, anyway? Milling around in my head as if he owns the place.*

"My, my, by the color of your cheeks, I'd say a lot more *nature* happened in that tent."

"Nonsense, Jo."

She pats her thigh and Martin jumps into her lap again. "He understands, don't you, Martin? He has a crush on the Pomeranian two doors down."

Anxious to change the subject, I say, "Did I tell you a squirrel attacked me?"

"You hate squirrels."

"I know. There I was, um . . . taking care of business in the woods, when a squirrel with claws longer than piano keys lunged toward me. His tail swept against my butt. It's a wonder I'm alive."

"Oh, Bree." She snickers. "You've never been one for the outdoors."

We laugh together and it feels good. Damn good to see she's not worrying about the 1058 form.

I'm worried enough for the both of us.

Jo reads on. *"We've followed the pair for weeks, trying unsuccessfully to catch a clear shot of Bree's man. But, as luck would have it, he's escaped our camera. Though I'm determined to get the perfect shot, something about Nick's evasiveness makes him all that more appealing.* I agree with that." Jo taps the paper before continuing. *"Nick doesn't want the sure-to-be-boy-band-like hysteria if his pearly whites are documented. But this reporter thinks it's more than that. It's more than self-preservation. It's not about him. This man's love is crystal clear, focusing completely on Bree, calling her simply, 'my lovely.'"*

"Wait . . . what?" I nearly choke on a pepperoni slice. "It says that?"

"Sure does. Right here."

I peer over Jo's shoulder.

My lovely.

Jo highlights the two words. "That's my favorite line."

Mine, too.

twenty-nine

I've given myself a stern talking-to. Lots of finger pointing at my reflection in the bathroom mirror while saying, "No more thoughts of Nixon. Perspective, Bree. Stay on target. You have a fiancé, for Christ's sake." And that's the thing. I *do* have a fiancé. But no one knows. Sometimes I forget myself because Sean's still in Denver and we haven't validated our engagement. It doesn't seem real and that's likely because we haven't celebrated and solidified its meaning. I know I can't tell *everyone*, but I've got to tell someone. That's what my heart and my mind need.

So, a couple of nights later, as the rain pours down and Andrew searches for an empty space in the crowded library parking lot, I tell him about Sean's proposal. It feels good to share the truth. This is one of life's most special moments. A man loves me enough to marry me. To join my name with his until death do us part.

Besides, if I reveal a bit of truth to Andrew, maybe he'll do the same. Maybe he'll divulge just what the heck he's been hiding from me.

"Sean just got a bit sideways, is all. A little scared. But we talked and agreed not to dwell on mistakes from the past. Everyone screws up now and then. You said so yourself." We drive along another row, packed with cars. "What's going on? Why is the library so busy tonight? Oh, there's a spot." I point toward the right. "Besides, Sean's been a constant in my life, we have *history*."

"You don't—"

"And I know better than most what it feels like to lose a part of your past. It sucks. Plain and simple. It sucks." Through my shirt, I rub my scar.

He parks the car and we dash across the wet asphalt lot into the library toward my Q&A session.

"You don't have to convince me," he says. "If you're happy, then I'm happy."

I recognize the fake approval in his voice but decide to let it go. "Thank you, Andrew. I *am* happy. We wiped the slate clean and gave our relationship a fresh start. He's taking me to La Valencia for a romantic weekend. You know, between Sean and work, my life's been a web of lies these past few weeks and I've had enough. That's why the next time I see Randi, I'm gonna tell her the truth."

"Are you insane?" He grabs my arm and digs his nails into my skin.

Um . . . ouch.

"No way in hell can you admit you're engaged."

"I know it's messy, but she'll understand."

"She'll kill you. Literally."

"Shush."

"What's the point?"

"Honesty is the point. What she chooses to do with it is up to her. Speaking of honesty, I know what you've been keeping from me."

"You do?"

"Yes, Andrew. The secret phone calls, the lunch at Ryoko's, the circled help-wanted ads. When were you going to tell me about the job?"

"Oh, Bree, I—"

"There you are," Randi says, approaching in a form-fitting red dress, a knockoff version of what Kate Hudson wore to a premiere three weeks ago.

"Randi? Hi. This is a surprise. What are you doing here?"

"Let's walk." She heads us toward the conference room.

"Actually, I'm glad you're here." I hurry to match her quick pace. "I've something I want to tell you."

"No, you don't," Andrew mutters.

"What is it?" Randi turns left rather than right, the opposite direction of my usual conference room.

"Randi, I'm the other way."

"Follow me." She doesn't stop until we stand outside a set of closed double doors.

I didn't even know they had meeting rooms in this wing.

Two women walk up from behind. Chatter engulfs the hall as they open one of the doors.

I sneak a peek inside the meeting room, the width and length of a basketball court and more crowded than Nordstrom's on the first hour of their anniversary sale. All of the tables are full and more women pack in along the walls.

"What's going on?" I ask Randi. "There must be three hundred women in there."

"You. You've developed quite a following." She points overhead at a banner hanging above the doors.

FALL IN LOVE WITH BREE CAXTON

"They're here for me?"

"I told you. I'm a sure thing. And I planned to wait until

the morning, but I just got the latest projections. Your preorders are up forty-seven percent, leaps and bounds above your competition. That's one of the sharpest rises ever seen with a debut nonfiction. The editor increased your first run. Again. And, the *National Tribune* is considering making you a biweekly installment."

"No way."

"We're right on track. Don't change a goddamn thing."

"Wow!" I raise my fists in triumph. "This is amazing."

"And everything you've worked so hard toward," Andrew warns.

And everything I worked so hard toward.

Wait until I share this with Jo. And Nix—I mean, Sean. Of course. I meant to say Sean's name first.

"So." She snaps her fingers. "Quick-quick. What is it you want to tell me?"

"Should she autograph her books with blue or black ink?" Andrew jumps in.

"What the hell do I care?" Randi reaches for the door.

"No, wait." This may be the most asinine professional move ever known to man, but I can't help it. Enough lies. Enough empty tubes of Cortizone cream. I have to be honest. "Randi, you need to know something first. Sean and I—"

Randi lifts her hand to stop me and looks over my shoulder. "Good evening, glad you could come."

I spin around and find a middle-aged woman with heavy jowls, Ray-Ban-style reading glasses, a buttoned-up gray cardigan, and dark brown pageboy haircut marching toward us.

Lucy Hanover.

Randi's cautionary words from a few weeks ago ricochet through my mind. *Lucy can make or break a new author by mere mention of their name on her show. She falls in love with you and you're golden.*

"Lucy, this is Bree Caxton. Bree, meet Lucy Hanover from *Gabbing with Gurus*."

"Yes, I know exactly who you are. It's very nice to meet you. I'm a big fan. Well, like most everyone American with ears." *With ears?* I shake her hand a little too hard. And too long.

"Pleasure." She yanks her hand out from mine. "In there?" she asks Randi, gesturing toward the conference room doors. "I'm a bit pressed for time."

"Yes, and please, go in and find a seat. We're only a minute out."

Andrew hurries and opens the door, once again filling the corridor with chitchat.

"Thank you." Lucy slips inside.

"I can't believe she's here. Hell, I can't believe any of those women are here."

"Get your ass in there. This is a very important night." Randi opens the door.

Hundreds of women are here to see me. To listen to my words of advice. To potentially buy my book.

Andrew is right.

No way I can reveal the truth now.

thirty

I'm nervous.

Which is silly.

I've given lots of presentations. So what if there are a few *hundred* more attendees than usual? So what if Lucy Hanover sits at the table nearest the front with my future resting in her hands? I'm good at this. I've done this job long enough to have an answer for any question, a solution for any scenario. Plus, Gwen and the gang are cheering me on from a table in the rear.

Not to mention, as I walk toward the podium dressed in a navy long-sleeved shirtdress cinched at the waist, black leggings, and black knee-high boots, I know that even if my presentation sucks, no one can knock me for my snazzy outfit.

Still, my stomach tangles into knots, recalling Randi's not-so-supportive words of advice prior to my stepping on stage.

"Don't fuck up."

I try to quell my jitters while the crowd takes their seats. I'm pleased to hear loud and lively conversation. People sound to be in great moods. One lady holds up a Vuitton bag while the rest of her table admires it. The women—plus the guy likely dragged here by the gal beside him—are all chatting and laughing, having a good time.

Except Lucy.

Talking to no one, she's angled her crossed legs away from the crowded table and scrolls through her phone.

It's not the stay-the-hell-away-from-me persona she throws off that worries me. It's her jiggling foot, pointed toward the nearby exit, wiggling faster than a hummingbird flaps its wings, that's got me flustered.

I haven't said a word and Lucy Hanover already wants out of here.

For Jo, for the book, for the house.

Sweat drips between my cleavage, soaking into my bra.

Can someone turn up the air?

My phone, resting on the lectern, chimes with a message from Nixon. His face pops into my mind and even though he made clear the pretense of our relationship, I find myself wishing he were here, standing close in a charcoal suit with hands slid inside his pockets, firm jaw, and confidence-boosting stare. I read his text. *I have your sweatshirt. Don't see you at library. I'll drop at the office.*

I chew on my lip before replying. *At library, different room. HUGE turnout for Q&A.* I press send. I wait a couple of seconds, then fire a second text. *Nervous.*

Room full of squirrels?

My nerves settle as I smile, glad to know he's no longer upset. *Vicious beast.*

A moon to remember.

I laugh out loud, then quickly cover my mouth with my hand.

He shoots me a final text. *Just be yourself. That's who people came to see.*

I stare at his words as a text from Andrew redirects my focus.

What's so funny?

I glance at him across the room and shake my head, imply-ing it's nothing. But it *is* something. Thanks to Nixon, I'm empowered. Knowing he's in my corner, I'm pumped and poised. Ready to impress the hell out of Lucy.

No doubt Sean would be equally supportive. He's champi-oned me for years. After all, it was Sean who encouraged me to channel my expertise and write a book in the first place.

It's just that Nixon and I were mere acquaintances a few weeks ago and now, make-believe aside, I'd like to think we're friends, good friends. He's stuck his neck out for me lately and I know once these interviews are said and done, we'll go about our separate lives, my focus shifting to my future with Sean. But, if I'm honest, I might just miss Nixon's snarky attitude. His rattle-my-cage approach. And, as long as no one can read my thoughts, I'll admit that I might just miss him.

Anyway, enough of that.

I grab hold of the lectern. Time to get this show on the road. *Just be yourself. That's who people came to see.*

"Hello, ladies and gentlemen. My name is Bree Caxton and I'd like to thank you for coming to the Fall in Love with Bree Caxton Q&A. I'm very excited to be here."

The crowd claps.

What a gorgeous roomful of strangers.

"Now, typically for these meetings, I pose a different topic and open the room to questions. I like to keep things fun and informal, like a chat among friends. If you've got something to ask or say, by all means, say it. With that said, let's get rolling. Tonight, I'd like to start things off and find out what you all think is the most important aspect to keeping a relationship alive."

"American Express Black card," a woman shouts.

The group laughs.

"Yes, well, that certainly doesn't hurt, does it?" I say. "Anything else?"

"Candlelit dinners," a woman says from way in the back.

"Kisses by the fireplace," adds a lady with bright pink lipstick.

"Skinny-dipping," a fourth woman says, and the group laughs again.

I hold up my index finger and wait for them to quiet down before saying, "So, given what you've said, is it fair to say the thing that keeps a relationship alive is romance?"

The crowd nods in unison.

"All right, good. And I agree. Wine, long glances, and soft music is never a bad way to spend an evening. Who doesn't love a quiet dinner for two?" I free the microphone from its sleeve and move toward the stage edge. "In fact, some say dinner is the slow seduction." I giggle to myself, knowing Nixon would likely roll his eyes. "But tonight, I'll explain why romance is total crap."

They gasp.

I take a moment and survey the room. The group is curious. They sit with elbows propped on the tables, resting their chins on fisted hands. Some lean an ear toward me while others hover a stylus over a glowing iPad.

They're hooked.

I have notecards on this topic stuffed in my purse. But I

don't need them. Now that I'm calm, the material flows effortlessly.

"Yes, that's right. Romance is irrelevant. Now, we can thank magazines and movies and Pinterest for convincing society otherwise. They practically cram down our throats that candlelight and wine, picnics and flowers, lingerie and diamonds are the cornerstones of a loving relationship. As if the number of chocolate-covered strawberries one is fed by a lover equates to happiness. But that's all a bunch of garbage."

Another collective "huh?" steeps through the room.

Lucy's foot stills.

Yes!

"Sure, we women appreciate the lovey-dovey stuff and so do men. But not for reasons you imagine. Lavender-drawn baths or rose petals shaped into hearts on the bed, or lack thereof, doesn't make or break a relationship. Romance means nothing if *one* key element is missing. Romance is a nice touch, pardon the pun, but only if it's complementing the most important component of a relationship. And, no, that component is not sex."

I let the anticipation build before saying, "The key component to a successful relationship, platonic or sexual, is *validation*." I pause for another moment, letting the word sink in. Murmurs and looks of doubt spread through the room. "I'm serious. Validation. Every single one of us, young, old, male or female, needs reassurance. We crave approval. We hunger to feel valued."

Deep down, isn't this what I want from Jo? To know that even though I made a terribly painful mistake, my life still has meaning?

"And what better relationship to satisfy this need than with the person with whom we're most vulnerable? Romance is arguably one form of displaying this core desire because we *feel* valued if the person we love shows us affection and attention. But a drawn bubble bath isn't the crowning glory of a relationship.

"Take, for example, the busy stay-at-home mom. Toddlers crawl up her leg all day, macaroni and cheese is stuffed in the DVD player, and Play-Doh is matted in her hair. If her husband hops up to change a diaper or pops dinner in the oven without being asked, even if it's a frozen pizza, she'll take notice. There's nothing inherently sexy about a man loading the dishwasher, but I guarantee you, the tired mama feels worthy because of it. She feels validated. And more than likely a gleam will sparkle like a firework in her eye. Make sense?"

The crowd nods.

"Good. So let's talk about the many ways to show validation in a relationship. We—"

A woman in an eyelet sundress raises her hand.

My first question. This is exciting. "Yes?"

"Can we meet Nick?"

"Sorry?"

"Is he here?"

"We all want to meet him," says a woman.

I glance at the guy.

He shrugs. "Sure."

"He sounds amazing and I'm dying to see his picture," the first woman says. "Got one?"

"Um, no . . . I . . . um . . . let's focus on the topic at hand, shall we?"

"It's just, we've all read your articles the last couple weeks. We're following your blog and planning to buy your book."

The crowd nods again.

"Thank you."

"Don't you see? We will have invested a lot of time in you."

"Yes, well, hopefully you've picked up a nugget of knowledge along the way."

"C'mon, share some of the nitty-gritty. Give us some first-hand experience. None of this blah-blah-blah stuff."

Blah-blah-blah?

"Give us an example of the perfect date with Nick."

"Yes, please."

"You don't want to know about us." Especially because there is no *us*.

A collective set of intense eyes are fixed upon me as if I'm about to reveal Apple's latest technology breakthrough.

"Tell us." A woman shouts from the back of the room. *Randi?*

"Well . . . um . . . okay, I guess we'd start off the day early, doing something active, like a long run or hike. Then grab lunch near the beach, somewhere with burgers and good beer. The late afternoon might include a few honey-do chores together, maybe a nap in the sun, searching for beach glass by the shore, or a movie, or an early dinner. But it all includes laughing. The whole day. You see, Nixon and I—"

"Who's Nixon?" asks a young woman with long blond hair.

Oh, shit. "Um . . . I said Nick. Most definitely Nick."

"Well, whoever Nixon is, he sounds like a good time. Is he single?"

The group laughs, even Lucy.

"Bree's right," says a thirty-something with a light gray cardigan. "This one guy I dated wasn't much to look at, but we laughed all the time. And so kind to me. One time I came down with the flu and he brought me an armload of movies and did my laundry." She shakes her head. "He was my best relationship ever. I don't know why I let that guy get away. I'm gonna call him."

"You should. And once you establish that mutual valida-tion, enjoy the romance that follows."

Twenty minutes later, after loads of questions and laughs, Randi pats her watch, signaling me it's time to wrap it up. "Well, that's gonna do it for today. Thanks for joining me. Hope to see you all next time." I step off the stage to a standing ovation.

∽

The crowd funnels out the doors and I overhear them saying things like "Totally fun" and "Lots of good information." One girl even said to her friend, "I really liked Bree's outfit."

"You crushed it." Andrew meets me at the base of the stairs.

Randi joins us a second later. "Hell of a job."

"Thank you. I hope I didn't sound too unsettled at first. Once I found my groove, I rolled with it."

Lucy Hanover steps close. "I enjoyed the presentation, Bree."

"Thank you. I'm glad."

"You captivated the audience. That's hard to do. I've been enjoying your book. Randi says it's coming out soon?"

"Yes, in a few weeks."

"I'd like to have you on my show. You free next Friday?"

"She's free," Randi answers.

"Great. Give me a call. We'll discuss particulars. Looking forward," Lucy says, waving good-bye.

Once out of earshot, Randi spins toward me and smacks my arm. "That's what I'm talking about."

I glance at the doors, still crowded with a long stream of *my fans*.

"Bree, Bree." Gwen waves, salmoning herself toward me through the mass. She clutches both of my hands. "That was a great presentation. Can you believe this turnout?"

"I know. Our little weekly group is little no more."

"No kidding. Even that cute man popped in."

"What cute man?"

"You know, the handsome guy you chatted with outside our conference room the other day, remember? The one with the little boy."

Nixon. "He's here? Where?"

She looks toward the back of the room. "Ah . . . I don't see him anymore. He must've just left. Anyway, great job. See you next week."

thirty-one

"C'mon, baby," Sean says, having just returned from Denver. He nibbles on my neck. "No one is here."

He's right. The office is empty. Jo's come and gone after sharing a tuna sandwich and chocolate-chunk cookie with me for lunch. UPS already made today's deliveries. Andrew left for a doctor's appointment. Or so he says. But he isn't sick, no raspy cough or unsightly rash. And who brushes their teeth and changes into a pressed oxford before a checkup, anyway? He left for an interview. I'm sure of it.

But the thing I still don't understand is why he hasn't come clean. Why won't he talk to me? And the little bugger slipped out before I had the chance to corner him and demand answers.

Sean murmurs in my ear.

"Sean, honey, wait. I don't want our first time back together to be on the edge of my desk."

"You didn't mind before." He slides his hand up my shirt and fingers underneath my bra strap.

"Let's wait for tomorrow night at La Valencia."

"You're killing me. Do you know that? I might be dead by tomorrow night."

"I'm sure you'll make it." I Eskimo-kiss his nose with my own.

"At least put this on. Give me *this* pleasure." He slides my engagement ring onto my finger. "I hate that you haven't shown it off to the world. I can't wait for this interview thing to be over."

"I know. Just a little while longer."

"Well, tomorrow night, you're all mine. I've reserved the best suite and instructed the staff not to disturb us our entire stay."

"It sounds perfect."

"And you don't have to bring a thing. I plan to keep you naked the whole time." He kisses my palm, then angles my hand, allowing the diamonds to catch the sunlight. "What the . . . ?" Sean slips the ring off my finger.

"What's wrong?"

"Is that residue or a scratch?" He squints, examining the stone. "Do you still have some cleaner underneath the sink?"

"I think so."

"I'll be right back."

"Okay." I busy myself filing a few paid invoices when Sara walks in.

"Hey, Bree."

Oh, Christ. What is she doing here?

"Sara? Hello. I'm surprised to see you," I say loud enough that I hope Sean will hear.

"I came to chat for a moment. May I sit down?"

Please, don't. "Sure, of course." I move close to the window so she'll face me, her back toward the break room.

She rests her sleek black purse in her lap and exhales.

"Everything okay?"

"Well, yes and no. I thought you should know, Nixon and I aren't seeing each other anymore."

"No?" I glance in Sean's direction again. "What happened? I thought you really liked Nixon."

"I did. I do." A wide grin illuminates her face. "But I called him and told him it wasn't working out. You see, something else happened. Something I didn't expect. Something extraordinary."

"Really? What is it? I'm all ears."

"Well, you're not going to believe this, but I fell in love with someone else."

"You did? That's wonderful. Who?"

"Sean."

I stare in at her in shock, as if she said her art gallery is now a strip club. "You *what*?"

"I know, I know." She waves her hand in the air. "I sound like one of those ditzy reality show girls."

Calm down, Bree. Breathe in. Breathe out.

"Quick, isn't it?" she says.

"Very quick," I say with total disbelief. "You don't really mean, *love*? Or *Sean*, right?"

"I can hardly believe it myself. But I'm tingly all over, can't eat a thing."

"Maybe it's the flu."

"I daydream about him for hours on end. I've no concentration at work, haven't gotten a darn project done all week."

"Maybe you're anemic."

She shakes her head and says with a playful voice, "I'm so distracted I mismarked an abstract oil painting, labeling it as a charcoal drawing. Don't I sound crazy?"

More like insane. I don't know what to say except . . . *what the hell?*

"And I have you to thank. If you hadn't introduced me to Nixon and given me the confidence that someone as charming and handsome as him could be interested in me, then I likely wouldn't have given Sean a second glance. I always thought men like Nixon and Sean were out of my league. I can't thank you enough."

Yeah, I'm a big hero. With an even bigger problem on my hands.

"Sara, let's not rule Nixon out completely. I mean, he's such a great guy. Don't you agree?"

"Yes, he—"

"And, he's got that cute little knot in his throat that wiggles when he laughs. Have you seen it?"

"Yes, but—"

"Everyone says he's the silent-but-deadly type. You know, guarded just enough to be sexy but not conceited. Come to think of it, you mentioned that yourself."

"Sure, all of that's true. And, Nixon and I had a great first date, but since then, we met only a couple times. And only to get coffee."

Coffee, eh?

"Nixon's wonderful," she says, "but I haven't felt this way about a man in a very long time. Sean's smart and funny and sexy as hell."

And my fiancé.

She leans close. "We haven't done anything *intimate* yet, but I'm ready. I bought all new underwear."

I rub my face with my hands. *How did this happen?* "Okay, Sara, let's talk about this. Remember what I said about taking things slow."

"I don't want to take things slow. I'm a thirty-year-old divorcee. Time is *not* on my side.

"I don't want to see you disappointed."

"You're sweet to worry, but there's no need. Something tells me he feels the same."

He does? I gaze in Sean's direction.

"That's all I came to say." She slides her purse strap onto her shoulder. "Wish me luck with Sean."

Sean steps our way, pinching the ring between his thumb and index finger and holding it high in the air. "Got it. Cleaned off a smudge of something. Look at it shine now."

"Sean?" Sara stands. "What are you doing here?"

"Oh, hi, Sara."

She opens her arms to greet him, jutting out her chin, hoping for a kiss.

Sean stiffens and moves toward Sara's cheek, giving her a quick peck.

Gag.

"I'm surprised to see you here." Her eyes dart between Sean and me. "I didn't realize you two were so chummy."

"Us?" I back away from Sean. "No, we aren't chummy. Not at all. Not in the least."

"Are you okay, Bree? Your neck is really red."

Where is my cream? Where?

"So, Sean, why are you here?"

"I . . . uh . . . well, I've just come by—"

"Sean?" Her eyes widen and her mouth drops open like a nine-year-old watching a magician saw his assistant in half. "Is that an engagement ring?"

thirty-two

"Sounds like you're walking through a tunnel."

"No," I tell Andrew. "I'm holding the phone away from my face. I don't want to mess up my makeup." I hop onto the curb after crossing the street. The tip of my pink-polished toenail catches my eye. "Damn. I should've stopped for a pedicure."

"It's radio."

"Exactly."

"You aren't making sense. Good thing your astrology reading is clear. The stars are on your side today. You're plotted for success."

His reasoning is fishy, but still, I'll take all the luck I can get. "Sounds good."

"What's today's topic?" he asks.

"Must-haves."

"I love that one."

"Jo does, too."

"She listening in?"

"Yeah, and you have to call in if no one else does."

"I will, but you'll get lots of calls. Don't worry."

"Thanks, Andrew. So much rides on my interview with Lucy. This could push me over the edge and into the pool of best-sellers." I wipe a bit of sweat from behind my neck. "I just hope I don't screw up or say something stupid."

"Relax. You'll be fine."

"Okay, I'm here. I'll see you later."

"Good luck."

"Who needs luck? The stars are aligned."

"Ha. Take care of you."

"Take care of you."

We hang up and I walk inside the glass-walled two-story foyer of the KMRQ radio station, clenching my stomach tightly, hoping to still the trembling in my thighs.

Randi stands between the coffee table and an L-shaped leather couch, wiggling her stiletto heel into the rug. Her cell phone is pressed against her ear.

I smile at the receptionist on the other side of the room and gesture that I'm waiting for Randi.

I'm glad my publicist is on the phone. It gives me a few more minutes to settle my nerves. Take in the moment. Remind myself of the importance of the interview, think of Jo's house and ignore the nagging thoughts rattling around in my brain about lying to Sara. And everyone in America, for that matter.

Thank God for Sean's quick thinking. He made up a story about it being his mother's ring and he had a loose diamond secured at the jeweler's nearby, then stopped in my office afterward to say hello.

Sara seemed disappointed, but honestly how could she think Sean bought her a ring so soon? Sean tucked the ring in his pocket before she could ask any more questions and, as luck would have it, his office called and he zipped off to San Francisco for a deposition with a client who had just arrived back in the country.

Once again, he's gone for a few days.

We canceled our rendezvous at La Valencia.

She clicks off her phone and walks toward me. "Nervous?"

"Yes."

"You should be. We're walking." She signals toward the doors at the far end of the hall. "I cannot stress enough the importance of this interview. Lucy Hanover is syndicated in all the major markets. You think Candace's reach is big, ha! Candace is the middle child in hand-me-down underwear compared to Lucy. We should have a good number of listener layovers, as you're slotted after the Gossip Guru."

We reach the end of a long hallway and are greeted by the man standing at the threshold of a control room. "Hey, I'm Trevor. Come in," He plops in a chair at the helm of a digital audio workstation with several monitors and a dizzying number of switches and buttons under his command. "They're just about done."

Lucy swivels her chair back and forth inside a glass-walled studio behind several laptops decorating her desk along with a fax machine, a printer, a framed photo of her shaking hands with Barbara Walters, several half-filled Fiji water bottles, and a microphone, suspended from a robotic arm, resting a millimeter from her lips. The earphones covering her ears look like English muffins. An ON AIR sign is illuminated above the glass partition.

We watch for a few minutes until they remove their earphones and the ON AIR sign switches off.

"Good, you made it," Lucy says, joining us in the control room.

"Sixty seconds," Trevor says.

"That's our cue," says Lucy. "Let's get started."

"Mention the book," Randi says. "A lot."

Lucy settles in her chair.

I sit across from her in the still-warm seat.

"Ready?" She slides on her earphones.

"Yes." I clamp mine on my head.

"Ten seconds." Trevor's voice echoes through my earphones.

Lucy nods in his direction and casts her gaze at a matching ON AIR sign on our side of the glass wall.

It lights up.

So do my nerves.

"Welcome back, everyone. Hope you enjoyed that rousing hour with the Gossip Guru. This hour we're joined by Bree Caxton, a Love Guru, and author of the highly anticipated debut, *Can I See You Again?* Welcome, Bree. Thanks for joining us."

"Thank you," my voice squeaks. "Thank you." I say again, with more confidence. "I'm happy to be here."

"So, as I mentioned, you're the author of the soon-to-be-released self-help book *Can I See You Again?* Owner and operator of Bree Caxton and Associates, the successful matchmaking service in San Diego County. And more adorable than a baby chick on Easter morning."

"Thank you."

"And you're here to assist the single men and women listening with their love life. So, what's the deal? What are you going to enlighten us with today?"

"Well, lots of my colleagues and fellow authors have discussed what to look for in a mate, where to meet people, what to wear on a date, when and when not to have sex, how to break down a wall. But that stuff is boring."

"Okay, then what new information are you bringing to the table today?"

"You."

"Me?" Lucy asks, pointing at herself.

"Well, no, not *you* exactly. Today I want to discuss what 'you' must have in a relationship."

"Must have?"

"Yes, traits that matter most to us, inherently. Habits or characteristics that a man or woman must possess for a mutually satisfying long-term relationship. These particular attributes, or lack thereof, are deal breakers."

"All right, listeners, let's talk about you. Call in and rattle off a must-have. Well, look at this, the phone lines are on fire. We've got twelve calls already. You're quite popular, Miss Bree. Keep calling, people. Bree is here to help." She presses the first blinking light on the workstation. "You're our first caller, give me something that in your heart and mind truly matters, a must-have."

"Nonsmoker," says a woman with a dog barking in the background. "I could never find myself close to someone who smells like an ashtray."

"Oh please, no one smokes anymore. Next." She pushes line two. "You're on the air."

"Christian values," says another woman.

"Gotta love cats and clowns," says a soft-spoken man on line three.

"You're gonna be single awhile." Lucy pushes line four.

"Wants kids," says a young woman with a bitter tone.

"Doesn't want kids," a young man hollers in the background.

"Uh-oh." Lucy clicks off the line.

"Yes, good. Well, not so good for the last guy. But these are all great examples of what I mean. Dig deep and discover what truly matters in your life. What you must have."

"Caller, you're on the air."

"Must like to act out the *Star Wars* movies. Not just the prequels," says a man with an unfortunate nasal tone.

"Ever had a girlfriend?" Lucy says, hanging up before the poor guy has a chance to respond. "Thanks for your calls, folks. Keep them coming. We'll be back in a few with more from Bree Caxton, the Love Guru."

She slides her earphones onto her shoulders. "Good stuff, Bree."

Trevor's voice echoes in the studio. "Randi wants Bree to mention the book."

After a minute, Trevor points in her direction and counts down from five on his fingers.

"And, we're back," Lucy says. "We're joined today by the lovely Bree Caxton, author of *Can I See You Again?* We've uploaded links to Amazon and Barnes and Noble on my website. Click it and buy it. This girl knows her beeswax. Okay, we're discussing what Bree calls the must-haves of a relationship. So, tell me, Miss Love Guru, from what I've gathered, without these must-haves, the relationship is doomed."

"For the most part, yes. Even the most perfect relationship ebbs and flows. And these values will ease the strain of the more challenging times."

"Let's pose a few scenarios. What if faithfulness is a must-have, it's important to me and my guy has cheated in the past, not on me, but in previous relationships."

"Walk away. A cheater doesn't change his spots."

"Okay, what if I don't drink, but my girlfriend does?"

"If no drinking is a must-have, then walk away because eventually the sheen wears off. If there's a deal breaker masked by newness and lust, it won't work once the relationship has dulled."

"So you're saying we fall into a relationship with someone without taking into consideration these must-haves."

"Exactly. And once the relationship grows to the point of T-shirts rather than lingerie, 'Honey, the Thai food didn't agree with me,' and socks scattered on the floor—"

"Your naked man props one foot on the counter and clips his toenails before bed without rinsing the sink clean."

"Personal experience?"

"Daily." She laughs.

"Well, if your must-haves aren't in place, if those qualities that run deeper than the surface aren't established, then it won't last. Simple as that."

"I'm curious, why do you think most clients seek you out?"

"They're tired of settling."

"For?"

"For nothing special. My clients are tired of either a string of meaningless relationships or a long-term relationship with themselves. They're seeking something wonderful." I glance at my scar. "I'm reminded every day that life is short. There's no reason to settle. That's what I hope to do. I hope to provide a bit of wonderful."

I answer a few more questions, enjoying the interview and the callers. Time passes quickly and I'm surprised to hear Lucy say we're through.

"I've learned quite a bit in this last hour. I'm certain our readers have too. Stay away from the naked toenail clippers of the world, people. Let's take a look at your book sales from our hour together."

I lean forward, trying to catch a glimpse of her screen.

"Damn, girl. Looks as if you've jammed the sites."

"Seriously?"

She nods. "All right, listeners, grab a copy of Bree's book before they're all gone. Literally. *Can I See You Again?* is a definite must-have. Thanks for joining us, Bree."

"My pleasure, thank you."

"Weather and news are up next." Lucy signals off and says to me, "Enjoy the spoils of a Lucy Hanover bump."

Randi clicks off her phone. "Well, that does it."

"Does what?"

"Congratulations, doll face. I just got word from my numbers guy. With these latest sales projections, and compared to those you're competing with on release day, no doubt about it, you'll make the list."

"I will?" A rush of excitement seeps through my body.

"You will."

"Oh, Randi, this is amazing. Thank you so much." *Wait until I tell Jo. We will celebrate with Champagne and dance around the house. Her house.*

"A pleasure. I told you I was a sure thing. So, should I mail or hand-deliver your bonus check?" she says with a wink.

I'm dialing Jo seconds after Randi finishes her sentence.

"Hello, Bree. Martin and I heard you on the radio. You sounded wonderful."

"We did it."

"Did what?"

"Secured a spot on the list. I'll get the check, Jo. I can save your house."

thirty-three

"I don't understand why you have to go." Sean lies on the bed beside my half-filled suitcase, pillowing his head with folded arms, having just flown in from San Francisco a couple of hours ago.

"I already told you. I promised Nixon weeks ago." I toss in an extra pair of jeans and an off-the-shoulder black sweatshirt for the ride home. "He posed as my guy for the paper and now I'm posing as his girl for the wedding. We made a deal."

"But you're *my* girl." He sits up, grabs my belt loop, and pulls me between his legs.

"I know." I pat his shoulder before pulling away. Aside from the few minutes at my office last week I haven't worn the ring since he proposed. "Just a couple interviews left."

"Then I can shout to the world we're engaged?"

"Once this whole thing has blown over, you can skywrite it above the city if you want."

"I might just do that. What time are you coming back?"

"Not sure." *Should I bring my bathing suit?* I wish Andrew were here to help me pack. He's great at this sort of thing, planning and picking out outfits. But he's probably too busy picking out his desk, discussing vacation days and sick time. His chipper smile was plastered across his face after returning from "the doctor" the other day, as big as I've seen it in some-time. And I hate it. Sure, I should be happy for him, especially if he's found another opportunity that makes him happy. But I'm sad for me. Mostly sad that he hasn't shared his good fortune with me. I thought we were tight. Seems all my lying has rubbed off on him.

"Don't let him keep you too late. Tomorrow is *our* night. Finally. With your busy schedule and my trips to Denver and San Francisco, I tell you, I'm about to explode. I can't believe it's taken us this much time to reconnect."

"You've been a patient boy. Don't worry, I'm certain the wait will be worth the pain." I open the drawer and fish for my black bikini and see Sean's note.

L'Straut Jewelers . . . ask Bree.

My mind detours to the first time I learned of Sean's note habit, right after we met at the barbecue. He got my work address from our friend, and starting with the following Monday, Sean had a florist deliver me a white rose, every afternoon, for two weeks. Each flower had a note card with an individual letter written on it. No name. Just a single letter. Alone, they made no sense. An *E* one day, an *R* the next, a question mark and a comma. But when the final rose came, I pieced the puzzle together—*Dinner, Friday?*

He called me minutes after the final rose arrived.

As I stare at the hundredth reminder I've seen since then, I'm thankful I didn't rip *this* Post-it into shreds. "I never told you, but I found your note."

"What note?"

"This one." I set it in his palm. "I found it behind the dresser."

"Oh?" He crumples up the paper.

Did he—?

He pitches it into the trash can.

Oh, my, God. I can hardly utter the words. "What . . . why . . . why did you do that?" I dig the Post-it out of the can and try to smooth out the wrinkles.

"What's the big deal? It's just a note."

"*Just* a note?"

"Yeah. Why are you freaking out?"

"I can't believe you'd throw this away. Don't you want to save the memento? Show our grandkids?"

"No."

Who is this monster?

"Why is a reminder about a battery so important?"

My eyes meet his. "A battery?"

"Yeah. My watch kept running slow. I meant to ask you to drop it off on your way to work but ended up taking care of it myself." He rubs clear a smudge on the face of his TAG Heuer.

"This isn't a proposal reminder?"

"A proposal reminder? Hardly," he says with a laugh, wrapping his arm around me.

"This isn't funny." I step out of his grasp.

"I'm sorry. I'm not teasing you." He pulls me close again and rubs his hands up along my arms. "It's sweet that you kept the note."

"When did you decide to propose?"

"I don't know . . . I suppose it was that morning I read about you and Nick. You looked happy in the photo. It scared me. I knew I had to have you back. I'm sure you felt the same when you saw pictures of Sara and me. But you fooled me. I had no idea you were pretending with Nick . . . Nixon . . . whatever his name is."

"So, it was a spur-of-the-moment decision."

"Yeah, you could say that."

No staying up all night, highlighting our times together, playing out proposal scenarios in his head. No being sick with worry I might say no. No heartfelt *she's the one* moment?

"And you only asked me because you thought someone else showed interest?"

"Yes. No. Don't make it sound like that. The situation brought me clarity, in a good way. I will never take you for granted again, soon-to-be Mrs. Bree Thomas. We have a lifetime of memories ahead, and I don't need a note to remind me how much I love you. Okay?"

"Okay." I stare at the wrinkled paper in my hand. He makes a good point. He asked me because he loves me. What does it matter the catalyst? So what if this Post-it isn't a proposal? I never liked these notes anyway.

thirty-four

"How can you not like weddings?" I ask Nixon, standing beside his charcoal gray Ford F-250 truck.

"They're a waste of money. Why obligate my friends to buy me a toaster?" He heaves my bag into the truck bed. "Jesus, it's just for one night, you know."

I hand him a second bag. "Maybe your friends want to buy you a toaster."

"How many toasters does one man need?"

The tension that blanketed over us the last time we were together has lifted. "Well, I'm sure your cousin is very excited."

My phone rings. *Hee-haw . . . hee-haw.*

Damn. I keep forgetting to change that.

"Excuse me, one sec." I step aside and answer Sean's call. "Hey."

"You on the road?"

"Just about." I comb my fingers through my ponytail. "What's up?"

"I'm gonna swing back by your place and grab the ring."

"Sure. It's in the drawer of my nightstand. Why?"

"When I cleaned off that spot the other day, I thought I noticed a loose stone. I didn't want you to worry if you came home and found your ring missing."

"Okay, thanks."

"Of course, I could've left you a note." He laughs. "Too soon?"

"Too soon."

Ding-ding.

"Hey, my other line is ringing. I better go."

"All right, I'll talk to you tomorrow."

I click over to Candace's call. "Hello."

"So glad I caught you. Scotty's at your office for a photo, but you aren't there."

"Change of plans." *On purpose.* "Nick picked me up at my house." Nixon and I high-five.

"Bree, this is becoming quite suspicious."

Shoot. She's getting antsy. How much longer can I fend off her need for a photo op? "Sorry, Candace, I don't know what you mean."

"Not only is Nick incredibly evasive, but we've yet to find a urologist matching his description in any of the physician databases, nor the Tough Mudder race results. Readers are questioning who Nick really is. They're upset, as am I, that we aren't getting answers."

I feel bad she's under pressure.

"Scotty can come to you."

I don't feel *that* bad. "What . . . did you . . . say? Dang, we've got crummy reception. I'm . . . losing . . . you . . ." I hang up.

"You do realize you'll rot in hell for all these lies?" Nixon teases.

"Someone's gotta keep you company."

"I'm a saint. Just look at all I've done for you lately."

"Yes, well, I'd like to think it's been less than awful posing as my boyfriend."

"It's tough, but I'm getting through."

"Ha. I'm the best fake girlfriend you've ever had."

"Yeah? Let's see how well you convince my family we're in love." He shuts the tailgate. "Let's roll."

Road construction and flashing pylons close the on-ramp to I-5 north, diverting us, along with a train of other vehicles, through a maze of side streets.

"I swear, they're always working on these roads."

"Job security," Nixon says, turning right. "There's an auxiliary cord in this console. Put some music on?"

"Yeah, sure." I plug in my phone and select my light rock Pandora station. Maroon 5's "Payphone" ballad reverberates through his speakers.

"Something else?" he says.

"What's wrong with this song?"

"Nothing, if the singer is *supposed* to sound like a drowning cat."

Jo said something similar once. They're both right. "Fine, Mr. Picky Pants, what music do you like?"

"Anything but this."

I search for a classic rock radio station and select the Red Hot Chili Peppers' "Californication." "Better?"

"Better."

We approach a stop sign and wait in the turning lane behind several cars.

I cast my eyes across the street toward a couple of young girls. They bounce and titter while coloring rainbows with sidewalk chalk underneath a tall pecan tree that shades the pathway. There's a gash in the tree's lower trunk, a foot-long deep slit that's healed but not forgotten.

It's as if a boulder drops onto my chest.

Is this . . . ?

I study the bordering houses and confirm what I feared. *Oh, God.* We came the roundabout way; I didn't realize we were in this neighborhood. The same neighborhood where fifteen years ago fire truck sirens blared and ambulance lights flashed, and fuel pooled at the curb before snaking down the street into the gutters. Police officers asked questions and told people to stand back. All the while, I sat numb, picking away at the tree's wound.

At once, the car's air is too thick. The sounds of the street too piercing. A decade and a half has passed and yet the pain is as raw as if the mangled steel of Dad's Jeep just now slices my forearm.

"Um . . . please . . . can you . . ." My voice is barely above a whisper.

"What's wrong, Bree?" Nixon shifts his gaze between me and the oncoming traffic, inching forward into the middle of the crossing streets, waiting to turn left.

I close my eyes and grasp the console. Digging my nails deep into the leather, I ready myself for the crunch of metal, the seat belt's burn as it cuts into my chest, Mom's screams.

I ready myself for the dizziness, the spins, Jo's cries as she falls to her knees in the hospital lobby, and the silence in the evenings, all the years later, when she and I sat alone in the big old house.

Nixon places his hand over mine.

We pass through the street unscathed and he pulls over. "You all right?"

Nothing happened, Bree. Nothing more than anxiety and paranoia taking control. "Yeah, sorry."

"Don't be sorry." He slips he hand away and pauses before asking, "Was that . . . *the* intersection?"

I nod, staring out the window.

"Anything I can do?"

"No, thanks. Let's keep going. I'm okay." It isn't until several blocks later that my stiffened back relaxes and I can inhale a couple of breaths, release my grip on the console.

My anxiety settles into embarrassment a few miles later. *What must Nixon think of me?* I claim to be this focused, assiduous businesswoman, and yet I shudder like a beaten dog at the sight of asphalt, an old tree, and a stoplight. Not to mention, I bullied him into joining my masquerade. Some noble, self-sufficient, forward-thinking woman I am. Allowing my present and future to hinge on my past.

After clearing the Southern California gridlock, we climb through the low mountains toward the paver-lined driveway of his parents' Spanish-style hillside home. The moment the beige stucco and terra-cotta roof comes into view, the skin on the nape of my neck prickles. Suddenly this doesn't seem like a good idea.

"Let's go in first," he says, "I'll grab our suitcases later. I need a forklift for yours, anyway."

"Wait." I grab him by the arm. "What's our story?"

"We've been over this."

"Humor me."

"We're casually dating. We met at your office. You like Maroon 5 and I'm willing to look past it."

"Be serious. I'm about to meet your parents." I check my reflection in the car's side mirror. *Damn, why didn't I do something with my bangs?* "Tell me more stuff about you, little nuggets to throw out in conversation."

"Like what?"

"Do you have any tattoos? Ever been in a bar fight? What's your favorite movie?"

"No. Twice. *Caddyshack*."

"You've been in two bar fights?"

He points to a hairline scar on the side of his right hand.

"Did you win?"

"Knocked him out cold."

I pinch my lips together. *Hmmm . . . isn't that sexy as hell.* Not that it matters here nor there . . . I'm just taking note.

"C'mon, you'll be fine. Let's go."

We follow the curvy sidewalk, lined with green grass. Rose-bushes decorate the property edge overlooking the valley and city. We near the front door and my neck flames with heat, but I recite positive thoughts in my head. *For Jo, for the book, for the house.*

"You should've worn a turtleneck."

"I know." I reach to scratch my skin, but Nixon grabs my hand and squeezes it tight.

"There's nothing to worry about. We've been at this for weeks now. Candace and Randi don't suspect a thing. No one else will, either."

"Okay, you're right. We're masters at deception. Funny thing is, it's been fairly easy pretending to be in love." *Wait . . . what did I just say?*

"What did you just say?"

Before I answer, Mrs. Voss swings open the front door wearing a *Last time I cooked, only three people got sick* apron. *"¡Mi chico guapo!"*

"Hi, Mom."

She kisses each of his cheeks, then wraps her arms around Nixon's broad shoulders and squeezes tight enough to leave handprints in his shirt. She turns toward me and clasps my hands with both of her own. "Welcome, Bree."

"Thank you. It's nice to meet you, Mrs. Voss."

"Call me Mom or Mama. When you're in my home, you're part of my family."

"Thank you . . . Mama." I haven't called someone that for fifteen years. It feels nice. *Really nice.* My scar tingles.

"Let me have a good look at you." She fans my arms wide and inspects me from head to toe. "Tsk-tsk-tsk."

What's wrong?

She says to Nixon, "*Tales caderas estrechas.*"

"*Sí.*" He laughs.

This isn't funny. What the hell are they saying?

"*Ella no será capaz de bombear más de tres o cuatro bebés.*"

"It'll be okay." Nixon pats her shoulder.

"*No lo sé.*" She frowns.

Nixon chuckles and says to me, "Mom's afraid with your narrow hips you can't pump out more than three or four babies."

Oh, God.

"We'll fatten you up at dinner." Mrs. Voss hooks her arm underneath mine. "I must say, Bree, I liked you that first day we spoke. I came home and told Nixon's father, 'Now that's a woman our boy should date.'" She peeks over her shoulder to Nixon. "Grab some wine, will you?"

"Sure." He opens the coat closet and reveals a couple of stashed cases of Francis Coppola Chardonnay.

"It's Southern California," Mrs. Voss says. "We don't need coats, but we do need wine."

"Absolutely!"

We head into the open-layout kitchen, circled with spot-free windows overlooking a lima-bean-shaped pool. A built-in stainless barbecue sits beside a rectangular teak table fenced with six wicker-backed chairs. "George, the kids are here."

The shape of Nixon's nose is mirrored in this man. It must be Nixon's dad.

George says nothing, nor does he look up from his *Los Angeles Times* crossword puzzle.

"I swear that man can't hear a damn thing I say."

"I can hear just fine." He sets the paper down and peers over his reading glasses toward Nixon. "How you doing, son?"

Nixon pats his dad on the arm. "Good to see you, Dad. This is Bree."

"Bree." He extends his hand. "It's a pleasure."

"Thank you. It's nice to meet you, as well."

"What's with the walk down memory lane?" Nixon points at an opened box of family pictures on the table.

"Your father thinks we had a white Honda. Bet me twenty bucks."

"He's wrong?"

"Of course he is. Thirty-seven years together and you'd think he'd be smarter than to make a bet with me. The car was as blue as the sky. Somewhere in that pile is a picture to prove it."

"What's a five-letter word for deep anxiety?" Nixon's father asks with his pencil hovered over his puzzle.

"Dread?" Mrs. Voss answers.

"Starts with the letter *A*."

"Angst?" I interject.

He smiles at me. "That fits."

I lean close for him to pat me on the head.

Nixon pulls out a photo from the stack and hands it to me. "Check me out." A sixteen- or seventeen-year-old version of Nixon is decked out in a black tux with polished shoes. He stands beside a curly-haired girl dressed in an off-shoulder floor-length chiffon gown. A pink carnation corsage is strapped to her wrist.

"Prom?" I ask.

"Yep."

"Here we go." Mrs. Voss hands Nixon and me a glass of wine. "Cheers to love."

"Cheers." We sip.

"Let's sit."

Nixon slides the chair out beside his mom, but she shakes her head. "No. No. That's for Bree. You sit across. Get the almonds from the pantry, too." She pats the seat and motions for me to join her.

"Thanks, Mrs. Voss . . . er, Mama."

We sift through the mound of pictures: Christmas mornings with bows taped in Nixon's toddler bed-head hair, various family birthdays, track and swim meets, he and a group of friends cheering at a Padres baseball game. We chuckle at a shot of Nixon dressed in his high school graduation cap and gown and muse on a tender photo of Nixon cradling his tiny newborn nephew at the hospital.

Tears line the lower lids of Mrs. Voss's eyes as she nudges her shoulder with my own. "I am blessed with a beautiful family."

"Yes, you are." I muster a softhearted smile, but shame strangles my heart. *What the hell am I doing? Chumming it up with Mrs. Voss. Calling her Mama. Pretending this moment is real.* This is wrong. So wrong. Nixon's family is lovely. Lovely. And I'm playing them for fools.

"What's a four-letter word for contemptible one?" George asks.

B-r-e-e.

"Liar," Nixon says.

Same difference.

Nixon's dad glances at Mrs. Voss, who stepped toward the refrigerator for more wine. He slides a picture from the pile and scratches behind his ear.

I peek at the photo. Mrs. Voss dangles keys in front of a Honda. A blue Honda.

"Hmm," he grunts.

I press my lips together, swallowing my laugh as he hides the picture underneath an artificial plant on the nearby windowsill. He winks at me, then says, "Need any help, Regina?"

"No, no. I'm fine. Thanks, dear."

"What time is the wedding?" Nixon asks.

"Sunset. At the Vista Inn on Nineteenth Avenue. Same place we held your dad's retirement party." She glances at her watch. "Oh, my. I better go beautify myself. At my age it's a process. Now you two get yourself settled. There are snacks in the fridge and clean towels in the bathroom closet. And Nixon, don't let your dad talk you into fixing the swamp cooler. I have a repairman coming Tuesday."

Nixon steps toward his dad as Mrs. Voss pulls me aside. "You let me know if you need anything."

"I will, thank you."

"He likes you."

"Sorry?"

"My boy is in love. I can see it in his eyes."

What? He . . . uh . . . what?

She disappears down the hall and calls out, "Stay off the roof, boys."

"Quick look?" his dad says with a mischievous grin.

"Sure. Let me show Bree the room first."

We grab our bags and I follow Nixon into the guest bedroom.

My boy is in love. She can't be serious. Can she?

"Here you go," he says.

The room is spacious, bright, and poolside, with a similar view as the kitchen. A puffy leather recliner sits in the corner beside an end table topped with hardbound copies of *Great Expectations* and *Pride and Prejudice*. Two books I promised myself to read. With CliffsNotes. At the far side of the room is a sprawling bathroom with an oval soaking tub, a vessel sink, and a stand-alone glass-walled shower.

"I'm through there." He points at a door on the opposite of the bathroom leading to an adjoining bedroom. "Why are you staring at me like that?"

Is it true? Is there something in his eyes? "Uh . . . nothing, sorry. This is a gorgeous room. I feel like a queen."

"Good." He laughs. "See you in a bit."

Half an hour later, I step from the shower wrapped in a towel. I hear voices in the kitchen and I think about how the Vosses have welcomed me into their home, the comfort and ease of sitting around the family table, laughing, teasing, and sharing intimate moments from their past. I've thought about what Mrs. Voss said and she's sweet, but surely mistaken. She's overzealous for grandchildren and would likely see promise if Nixon brought a blow-up doll. Besides, Nixon made it clear, *these past couple weeks have all been for show.*

Prickly thoughts of Sara enter my mind. Nixon and his family are great. Really great. *How could she let him go?*

Rubbing clear the fogged mirror, I catch sight of my scar. I know this was Nixon's idea, but my parents would be disappointed in me, toying with this family's emotions for my own benefit. And what about Nixon? He's stood beside me these past few weeks and though he hasn't asked, I haven't told him about Sean. Doesn't he at least deserve the truth? I hear him meandering about in his room. No time like the present.

"Come in." Nixon, dressed in dark gray slacks and a soft-blue shirt, stands by the window tying the knot of his silk tie. *Handsome.*

"Everything okay?"

It takes a moment to find my voice before I say, "We can't do this."

"Do what?"

"Hoodwink your family." I repeat the word Mr. Voss spelled on his puzzle earlier. "You have such a nice family."

"I do."

"A beautiful family."

"They are. Relax, now. It's only for one night. We'll be gone in the morning. You're just a prop, remember?"

I nod, slightly offended by his apathetic attitude. I did buy a new dress, after all. And my Christian Louboutin tan leather pumps did not pay for themselves. But I'm quickly reminded of Sean and what I came to say. "Nixon, there's something else I need to share with you."

Mrs. Voss knocks on the door. "Nixon?"

"One sec, Mom."

"Your father's on the roof."

"I'll be—"

She raps the door again. "He'll fall off and break his head. Or worse, foul up the repair even more. I need you this instant."

"She'll kick down the door if I don't let her in."

"You better go."

"We'll talk later, okay?"

"Yeah, sure."

He starts to leave, but turns and says, "Are you wearing that to the wedding?"

I glance at my towel. "Too casual?"

"Actually, I like it."

And with that he's gone, leaving me alone with a damn little flutter.

∽

Twenty minutes later, after I'm zipped snug in my dress and my hair is wrapped in a loosely braided side bun with a few wispy tendrils framing my face, I dab my lips with pale-pink lip gloss and head out the door.

Nixon stands in the living room, fiddling with his cuff links. He turns toward me and smiles. "You look amazing."

"Thank you. So do you."

"No, I mean *amazing*. The bride's gonna be pissed. We'll have to hide you in the back or something."

"Oh, stop," I halfheartedly protest. "Or compliment me all the way to the church. Whatever floats your boat."

He laughs. "Let's go."

Half past the hour, we arrive at the Vista Inn, a Mission Revival–style historic hotel in downtown Encinitas.

"This is beautiful," I say as we stroll under the thick arched entryway and into the courtyard. We're surrounded by white-plastered walls veined with red-flowering vines, heavy concrete tiered fountains, and the smiles of family and friends.

Nixon says hello, shakes hands, and introduces me to other guests before we settle into our seats in the second row behind the altar.

The ceremony is tender. The bride glows. And to my body-language-heart's content, the groom's shoulders are relaxed and his focus never wavers as she walks down the aisle. *Good sign.*

Before long, the newly married couple seals their union with a kiss and walks the aisle, whispering and giggling to one another as if no one else exists. *Another good sign.*

Wiping a tiny tear away, I say to Nixon, "See now, how can you not like weddings?"

We make our way to the reception held in an adjacent

banquet hall. The festive music plays loud, matching the vibrance of the room decorated with orange, red, and yellow flowers, white tablecloths, and dome lights.

We find our table with the personalized placement cards, cream linen card stock wrapped with a chili pepper attached to a raffia bow.

I smile at the recollection of my conversation with Mrs. Voss a couple of weeks ago. "It's insensitive to have a reception without assigned seats, leaving people to just mill around, don't you think?"

Nixon and I claim our seats. We chat with the six other guests at our table during dinner, clink Patrón-filled shot glasses for the wedding toasts, and eat our heart-shaped churros dipped in chocolate for dessert. It's a perfect evening.

Nixon's pulled aside to chat with a family friend.

I take a moment to study the room.

A cluster of people fill the dance floor, others gather around tables laughing and chatting, and a group of groomsmen are shouldered at the bar. The party is in full swing. And not a single person without a smile.

My thoughts drift to my own wedding. Sean and I haven't talked about a venue, or a date—haven't talked about much of anything, really—but I'm certain once the interviews are over, we'll start planning. Or at least I will. Sean, like most men, won't get too involved in the preparations. He'll leave the decision making to me, asking only when and where he's supposed to show up, letting me pick exactly what I want. *What do I want?*

"Drink?" Nixon's voice startles me.

"Yes, I'd love one."

Before we have the chance to grab a cocktail, Mrs. Voss with her nearly drained margarita approaches us. "You two need to get in line. They're about to form the path of love."

"What's a path of love?" I ask.

"Hurry, they're doing it now." She points across the room to a dozen or so men standing in a long row opposite the same number of women. Each pair raises their joined hands, canopying a walkway like a roof. Lots of couples form a line to enter the human tunnel. The bride and groom sit at the exit, sipping Champagne and clapping to the music. A basket of rose petals rests near their feet.

Mrs. Voss swallows the last of her drink. She sets the glass on a nearby table and motions toward the group. "All lovers need to get in line and walk through the path of love. *¡Vamos!*"

"No, that's okay. We'll just watch. We—"

"*¡Vamos!*"

I stumble half a step back.

Nixon snickers.

"It's bad luck for the bride if you don't." She pushes us toward the line. "Do you want to doom the marriage?"

"God, no."

"*¡Rápido!*" she insists.

"Guess we better do this." I slide my hand into Nixon's, realizing he didn't offer.

We follow Mrs. Voss as she wiggles her way into the middle of the chain, joining hands with Nixon's dad.

The music is bouncy and the tequila I had with dinner relaxes me. I find myself swaying along as we inch forward in the line, waiting our turn.

We watch others before us dance through the path of love, twirling and twisting toward the newlyweds. Once there, they sprinkle a handful of rose petals at the bride and groom's feet.

"If I didn't know better, I'd say you might actually be enjoying this," Nixon says.

"You think so, huh?" But Nixon's right. I *am* enjoying this.

"Ready?" he asks. The last couple in front of us exits the tunnel.

"Try to keep up."

Nixon and I groove under the canopy of arms, our hands still linked together. We sway and sashay down the aisle, smiling, laughing, waving to the cheering crowd. The energy in the room is contagious. The affection of friends and family glides through the air. The body language is obvious. Pure love and fun.

And, I have to admit, I'm impressed with Nixon's swagger. His hips slink and jut with the rhythm. His shoulders rise and dip, matching the beat. He's got moves. They say a man's dancing skills are a direct reflection of his bedroom—*Jesus, Bree. Focus.*

We're halfway through the line when Mr. and Mrs. Voss's arms drop to our waist. They clutch us tight.

What the . . . ?

Breaking the tunnel, the remainder of the group forms a circle. The Vosses claim a spot and they all swirl around us like a whirlpool. We've no escape. Everyone cheers. *"¡Besar, besar, besar!"*

Besar?

I glance at Nixon. There's an interesting look in his eye.

This isn't some sort of cult ritual, is it? I don't have to drink potion from a skull or pierce my eyebrows, right?

The group continues to spiral around us like a bunch of sharks stalking two defenseless seals. They chant. *"Besar, besar, besar."*

Okay, first off, everyone needs to settle down. And second, what the hell does *besar* even mean? *Damn, I knew I should've taken a foreign language in college.*

"It's bad luck for the bride if you don't," a woman shouts.

Yeah, I've been told that already.

"You don't want the marriage to fail, do you?"

Heard that already, too. I'm beginning to think this whole path of love is some sort of scam. A cheap ploy to draw a laugh.

"*Besar*," Mrs. Voss yells with an adamant tone.

"Okay, fine. You win." I'll be the sucker. "*Besar.*"

"You sure?" Nixon asks.

"Yes. Let's get it over with."

But I'm totally *not* prepared for what Nixon does next.

He slides his fingers toward the nape of my neck. Cradling my head in his hands, he strokes my cheek with his thumb. He leans toward me; his breath hovers above my skin. His mouth finds mine. He parts my lips with his own. Nixon kisses me long, soft, and slow.

The music stops.

The crowd falls silent.

There is something about a wedding. Whether it's the amorous bride and groom, the clanking spoons sparking kisses, the smell of flowers, the flow of Champagne, the proud parents, the hunt and seek of groomsmen for bridesmaids, or the elderly couple that jitterbugs long into the night, the occasion always stirs a wistful tone within me.

It must be the promise of this day that is making me quiver as Nixon glides his hands toward my hips. The spirit of the ceremony is why my body is weakened by his touch, as he pulls me closer. It's the vows for a new love that warm my skin as Nixon breaks our kiss, then presses his forehead against mine.

We share a breath.

"Now that's what I call good luck for the bride and groom." Mrs. Voss cheers.

The crowd claps, then breaks its circle and dances to the restarted music.

Nixon and I remain still.

The music slows to one of my favorite songs, a Dire Straits ballad, "Why Worry?"

"Dance?" Nixon whispers.

"Yes."

He clasps my hand in his.

"Baby, when I get down I turn to you. You make sense of what I do . . ."

We sway, moving slow, body to body. Aware of nothing else. No one else.

I forget all about the lies. I forget about Randi, Candace, his family, Jo. I forget about my book. I forget about the 1058 form. I forget about Sean.

૭

The following morning, I sit alone on a bench swing in the Vosses' backyard. The tequila has worn off. The bride and groom are gone. The toasters packed up and hauled away. Only my guilt remains.

With my laced hands together, I pillow my aching head and recall all the lies I told Nixon's family and their friends. *Yes, Nixon and I enjoy art museums. No, we haven't seen that movie. Yes, we'd love to visit south Florida sometime. Blah-blah-blah.*

God, I'm so sick of hearing myself spew one half-truth after the other.

Not to mention, I still haven't told Nixon about Sean. What the hell do I think I'm doing? Yes, I know Nixon said these past weeks were pretend. And I know we had no choice but to march through the path of love, but when he kissed me . . . I didn't pull away.

I'm engaged to Sean. I love him. I've *loved* him. I criticized him and nearly threw everything away because of one short-lived lapse of judgment. But look at me now. Am I any better than him?

God, all I want to do is get home. Take a long shower and wash away my behavior.

Thank goodness Sean and I have our special night at La Valencia this evening. I will rush into his arms and never let him go.

Point is, I'm crawling out of my skin, dying to get my *real* life started. Enough of this make-believe.

Until then, Nixon will drive me home. We'll wrap up the interviews and go our separate ways. I'll forget about his family. I'll forget about the kiss.

"Morning." He stands beside me in gray jeans and a white T-shirt clinging to the outline of his chest from the breeze.

Forget about his body pressed against mine.

He kneels down and plucks a small yellow wildflower from the grass and hands it to me. "Thanks for posing as my date."

I twirl the flower between my fingers. "Yeah, well, it wasn't easy."

He laughs. "Thanks for soldiering through. You ready to go?"

"All set."

We hug and thank his family, saying good-bye to everyone. And though Mrs. Voss asks that I visit often, I don't expect to see the Voss family again. Still, I'm grateful they allowed me in their home and to celebrate a special moment with their family.

Forget about his family, too.

"Remember, when you break up with me, make sure they know what a good time I had."

"I will, thanks."

Nixon says nothing more about last night, about the kiss,

or my head resting on his shoulder while we danced. We're silent during the drive, as if none of it ever happened. And yet the air has changed between us.

You need to know, these past couple weeks have all been for show.

Yeah, well, I wish he weren't such an amazing actor.

We follow a different route home. No freeways, no honking horns, just quiet side streets. Though I'm eager to get to Sean, it's nice meandering our way back. We drive slowly past women digging in flower beds, dads washing cars in the driveway, kids spraying each other with the garden hose. The ease of a Saturday morning.

We're still a few streets away from my house when Nixon pulls curbside.

"Something wrong?"

"Nope." He hops out and walks around the car and opens my door.

"What's going on?"

He tosses the keys in my lap. "Drive."

"What? I . . . I can't."

"You don't know how?"

"Of course, I know *how*."

"Do you have a license?"

"Yes." I got it when I turned eighteen, even drove for a year before another driver nearly sideswiped me on the freeway and my memories overwhelmed me.

"Then drive."

"It's not that easy."

"Sure it is."

"No, it's not!" This must be what a panic attack feels like. My heart is pounding. My fingertips grow numb. "Nixon, I—"

"Hate me if you want. But don't spend the rest of your life letting the world pass you by. Literally."

"I can't drive."

"You can't? Or you won't?"

"Nixon, please."

He stands with a wide stance. Arms crossed about his chest. Any body language expert will say his posture is certain and resolute. But I think he looks like a jackass.

"You're being a real jerk, you know that?"

"I do."

As much as I hate to admit it, he's right. I do want to drive again. I don't want to depend on Uber for the rest of my life. Even Andrew pointed out time and time again that if I'm ever lucky enough to have children, how pathetic will I look strapping a car seat into the backseat of a glorified taxi?

"I'll be right beside you," he assures me.

"Fine. Fine. Fine." *Not fine.* The keys jingle within my trembling fingers as I slide into the driver's seat. Sweat drips down the nape of my neck.

"When did you drive last?"

"I was eighteen or nineteen years old."

"Well, it's like sex."

"How is driving like sex?"

"Think you'll ever forget how?"

I laugh in spite of myself, thankful for the comic relief.

"Don't be nervous, you'll be fine."

I slip the key into the ignition and start the engine.

"Step one complete. Adjust your mirrors and put on your seat belt." He fastens his.

Oh, God. I can't believe I'm doing this. With a shaky hand, I shift the truck into reverse and then, once it's clear, inch out of the spot. My palms sweat underneath my iron grip on the steering wheel. I turtle down the street.

"If you go any slower, we'll roll backward."

"Shush."

"Make a right at the light."

I steer toward the intersection, not hitting a single car or tree. *Hooray for me!*

He reaches over and lifts the blinker.

"Oh, right. Thanks."

"You're doing fine."

I drive for another mile or so, quite well, thank you very much—only two people flipped me off—and relief seeps through my body. "For the record, this is nothing like sex."

"No, not exactly."

For the next several minutes, I steer and navigate, stop and start. *Look at me, I'm driving!* Sooner than I like—I am enjoying the hell out of this—I swing in close to my curb, rubbing the tire only a little bit, and shut off the engine.

I hop out and jump up and down like a toddler standing at the gates of Disneyland. "Did you see that? I drove. Me. I can't believe it. This is totally liberating. Now I can drive Jo to her appointments and bridge club games. Hell, I can even take Martin to the dog park." *Well, maybe not so much.*

"You did good. I knew you would."

"Thanks, Nixon." I nod. "I mean, really, thanks."

"No problem." He walks me to my front door and sets down my bags.

One of Sean's sticky notes is stuck to my front door.

Love you.

I quickly tuck it into my pocket.

"Why is your porch all wet?"

"Leaky sprinkler valve, remember?"

"You should—"

"Get it fixed. Yeah, I know."

"Well, thanks for coming to the wedding," he says. "My family totally bought into it. A spot-on performance."

"Yes, yours, too. You displayed one heck of a show."

Especially with that kiss. "Your family is amazing. I had a great time."

"I did, too."

"And thanks once again for twisting my arm. I'm glad you made me drive."

"You're welcome."

It seems unnatural *not* to hug Nixon good-bye. We may not be lovers as everyone suspects, but we are friends. At least, I'd like to think so.

Nixon leans toward me and I wrap my arms around him for a long body-molding-to-body hug.

We part and he says, "One more interview and that's it."

"Then you're free of me."

"I'm counting the days."

"Yeah, whatever. You know, people might miss reading about Nick the urologist."

"Nah, in a few weeks you, along with the rest of America, will have long forgotten about me. Out of sight, out of mind. I'll be a thing of the past."

He's right. Outside of a professional relationship, our contact will be minimal. In a handful of days Nixon and I will be *history*.

Something tells me Nixon will be hard to forget.

thirty-five

"Baby." Sean greets me with a kiss at the door of our La Valencia suite later that evening. "I'm glad you're here. You look gorgeous. No, I take that back. You're glowing."

I stand before him in a strapless gray cotton maxi-dress and black flip-flops. My hair is pinned loosely in a side bun, my scar is hidden underneath my thrice-wrapped gold armlet, and I *am* glowing. Inside and out. Because my heart is full enough to explode. Not only am I happy to be here with Sean, ready to start a new chapter in the story we've created over the last four years, but because—thanks to Nixon—I've rented myself a Prius for the week and just came from Jo's house, where I showed it off.

Thrilled to find me behind the wheel, she clapped her hands and everything, said she was glad I'm no longer anchored by my fear.

Martin wasn't as impressed. When I jiggled the keys in Jo's direction, he snarled and lunged toward me, tugging at my dress until he formed a tiny hole in the hem. But the furry little pissant didn't dampen my elation. Truth is, I'm glad he wanted nothing to do with a car ride. I worried he'd piddle on the floorboard and I'd get hammered with a cleaning fee.

Jo and I hopped in the Prius. We cruised with the windows down and the radio up, singing along to Van Morrison's "Brown Eyed Girl." Sharing a mint-chocolate-chip triple-scoop sundae at Crystal Pier, we talked about driving to the Temecula wineries next weekend. We didn't talk about the house, but I can tell by the lift in her shoulders and the brightness in her eyes, she's relieved.

And that makes me happy.

"Thanks," I say to Sean with a broad smile, tossing the car keys into my purse.

"Wait . . . did you drive here?"

"Yes, isn't it great? I rented a car but I'm half thinking of buying one of those snazzy BMW X6s. Jo said she'd come along and help me choose a color."

"Whoa . . . slow down. When did you start driving?"

"Today. Nixon taught me—strong-armed me, actually—on our way home from the wedding."

"Nixon, eh?"

"He's a nice guy," I say with an edge to my voice.

"Hey now, I'm sorry. Let's not get started off on a bad foot. Tonight is about us."

"Yes, you're right."

"First things first." He slides on the engagement ring and kisses my fingertips. "Isn't that a beautiful sight? And, rest assured, the stones are secure."

"Looks like they cleaned it, too. It's so shiny."

"Yes, they did. Wine?"

"I'd love some." I step out onto the balcony, overlooking the rectangular pool, breezy palm trees, and endless Pacific Ocean. "I could get used to this view."

"I thought the same thing. Maybe this should be our new

anniversary spot?" He uncorks a bottle of Merlot and we clink glasses. "To us."

"To us."

"What do you say to dinner served here, on the balcony? I'm thinking the grilled swordfish. And the bellman said they have the best crème brûlée in all of La Jolla."

I stare at the sand, just past the pool. Spotted with fire pits, the beach reminds me of Idyllwild. "You know what? Instead of this fancy stuff, how about we grab a package of hot dogs and a six-pack of beer. We can build a fire on the beach."

Sean laughs. "Since when do you like hot dogs? Aren't they processed junk?"

"I know, but it'd be fun. Casual."

"Now I know you've gone crazy." He pours more wine. "Besides, aren't we supposed to be incognito?"

"Yeah, I guess you're right." I offer him a smile. "Maybe another time?"

"Anything you want." He kisses my shoulder, then traces down my arm with his fingertips, lacing our hands together. He wraps our arms behind his waist and pulls me close. "To hell with crème brûlée. I'll have you for dessert. And I'm hungry now." Setting my glass on the table, he kisses my neck soft and slow, then leads me toward the bed and lays me down on the comforter.

"Eww . . . gross."

"Huh?"

"No, sorry, not you." I know I shouldn't complain. This is a huge moment for us, consummating our engagement and all that. Closing the door on his confusion. But I can't relax, let alone strip off my clothes and lie naked, I mean, this comforter is likely *never* washed. "Get up."

"I'm trying to." He points at his manhood.

"Funny. Now seriously, get off the bed."

"What are you doing?"

I scramble to a stand—resisting the urge to pop in the shower for a quick rinse-off—and fold the comforter in half. Then half again. Then I take the whole damn thing off and drape it over a nearby chair.

"Better?" He laughs.

"Better."

Sean unclips the latch on his watch and rests it on the nightstand. He unbuttons his shirt and slides my arms around his smooth-skinned waist.

This is nice. This is . . . dammit. Why is the balcony door still open? What if someone outside hears us?

"It's been too long." Sean nibbles at my neck.

The sheer curtains kick up in the breeze.

Aww . . . for Pete's sake. "One sec."

"What the . . . ?"

"Sorry, I'll be right back." I slink away from him, shutting the door and curtains. I fasten the lock for good measure. How embarrassing would it be if a burglar broke in and caught sight of my bare bum. I mean, I work out and everything, but . . . why am I so nervous?

"Bree?" Sean regains my thoughts, though his tone isn't quite the same playful tenor as a moment ago. "Want to check for chips in the shower grout? Maybe the Internet connection?"

Bree, you're ruining this special moment. Knock it off! "No, sorry. I'm good." I saunter toward him and peel off his shirt. I stroke his bare chest with my fingertips, following behind with tiny kisses. He's right. It has been too long. I wander up his neck and blow softly behind his ears.

Sean moans. "God, I've missed you like this." Once again he lays me down and straddles me on the bed.

His lips find the crevices of my neck and my ears. His hand

snakes toward my hips. Without moving his mouth from mine, he gathers the skirt of my dress and inches it above my thighs.

"Sean."

"I love you, baby." He slips his fingers underneath my panties.

"Sean."

"It's okay. We'll go slow."

"Sean." I grab his wrist.

"What's wrong now?"

"We can't."

"What do you mean we can't? I'm quite certain we can."

I stare over his shoulder, embarrassed. "No . . . I can't. It's my time of the month."

His head drops onto my chest. "You're killing me."

"I'm sorry."

His sigh reminds me of a city bus coming to a stop. "It's okay." He kisses my forehead, then forces a sweet tone. "We have lots of nights to make love."

"Yes, we do. A lifetime."

He rolls off me.

Turns out neither of us is hungry. Sean finishes the bottle of wine as we watch *The Secret Life of Walter Mitty* on the suite's flat screen. Sean falls asleep before the credits roll.

I slide off my ring and set it next to his watch, then close my eyes.

Hours later I wake, finding the sun about to rise.

Sean snores peacefully. He had a long week of traveling and working late into the night. It'd be a shame to stir him.

I tiptoe from the bed, slip into a sweatshirt and jeans, then hurry along the cold sand to a secluded spot on the beach. Wrapping my sleeves over my hands, I hug my knees against my chest and listen to the waves splash onto the shore before receding out to sea. Ebb and flow. Give and take. A lot like love.

The sun peeks above the horizon and within seconds the sky is ablaze with bands of orange, red, and yellow. The swaying palm trees are silhouetted against the brilliant sky, and the ocean reflects the sun's colors as if the water is one boundless mirror. And though Tahquitz Peak is nowhere within sight, I gaze across the rolling waves toward the tumbling mountains, hoping to catch sight of the man searching for his bride.

With my pinkie, I engrave a heart shape in the sand, over and over, deeper and deeper, outlining the symbol of love.

I glance over at our suite's balcony. The curtains and door remain closed.

I wonder if Sean knows I slipped out.

I wonder if he knows I lied about my period.

thirty-six

Thirty minutes later, I climb the steps to Nixon's second-floor town house and knock on his door.

"Bree?"

I try not to notice the morning sunlight reflecting off his bare chest.

I try not to notice the smell of sleep on his skin.

I try not to notice that the top button of his jeans is undone.

"What are you doing here?"

What am I doing here? "Sorry, it's so early."

"It's fine. You want to come in?"

"No. I . . ."

"I don't bite." He steps aside.

"Right, of course not. Sure, just for a minute."

His home smells like laundry detergent. A dryer tumbles clothes in the next room.

"Want a cup of coffee?"

Before I answer, a sleek and silent white cat slinks between Nixon's feet, then dashes toward a tennis ball in the living room. He swats the toy with his paw before jumping onto the neck rest of Nixon's leather recliner.

I laugh out loud. "Who is that?"

"That's Sketch."

"He's cute."

"Don't let his sweet eyes fool you." Nixon scratches behind the cat's ears, and the cat arches his neck in thanks. "Sketch is a direct descendent of the devil."

A relative of Martin, then?

"So, how about that coffee?"

"Yes, thanks."

"Make yourself comfortable. I'll just be a second." Nixon disappears into the kitchen.

I move wide past Sketch—Martin doesn't like me and there's no telling what this evasive cat might do—into the living room flanked with two large glass windows.

On the iron coffee table sits a framed picture of Nixon's parents on their wedding day. Mrs. Voss and her baby face look too young to be married. I think about my mom and dad. Too young to die.

Beside the picture rests a pile of *Smithsonian* magazines topped with an old film-style Canon camera. I trace my fingers along the leather strap, then step toward the opposite wall lined with five or six black-and-white framed photographs of La Jolla's windswept rocks, beaches crowded with dilated umbrellas and lifeguard towers, and a simplistic yet powerful shot of a young woman's ankle as she steps from a cab onto the boardwalk, the chaotic city traffic blurred in the distance. They're bordered with the same frames as I have at my office. Funny he never mentioned it.

I examine the remaining prints, drawn to one in particular. It's a ground-level perspective of a long and rutted wood-planked pier. The end disappears into the horizon, but Nixon's zoomed in on a shattered lightbulb, dropped from a weathered metal light post and sprinkled on the floorboard. From this viewpoint, I can practically hear the glass crunch underfoot, smell the sea salt and kelp, feel the sun's warmth. It's powerful, intense, gorgeous.

Like Nixon.

"Hey." He hands me the coffee.

"I have to admit, I imagined your place to be different. It isn't cold and sterile like I thought." It's warm and sensual.

Also like Nixon.

"You were right about the expired milk, though. Hope you take your coffee black." He hands me a mug.

"You take these?" I point at the photos.

"Yeah, took this one just the other day." He motions toward the pier. "I converted my guest bathroom into a darkroom, got the stabilizer baths, tongs, and everything." He shrugs. "A dumb hobby."

"Hardly a dumb hobby, Nixon. You're really good. These are beautiful."

He reaches to straighten a frame, then lowers his arm, touching mine.

If I remain still, maybe he won't move.

There's no denying that I find myself relaxed and comforted by his composure. Charmed and absorbed by his humor, his generosity, his sincerity.

Standing this close to Nixon, I allow myself thoughts that I've sequestered the past few weeks. I think about his tall, chiseled frame mirrored against mine, palm to palm, belly to belly, thigh to thigh. I picture the want in my eyes, reflected in his own, as he lowers himself onto me.

I know what I'm thinking is wrong. What I'm *feeling* even more so. I'm engaged to another man. But there's something about Nixon's presence that cushions my vulnerability, makes sense of my wrongs.

It's ironic. For the expert I claim to be in body language, I didn't figure him out. I never pegged him to be this kind, handsome, addictive man. I pegged him as shallow and narcissistic. But I was wrong. Turns out, he's pretty great. And, if I'm truthful with myself, I miss him when he's not around.

He steps away and opens the living room shutters, welcoming in a view of the ocean. Just beyond a couple of rooftops and a two-lane road, a long stretch of smooth-sanded beach spreads into rolling waves and the same weathered, wood-planked pier from his photo.

"My God, Nixon. This view. I didn't realize you were so close to the water." I point through the window at a lady walking along the shoreline, sipping from a to-go coffee cup. "You can practically read the type of drink she ordered."

He laughs. "I don't know about that."

"I bet you spend a lot of time in the sand."

"I used to, but now one of my favorite things to do is sit on the porch and watch the surfers on Sunday mornings. The beach is usually empty at that time of day, just a handful of guys and girls who come every week to ride the waves. I hardly ever miss it."

"You don't surf?"

"Nah. After swallowing a couple lungfuls of salt water and getting tossed ashore, I hung up my board. Rough waves are too much for this old guy."

I imagine him sitting shirtless on the porch steps, sipping his coffee, feet propped on the porch railing.

"Sit?" Nixon breaks my spell and points to a cream-colored leather couch decorated with burnt orange throw pillows.

Hee . . . haw. Hee . . . haw.

"Need to answer that?"

Probably. I pause before mustering the courage to say, "I watched the sunrise this morning. I thought of you and your family and everything you've done for me and how these interviews are almost over . . ." I clench my jaw. *Say it, Bree.* "I thought about how you make me feel and . . ."

"Bree." He slides his hand onto my knee.

My thighs tighten from his touch, but I shake my head as my eyes well up with tears.

He pulls his hand away. "Look, I didn't mean to push something that—"

"No, it's not your fault. Nothing like that."

Tell him you're engaged.

"Do you remember before your cousin's wedding, I had something to tell you?"

"I didn't until now, but actually." He licks his dry lips. "If you don't mind, I'd like to say something first."

"Sure, go ahead."

Nixon folds his hands in his lap and stares at the ground.

In all the times we've spent together, I've never seen him like this. His shoulders are curved inward. His eyes are narrowed. Sweat trickles below his brow. I've never seen him nervous. Insecure.

"What is it, Nixon?"

"All right, here it goes." He smacks his hands on his knees, his confidence back. "So, you've heard me say, many times, that the last few weeks have all been for show."

That's what you wanted to say? Gee . . . great. "Yes, you've made yourself clear." *And I clearly feel like an idiot.*

Nixon catches my tense nod. "No, that's just it. I haven't made myself clear." And without pause, he grabs my hand and flips it over, just like he did during our first interview. But now, no one else is here. No observers. No cameras. No questions. Just us. Surely, in this very second, just he and I, him holding my hand, isn't *just for show.*

"Look, Bree." His fingers follow their familiar course

across my wrist, one after the other, prickling my skin. His eyes find mine. "I don't know if this is the right or the wrong thing to say, but I've got to tell you—"

Loud as a shotgun blast, the mail slot's door bangs open and the newspaper plops onto the floor.

Sketch vaults off the recliner and pounces on the *National Tribune*, clawing at the rubber band, tearing at the newspaper, shredding the pages. Tattered bits of paper scatter across the floor.

"Take it easy, Sketch." Nixon lets me go and scoops up the paper and the cat, setting Sketch by his tennis ball. "See what I mean? He's nuts. Not much left of this." Nixon frees the fragmented rubber band and the *Tribune* unfolds. The *Close-Up* article falls onto the ground.

But I don't care what the article says. I don't care what charming anecdotes Candace inscribed or what comments readers sent in. All I want to hear is Nixon's words. I want to watch his lips move. I want to hear what he started to say.

But the atmosphere between us turns toxic the minute Nixon reads the article's headline. Anger and surprise flash within his eyes. The lines between his brow deepens. His shoulders stiffen. The tenderness of a moment ago is gone.

"What's wrong? What does it say?"

"Shit, Bree." He flings the paper onto the couch. "You're engaged?"

thirty-seven

BREE CAXTON IS A FRAUD.
Shocked, America? So are we.

"They think . . . Oh, God, Andrew . . . America thinks . . ."
My throat tightens and I swallow hard, reading the headline
over and over.

Andrew pours us more Merlot, then scoots close to me on
my couch. "Bree, don't—"

"No, they're right. I deserve this. I've lied the whole time. I
lied to Jo, Randi, Candace, and my readers. I lied to Nixon, his
family, and their friends. And worse yet, I lied to my fiancé.
Just this morning I made up a story when I returned to the hotel,
said I went for a long walk. I bold-faced misled the man I'm
about to marry."

Jesus . . . I am such a piece of work.

My hands start to tremble and I can hardly focus on the
article's words. Which, honestly, might be a good thing.

Andrew squeezes my hands. "I'm sorry, honey."

Turns out our beloved matchmaker is too good to be true. Take a look at these pictures captured shortly before print time. First we have Bree hugging Nick . . . or do we say Nixon Voss?

With utter dread, I glance at the photo of Nixon and me clutching one another outside my front door. My suitcases from the wedding rest beside us.

So tell us, Bree. If you're hopelessly in love with Nixon, why are you sipping wine with Sean (yes, that Sean . . . uh-huh . . . THAT Sean) at the romantic La Valencia? And isn't that an engagement ring on your finger?

The second photo shows Sean and me standing on the balcony with our wineglasses. An inset snapshot zooms in on my shiny diamond ring.

"How'd they get these photos?"

Sources confirmed, the two are engaged.

"Sources? What sources?"

Sara, the duped client, says, "I am done with Bree Caxton. First she sets me up with a felon and I spent the evening in a jail. Jail. But the goodhearted person I am gave Bree a second chance. And what did that get me? She stormed into my workplace, demanding that I host her drunken cocktail party at my brand-new art gallery at which someone spilled red wine on my new floor and I'm yet to be compensated for."

"I didn't storm into her gallery. Or demand anything," I snap. But the jailhouse bit is true.

"And, a few weeks later, I catch her and Sean acting all chummy at Bree's office. He held a diamond ring in his hand and I mistakenly believed the ring could be for me. Ha! But the two cast it off, having the nerve to lie to my face, claiming it was his mother's ring. Playing me for a fool. I am not a fool. Then I come to find out she's not only fake-dating a man she set me up with, but she's engaged to the other man she set me up with. A man that I fell in love with. Yes, I may look ridiculous falling in love so quickly, but at least I'm not a liar. Honestly, who the hell does she think she is?"

The paper falls from my hands. "Christ, Andrew, this is bad. Unbelievably bad. I've disappointed so many people. Anyone else I can hurt? Any puppies' paws I can step on? Old men whose canes I can sweep out from underneath their feet? How did all of this happen?"

"Don't be so hard on yourself. You thought you were doing the right thing."

"I don't deserve your sympathy." I shake my head. "I *am* a fraud. Everyone knows it. How did they find out we were at La Valencia, anyway? It's like they have little moles, sneaking around in my business. I mean, no one even knew we were going to that hotel except . . . *you.* Andrew . . . my God . . . did you tell Candace?"

"No." He shakes his head, staring at his lap. "I told Scotty. I'm so sorry. We were making conversation, it just slipped out." He gasps at my laugh. "This isn't funny. I feel horrible."

"I know you do. And you should." I keep giggling. "But think about it, your lying boss who's in love with the man America thinks she's dating but actually is engaged to Sean, who America thinks is dating Sara. Jesus, what a joke."

"I'm sorry, Bree."

"I know. Thing is, I'm a bit relieved the truth is out." Panic sets in as Jo's face comes to mind. "Oh, shit. Jo. Her house. This means . . . Oh, God. I gotta go. I need to see her."

"How about I drive you?"

"No, I'm fine." Not wanting to waste another minute, I slip into flip-flops, disregarding the coffee stain on my white T-shirt and the hole in the knee of my gray sweats. "I'll see you later, Andrew. Lock up when you leave."

"Yeah, I'm right behind you. Take care of you."

"Take care of you."

I drive toward Jo's, hoping to suppress my growing worry. I fear my stupid decisions will smash the framework we've rebuilt like a wrecking ball and dissolve all possibility of saving her house. *Her house.* What is she thinking right now? Is she confused? Mad? Disappointed? *Oh, God. Will she hate me?*

Fifteen minutes later, I'm knocking on her door. "Hey." I muster an optimistic voice and a wide smile when she answers the door, trying to pretend my world isn't collapsing all around me.

She doesn't unfasten the chain lock and welcome me inside. She doesn't scoop up her barking four-legged friend and protect me from his hungry canines. All she does is say to Martin, "It's just Bree."

Just Bree. We're back to that. My fears are confirmed.

She stands there with a rigid look in her eyes as if I'm a door-to-door salesman peddling discount oil changes at Auto World.

"Is it true?" she asks.

"Is what true?" A silly question. She's obviously seen the article. But I ask anyway, buying time, uncertain how to explain.

"The article, Bree. Did you do what they claim?" Her voice is curt. But I hear a familiar quality in her speech. It's the same clipped tone as Mom's on the night of my parents' accident when she pulled me from the party and asked why I disobeyed their rules.

Tears dampen my eyes. "Yes, it's true. But please let me explain. Let me come in and I'll tell you everything." I pause. "I know it sounds stupid to say at this point, but I didn't mean for this to get so out of hand. I never intended for anyone to get hurt. But obviously, I didn't think things through."

"If that's all."

"No, Jo, please don't shut me out. Let me explain. You have to understand that I did this for us. I know it seems crazy, but everything I did and said—"

"You lied for us?"

God, it sounds so much worse when she uses that voice. "Yes, I did. All I want, all I've ever wanted, is to be your granddaughter, to have a relationship with you. I thought if I reached the bestseller list you'd be proud of me. You'd forgive me. You wouldn't . . . hate me."

"All this shows is how little you think of me. You don't respect me or you would've told me the truth. You sat at my kitchen counter and let me read these articles, week after week, and all the while they were a bunch of garbage. You say I'm special to you? You fooled me just like everyone else." She starts to close the door.

I press my hand against the wood panel, stopping her. "Jo, please."

"Caxtons don't lie. I'm disappointed in you."

It's as if she punched me in the gut. "Without a bestseller, without the escalator clause, I can't save the house." But my desperation bounces off a closed door.

She's gone.

I spend the next couple of hours wandering the beach, picking up sand dollars and wishing I could jump back in time.

It's a beautiful day: warm, cloudless, crisp air. At least God isn't mad at me.

I pass Antonio's, and staring at it from the shoreline, I think of Sean.

For four years, he's all I've known. We've spent Thanksgivings, birthdays, barbecues, and long weekends together. We've picked up one another from the mechanic's shop when our car needed new brakes or if we were loopy from a dentist visit. We've played numerous games of Scrabble and strip poker, filled a vase with shared wine corks, and shared knowing glances in a crowded room for as long as I can remember. He's been my everything.

"This is great, actually. We won't have to sneak around anymore," he said. "And you gotta admit the picture of us is good. Come to think of it, we're going to need a wedding announcement photo. Maybe we can use this one?"

I appreciated his attempt to cheer me up but still turned down his invitation for lunch. I want to be alone.

My mind stays focused on Sean. Yes, I accepted his apology and promised to wear his ring, and yet I can't help but think his actions started this mess. Would I be in this position had he not ended things?

I suppose it isn't fair to pass all the blame on him. He may have started this chain of events, but I added links. I'm the one who built the fence.

And then there's Nixon. What must he think of me? I apologized, clutching the incriminating newspaper in my hand.

He said nothing. He didn't have to. His facial expression said it all, demonstrating all but one of the universal facial expressions, everything but happiness.

Andrew texts me throughout my walk, saying things like, *This will blow over. Nothing gets remembered for very long. Ready for the wrath of tomorrow?*

No.

Before you soak in the bathtub with your hair dryer,
    remember I get your Frye combat boots.
No can do. Gonna use them to kick my own ass.
You're not a bad person. Take care of you.
Take care of you.

We click off and I drive home, stopping at my porch steps to sort through my mail.

The sprinklers kick on and I hop out of the spray in anticipation. But nothing happens.

A shiny new irrigation valve holds the water tight.

Nixon. He must've fixed it when I was at the hotel with Sean.

Yep, it's official.

I'm the worst person on Earth.

thirty-eight

"What the hell is this all about?" Randi slings the *Close-Up* article onto my desk the following morning, scattering my paperwork onto the floor.

Gee, if only I were an expert in body language and truly understood Randi's feelings.

"Bree?" Andrew covers the office phone's mouthpiece with his hand.

Um . . . Andrew, I'm kinda busy at the moment.

"You better have a damn good, like bloodsucking-aliens-snatched-you-into-space-and-replaced-your-brain-with-an-idiot's, excuse. That's the only explanation I will accept."

"I realize how things look, but—"

"I don't think you have a fucking clue." Her abrasive tone is enough to strip the enamel from my teeth. "Candace is furious. Lucy Hanover retracted her endorsement. Three quarters of our presolds canceled. People are questioning the *National Tribune*'s ethics for not vetting you closely enough.

I look like an asshole for representing you. And the publisher is threatening to sue. Sue. So." She leans closer and says with a clamped jaw, "You better find a way to crawl out of the goddamn hole you've gotten us into."

"Bree, it's important." Andrew points at the phone.

"What is it with him always interrupting us? Whatever it is, it can wait," Randi barks.

Andrew ignores her. "You need to take this, Bree. It's San Diego Medical Center. It's about Jo."

I'm out of the office before Randi screams another word. I zip through the streets, passing cars with the speed and expertise of a race car driver, pushing aside my fears and memories of driving. My focus is on the path to Jo.

The emergency room's lobby is filled with patients waiting to be seen. I'm sure the construction worker and his bandage-wrapped hand, the older gentleman with a sour cough, the middle schooler clutching his swollen elbow, or any of the others waiting are important, but I don't care. I need to see Jo.

"Excuse me." I lean through the patient window, grabbing the attention of the nearest admitting nurse. "I'm here to see Jo Caxton. *C-A-X-T-O-N.* I'm her granddaughter. Is she okay? Please tell me she's okay."

"Ma'am, have a seat. We'll be with you in a moment." Other nurses scurry behind her answering phones, reviewing charts, pushing random buttons on their computers.

"No, I don't want to sit. And I don't have a moment." Urgency charges through my body in a way I've never experienced. I want to grab the nurse and shake her like a rag doll until I get my answer. *Where is my grandmother? Where?* I've never felt so helpless, so out of control. Never felt such *need.*

"We'll get to you as soon as we can."

"No, please. Tell me what happened. Tell me she's okay."

"I'm sorry, but the HIPAA laws—"

"Fuck the HIPAA laws!"

Her eyes widen with shock.

"I'm sorry. I just need to know, something, anything." Streams of tears slide down my cheeks. "She's my grandmother. We fought the last time we saw each other and now she's here. Angry with me. Can't you just tell me if she's all right?"

What if she isn't? What if the last time we spoke, it ended in a fight? Just like I did with Mom and Dad.

The nurse pats my hand. "Let me find her chart."

I'm not a spiritual person. Never spent much time in church. Never knelt bedside and folded my hands in prayer. I've taken the Lord's name in vain more often than not. But now I'm reaching out, hoping it's true, hoping he is listening like his followers always claim. Now I'm silently praying, *Please, God, let Jo be okay. Let her sit up and yell at me, tell me how awful I've been. It's okay if she hates me, just don't take her from me like this. Please, God, please let Jo be okay.*

I wait, chastising myself for the person I've become. The lies I've spun. The people I've hurt. Several minutes pass and I'm tempted to climb through the window, track Jo down myself, when the nurse calls me from across the room.

She ushers me through a set of double doors and pulls me into a used exam room, clutching a chart against her chest. "I'm not supposed to do this, but I recognize you from the newspaper. I just love following your story. I haven't read yesterday's edition, so don't tell me what happens."

Who cares about the damn article? The fallout from the interview seems a million miles away. "How's my grandmother?"

"Right. I spoke with her doctor. Your grandmother suffered

a fall at her home. She tripped over a rug in the kitchen. They're monitoring her for a concussion. The good news is her fall activated her Life Alert and the paramedics arrived within minutes. She's been under our care since almost immediately after the incident."

"Did she break anything? Can she walk?"

"I'm sorry. That's all I know."

"May I see her?"

"The doctor said just for a moment."

"Where?"

The nurse refers to her notes, then says, "Far end of the hall, last room on your right, number one thirteen."

I hurry down the cold, sterile hallway bordered with curtain-drawn exam rooms. I dash past bleeping machines, medical carts, lab-coated doctors, and blue-scrubbed nurses who zoom in and out of my path. The smell of bleach, blood, and fear floats through the air. My breath quickens with each step.

But as I reach the door of room 113, I stop, petrified to enter. At once, I'm taken back to the last time I visited a hospital. The night my father lay on the operating table where the doctors clamped, sutured, pumped, but nothing saved him. Mom was already gone.

Just like that night, I inch through the door, terrified of what I'll learn.

This time, Jo's not hunched over and sobbing. This time, she lies in bed with her eyes closed and a blanket draped over her thin body. A fist-sized bandage is taped above her left eye. She's connected to a web of tubes and monitors. An IV is strapped to her age-spotted left hand. Her right wrist is wrapped in a splint.

Sweet Jo.

The female doctor—who looks no older than a Girl Scout—lifts her stethoscope from Jo's chest.

Another nurse stands behind the doctor, adjusting the tubing of Jo's clear-fluid drip.

"You must be the granddaughter."

"How is she?"

"She's stable. She suffered a supraorbital ridge laceration, a possible concussion, and a distal third scaphoid fracture."

I'm sorry, what?

The doctor recognizes my confusion.

"Cut her forehead. Bumped her head. Broke her wrist. We stitched her up and now are monitoring for any peculiarities, as her blood pressure spiked quite high upon her arrival. We're waiting for the CT scan results to rule out a concussion." She lays her hand on Jo's splint. "But all in all, the scaphoid is minimally displaced, mitigating the need for surgery. I think with a short cast and a lot of rest she'll recover quite well."

"Okay, that's good." Relief pours through my body. I step closer to the bed. "May I . . . speak to her?"

"Sure, but only for a couple of minutes."

"Hi, Jo." My voice cracks as I slide her hair from her eyes, careful not to touch the swollen spot. "I don't know if you can hear me. I don't know if you even *want* to hear me, but I'm here. I'm right next to you. You're going to be okay." I want to scoop her into my arms and squeeze away her pain. But she looks so frail I'm afraid she'll crumble like one of the dried-out sand dollars I collected. I slide the blanket to her waist and make a mental note to bring her favorite throw from home.

If she were to sit up, what would she say? What does she see when looking at me?

Please be okay, Jo. Please. You're all I've got.

"I'm sorry, but she needs her rest," the nurse says, standing at the door.

"Please let me stay. I won't make a sound. I can sleep on this chair."

She steps fully inside the room. "Wait a second. You're Bree Caxton, from the *Close-Up* article?"

"Yes, I am." Who knows, maybe my fifteen minutes of fame will pay off and she'll let me stay. Maybe she hasn't seen yesterday's article.

"People are pissed at you."

Or maybe she has.

"Yes, that's what I'm told." I stare at my feet, then offer a coy plea. "So, can I stay? Please?"

"Sorry, but hospital policy doesn't allow it." She shrugs. "I don't have the authority to say otherwise. But we'll call you if there's any change."

"Promise? No matter what, you'll call?" I realize that I sound like a child, but I can't help it. I *feel* like a child. Helpless. Confused. Scared. I want to climb into the bed and snuggle with Jo, smell the black cherry on her lips.

The nurse pulls Jo's chart from the slot near the door. "I almost forgot. The paramedics said something about a dog left at the patient's residence. They're asking if they should call animal control."

Martin.

I glance at Jo and almost smile. *Did you do this on purpose? Even asleep, you get the last laugh.* "No, don't call animal control. I'll take care of him, thank you."

"All right, then."

"What time can I come back in the morning?"

"Eight a.m."

"Okay. Call if anything changes." I rattle off my cell phone number.

"We will." She pats me on the back and escorts me through

the door. I start to walk away when she calls after me, "You know, it's too bad."

I spin around. "What is?"

"You and Nick. I really thought you two were perfect together."

thirty-nine

I pull up at Jo's curb when Sean calls me.

"Hey."

"It's as if you fell off the face of the earth. I phoned and texted you several times. Andrew said you left the office this morning in a hurry. I saw the paper. Everything all right?"

"Jo fell. She's in the hospital."

"Is she okay?"

"I think so, but she cut her head and broke her wrist."

"Want me to come?"

"No, that's okay. I'm picking up Martin, then heading home."

"When can I see you? Like I said, we're no longer a secret. All of America read that article. My phone's been ringing all day. My friends are stoked. Except Mom. She didn't like learning of our engagement through the article." He laughs. "We'll have some damage control there."

"Yeah, can we talk later?" I haven't explained the escalator clause fiasco and don't feel like doing it now. "I'm at Jo's house now. And I don't want to miss a call from the hospital."

We hang up and I grab the newspaper off Jo's doormat, then slide the key into the lock. Prepared for Martin to lunge at my feet, I grip the *National Tribune* tight, ready to swat his little ass out of the way.

But when I open the door, Martin's not there.

"Martin?" I step into the kitchen. There's a pool of dried blood on the floor next to the wrinkled kitchen rug. Must be where Jo fell. *Oh my God. Poor thing.*

I right Jo's toppled-over chair, then check the dining room for her fuzzy buddy.

"Martin? Come here, boy." I check the living room, too, but he's nowhere. I'm about to leave Jo's bedroom, uncertain what to do, when I see the tip of his tail poking out from underneath the bed.

He's shaking.

"Hey, Martin." I crouch to my knees and touch his tail. Slowly, I slide my hand toward his back and stroke his soft fur. He doesn't bark or growl, just trembles. "It's okay, little fella." I curl my hands underneath his body and gently pull him out from under the bed. He doesn't jump out of my hands. He doesn't claw at my face. He doesn't growl. The six-pound fur ball falls limp as I clutch him against my chest. "I miss her, too. She's gonna be okay."

She has to be.

I gather his leash, dog food, bones, chew toys, and his favorite bed. I climb into the car and set him on the passenger seat.

Martin whines, then hops into my lap and curls into a ball.

"Okay, you can stay here." I pat his head.

Martin and I arrive at my house and I set his things on the kitchen floor, filling his food and water bowls. He's not hungry.

Nor am I.

Martin follows me into the living room, where I plop on the couch and call the hospital.

The nurse tells me there's been no change, that Jo's resting comfortably and that they would call if necessary.

I glance down at Martin, who sits by my feet. He doesn't crawl into his bed or eat his food. He doesn't bark or growl. He doesn't gnaw the skin off my ankles. Instead, he stares at me with heartbroken eyes.

"You want up?" I reach for him and settle him into my lap. The two of us lie there on the couch, missing the most important person in both of our lives. Worst of all, we're unable to help. Nothing we can do but wait.

Worried about Jo, I'm up half the night. So my seven a.m. alarm jars me from a deep sleep. I hop into the shower, throw on a pair of jeans and a T-shirt, brush my teeth, and wrap my hair in a loose bun. I feed Martin and take him for a walk, where he sniffs and piddles on every single bush around my block. Once I'm certain he's exhausted and will sleep while I'm gone, I toss him his bone. "Okay, little buddy, I'm gonna check on Jo."

Martin lifts his ears as if he understands.

"I'll be back later. Be a good boy. And by *good boy* I don't mean eating my ficus leaves. Or chewing up my *other* flip-flop."

With her favorite throw in hand, I grow nervous, uncertain how she'll react to seeing me. After our conversation at her door, I fear our relationship is in jeopardy.

But I'm not giving up.

I text Andrew, asking him to cancel my appointments for the day.

Who am I kidding? Since the article released, I have no appointments.

A few minutes later, I knock on her opened door and walk inside.

A different and older doctor stands by her bed.

"Oh, sorry. I didn't mean to interrupt."

"No problem. We're just giving Ms. Caxton a quick peek." He checks her pupils and heart rate, then lifts the tape to check her laceration.

She's awake. There is color to her cheeks and a clean bandage on her head. But she doesn't look in my direction. Doesn't wave. Doesn't wiggle a pinkie.

"On a scale of one to ten, ten being the worst, what's your pain level?"

"About a four," Jo says. "I'm real tired and sore and feel like an idiot for slipping on my fanny, but other than that I guess I'm okay."

"Well, that's to be expected. You're certainly not an idiot, but your body did suffer a great deal of shock." He checks the mobility of her fingers. "Depending on how your wrist looks once the swelling is down, we'll address the cast situation." He wraps the stethoscope around his neck. "You had one heck of a scare. We want to monitor you for another couple of days, but if you keep at this same pace, you'll recover quite well."

"Thank you."

I say the same.

"My pleasure." He nods and steps out of the room.

"So . . . hi . . . Jo," I say with trepidation. "How are you feeling?"

"Didn't you hear what I told the doctor?" She presses at the tape of her IV.

"Yes, well . . . I brought you this." I show her the blanket.

"I'm not cold."

"Okay, I'll just set it on this chair." *Next to my sorrowful heart.*

A stocky male dressed in scrubs walks inside with a huge bouquet of yellow daisies, carnations, and roses. "Someone's got an admirer."

Damn. I didn't even think about sending flowers.

"Well, now, aren't they beautiful. I have to admit, I laid here a bit depressed in this boring old hospital room. Nothing but tubes and monitors and cheesy wallpaper. Flowers just liven up the place. Don't you think?"

"Where do you want them?"

"On the table over there is fine. Read the card. Tell me who they're from."

The attendant says, "From your family at Life Alert."

"Those gals are so sweet."

"Have a good day, ladies."

Jo smiles at the bouquet.

"So." *Yoo-hoo! I'm over here.* "I thought you should know I have Martin and—"

"You have him?" She grips the bedrail. "Dear Lord, I've been worried sick. The nurse said a young lady picked him up, but seeing how you don't like Martin, I figured someone else had him. Where is he? How is he?"

"He's at my house. I fed him and took him for a long walk before I came. He's fine—so comfortable, in fact, he chewed up my favorite flip-flop."

"Don't worry. I'll call one of my friends to pick him up straightaway."

"No, no, I didn't like those flip-flops anyway. Martin's no trouble. I'm happy to have him. I want to have him."

"He's very important to me."

"I know that, Jo."

The air is silent and awkward between us.

I suppose there's no reason to dance around the elephant in the room. She's mad. I feel bad. Let's get this shit worked out.

"Jo, I want to apologize again for the article and the lies. I want to explain—"

"I'm tired. I need to rest."

Or not.

"You'll take care of Martin?"

"Yes, of course."

She closes her eyes and folds her hands across her belly.

"Sure, right. I'll go." I walk out wanting to press the code blue lever. *I need a doctor. STAT.* Someone to suture my broken heart.

At least now I know. My questions are definitely confirmed. Jo never looked me in the eye. Not once.

Just like the rest of America, she hates me.

forty

Crickets. That's about all I heard the last few days at my very quiet office. The phone only ringing when Randi called to berate me. *Again*. And today's e-mails consisted of nothing more than a dozen clients withdrawing their applications. Such a slow day, I pitched my water bottle cap at Andrew's head when I caught him nodding off.

Totally disheartened and bored, feeling hopelessly sorry for myself, I spent the afternoon Web-surfing time-shares in Puerto Vallarta and ordering new wineglasses from Crate and Barrel, and bought myself a turquoise bolero. Not sure why.

Although my mind is cluttered with guilt and regret—not to mention, I rolled over Martin's tail with my office chair—add financial stress to my mix, fearing that if today's any indication of my business future, I'll be living off canned beans by month's end.

All the more reason I'm looking forward to tonight's Q&A.

There's a bounce in my step as I walk into the library a couple of hours later. Knowing the crowd won't spill out into the hall like last time, I'm still eager to be welcomed by Gwen and the gang. After the past couple of days, I could use the love and their comic relief. Andrew's right. I do need them. Tonight more than ever. I've got two bottles of Chardonnay tucked into my bag.

And this time I don't stroll the long way, passing Kid Town. I don't want to see Nixon tonight. Well, I do, but only if he can have an acute case of amnesia, forgetting all that I said and did to hurt him.

But when I turn the corner toward my usual conference room, the light is off. The door is locked. The blinds drawn.

"No one left a message?" I ask the librarian as she assigns me the door key.

She shakes her head. "Sorry."

"They must be running late." I force a smile, then glance at my watch, ignoring the voice in my head that says, *They're never late.*

Twenty minutes later, I still sit alone. *You did this. You deserve this. And no, don't smash a bottle of wine over the table and guzzle it down.* I bury my head in my hands.

"Let me ask you something."

Nixon stands at the door dressed in a black suit and light yellow tie.

My heart beats wildly against my chest, wishing I could read his emotion. So much for my inherent ability to read people. Is he angry? Sad? *Nothing?*

"How long?" he says.

Now I know what he's thinking. "A couple of weeks."

"You were engaged before the wedding, then?"

"Yes. I . . . I didn't know how to tell you. I—"

"He's your guy?" Nixon picks at the edge of the doorjamb.

"What do you mean?"

"When you have a bad dream, a shit day, the lights go out and the entire house is dark, can't see one foot in front of the other, Sean is the first person you think of? He's your guy?"

"Sean and I are familiar, comfortable."

"Ah, yes, convenience. The cornerstone of every relationship. Didn't Shakespeare write that?"

"We have history," I protest.

"You're overlooking his uncertainty and all the pain he caused you these past few weeks because you two have backstory?"

"Yes, fine. Sean and I have a lot to sort through. But there's something to be said for history."

"Yeah, it's called settling. I heard it on a radio show once." He starts to walk away.

"Nixon, wait." I stand up and reach for his wrist. "I'm sorry. I tried to tell you, but I didn't know what to say. You're the one who said these past few weeks—"

"It's no big deal. No reason for you to share your personal life with me. Who am I, anyway? Just a guy you made a deal with, nothing more. You held up your end of the bargain. So did I."

"Look, you have to know the time we spent together, the wedding, camping, and . . . well, everything, it meant a lot to me. All of it."

"Nah, forget it. You don't need to explain. For a second I forgot my place in your life."

"C'mon, Nixon, that's not fair. I didn't mean to hurt anyone. All I wanted, this whole time was for my book . . ." I stop, realizing how shallow I sound.

"Oh, that's right, your precious bestseller. Jesus, Bree. It isn't Jo. It isn't this book. It isn't your parents. It's you. You control your life. No one else."

"Well, you'll be happy to hear I screwed up. Everything I've worked so hard for—Jo, Jo's house, my book—it's all gone. All of it."

"That's my goddamn point. Why put yourself through this? Why put me through this?"

"Oh, I'm so sorry I've made your life miserable. I'm sorry spending fake time with me really sucked." I pause. I shouldn't yell at Nixon. He's helped me. "Because she's all I've got. And I want her to forgive me. Forgive me for taking my parents away from us. For being responsible for all that we lost."

"You weren't behind the wheel. Accidents happen at all times of the day or night. It's not your fault."

"This isn't a joke to me."

"This isn't a joke to *me*." His tone is bitter. Hurt. "Why do you think I turned down eleven dates?"

"Because you're self-centered and arrogant." I know this isn't true, but I'm mad. Mad at myself. Right or wrong, I'm mad at him.

"Yep, you're right." He raps his fist on the doorjamb. "You know, for an expert, you certainly miss a lot of signs. Tell me, Bree." He shuffles half a step closer and the tiniest whiff of his toothpaste floats off his lips. "What exactly do you think I've been doing the last few weeks?"

"Doing what you're told." I snap.

"Yeah, well, you didn't tell me to care."

forty-one

The smell of wet grass floats through my car windows as I drive along the rolling hills of Mount Hope Cemetery the following morning. Dotted with headstones, shade trees, and concrete benches, the graveyard is a sad but beautiful sight.

I marvel at the growth of the trees, the annexed parcels, and the vast number of graves as I follow the curves to my parents' shared plot.

Gosh, where have the years gone? Fifteen years have passed and Jo still resents me just as on the day we buried my parents.

Fifteen years.

It doesn't seem that long ago when Dad stood at the kitchen counter and poured Cheerios into his bowl as I munched on cinnamon-sugar toast.

Mom stumbled into the kitchen, cinched her robe, and yawned. "Morning. Happy anniversary." She kissed Dad's cheek.

"Do you remember how I met your mom?"

He'd told me every year on their anniversary.

"Tell us again," Mom had said.

"Well, your mom worked at Vons as a checker, two streets away from my first apartment. Holy hell, she had the most startling blue eyes. Still does." He winked at her. "They're the exact color of the Extra peppermint gum label."

"He should know. He bought a pack every day for six months."

"The only way I could see her and talk to her." He laughed. "Wrappers covered my backseat." But eventually the store manager questioned why I bought so much gum and threatened to kick me out. So, with time running out, I mustered up the nerve and asked your mom out for dinner. And you know what she said?"

"What?" I asked, already knowing the answer.

"I don't like gum." Dad laughed and pointed his index finger at me. "But she smiled when she said it. You could've shot me dead at that very moment and I would've died a happy man." He slid toward Mom and pulled her close. "Happy anniversary, honey."

Their last.

"Sorry I haven't visited in a while," I say, now seated beside their headstone. "I know it's no excuse, but I've been busy. Busy enough to have worked myself into a mess and lost focus on what mattered. Now I don't know what to do. Jo's mad at me. I've hurt Nixon, who's this guy you don't know but would really love. Especially you, Mom. You'd appreciate his rugged sweetness." I pick a blade of grass and run my fingers along the waxy surface. "Besides them, I've disappointed my colleagues. I've blown my chances at a bestseller . . ." I turn and face their names and say after a long sigh, "Worst of all, I've lost Jo's house. G-pa's house. *Your* house. I'm sorry. So very sorry. I guess it's fitting that a good portion of America hates me. I kinda hate me, too."

I watch a funeral procession wend its way toward a few

rows of white chairs and an aboveground coffin. A couple dozen people step out from their cars, hugging and consoling one another as they drift toward the service, their voices carried toward me by the breeze. It's an awful day for them. No other way to describe it. Simply an awful day. Someone, loved by someone else, is now gone. The survivors left to grieve. Tonight will be their longest.

A young girl—six or seven years old maybe?—dressed in a lavender-colored dress, white stockings, and sandals, walks behind the group. She carries a clear Plexiglas box topped with a silk blue bow. A handful of monarch butterflies flutter inside. Heading toward her chair, nearest the end, the sweet girl is focused on her job, concentrating on the winged insects.

What is she thinking? Does she understand the reason for the butterflies? Does she grasp the fact that whomever these people have gathered to mourn is gone? Or does she just think the monarchs' spots are pretty?

The day we buried my parents, I had a hard time making sense of why life just *carried on*. The world didn't pause, not even for a moment. Cars still zoomed past on the freeway. Cemetery workers repaired a sprinkler line on the far side of the hill. People ate lunch. Paid bills. Watched TV. Laughed at jokes. Life didn't stop.

Worse yet, people gathered at Jo's house after the service and offered condolences. Dad's coworkers, Mom's friends, *strangers* would squeeze my shoulder or grasp my hand and tell me how sorry they were. Then, after appeasing their conscience, they'd move on to other friends and start talking about last night's doubleheader or snicker at a stupid joke. My parents all but forgotten.

I talked to no one. Smiled at no one. I didn't care that our neighbor brought a vegetable lasagna or Jo's bridge club friend left a tray of peanut butter cookies. I didn't care that so-and-so thought my parents were wonderful people. That didn't bring Mom and Dad back. Cookies didn't bring them back. I *knew* they were wonderful people and I wanted them here, with me.

I'm not sure what I expected, but watching the guests help themselves to another deviled egg or second glass of wine infuriated me. I wanted to scream *Get off my dad's recliner. Pick that bread crumb off my mom's rug. Get out of my house.*

I stand and face my parents' headstone.

What would they say to me now? What advice would they give me? Would they be disappointed in me, too?

Cries from the girl catch my attention. She's tripped and fallen face-first into the grass.

The box's quick-release lid popped off.

The butterflies are flying away.

An older man, likely her grandfather, rushes to her side and helps the sweet child to stand up. He brushes grass off her knee-stained stockings.

"I wasn't supposed to let them go yet," she wails. "Mommy's gonna be mad at me."

Mommy? Is that who passed?

My heart aches for the girl. *No, please, no. It isn't your fault. Say something. Tell her, she's not to blame. Don't let her assume the same burden I have.*

"Come here now, sweetie." He clutches the girl close. "Your mom's not going to be mad. She could never be mad at you."

"But they flew away already."

"Good." He tucks her hair behind her ears. "They'll reach your mom that much sooner. She'll like that."

The little one buries her head in the man's neck as they sit down.

One of the butterflies lands on the edge of my parents' headstone. It flaps its wings but remains fixed in place. I stare at the orange-and-black-winged insect, lined with tiny white dots. It's beautiful, really. Aimless and free. I reach for it just as it flies away.

It sails through the air and I hope the butterfly finds my parents.

I miss them so much.

Through tears, I trace along the curves and swirls of their names embossed on the headstone, following through the year they were born and the year they died.

Though I'm saddened and lonesome, this time, the feel of the letters underneath my fingertip brings me clarity.

Mom's determination and Dad's integrity lift me like the butterfly gliding through the air.

My scar reacts to my feelings.

It's not your fault.

And for the first time in years, I know exactly what to do.

forty-two

Sitting in my Prius, I call Randi and leave the message that I am sorry for the hole that I got us into and have a plan to dig us out.

My next call is to Candace.

"I can't imagine why you're phoning me, Bree." Her tone is sharper than an assassin's blade. "Haven't you done quite enough?"

I could've bled to death from her razor-edged tone, but I lifted my chin, straightened my back, and said, "Yes, I'm sorry. Very sorry. But we signed a contract. A five-week installment and I have one more interview to give. Meet me at my office, tomorrow morning."

It's either the grace of God or generosity from the karma gurus that got her to agree.

The last thing I had to do was find Sean, and it didn't take long.

I find my fiancé lying on my couch scrolling through his phone. A Post-it pad and pencil lie beside a note he's scribbled and stuck on the edge of my coffee table.

"Hey, there you are." He tucks his phone into his pocket

and sits up. "I've been here for over an hour. I began to worry about you."

"What are you doing here?"

"Thought I'd surprise my fiancée. Where were you?"

"Visited my parents."

"Really? How come?"

For some reason this irritates me. Or maybe I'm already irritated. Why do I have to have a reason to visit my parents' grave? Isn't the fact that it's a *grave* a justification in and of itself? "Just needed some clarity."

"Well, I hope you found it. Want to grab dinner tonight?"

"No."

"Why not?"

"Because we need to talk."

Martin barks off in the distance.

"Where's Martin?"

"In his kennel."

Sean left him in the small kennel I set up in my bedroom and stuffed with one of Jo's T-shirts so that he would recognize her scent. Martin starts to bark when he hears my voice. "Why didn't you let him out?"

"Was I supposed to?"

This inflames me even more. What kind of man ignores a dog? They're *man's* best friend, for Christ's sake.

I hurry into my bedroom. Kneeling beside his kennel, I free him from his cage. "Sorry, little buddy. I should've let you out sooner."

He hops into my lap and jumps toward my chin with kisses.

"I've missed you, too."

"Dang, Martin gets all the attention." Sean jokes from my door's threshold.

Martin springs from my lap and growls at Sean. The hair on his little back rises like a mountain ridge.

Sean poses his stance like he's about to attack. He jerks toward Martin.

The little fella whines and runs with his tail between his legs around Sean and out the door.

"Stupid dog," he laughs.

"He's not a stupid dog." I chase after him, finding him hiding underneath the coffee table.

The air conditioner kicks on. Sean's note flaps in the breeze. *God, I hate those damn stickies.*

After I fill Martin's food and water bowls, he calms down and starts to eat.

I meet Sean in the living room.

"I almost forgot." He pulls my engagement ring from his pocket and slides it on my finger. "Now that this interview stuff is over, you can wear this all the time."

I stare at the large diamond overwhelming my small finger and think of the misery that consumed me after that night at Antonio's. And how the hours and days passed with such puzzlement and pain, as if my heart forced itself to beat.

Then Nixon came along.

And made everything right.

But aside from how I may or may not feel about that man, this isn't about him.

It's about Sean.

It's about me.

I glance at the ring again, the stone's brilliance blinding me with clarity. *This* isn't right.

"You hurt me, Sean. Really hurt me. And when we were apart, I missed you."

"I missed you, too." Snagging my belt loop, he pulls me closer.

"No." I inch away.

"What's wrong, Bree?"

"I don't want to be married to a man who isn't sure. I don't want to marry because it's safe. I don't want to marry a man out of convenience."

"Where is this coming from? You said you've forgiven me."

"I may be able to forgive what you did, but I can't forgive the way you made me feel."

"What are you saying?"

I slip the engagement ring off and set it on the table. I tear off a Post-it and scribble *You're a lawyer, figure it out* and stick it on his forehead.

And with that, I close the story of us. I know without a doubt, Sean's and my history has become just that, *history.*

forty-three

Candace walks in the following morning with a scowl so deep not even a vat of Juvéderm could fill it.

Stay calm, Bree.

This time there is no rearranging of chairs or spiffing up my office with rugs and flowers. This time Candace sits with her legs crossed and an ankle wrapped around the other. She's angled herself, offering more of her profile, rather than her whole face. Proving she's interested in anyone or anything but me. Her body is closed. So is her mind.

"Water? Coffee?"

"I don't have much time." She clicks on her recorder. "Get on with what you want to say."

And here I feared this wouldn't be fun. "Let me start by apologizing again."

"You've done that already."

"Okay, fine. Let's cut to the chase, then. I lied."

She sits forward and scoots her recorder closer toward me. "Talk louder."

"I pretended to date a man, a man I barely knew, for this

article. And, yes, Sean and I dated for four years. Yes, he asked me to marry him. And yes, I played Sara for a fool."

Candace reaches for her notebook and scribbles as fast as I talk.

"It's my fault. I own all of it. The lies. The deceit. Everything. But they weren't my intentions. I was thrilled at the opportunity this segment afforded me. And I promised myself to use this article as a platform to promote my book and be the best damn interviewee you've ever had. But on the eve of our first interview, Sean broke up with me. Out of the blue."

"No!"

"Yes." I continue, thankful the tension has lifted. "Now, please understand, I'm not asking for pity. This isn't a 'poor-me' appeal. But, at that moment, I didn't know what to do. Obsessed with a successful book, I panicked. I begged Nixon, a client already, to pose as my boyfriend." I stare through the window at the rolling ocean waves. "Everything about him is true. He is kind. He is handsome. He is the truest person I've ever met. He's the man I think of when I have a bad dream, a crummy day, when the lights go out and the entire house is dark. But I've hurt him."

"Go on."

I pause before saying, "Truth is, I'm no good at love. My boyfriend of four years says I suffocated him. And Nixon, the man I fell in love with over this past month, won't return my calls. I've jeopardized my family. I've hurt Nixon's family. I've embarrassed people that I care about. I've lost my grandmother's house."

"What's your takeaway from all this? Where do you go from here?"

"Good question." I swallow hard. "I will continue to work hard and find love for my clients." *Those I still have left.* I laugh in spite of myself. "Not that anyone cares, but I've learned a lot along this little journey. I've learned that success—or in my case, lack thereof—is never worth hurting others for. Especially those you love. I've learned that I'd rather be alone than settle. I've learned that squirrels are as feisty as I feared, zip-ties are remarkably effective, and hot dogs taste like heaven straight from the fire. I've witnessed the innocence and beauty of a mountain sunrise. I've shouldered the pain of lies and regret. I've learned to drive. I've learned to believe in chance." Tears line my eyes, but I don't blink them away. "I've learned what it's like to kiss a man with every bit of my body and mind. To be stilled by his touch, silenced by his breath on my skin, honored by his smile. I've learned what it's like to *feel*. I've learned what it's like to lose him."

forty-four

I'm set to leave for the hospital. It's futile, really. All week she's either pretended to be asleep or requested her bath the moment I arrive.

Martin whimpers at my feet.

"I can't bring you to the hospital."

He rests his head on my foot.

Nice ploy.

His swishing tail gives me an idea. "Okay, fine, but you can't bark."

Jo doesn't want me to visit, but I'm certain she'll love to see Martin. Besides, the nurses asked that I stop calling for updates and what flavor of Jell-O she ate that day.

I grab a tote bag and stuff Martin inside. He lies down, sandwiched between the canvas, ready for the ride.

We walk the hallway toward Jo's room knowing, mentally preparing for the worst. *She won't be thrilled to see me, but she will Martin.*

Jo's watching an infomercial on tire cleaner with a tray of eggs, toast, and fruit cup on her lap.

"Hi, Jo."

She clicks off the TV. "They're releasing me today."

"Oh, good. Okay. Let me gather—"

"I saw the article."

Candace ran a "Special Edition" segment, posting the interview the day after we met, rather than waiting until Sunday. Guess she wanted to watch my book sales tumble even further that much sooner. "Yeah, well, I suppose it—"

"I'm proud of you."

I squeeze my fists tight around the tote bag's strap. *Did she say what I think she said?* "You are?"

"I am."

She is?

No snappy tone? No distant, disappointed look in her eye?

"You're a smart woman. A lovely woman."

"Thank you, Jo." I shake my head, delirious with joy.

She picks at her toast. "Sitting here, all alone, I've realized what a sour old fart I've been. Oh, honey." Jo sighs. "I'm sorry if I've ever made you feel ashamed."

"You have reason to be mad at me."

"No. No, I don't." She pushes her tray away and pats the edge of her bed.

I sit beside her.

"I'm mad at the world. I'm mad at the damn drunk driver that took your parents away. I'm mad at the doctors for not saving them. I'm mad at the bartender who served the guy too many drinks. I'm mad at the car dealer for selling him a car. Hell, I'm mad at the wind when it blows the wrong direction. I'm mad at everything. But I'm not mad at you. I never have been. And I never will be."

We're both crying. Jo's proud of me. She loves me.

"You know, with my colossal screw-up, it means I can't save your house."

"I know." She pats my hand, likely recalling all the years of joy spent in that house. After a moment she says, "It took a lot of courage to do what you did. I'm honored to call you my granddaughter."

"Oh, Jo. You have no idea how wonderful this makes me feel. I'm . . . I'm just speechless."

I bend toward my grandmother and hug her tight, soaking in the forgiveness, the memories, the love. Everything else in the world can kiss off. I have my Jo.

Martin barks.

Jo gasps. "Is that—? Where is he?"

"Right here." I scoop the little lovebug out from the bag and rest him in Jo's lap.

"My baby."

His tail wags fast enough to make me dizzy.

Jo's beaming smile is contagious as we chuckle at Martin, who alternates kissing Jo's hand and spinning in happy circles on her lap.

After he settles a few minutes later, Jo asks, "How's everything else going?"

"Well, let's see. The man I care for won't talk to me, my career is headed down the toilet, and all of America loathes me. So, all in all, pretty good."

"Who needs 'em? I always say, if plan A fails, you have twenty-five letters left."

"You're right, Jo."

"Now get me out of this prison."

"Wanna go somewhere with me? If you're not too tired."

"I've been lying around all week. Where we going?"

I roll up my sleeve. "Going to do something about this."

"Bree . . . it's a scar. You don't need—"

"No, I'm not ashamed of it. Not anymore. I'm going to give it the respect it deserves."

"How's that?"

"Come and find out. I can use a hand to hold."

An hour and a half later, Jo and I examine my new tattoo. My parents' initials—though red and puffy—are scripted and swirled around the four-inch reminder that shaped my life. Now, when I look at the scar, I won't see pain and disfigurement. I'll see beauty, art, and history. I'll see life. I'll see *me*.

"People are going to ask you about that, you know," Jo says.

"I hope so."

She smiles. Real and genuine. The type of smile I haven't seen for fifteen years.

"People are going to ask you about *that*, you know." I point to my parents' initials decorating her left ankle.

"I hope so."

⁓

The following Tuesday, my book is released. The golden day is finally here.

Andrew sent me a beautiful bouquet of flowers with *congratulations* spelled out across the card. And Jo called, asking me to drive her and Martin to Barnes & Noble.

Turns out, she picked the store from years ago when I stole the book.

Hope the same manager isn't on duty.

The publisher still released the book and though likely only a few people will buy a copy, there's something magical about walking with my grandmother's hand linked around my arm into a bookstore that captivated so much of our time over the years. And today we're here, celebrating a book that I wrote. *I wrote*. Books are such a staple in our relationship. My release solidifies our past.

It doesn't take more than a few steps before Jo's eyes widen and my heart pounds. Right near the entrance is a round three-tiered table with *Can I See You Again?* stacked and fanned in a beautiful display of my creativity.

We each grab a copy and examine the glossy cover. *Can I See You Again?* is emblazoned in a creamy white font over a closed cardinal-red front door. The flowers held behind the woman's back are embossed and I trail my fingertips over the raised petals.

"Pretty neat, eh?"

"Pretty neat," she says.

We head into the nonfiction section and nearly jump up and down when we find a dozen more copies lining the shelves. Jo pulls one out, placing it perpendicular to the others.

"It should stand out," she says.

God, I love this woman.

After lunch and laughs, I drop Jo and Martin at her house, then head toward my office.

"So, how'd it go with Jo?" Andrew asks.

"Awesome. Jo insisted we purchase all the books, but store policy limits customers to ten per transaction." I laugh, then say, "Jo paid for her first batch, walked out, walked right back in, and bought ten more."

"I've done the same." He points to two large bags behind his desk. "Guess what my friends are getting for their birthdays this year.

"Thanks for your support, it means a lot. Any calls?"

"Yes, a few."

Any of them from Nixon?

I spend the remainder of the week answering questions, commenting and discussing my way through blogs and Web chats Randi's team arranged. It's a whirlwind of activity for which I'm thankful; it helps keep my mind off Nixon. And, kudos to me, I've only started to call him less than a dozen times. Which isn't that unhealthy. I don't think.

Randi marches into my office a week to the day after my book's release and sits her booty on the edge of my desk. Her bug-eyed black sunglasses reflect the office's overhead lights, and her polished red nails are long and fierce.

I haven't seen her since her rage-filled rant.

"You want the good news or the bad news?" she says.

"Is the paper still going to sue?"

"No."

I slump against my chair rest with relief. *Thank you, Lord. Thank you. Thank you.* Then I remember the counterpart of her question. "What's the bad news?"

"You didn't make the top twenty."

"Yeah, I figured as much." *Didn't even bother to check the* NYT *Web page.* "Truth is, I'm lucky to have gotten to this point. Sorry to ruin your stellar reputation. Probably would've been easier if I wrote a book of French Provincial cabinetry, eh?"

"Would've been easier if you didn't lie."

Or that. "Where am I, though? High eight millions?"

"Let me finish, goddammit."

"Oh, right, sorry."

"You didn't make the top twenty."

Yep, got that part.

"You made the top ten."

"What?" I nearly jump off my chair. "You're kidding me."

"I told you, I never joke about money. Your book debuted at number seven. Seems people like the truth. Welcome to the *New York Times* bestseller list."

∽

A few days later, Randi drops off my bonus check for twenty-five thousand dollars. Before the ink is dry I grab Jo. "Let's go save your house."

Never have I felt more proud. My steps are light. My cheeks ache from my fixed smile. Jo's tender hand is protectively clasped within mine. She won't lose her home.

We walk into the courthouse, turning down the long, cold, sterile hallway lined with various departments and posters citing the benefits of vaccinations and how to prevent the spread of viruses. We find our door and walk inside the assessor's office.

An older lady with her graying hair pinned behind her ears smacks on her chewing gum and says, "May I help you?"

"Yes, please. We're here to satisfy a lien." I slide her the paperwork and open my checkbook. "Just need to know the exact amount."

The woman hammers at her keyboard.

"I can't believe you're doing this for me, Bree. You've saved G-pa's house. I know he's looking down on you right now smiling. I just know it." She wraps her arm around my shoulder and squeezes it tight. "Thank you, Bree. I'm so proud of everything you've done."

My heart swells. My body literally feels like it might—

"The lien's been satisfied." The woman slides over the paper. "Next."

"Wait . . . what? It couldn't have been. We're just here now."

"It was."

"Please, this makes no sense. Can you double-check?"

Her finger follows along the screen as she reads: "The property was sold to RNC Investments, Inc., at 8:09 a.m. this morning."

"That's impossible."

"My computer says otherwise."

"Hell with your computer. We have the money. It's my grandmother's house."

"Bree, what's going on?"

"I'm sorry," the clerk says, "there's nothing I can do. On the positive side, they've given you ten days to evacuate. You don't see that very often."

"What does this mean, Bree?"

Someone else owns her house.

⁓

Driving toward Jo's house a few days later, I'm still sick about the whole situation. How did the auction slip through my fingers? How did I miss it? The paperwork mentioned the date. Did it list a time, too? How did I not see the time? *Oh, God. I've screwed up. Again.*

"What are you doing?" Several half-filled boxes litter Jo's living room floor as I let myself in. Obviously, I know what she's doing. She's packing, and she agreed to move in with me until we can find her a new place. And, obviously, I know why she's doing it, but to witness her life wrapped up in yesterday's newspapers is almost as painful as the disappointed look across her face.

I can't take it.

I don't wait for an answer.

I march out the door and return to the assessor's office determined to gather more information about RNC Investments. Determined to find out who bought Jo's house.

No luck.

Defeated, I sit in my car in the parking lot with my head pressed against the steering wheel. I don't understand. What could RNC Investments possibly want with a forty-year-old house? Yes, the neighborhood is nice, but there are zoning restrictions in the area. It's not like someone can come in here and flip the house, make a killer profit. I've scoured the internet for RNC Investments to no avail. It's as if they don't exist. I think of Sean. *Can he help?* But, no. I will not call him. I'll figure this out on my own.

A screech of tires in the nearby intersection catches my attention. It's then, across the street, I notice the Corporation Commission building. And I remember filing with them when Bree Caxton and Associates incorporated. The information there is public record. Maybe RNC Investments is a corporation. Worth a shot.

I hurry into the office, wait what feels like three days before my number is called, then nearly fall off my chair when the clerk reveals the name of the president of RNC Investments.

Randi Noreen Chapman.

My publicist.

"You bought it?" I step outside and call her straightaway.

"Jesus, woman, I was wondering how much longer it'd take you to figure it out. I was about to leave a trail of cookie crumbs from her house to mine."

"I don't understand."

"What's there to understand? It's a well-built house in a great neighborhood."

"Yes, but it's my grandmother's well-built house in a great neighborhood."

"I know."

"Randi—"

"Listen, missy, stop right there. I have a grandmother, too. She's tiny and ornery, has cotton-candy-thin hair, but is tough as nails. She raised me. I owe everything I am, and everything I'm not, to this woman. Grandmothers are special."

"What are you saying?" I ask, with a tentative voice.

"Bring me a check, I'll quit-claim the deed."

"Are you serious, Randi?"

"I already told you. I never joke about money. I didn't buy

the house for me. I bought *time* for you. What the hell am I going to do with a well-built house in a great neighborhood?"

At the mention of reclaiming the house I feel ten pounds lighter. I bounce around the sidewalk as if springs are fixed to the bottom of my shoes. "Thank you, thank you. Dare I say it, Randi, you have a soft center." Just like Nixon.

"Don't you tell a soul. It'll ruin my reputation."

I laugh. "When can we meet?"

"Tomorrow."

"Oh, God, thank you. Text me the exact amount, I'll bring a cashier's check." We're about to hang up and I ask, "Randi, before you go, how'd you know about Jo's house anyway?"

"Andrew may be adorable, but he's a terrible secret keeper."

"That he is."

Minutes later I rush into Jo's house, sweep my arms across the room and say, "Stop the packing. Right now. All of it."

"What? Why?"

I pull several picture frames out of a half-filled box, return them to the bookcase, and scoop Martin up. "Because this house still belongs to you."

forty-five

Andrew's right. It's three weeks later and the media frenzy has settled down to nil. The *National Tribune* moved on to bigger and better stories. Like Lindsay Lohan's crotch, no one cares about it anymore.

I'm not complaining. I wasn't a fan of the media attention, anyway. Though my book sales benefited from the circus—I've held strong at number thirteen on the list—it's nice to get back to my quiet, mundane reality.

The office has maintained a nice bump, too. Andrew signed fourteen new clients last week alone, including Candace's sister. She has a date with Lawrence Chambers on Friday. Seems as though people respected my initial intentions and don't fault me for my subsequent actions. A nice pat on the back from humanity. One client went as far as to say he admired my quick thinking with regard to Nixon posing as my boyfriend. The man offered his services—along with an eight-by-ten glossy of himself flexing in a Speedo with his pet macaw on his shoulder.

When God closes a door . . .

Jo's nearly healed and feels much better. *We're* nearly healed and much, much better. Just this morning, I earned the coveted spot on Jo's half-moon cabinet.

To top it off, Martin hasn't tried to bite me in nearly a month.

All in all, my life is good.

You'd think I'd be happy.

And I am.

Except for the fact that I lie alone.

Missing Nixon.

I took a chance and left him a message a couple of weeks ago. He never called back. So that's that. Like it or not, the time spent I with Nixon *was* all for show.

Determined not to pout any longer, I hop out of bed and take advantage of this beautiful Sunday morning. No wind. Warm sun.

I slide into a light sweatshirt, capri leggings, and running shoes. When's the last time I went for a run? *Don't answer that, Bree. It'll only make you feel worse.*

Plus, running clears my head. It allows me to think about things without distraction. And with the onslaught of new clients Bree Caxton and Associates has received, I've got lots of planning to do.

After a quick stretch, I jog down my street, turn left, and within a few minutes reach the water. The boardwalk is quiet this time of day, no more than a few fellow runners and bicyclists. Coffee shop and restaurant owners hose down tables and outdoor seating areas in preparation for the breakfast rush. I follow along the cracked sidewalk listening to the squawking seagulls. My feet bound against the concrete. I welcome the blood coursing throughout my legs.

Thirty minutes pass and I'm pleased—and surprised—with

my endurance, glad to see that the discipline from my half marathon training hasn't worn off. And good news, I may have an unsettled longing in my heart but at least I won't have a saggy ass to go with it. I keep running with no particular course.

Another half hour later, mentally refreshed and physically spent, I opt for a latte, then walk down the stairs toward the beach. I slip out of my shoes, sink my feet into the cool sand buried underneath the warm surface layer, and, with no destination in mind, meander along the beach. I squat in a spot between a lifeguard tower and the pier, watching the waves crash onto the shore. There's no better way to start a day than with sweat-pinked cheeks, a cool breeze along my neck, and sun on my shins.

Thirty feet away, toward the pier, a dozen or so surfers catch my attention as they wedge their boards in the sand. I smile at them, uncertain if their hair is bed head, hungover, or the "surfer" look. They slip into wet suits, some full, some cut to the knees, then carry their boards to the ocean, paddling out past the breaking waves.

Surfing. Maybe I should try it someday.

A surfer catches a wave, then is thrown off into the rough sea. His board shoots ten feet in the air and misses smacking his head by a few inches.

Or not.

With my pinkie finger I once again carve a heart in the sand, noting the irony. I spend my weekdays orchestrating love and my weekends feeling sorry for myself that I've lost it. Good thing none of my clients have mentioned that little nugget of truth. Not something to advertise on a brochure. Although, come to think of it, maybe that should be the title of my follow-up book? *No, You Can't See Me Again Because I'm a Lying Fool.*

The laughs and cheers from the gaggle of surfers grabs my attention. One of the guys in a full wet suit catches a long wave, carving in and out above the breaking water. He's still going; he nears the pier.

His friends cheer louder.

What about the pier? I stand, scanning the beach and boardwalk. No one is alarmed but me. "He's gonna crash into the pier," I shout.

But the moment the words leave my lips, the guy, with incredible precision and skill, effortlessly slaloms his board in between the columns. The wave shrinks to a ripple on the other side. The surfer kneels on his board and raises his fist in victory.

His friends erupt with whoops and hurrahs.

I find myself clapping and bouncing up and down. "Amazing," I yell. And it truly is. He maneuvered himself through the wood poles and—

It's only then I notice yellow caution tape wrapped around a light post on the pier. A light post missing a bulb.

Nixon. He took a picture of this pier. Hung it in his living room.

I spin around and glance toward the street. Above two condos, I recognize Nixon's front porch.

Oh, God. I didn't know I'd run this close. *He's so close.*

And it's Sunday. Is he watching the surfers? Did he see that guy? Does he see me?

The heart dug into the sand gives me an idea. A beautiful idea.

Just like Nixon said, aside from the surfers, the beach is clear this time of day. The high tide washed away footprints, chair imprints, and castles, leaving the sand smooth.

A perfect landscape.

With the help of a foot-long piece of driftwood, I line up just so and etch my plan into action. My biceps and shoulders ache from my efforts. *Jesus . . . I should've written something shorter.* Sweat drips down my back. My heart swells.

"What are you doing?" a dripping surfer says once I've finished.

"Careful where you step."

He hops over my carved words and reads aloud. "'Can I See You Again?' Me?" the surfer says. "Yeah, all right."

"No, not you. Him." I point toward Nixon's house, brushing the sand off my knees and shins.

The guy shrugs. "Later."

My message to sweet, charming, aloof-just-enough-to-be-sexy-but-not-conceited Nixon spreads thirty feet long and at least fifteen feet tall. Yes, it's a mite crooked and the second *N* looks like an *H*, but surely he'll get the gist. Though I don't spot him on the porch, his shutters are open. Surely he can read this from his house. Didn't he say he always watches the surfers? Didn't he say he *cared*?

But an hour later, moms, toddlers, football-throwing dads and sons, and a group of giggly teenagers have settled their beach day close to my plea.

"What does that say?" asks an eighteen- or nineteen-year-old girl with an itty-bitty yellow bikini tied around her flat-stomached and olive-skinned body. It should be illegal for someone so adorable to stand next to me. "Is it like a love note or something?"

"Something like that."

"Cool."

I glance for the two hundredth time at Nixon's porch, sweep my eyes along the boardwalk, peek at the stairs, and glimpse along the shoreline.

Still no sign of Nixon.

And when a rogue wave—much like the ones Nixon described

when he surfed—pounds onto the shore, seeps up the sand, and washes away part of my message, I gather my things.

Before I leave, two toddler boys smash their Tonka trucks through the heart I originally dug, etching a new track, destroying the shape.

Seems fitting.

forty-six

"What's that?" I ask Andrew, pointing at his computer.

"Huh?" He closes a file labeled *RÉSUMÉ* and yanks out the flash drive. "It's nothing. I'm gonna go. Take care of you."

He's gone before I can say, "What the hell?"

But, what the hell?

I've had just about enough. Along with his hushed conversations, Andrew's been late several times the last few weeks, forgot to finalize two clients' portfolios yesterday, and just this morning changed his phone's password. *It's not really snooping if he leaves it on his desk while stepping to the restroom, is it?* Well, anyway, how the heck am I supposed to see what's going on now?

I overheard him mention drinks at The Grill tonight, so like any good employer does, I'm going to spy on him. I'm going to find out who he's leaving Bree Caxton and Associates for.

I'm still brokenhearted that he hasn't confided in me. Hasn't come clean and alerted me of his plans, allowed me time to prepare for his replacement. Time to cry. Well, if he doesn't have the decency to own up to his intentions, maybe I won't have the decency to write him a glowing recommendation letter.

Who am I kidding? Other than the fact that Andrew dips his French fries in mayonnaise, I can't think of a bad word to say about the guy.

Andrew sits with his back to me at a high table in the corner. He's with someone else, but thanks to the dim lighting and reflection off the glass tabletops, other than it's a man, I can't make out who it is. What I can see, however, is that Andrew changed his clothes after work. He's now dressed in pressed khakis and a black blazer. His companion is equally decked out in interview-like attire: ivory shirt, dark tie, and slacks. The two are reviewing papers Andrew pulled from a manila folder.

Résumé?

Andrew swigs his beer, and then his shoulders give way to a laugh. For a moment, I'm offended. Who is he laughing with? Who's more funny than me?

I creep closer, ready to catch him in the act. *Who is this joker trying to steal my Andrew?* If it's another matchmaker, I'll kill him.

But I'm shocked when Andrew climbs off his bar stool to reach for a fallen piece of paper and the man's face comes fully into view.

Scotty.

"Bree?" Scotty says with alarm.

"Scotty?" I say out loud, just as shocked the second time.

Andrew spins around. "Bree? What are you doing here?"

"Me? What are *you* doing here?" I catch him glancing at the entry door. "Ah, so that's it? Scotty is your go-between. Candace is on her way here, right? You're leaving me for a job at the newspaper."

"Can we talk about this later?"

"Why didn't you tell me?"

"Please, Bree. I—"

"Hello, Bree." Andrew's father, a salt-and-pepper-haired man with a lumberjack's build, walks toward us. "It's been a long time."

"Yes, hello. How are you?"

"Just fine. You?"

"I'm good, thanks. I'm . . ." Out of the corner of my eye I notice Andrew adjusting Scotty's tie.

"From what I hear," Andrew's father says, "Andrew's . . . um . . . *friend* . . . has a real talent for tile work. I'm looking for a new flooring man."

His friend?

"Excuse me, but I need a quick second with Andrew."

"Sure, I'm gonna grab a beer anyway."

"Scotty?" I pull Andrew toward me by his elbow. "He's your *friend*? He's the person you've been sneaking around with, whispering into your phone, smiling like a two-year-old at Disneyland."

"I didn't want to tell you."

"Why not?"

"The interview, conflict of interest, I don't know."

"Does Candace know?"

"Yeah," Scotty says.

"What?" I smack Andrew's shoulder. "Candace knows but not me? Randi?"

He nods.

"Jo?"

"Yep."

Okay, now I'm mad. But, then I see the terror across his face. He's like a week-old puppy. How can I stay mad at that? "Does this mean you're not job hunting? Or are you and Scotty both?"

"What are you talking about?"

"The newspaper. The circled help-wanted ads. The résumé."

"All for Scotty, he's the only one looking for a different job. Since he's got a background in tile and flooring, I called my dad. We talked, sorted out a lot of baggage, and he agreed to meet with us."

"Wow, Andrew, your father? Meeting Scotty? And maybe hiring him?"

"I know. This is huge. We've come a long way the past few weeks."

"I'd say."

"Don't tell Candace, okay? That's why I kept it from you, as well. Scotty wants to secure a job before putting in his notice."

"Tiny white lie?" I tease.

"Something like that."

I sneak a peek at Andrew's father chatting with Scotty, even smiling.

"You happy with him?" I say to Andrew.

"I am." He glances over his shoulder at the two men before whispering back, "Thinking of introducing him to Jo."

"She'd like that." I pull him close and hug him.

"I better get back to them."

"Yeah, go ahead."

Just like I thought, my little boy is growing up.

⁓

Three days later, I'm working late at the office. Andrew's long gone; he and Scotty are going paddleboarding with Andrew's parents. I'm busy burying my embarrassment and regret into client files, when Nixon slides into the chair opposite my desk in a gray suit, white shirt, and black tie. The same chair he sat in weeks ago when the paper clip stuck to his butt. The same quiet, sexy masculinity spews from his pores. The same smile that certainly does have its charm.

How I'd love to jump back to that day and have a do-over. Come clean about Sean right off the bat. Spare Nixon my troubles. Lie less. Love more.

"Hello, Bree."

"Hello." I can barely get the word out. Some professional I am, clamming up like a teenager at the sight of a cute boy. "How are you?"

"I'm good. You?"

"Okay," I say, noting the chill in the air between us. An outsider might suspect Nixon was an insurance adjuster rather than the man who clutches my heart in the palm of his hand.

He says nothing about the latest *Close-Up* article or my beach message. Maybe he didn't see them? Maybe he *doesn't* care.

As I take in his soldierlike posture and clenched jaw, I realize the latter is likely the case. But good news, for the first time I'm clear on his body language. I'm not misreading him. I *am* good at this stuff. See there, his rigid stance oozes hostility, matching his narrowed lips and curt tone of voice. He's still pissed at me. So, hooray for me, I've finally got him figured out.

"I've come to terminate my contract," he says. "I won't be needing your services any longer."

"Oh, right." I knew this day would come. Only a matter of time. I've hurt him, embarrassed him, why would he stay? Did I honestly think some silly message in the sand would change that? Still, I'm disappointed, wishing it weren't true. If nothing else, I'd hoped to still see him from time to time. "I'm sorry to hear that."

"You know I never like this arranged-dating thing."

"Yes, I know."

"It just makes sense," he says, "given everything we've been through."

"No, no, you don't need to explain. I get it."

"No hard feelings?"

"My gosh, Nixon, no. How could I possibly?"

"Great, because actually, there's something else."

"Yes?" My mood perks a tiny bit.

"I hope you don't mind me asking you about this."

What's that? Erase the last few weeks and start over? No, I don't mind at all. Happy to do it. "What is it?"

He trails his palms along his thighs. He's nervous.

Why? Might there be a chance?

"I met a girl."

Oh.

My gasp draws his stare. *I met a girl.* Pressure builds around my throat and I swallow hard. Of course he met a girl. Look at him. He's beautiful. *Do not tear up, Bree. Do not.*

Though I'm certain despair clouds my eyes, I maintain my composure and force a smile. After all, he owes me nothing. It saddens me to know that not only has another woman captured his heart, but I've blown my chance at a relationship, even a friendship, with this guy. This lovely man. It says a lot about the type of person he is, showing up today, handling our business breakup face-to-face, rather than with an impersonal text. He's a great guy. And, though it sucks—*Lord, does it suck*—I need to accept the fact that just because I fell for him doesn't mean he fell for me. Everything was for show.

"Okay . . . um, certainly . . . a girl . . . yes, that's what I'm here for . . . that's good."

"I hope you don't mind me asking you for advice . . ."

"No." I purse my lips. "Of course not."

"We've been through a lot, but water under the bridge, right?"

I'm drowning in the water, but go ahead. "Right."

"And since I've curtailed your success rate—didn't you say

I'm your two percent?—this new relationship of mine bumps up your odds."

Yes, okay, I got it. You like a girl. "It's no problem. What can I do to . . . help?"

He leans forward.

Whoever she is will get to stroke her fingers through his thick hair and— Enough, Bree. It's over.

"You see, I'm confused." He laughs, tossing his hands in the air. "You women are so hard to figure out."

"Yes, well . . ."

"She wrote me this note but it makes no sense. I'd hate to misinterpret a clue. I swear you women speak a different language. I'm hoping you can decode the meaning."

Read your love note? Gee . . . what fun. "Sure, what does it say?"

"That's the thing. I have no idea. But here, I took a picture of it." He scrolls to a photo on his phone and hands it to me.

It nearly slips from my grasp as I stare at a picture of my giant sand plea. I read the message washed away by the waves. Ca—I—Yo—Aga.

"Oh, God, Nixon, I—"

"Hush," he teases. "Can't you see I'm trying to flirt here?"

His smile pulses heat through every neuron in my body. I press my lips together, holding back my wide grin. "Sorry. Go on."

"What do you think it means?"

"It means that she's incredibly sorry to have been reckless with your heart. It means that you make her a better person. It means she misses you."

"Wow." He shakes his head. "You got all of that from just a few letters?"

"Well, I am good at what I do."

He stands and tucks his phone into his front pocket. "That

answers that. And, Bree, I'm glad to see you're no longer hiding your scar."

I peek at my new tattoo. "Yeah. A friend of mine said I shouldn't."

"That friend sounds super smart. Thanks for your help." He turns to go.

"Wait." I hurry around my desk and meet him, face-to-face. "You're going?"

"Yeah? Why?"

"Um . . . because . . ." *Why are you going?* "I hoped you'd stay. I hoped to talk a little more. Maybe we could grab a cup of coffee or something?"

"Coffee?" He folds his hands across his chest. "Someone once told me dinner is the slow seduction."

My heart flutters alive again. *He does like to see me squirm.* "That person is a genius."

"I don't know. It took her a while to figure things out."

"Yeah, I bet she foolhardily considered herself an expert on reading people and completely misread you."

"You think?"

"I do."

"What happened to history?"

"What do they say? The past isn't meant to be repeated."

"That's the best you've got?"

"Yeah."

"Pity." He drifts closer.

We stand inches apart, separated only by our breath.

"Tell me, Nixon Voss." I lift my lips toward his. "Can I see you again?"

He reaches for my forearm and tenderly kisses along my scar before placing my palm against his chest. Then he lifts my chin with his finger, hovering his mouth above mine. "No coffee." And with that, Nixon kisses me.

His lips explore mine, soft and slow.

His body presses tight against my own, solid and certain.

And while I'm wrapped in his strength and his tenderness, I take notice of his body. My mind wanders from his mouth to his neck, down his chest to his legs, mapping the feel of his skin against mine, his curves, his angles, his bends.

I realize he and I have no lengthy history, no shared past. No comfort of the common.

His body, his mind, his soul—*all of him*—is new and obscure. Unknown.

But this no longer frightens me.

I no longer crave safety of the familiar.

I no longer yearn for the past.

I let myself go, lost in Nixon's kiss.

It's time to make new history.

Don't miss Allison Morgan's
funny and endearing debut novel

The Someday Jar

Turn the page for a special excerpt . . .
Available now from Berkley!

Don't panic, Lanie.

Don't freak out.

Don't shove your hand into the paper shredder. It won't fit.

Sifting through the contracts piled high on my desk—I swear twelve trees are chopped down each time a house is sold—checking the trash can and digging through my purse, I find nothing. Nothing!

How is this possible? I'm twenty-seven years old with dental floss, multivitamins, and spare staples in my desk drawer. I have no past due library books or expired tags on my car. I never litter. Never chew with my mouth open. I lift heavy things with my legs, not back. A responsible adult by any account. Yet, someway, somehow, I've carelessly gone and lost the single most important thing I *shouldn't* lose. My engagement ring.

"Lanie?" Evan, my fiancé, calls from his office.

Crap.

"Just a minute." I push my chair aside and search underneath the desk, finding no more than a few paper clips and a fuzz ball. Apparently, the maid has gotten a bit lax with the vacuuming. Oh right, that's me.

"Where are you?" he calls, sounding closer this time.

Quick to stand, I bonk my shoulder on the desk and hear the silver picture frame of the two of us from last year's Realtor Awards ceremony fall over.

"Oh, there you are." Evan strides toward me in his crisp Armani button-down shirt and creased pants, with a smooth gait that only good breeding spawns—his mom's a tenured English professor at Stanford and his dad's a venture capitalist. Evan is smiling, the same smile that garnered him a number six spot on last month's most-attractive-businessmen poll in the *Arizona Republic*. More than his Ken-doll good looks and crackerjack genes, Evan's a proven asset in the real estate community. He's respected and admired.

And he's mine.

But great. Just great. I've gone and lost his token of love.

Obviously, I could ask him to help me search, but what would I say? *Hey, funny thing, I've misplaced my ring. You know the one—diamond-encrusted platinum band, passed from generation to generation. Wasn't it your great-grandmother's?*

As a perfectly timed distraction, the office door swings open and in walks my dear old friend, Hollis Murphy.

He's decked in his usual navy blue, one-piece jumper. The matching belt droops around his waist. He smooths his thin white hair with a finger comb, and his cheeks and nose, laced with a few broken capillaries, flush pink.

My whole world just got brighter.

"Hollis, what a nice surprise." I slide around the desk and open my arms for a hug.

His skin is cool and clammy, he smells of too much cologne, and staleness heavies his breath, but I don't care. I love this old man.

We met several years ago, when I crashed my shopping cart into the side of Hollis's truck. In my defense, *People* had just released the Sexiest Man Alive issue and a shirtless Ryan Reynolds, along with each one of his gloriously defined abs, was pictured on page thirty-seven. Who wouldn't be distracted? Besides, it was only a scrape. Okay, dent. But Hollis was forgiving and we've been friends ever since.

He grasps my hand and says, "Zookeeper chokes to death eating an animal cracker."

Nearly every time we talk, Hollis rattles off a peculiar obituary. It's a sick ritual and I'll likely rot in hell for making light of someone else's misfortune. Still, I can't help but chuckle. "That's awful."

"Good one, don't you think? My Bevy clipped it out."

"How is Mrs. Murphy?"

"A slice of heaven. Today is our fifty-fourth wedding anniversary."

"Congratulations!" I say, making a mental note: *Send Murphys wine.* "Any special plans?"

"She's making meatballs tonight. My favorite."

"Sounds perfect. When will you bring Bevy by? In all this time, I still can't believe we've never met. I'd sure love to meet her."

"She says the same about you, but I swear that woman never has any free time. She's busier than the tooth fairy at a crackhead's house."

Evan approaches, extending his hand. "Mr. Murphy, it's nice to see you."

"Likewise."

"To what do we owe this honor?" Evan asks.

Hollis fishes in his pocket and pulls out a candy cane, his favorite treat that he carries year-round. He offers it to me. "Just came by to give Lanie-Lou something sweet." He eyes me, waiting for my answer.

"Because every woman deserves a candy cane."

"That's right." He squeezes my arm and says, "Everything good?"

"Everything's great, thank you." *Except for the fact that I can't find my ring.* I quickly scan the carpet.

"All right," Hollis says. "I'm off."

"Good to see you," Evan says.

"Give Mrs. Murphy my best," I say, walking Hollis outside.

"I already gave her my best this morning," he chuckles, and then he drives away.

Evan waits for me beside my desk. He holds out his open palm. "Look what I have."

Damn. He found it first.

I step toward him, conjuring up a witty explanation like, *Silly little bastard, that ring must have legs*, but words escape me as I stare into his hand.

He doesn't hold my ring. He doesn't hold the symbol of my future. He holds a piece of my past. My Someday Jar.

"My God." I try to hide the tremor in my fingers as I reach for the glass crock. Nostalgia surges through me like a desert flash flood and all at once I smell my dad's cologne masking his one-a-day cigarette habit and hear his voice, usually light and high-spirited, pivot adamant and stern when he said a dozen years earlier, "This jar is for your goals and aspirations, Lanie. None too big. None too small."

"Where did you find this?" My voice is no steadier than my hands.

"In a box at the bottom of my office closet. Found your ASU graduation cap, too. Maybe you can wear that to bed later?" He teases, but he must see the focus in my eyes because he strokes my arm. "What is it?"

I lean against my desk, my body heavy with sentiment. "This is my Someday Jar. A gift from my dad. God, I haven't seen it in years." The last time I held this, I wore bubble-gum-flavored lip gloss and braces dotted my teeth. With the jar close to my ear, I give it a little shake and listen to the slips of paper tumble inside.

"What's in there?"

"Fortunes."

"Fortunes?"

"Yeah. Every year for my birthday Dad took me to the Golden Lantern, a Chinese restaurant in Mesa." I half smile, remembering the dome-shaped chandeliers covered with crushed red velvet and dangling tassels decorating the dining room. "They had this wall with dozens of fortunes pinned to it. Dad plucked a handful of slips, flipped them to the blank side, and said, 'Write your own fortunes, Lanie. Create your own path.'"

I remember scribbling *Learn something new* on the first slip, thrilled with his nod of acceptance as I tucked the goal into the jar.

Now, as I rub my thumb along the nicks in the glass, a lump forms in my throat. "Dad made me promise that I'd empty the jar. He made me promise I'd claim my own stake in the world, fulfill my desires and dreams. He made me promise I'd do this . . . before I got married." I'd forgotten that last part until just now.

Evan tucks a strand of hair behind my ear. "Your dad was never afraid to throw caution to the wind, was he?"

"No, he definitely wasn't," I whisper, staring at the jar.

"You okay?"

I shake my head to clear it and force a little laugh. "I'm fine. It's just an old piece of glass that brings back a lot of memories, I guess."

Evan pulls me close and holds me for a minute.

Though it serves no purpose but longing and regret, I let my mind wander to my childhood days with Dad. The days when pancakes were dinner, chocolate cake was breakfast, and jokes and laughter filled our bellies in between. I hate to admit it, but I wonder what Dad would think of me now, so different from the carefree teenager he knew. Would he be proud of the woman I've become or disappointed by my structured life? Worse yet, indifferent?

Evan steps back and says, "Listen, I don't mean to rush this moment for you, but I'm in a tight spot and sure could use a favor."

I blink away tears foolhardily forming in my eyes. "Yes, of course. What is it?"

"Can you pick up Weston Campbell from Sky Harbor Airport, executive terminal? He's flying in from Los Angeles."

"A new client?"

"No, a business associate of my parents turned family friend. You've never met him?"

"The name doesn't sound familiar."

"Well, anyway, he's going to lend me a hand with an upcoming project."

"How will I spot him? I have no idea what he looks like." For some reason, the name Weston Campbell evokes an image of a wirehaired and well-fed Irish farmer stabbing bales of hay with whiskey breath spewing from his toothless grin. I should work on being less judgmental, but honestly, where's the fun in that?

"No problem recognizing him." Evan aims his phone's camera in my direction. "Smile."

"Wait." I set the jar on my desk and comb through my shoulder-length brown hair, fluffing the bangs that hover over my Irish green eyes, thankful I wore my favorite sleeveless dress cinched above the waist with a ridiculously cute Michael Kors belt. "Okay, go."

He snaps a photo of me.

Dang. I think my eyes were closed.

"This is Lanie Howard." He punches at the keys. "There, I forwarded your picture to him. All you have to do is stand outside the security gates and he'll find you. The executive terminal isn't very big." Evan slides into his jacket and steps toward the leather-framed mirror hanging on the wall to study his reflection. He swivels his head side to side and checks for any budding "parasites," as he called the two gray hairs discovered earlier this year on his thirtieth birthday. "I'd go myself, but Weston changed his flight and I've got that 1031 Exchange lecture tonight."

"What time is Weston arriving?"

"Six." Evan spins around and catches me peeking at the clock. "I know, the Cardinals game. Maybe you'll miss the first half, but you'll be home in time to catch the rest. I'll make it up to you tomorrow." He winks. "You'll take care of Weston for me?"

Waiting in a stuffy airport is the last thing I feel like doing, especially if it means missing a Monday Night Football game. But Evan's in a pinch and business outweighs pleasure, so I hide my discontent with a smile and reply, "Sure."

"Great. Weston's staying at the Biltmore. Just drop him there." Evan slips his hands around my waist and pulls me toward him again, my Someday Jar wedged between us. His lips brush my neck and he whispers, "I'm such a lucky man."

After his quick kiss, I watch his Mercedes drive away, then slump into my chair. With the tip of my forefinger, I trace the jar, top to bottom, following a crack. "Promise me you'll explore life," Dad had said with narrowed eyes and hands clasped around mine. "Promise me you'll color outside the lines."

Now, here I am, a grown woman, many years later, wondering if I should twist off the cork. Reach beyond my comfort zone and tackle my ambitions, challenge myself like I vowed. *Should I color outside the lines?*

My inbox chimes with an e-mail, jarring my thoughts to the present. Glancing toward the computer and spotting the lotion bottle, I'm reminded why I took my ring off—for age-defying, triple-moisture smooth hands—and see the jewel behind the knocked-over frame.

Thank God. With relief, I slip the ring on my finger and decide that my future is what deserves my attention, not the painful reminder of days behind. I tap the jar's brittle cork and drop the keepsake into my purse. *Those days are gone*.

An hour later, I lock the office and head toward my car, juggling an armful of files and a ringing cell phone.

"Hey," says Kit, my best friend of countless years. She's chewing on something, odds are a papaya granola bar, as she lives off those things, admitting they taste like cardboard, but loves the fact that they can double as a kickstand for her son's bike, should the need arise. "Want to catch the game and share a plate of greasy potato skins?"

"God, I'd love to, but I'm on my way to pick up a colleague of Evan's, then hurrying home to catch what I can of the second half with a mound of paperwork piled on my lap. Dammit," I say as much to myself as her, "I need to swing by Nordstrom's. Evan's out of shaving cream."

The judgment in her silence is deafening.

"What?" I ask.

"I'm just wondering what happened to my nutty BFF who used to hustle pool tables and dance on the bar after a couple drinks. Has she been eaten alive by the responsibility monster?"

"I don't know what you're talking about."

She chews another bite, then says with confidence, "The Vine, Labor Day weekend, senior year. You danced on the bar in that denim miniskirt. The bartender's arm was sticky from your sloshing lemon-drop martini. He was pissed."

I can't help but laugh. "Next time we'll grab drinks."

Kit sighs. "Okay. Just promise me that cheeky girl I've known since grade school is still in there."

"She's there." *Somewhere.* "I've been busy." *For three years.* "Did I tell you? We have nineteen listings in escrow right now. Evan Carter Realty is poised to rank number two in residential sales this quarter, in all of Phoenix. Evan's worked really hard."

"*You've* worked really hard. Come out and play sometime."

"I will."

"Swear?"

"Swear."

"Okay, I'll talk to you later."

"Sounds good. And Kit, for the record, it wasn't the Vine. It was Club 99. I rocked the hell out of that miniskirt."

⁓

Interstate 10 is the direct route to Phoenix Sky Harbor, but since traffic is light and I've a few extra minutes, I find myself steering through the side streets of downtown. I turn onto Washington Avenue and pull up curbside at the almost completed City Core construction site. Chain link surrounds the seven-acre urban complex, which combines condos and commercial space built within two sharply angled towers. I don't know much about the project, other than I'm impressed by the architect's vision, for he or she must've known that at this time of early evening, the towers' glass captures the sun setting over Camelback Mountain and reflects on the city, dual sixty-story murals of the desert's incredible landscape.

I step from my car and wrap my arms around myself, grabbing hold of the fence, uncertain if I'm chilled from the hint of fall in the breeze or the memories from where I stand. The City Core is very different from the building that once stood here, the one my dad worked in when I was a kid. The one with the corner deli where he let me order my own coffee. Side by side, we spent mornings sorting through photographs of him rafting, hang gliding, rappelling, choosing the best shots for his next freelance magazine article.

"Are these dreams from *your* Someday Jar?" I'd ask, holding a glossy photograph of some snow-covered mountain range, praying I didn't sound too eager. Too much like a child.

"Nah, I don't need a jar." Dad nudged my elbow with his own. "You're my greatest adventure."

My heart flickered. Actually tickled inside my chest when Dad said those words. *You're my greatest adventure.* I'd never felt more loved. Or more protected. The most important person in his world.

He moved out six weeks later.

I release my grasp on the fence as if it's buzzing me with voltage and chastise myself for letting a silly childhood token rattle my thoughts. Honestly, what has gotten into me?

As I drive toward the airport, my engagement ring catches the sun's light and I think about my life. In three months I'll be married to a beautiful man full of integrity and principle. A man who is kind to my mom, finishes my crossword puzzle, and still half stands when I join him for dinner or return from the restroom. Thanks to this man, I have a solid job with clients I adore. A stable future.

I nudge the jar deeper into the depths of my purse. I'd be a fool to uncork the pain and splintered promises of my past. Yes, my dad is the first man I ever loved. But he's also the first man who broke my heart.